CHAOS SPACE

Two hundred millimesurs until maximum excitation.

Adrenalin shot through her. Her entire body tightened with anticipation – and dread. Could she navigate them through? . . . *The result of an inexact res-shift is catastrophic and will have an irrevocable impact on humanesque tissue. Vibration calibration must be precise or molecules in the tissues will implode the flesh* . . . Why did she have to remember that passage from the manual so exactly?

'Rast,' she whispered. 'Shift imminent.'

A fraction of her awareness saw Randall run for her tubercle, saw Catchut crossing himself again, saw Latourn curled up in a ball.

Then Mira stared straight into the face of both her deepest longing and her darkest fear – and wondered which one would say her name.

BY MARIANNE DE PIERRES

CHAOS SPACE

Book **2** of *THE SENTIENTS OF ORION*

marianne de pierres

orbit

www.orbitbooks.net

ORBIT

First published in Great Britain in 2008 by Orbit
Reprinted 2009, 2010

A CIP catalogue record for this book
is available from the British Library.

ISBN 978-1-84149-429-6

Typeset in Caslon by Palimpsest Book Production Limited,
Grangemouth, Stirlingshire
Printed in the UK by CPI Mackays, Chatham ME5 8TD

Papers used by Orbit are natural, renewable and
recyclable products sourced from well-managed forests and certified
in accordance with the rules of the Forest Stewardship Council.

Mixed Sources
Product group from well-managed
forests and other controlled sources
www.fsc.org   Cert no. SGS-COC-004081
© 1996 Forest Stewardship Council

FSC

Orbit
An imprint of
Little, Brown Book Group
100 Victoria Embankment
London EC4Y 0DY

An Hachette UK Company
www.hachette.co.uk

www.orbitbooks.net

For Marcus and Jules

ACKNOWLEDGEMENTS

Thanks to Tara Wynne and Darren Nash for their unfailing support, and to Nicola Pitt for being so calm when books go missing.

MIRA

The edges of the Dowl shift-sphere were a frenzy of spacecraft. No order in their behaviour. No etiquette. Only panic.

Mira/Primo writhed in vein-sink, her senses deluged with information upon which her imagination piled fear. *What have the Saqr done to Dowl?* That and a hundred other questions prickled her subconscious. But only one found its way to the top. *Insignia? Can we shift?*

The biozoon hesitated. *Dowl's shift system is compromised.*

Then we are trapped here!

I *am not. We use your stations as an act of good faith – not necessity – and to protect our humanesque Innate.*

You do not need to use our shiftspace?

*I do not need to use your **systems**. I am bred with Resonance ability. However, your stations are located at our optimum resonance points. I must use this space.*

Then we can still resonate?

As I said . . . yes.

Mira's relief translated into a surge of energy. *Go, then.*

Insignia slid precariously between the mêlée of stranded ships. Some were already changing direction, their auras exuding bursts of magnetic waves.

What are they doing?

They are opting for sublight travel. Maglev is still oper-ating but unstable.

That meant someone on Dowl station was battling to keep maglev function available. Mira trembled at their courage. Insignia – *go! Leave here!*

A visual representation of the shiftsphere blossomed on Mira's retina; a magnificent kaleidoscope of pulsing, spinning concentric rings. Then a low thrum started as *Insignia* unfolded her cephalic fins. Mira knew that the sound would escalate to something beyond her hearing range. Soon she would be immersed in the thing she had most longed for.

As they entered the outermost ring of the sphere, Mira/Primo lost all connection with her physical self. She became a force amongst other forces, an energy thrusting forward against returned energies.

It's like swimming, she thought. *I am swimming, not flying.*

Yes, *Insignia* agreed jubilantly. *We are. And it has been too long . . .*

With each ring they traversed the hum-pitch rose and the opposing forces strengthened. Mira/Primo lengthened her stroke, absorbed in the rhythm and effort of her propulsion.

Then a faint disruption occurred, like a splash disturbing the perfect ripples of her movement.

A craft slid across their wake, travelling with ragged momentum.

What is it?

Desperation, replied *Insignia*. *They are trying to shift. But we are only partway in.*

The ring ahead of us is designated for refuse ships.

They have a different shift point?

Yes. In case there is a spillage or an accident during resonance – so that ultimate shift space will not be compromised.

But they are not resonating at perfect pitch. How—?

Imperfect Shift is possible.

Insignia sent the equations and logistics tumbling into Mira/Primo's mind. In less than an instant she understood. Imperfect Shift *was* possible, though high-risk, and if they were caught in the wake of it, they would be dragged into Failed Shift.

A warning from Mira's Studium instruction manual flashed into her mind. ***The result of a Failed Res-shift is catastrophic and will have an irrevocable impact on humanesque tissue. Vibration calibration must be precise or molecules in the tissues will implode the flesh . . .***

Insignia?

I am ahead of them still and I am able to accelerate but in doing so I will disrupt their accumulated speed. They may be forced into a Failed Shift.

What other option is there?

You know it.

Mira/Primo's fingers clutched at the vein's viscous cushioning, her eyelids fluttering – though she had no awareness of it. *Death to them? Or Death to us?*

Yes.

I cannot choose such a thing. I cannot!

Insignia had no sympathy for her. *I can. It is very clear to me.*

Oh?

If you choose the riskier option for us your baby will die.

An instant? Or protracted moments? Mira/Primo didn't know which it was, but she felt *Insignia*'s satisfaction as she thought the words . . .

Us. Save us . . .

Sole

closer closer/luscious luscious
find'm secrets/know'm all
bring'm home/bring'm home

THALES

Thales prostrated himself for the last time that day. As he lifted his lips from the cool marble floor of the Jainist upashraya, he sent a message to his moud: *Quesadillas for dinner with spiced ratafia and a side of hot meat-stuffed peppers.*

It was really too mild a time of year for such a meal but he could already see the smile on Rene's face when the moud filed the dinner menu to her inbox.

He retrieved his slippers from the racks in the entry recess, shoved his feet into them and pummelled the muscles in his back. Sometimes he longed for a more active lifestyle. Already he could feel a slight softening of his torso, the natural tone of youth stealing away like a mistress at dawn. Prayer and contemplation were no substitute for physical exertion.

Thales paused in the entry of the basilica. It was small in comparison with many on Scolar but no less grand for the religion's inauspicious Cerulean beginnings. It was probably part of the attraction for him, he mused.

He had discovered an innate perversity in his nature that he had recently stopped suppressing and begun to acknowledge. Scolar, the much-lauded hub of ideas and learning in Orion, was becoming as staid and intransigent as a Balol monk.

Oh, and chocolate linguine with pig peaches, he added to the menu.

Perhaps extra carbohydrates would give Rene the energy to make love tonight. She seemed to be gripped by preoccupations these days; a mental fatigue that affected her interest in his manliness amongst other things.

If only she would agree to have a child.

Thales craved one as deeply as he craved new knowledge. At night when he woke and couldn't get back to sleep, he made lists of the things he could teach a child of his own, the wonders he could show them.

But Rene would not be enticed. Although she had never said as much, Thales knew that she found the whole idea slightly primitive. Sensitive to her preferences, he had instead broached the subject of non-biological parenting.

Her reaction had been clear. *How could I care for a child that is not my own?* It was, perhaps, the only time that he has been disappointed with her.

Sighing, Thales looked to the shards of violet light stabbing downward onto the marble surface where he'd been lying in prayer. They fell like swords from the twists of cut amethyst inlaid into the domed roof. On suns' set, all the basilicas in the Hegel quarter burned with refraction rainbows. Each one of them had been built to capture the rays at rise and fall of Scolar's twin suns. It was as if the universe sent its most vibrant, imperious shades cascading down to Scolar to rejoice at the City of Ideas's importance.

Thales turned from its flaunting display and walked out onto the avenue. Others emerged from their prayers and study, and queued to enter the conduits. Thales caught glimpse of faces he knew – the Cerulean, Msr Lacroix, from the Zionist temple and the uuli near-elder Uumau. But today they avoided acknowledgement of him as though somehow pre-empting the next moment.

Thales?

Yes, moud?

A priority message has been logged.

Thales's heart pumped. His petition must have been approved. He would be the first scholar to be sent to study the Entity on Belle-Monde. *Proceed.*

Sophos Mianos wishes to inform you that tomorrow you will take up a new post as Grievance Adjudicator at the OLOSS offices in the Bureaucratie district.

Shock caused Thales to sway as the conduit raced past the blossoming cherry trees towards his domicile in the Kant district. Only steady meditative breaths kept his anger on a leash. He grappled with it until he reached the sanctum of his apartment.

Rene was home already, seated at her studium-adjunct, scanning through her most recent treatise.

Despite his distress, Thales paused to admire her gracefulness as she bent over the desk. She seemed thinner than she had this morning, her frailty accentuated by the freedom she had given her waist-long hair. He often begged her to let him braid it but she said he was clumsy and preferred their maid's adept fingers. In the evenings, though, she would let him unravel it and stroke it loose. She would lean into him, her body as light as the stalk of a sunflower, her eyes unfocused and trusting.

'Thales, calm down.'

He opened his mouth in surprise. 'How did you know?'

She turned to him and he soaked in the sight of her intelligent oval face. 'Your step was rushed and you spoke to Alambra brusquely.'

One of Rene's more delightful quirks was that she never thought of their shared Made Intelligent moud as anything other than sentient. 'But, as you ordered my favourite dinner foods *before* you left the upashraya, I'm assuming that whatever upset you occurred on the conduit.'

She held her arms out.

Thales ran to her like a child, kneeling to bury his head in her lap. A sudden desire somehow to subsume her into his being beset him. She was older than he but more beautiful than all the young women on Scolar. She would always be so. The beauty of her intellect held him in far greater thrall than any physical loveliness.

Rene let her hand stray through his hair. 'Dear Thales,' she whispered.

Hurt pride tore loose from a burning spot in his chest. 'They have ignored my petition to study under the Entity and are moving me to OLOSS to be a Grievance Adjudicator at the Bureaucratie, Rene. This is because I oppose their staid ideals. The entire Sophos Pre-Eminence treat my arguments against their theories as though I am diseased. What happened to the acclaimed dissension of Scolar? What happened to lively discourse and the intersection of ideas? This place is dying, Rene. And we are in danger of becoming as stultified as them. It is little wonder that the great philosopher Villon abandoned this place.' Thales stared up into her face.

She stroked his cheeks but her expression tightened.

'Villon was a malcontent. We are a better society without him.'

'I don't agree,' said Thales hotly. He pulled away from her grasp. 'His dissent was what kept us honest. He believed in argument *and* change.'

Rene smiled. 'A philosopher for the youth. Change cannot always justify itself.'

'Don't denigrate his beliefs, or mine, by such a bland dismissal. It is true that Villon challenged everything, even himself. But that is the only way to ensure that our ideas advance.'

'Villon challenged the Pre-Eminence. He sought to displace them with an anarchic model of leadership that would have allowed anyone into governance. That might have made him a champion to the younger and the less prudent, but how could you know what his motivations were? Perhaps he simply sought influence and his own kind of repectability.'

'Respectability! Rene! How stolid you sound.'

'And you sound like a boy suffering from hero worship. Thales, you did not know Villon. It is most likely that he used dissension as a tool.'

'A tool? *Dissension* has been Scolar's life blood. We are not taught to study in school, we are taught to think. Why assume that anything is how it seems? Or how we are told it is? And yet we are governed by old men who want nothing more than the status quo.'

'I do not need a lecture on Scolar's education methods, Thales. Or a mocking precis of the Pre-Eminence. Have you forgotten that my father is among them?'

'Have *you* forgotten what we learned?'

Rene frowned, and pressed her fingers to her forehead. 'Dissension creates conflict. I do not seek conflict, especially not with you. It is uncivilised and stressful.' She dropped her hand from her face and gave Thales an almost pleading look. 'Equilibrium is our secret weapon, dearest.'

'It is an excuse for much to be left undone.' He grabbed her pale smooth hands to his chest. 'We should leave. You could apply to study with the Sole Entity on Belle-Monde. The Sophos would not be able to deny you as they have me. The tyros are only Dicter's, Lawmon and Geneers. How could they have a true dialectic with the Entity without a philosopher? It could be a new start for us.'

'Thales, my exposition is almost finished. When it is accepted, you know I will be made Provost Laud.' Rene's expression softened. 'Don't you enjoy our lifestyle?'

Petulance boiled up in Thales. 'You will call it a symptom of youth, Rene, but lifestyle is not all. *Knowledge* is all. It used to be that you thought that way as well. Now you seem more moved by status and position. I think that sometimes you prefer the company of your father and his antediluvian Sophos to mine.'

As the words tumbled from his lips, Thales saw his hopes for the evening evaporate. Yet he could not stop himself. Anger had gripped him – righteousness felt more gratifying than any judicious reply.

Rene pushed him gently away and stood. 'I will be in muse when you are ready to be rational. I have made many sacrifices for you, Thales. It is unkind for you to reward me with such childishness.'

Thales could not let it drop. 'What sacrifices? How have I encumbered you?'

But she had turned away already, rebuff apparent in the frail set of her shoulders, the tremor of her thin fingers.

Contrition played him. 'Rene, please . . .'

'Go for a walk, Thales. *Young* men need exercise.'

She shut the door between them quietly.

MIRA

'Fedor? You still with us? Or are you napping again?'

Rast/Secondo's voice vibrated through vein-fluid and disseminated into Mira/Primo's mind. Her several days of immersion with the organic ship *Insignia* had robbed her of any interest in the mercenary's needs or demands. She was enthralled by the biozoon's unique biology, its adaptation from water to space.

Yet the speech vibrations became insistent and louder.

'Hey! Baronessa! Answer me or I'll come over there and rip you out of your cosy little bed!'

Mira/Primo sighed at the banality of the threat. The Primo vein could resist any attempt at forcible entry short of res-shift error. Even then, there was a possible chance of survival, although 'where' Mira/Primo was not sure. The composition of the Eter-nix was sheer theory.

With reluctance she began the process of separation from Primo, finishing with an instruction to the vein to release her body. It disgorged her into an upright position, supporting her gently while she regained her balance.

Rast, no longer in Secondo, was already waiting for her. The mercenary lay on her side still, flicking the black scrawls of drying vein-fluid from her skin as she clenched and unclenched her muscles. A pistol bearing the Cipriano crest lay propped against her stomach.

Mira felt the last reassuring intimacy of the Primo drop away, leaving only the faint and dissatisfying distance of waved interface. She could feel and hear the biozoon but she was no longer *it*. 'Where did you get that?' Her voice rasped with suspicion and the after-effects of immersion.

'This is the flagship of a war fleet, Fedor.' The mercenary waved a hand at the luxurious trimmings that disguised the fact that they were in the biozoon's cheek. 'Where do you think I got it?'

Mira felt a twist of indignation. Perhaps the Primo influence was upon her still. Or maybe she was more patriotic than she thought. 'The biozoon is not a weapon ship; it is a sophisticated macro-organism.'

Rast shrugged. 'Whatever. It still carries a weapon stash that will do me nicely, seeing as I never got paid for the whole frikked-up mess down there. Now you will take me where I want, and on the way we can negotiate how you might get out of this with your skin on.'

The memory of their situation flooded through Mira's mind. The invasion of Araldis, Faja's death, Trin Pellegrini and . . . She closed her mind to the last thought and studied Rast.

The mercenary's face was pale, and her injuries had not been repaired by the Secondo. The veins were only matched to heal the Cipriano genotype.

She was a mess.

Mira rubbed the back of her hand and watched vein-flakes slough into the air. She imagined she looked much the same. 'I left a child . . . *my* child on Araldis in the care of an unstable man while my world is being violently colonised by alien creatures. I will not take this macrorganic anywhere but to the nearest OLOSS protectorate where I will get help for Araldis. According to *Insignia* that will be Scolar in the Utmos system.'

Then she added softly. 'I do not care what you threaten, mercenary. I will go to Scolar. You cannot res-shift without me. But I will take you to where you wish to go – when I can. And now I am going to clean myself.' Mira didn't wait for Rast's reaction or answer. She stood and walked unsteadily across the buccal towards the uneven skin folds that the biozoon had grown to create a sphincter between spaces, and pressed her fist into its centre.

'Fedor?'

Mira paused, waiting for the pucker to retract. But she did not turn back.

'You made the right decision back there when that ship turned up on our tail. Tough call, but the right one.'

It was meant as a compliment, perhaps, a vote of confidence – but a weight settled on Mira's chest at the reminder of what she had done. 'Was it?'

She stepped out, turned and walked along *Insignia*'s ridged sloping strata, looking for somewhere to wash. Choosing a random pucker, she pushed her fist gently into it. It opened with a sucking noise.

Catchut was inside, bent over the cocooned form of her fellow mercenary Latourn. Surrounding them was an array of medi-tools.

'How is your . . . friend?' Mira asked.

Catchut nodded wearily. 'The 'zoon has top medic. Never seen nuthin' like it before, though. Bring you back from most anythin' . . .'

Mira allowed herself a small smile. 'Fit for royalty.'

'Lucky for Lat,' said Catchut.

'Remember that, mercenary. Remember that Cipriano wealth saved your friend.'

Mira stepped back out into the stratum and took the next upward channel, pressing more puckers until she found an empty space with a bed and a separate wash compartment. From the modest nature of the furnishings she deduced that it was meant for the lower castes.

She removed her torn and filthy fellala and sank down into the steam couch. The heat lifted the dirt from her pores, leaving her skin almost tender.

Insignia?

Yes, Innate Mira.

How do I get cool water?

Water burst from a slit in the wall above the couch and cascaded over her.

Her skin tingled. *Thank you.*

I am preparing a replacement fellala for you. What colour is your rank? asked the biozoon.

'Elite, of course,' she said aloud without thinking.

I have never exfoliated during Prime before. It is a previously unproven limit for me. I am pleased to have that knowledge. I . . . enjoyed our union. It has been some time.

'Th-thank you,' said Mira. Now that they were separated, the reminder of her intimate immersion in the ship's biologics embarrassed her a little. And yet she had so longed for it – like desiring a stranger from afar to find out, once you had been intimate with them, that they were still only a stranger. 'Are you quite recovered from the exfoliation?'

For the most. Although a salt rub would be pleasant. Indeed, though, it is refreshing to be resonating again. I have spent much time in dust and inactivity. My sonics lacked tune, and my fins are stiff.

Their conversation faltered as Mira dried in jets of warm air. She tried to think of how to draw the biozoon out. 'Do you understand what is happening on Araldis?'

Yes. I believe so. Although my concerns remain entirely with my Innate and myself. Worlds and their politics are beyond my control and my interest.

Mira thought of the hybrid biozoon, Sal, the one she had encountered on Araldis which had been treated poorly. 'What if your Innate turns out to be cruel or untrustworthy?'

If our own relationship is satisfactory I would not be bothered. I am not concerned with moral judgments. I am concerned with the enrichment and survival of my species.

'What if the person – your Innate – threatened your species? Or you?' On impulse, Mira leaned over and scraped her nail down the biozoon's skin.

A shock stung her arm, throwing her across the space onto the bed where she knocked her head.

Intention determines my response. I am not unintelligent, Baronessa. I am merely . . . your word would be . . . egocentric. In my genus it is an admirable, in fact necessary, quality.

'M-my apologies,' Mira stuttered. She rubbed

her arm, then her head. 'I-I needed to know.' Then she added: 'And we are not unalike. Our species is also egocentric, only . . . we do not consider it a strength.'

Insignia made a hissing noise that could have been laughter. *When we fuse again you will learn much more about me. For a pilot you are naive.*

'I am studium-trained only. I am also the first woman born into my line to bear the pilota gene. It made it difficult for the Principe. He was not disposed to encourage me.'

Woman? I hear your people use that term frequently. What does that mean?

Mira left the wash compartment to lie down on the bed. 'I am the female of our species. Male – female. Surely you comprehend that?'

You are different to my other Innates – yes, I see that. But the humanesque nuance of it escapes me. Our sexuality is diverse and subtle.

Mira's thoughts circled to Trinder Pellegrini, his breath suffocating hers, and his brutal thrusts. His men with their hands bruising her shoulders. She rolled to her side and brought her knees up under her breast. 'We are not a subtle species.'

I need several of my own kind to reproduce. It is our way of keeping our species strong. Unlike you who have genetically limited yourselves to a single choice.

And sometimes none, Mira thought bitterly.

You are not happy to be bearing life?

How did you know I was?

This time there was no mistaking *Insignia*'s amusement. *How could I not? Your blood, your neurology, they are as my own when we are immersed.*

Mira pushed herself upright. 'You must not tell anyone,' she cried aloud.

And how would I speak of it, Innate? You are the only one with which I can directly communicate.

But what of the person in Secondo?

You are the only one with which I can directly communicate, repeated *Insignia*.

A gentle burst of energy crackled over Mira, running down the lines of her body to her toes. The panic within her subsided and she sank down into the bed again. *What was that?*

Thought is not always an adequate way of communicating. I emitted a calming scent.

Mira lay still, fighting the fog that was sliding across her thoughts. *Can you tell . . . do you know . . . i-is the baby well?*

Yes.

It is a boy. A statement, not a question.

Perhaps after I have had further time fusing with your unique biology I will be able to tell.

It will be a boy. That is what he wanted; an heir.

You are not pleased?

I had no choice. I-is choice important to your kind?

Indeed. I chose this symbiotic role. However, when I contracted to the Cipriano Clans I did not expect such dreariness. I wished for enrichment.

Mira's heart thumped out of rhythm, rousing her drifting concentration. 'Contracted? You have a contract?'

Yes, Innate Fedor. And I should inform you that you have an irritating habit of repeating thoughts. The contract was for schika – *two hundred Araldisian years. I have only a short time left.*

'And then?'

Insignia paused for an age before answering. Even then Mira was not sure if she had dreamed it, for exhaustion began to pull her down to into the dark.

That depends entirely on you.

Trin

Sleep had become Trin's hell: a semi-consciousness that harboured fear and contrition. It was in that state that Mira Fedor was with him most often; her dust-caked skin and exhausted eyes, her overly thin body, the thick-ridged tight pressure of her virginity as he took it from her.

You must understand . . . he told her over and over while he slept . . . *understand why I did it.*

But the Mira in his dreams did not understand. She thrashed against him, outraged and desperate. At times she transformed into his mother and he was the one who cried and begged to be left alone.

'Principe! Wake up! Trinder, what is it?' a voice whispered.

Joe Scali was on the floor next to him in one of the mine's labyrinth of tunnels. The central shaft ran for over a hundred mesurs with mined shafts cutting off it at short intervals. Many of the worked shafts were partially or fully blocked where the machines had scraped the seam of mineral and collapsed the tunnel behind them. It was a primitive way of mining which left sunken trenches at ground level and played havoc with the ventilation.

Trin couldn't see his friend's expression in the gloom – he didn't need that kind of vision to know that Joe had lost all his vitality. It had drained from him on the day the alien Saqr had drained the life from Rantha's skull.

All that remained of Joe was his belief in Trin: that Trin would see them to safety and that he would find a way to restore order and exact retribution.

Djeserit – Trin's half-breed woman – held the same belief.

Trin loved them both for it – and loathed them. Their foolishness in thinking that he was better or stronger in some way.

He strained his eyes in the semi-darkness to find Djeserit. She was serving rations to those closest. Three hundred or more people spread out behind them down the tunnels; all that was left of the true Araldis.

'We are close to the end now?'

Trin dragged his attention back to Scali. 'The scouts say only a few more hours of walking before we see the sky again.'

'And then?'

'A night – no more – to the islands. There will be food and water at the vacation palazzo. We can treat the injured in the medi-lab.'

'What if the creatures are waiting for us when we leave the tunnels?'

Trin shuddered. That notion plagued his waking state as Mira Fedor plagued his sleep. The Saqr had followed them into the tunnels, he knew that. But they moved slowly and were still some mesurs behind. Yet Joe's concerns were his. What if the Saqr had found a way to get ahead of them? They would be trapped underground and cannibalised for their fluids.

'It is possible but unlikely.' He spoke in a hoarse

but confident voice – loud enough for those nearby to hear. His words would be passed along. Everyone hung on the Principe's words. 'Only a few govern the invasion. And I wager my birthright that they will be at Dockside.'

Wager his birthright . . . The murmur spread. The Principe was confident that their path to the Islands would be clear.

Djeserit returned and sank into the small space between Joe Scali and Trin. She leaned into Trin's shoulder and he smelled her unwashed alien smell.

'Do you mean it?' she whispered. 'Will our way be clear?'

He shrugged, unwilling to share his fears even with her.

'The last of the dried quark is gone. We have a little kranse and some desert figs left.' Djeserit fumbled in the sack strung around her waist and slipped some bread crumbs and a fig into Trin's hand.

He hid his head behind his raised knees and chewed. Djeserit fed him more than the rest but was discreet about it. He valued that in her, her instinctive ability to read situations. It would be an asset to him when he re-established Pellegrini rule. He would claim his son from Mira and Djeserit would be in the background of his life, smoothing paths, supporting him.

His fantasy ran its course until it reached the same obstacle. Would Mira Fedor return? Would she bring OLOSS help? He had gambled everything on the fact that she would come back for the Pagoin infant that she had saved from Villa Fedor. Mira was as stubborn and determined as her sister Faja had been. It was not an attractive trait in a woman but it was one that he could manipulate.

For the first time since fleeing Lois, Trin thought of his friends and cousins, the Silvios and the Elenis. A tiny part of him mourned them, but the greater part felt liberated. He could begin again. Instil a new set of rules. He knew he would make a superior Principe. Smarter and less hampered by tradition and a tight association with the Malocchi dynasty. The Scalis would be his new Cavaliere.

A scuffling noise came from the darkness ahead of him – not from behind where the three hundred or more refugees huddled. A scout had returned. Juno Genarro, he guessed. What news would he have?

'Principe?'

Trin raised his head from his knees, his breath catching tightly in his throat.

Genarro had knelt in front of him by custom, and from exhaustion. The light was so dim and the scout's face was so lined with weariness that it was impossible to read his expression.

'Well?'

'There is a small rockfall, but around it the way is open, Principe. We must hurry now, though, to be there by night.'

Trin's heart leapt and those around him gave a little cheer. He unfolded his cramped body and stood in the stooped manner that they had all been forced to adopt while walking through the smaller shafts. 'Pass word along,' he said. 'The way is clear. We must hurry now.'

He pulled Genarro to his feet. 'Take fresh help and go ahead,' he said in the man's ear. 'Clear the entrance.'

'Be quick, Principe.' Genarro swayed with fatigue. The stocky scout had covered more mesurs than any of them. Dutifully, though, he turned and headed back the way he had come. He knew as well as Trin that once the entrance was cleared and visible it would signal their intention to surface at that point. There would be no retreat.

A trickle of energy suffused Trin's muscles. Fear combined with anticipation. Soon they would feel the blast of the hot nightwinds on their faces. It would blow the stink of cramped unwashed bodies from his nose. It would also rob his body of moisture. How many of those without functioning envirosuits or robes would survive the night's walk to the Islands? Many of the women whom Mira Fedor had helped to escape from Ipo struggled merely to breathe.

A figure made its way along the tunnel, stepping over the others' legs, speaking harsh apologies, until it stopped, hunched over before Trin.

It was a woman with a babe in her arms. He knew this one and the child she carried: Mira Fedor's ally carrying the Pagoin infant that Fedor called her own.

'Si, Signora Mulravey? What do you want?'

'Your men are all wearing suits or fellalos. Some of my women have nothing. They will not survive in the nightwinds.'

'They made it to here.'

Trin heard the intake of her breath, as if she had held in a sharp retort and replaced it with something else. 'They did, but I can tell you one thing for certain, Principe Trinder Pellegrini. They will make it no further.' She leaned towards him then. 'And what will your men survivors do with no women?' The last she spoke in a broken whisper.

Next to him Djeserit stiffened. Trin wanted to stroke her arm, to reassure her, but not while this bold woman was their witness.

'The Carabinere are your protectors. It is only logical that they should remain suited. If they need to fight . . .'

'Fight?' The woman raised her voice a little and it carried too far. 'What need is there for that? You have given the word that the way is clear.'

Trin lowered his own voice. 'We cannot know such a thing absolutely. You must understand that, after what you have been through.'

'The women must have protection.'

'I will consider it.'

'You will do better than that.' Mulravey lowered her own voice and her breath laboured with emotion. 'What – did – you – do – to – Mira – Fedor?'

'Mira Fedor stole an AiV. She deserted you. All of us.'

Mulravey shuffled closer until her stale breath was hot on Trin's face. 'By all the useless gods in this universe I do not believe that. And if you do not give my women suits to wear I will make sure that everyone else does not believe it either. Then we will see what respect you garner, *Principe.*'

Trin pressed one hand against the rock wall, resisting an urge to thrust the woman away. Djeserit's hand slipped into his other, and squeezed. He understood her message. She wanted him to listen.

Mulravey had influence among her own, and not only with the females. A contingent of non-Latino males listened to her. Better that she should remain an ally for as long as possible. *Mira Fedor must not become admired.*

'I do not like threats, Signora Mulravey, but I do understand compassion. Bring the worst ones forward and I will see what I can do,' said Trin.

The woman rocked back on her feet, suddenly drained of energy. What had it cost her, he wondered, to challenge the Principe?

The reminder of his authority brought a warm flow to his veins. He could afford some benevolence. It was a lesson that Franco had never learned. He squeezed Djeserit's hand and then let go.

They had to move on.

The last stretch was a steep uphill crouched walk, very different to the wide road and gentle gradient at the beginning of the Pablo mine maze. They had travelled several hundred mesurs underground and the hardest section was the last.

Juno Genarro and Seb Malocchi had gone above ground to clear away the rocky plug, allowing the waning sunlight into the vertical shaft. The final climb was by ladder and cut-in steps. Some would be too weak to make it unassisted.

Trin stood at the bottom, blinking up into the light. He could barely contain his relief. Near him some of the Carabinere were shedding their fellalos at his order. Cass Mulravey stood by, making sure that the weakest of her women received the protection. For some inexplicable reason it angered Trin to know that his men were close to naked.

'It is the right thing to do,' whispered Djeserit as if she knew his thoughts. 'It will draw them to you.'

He stared at her in the shaft of sunlight. Her papery Lostolian skin was dry and cracked, and grime coated the ridges of her neck gills. He noticed the slight breathiness in her voice.

'What is wrong with your breath?'

Djeserit turned her head away in the way unique to the young; a way that told Trin that she did not want to answer his question. For the first time he saw the child in her and guilt surged through him. Had Mira Fedor been right? Was his relationship with the half-breed Miolaquan a corruption? He thought of Luna il Longa and all his father's paramours. It was expected for a Principe to take many women.

Had beautiful Luna died at his father's side? Had Franco seen her as he drew his last breath? Or had his wife been with him?

Trin did not want to think of his mother. It filled him with uncomfortable twisting emotions. In the way of most sons, he knew that something solid had been lost to him.

'Principe!' Juno Genarro called to him from the top of the shaft. 'The sun fades.'

'*Vada!*' Trin instructed his Carabinere. Then he sealed his fellalo and began the difficult climb.

JO-JO RASTEROVICH

Jo-Jo Rasterovich was pissed off for a couple of reasons.

Being stuck in a Dowl confinement cell with a raging case of claustrophobia was forcing him to use up his HealthWatch's narcotic allowance to stay calm.

His ship *Salacious* had been stolen by a man he knew only as Jud. *And* he couldn't get at his Gal Bank account while he was officially a criminal, which meant that bribing his way out of this craphole wasn't feasible.

So, with narcotic-assisted patience, Jo-Jo began teasing out means for blackmail. He had learned within the first month that his humanesque gaolers were either wine-sopped young Latinos who couldn't cut it in the local Carabinere police outfit or discontented tourists stuck on Dowl for one reason or another and forced to work.

His fellow inmates were an uninspiring string of petty offenders and addicts who changed on a daily basis. Only two appeared to be in there for the long haul: a teranu called Petalu Mau who'd been busted with a container of space borers that he'd been grinding into a fine powder and selling as exotic spices to the Dowl Kafe, and a sallow-skinned female with stringy hair who couldn't, or wouldn't, stop crying.

Their triangular cells touched each other at one central point. If they so wished, the inmates could sit in a circle to talk like a group of friends around a campfire. Only in this case the 'campfire' was the intersection of a containment module and gave out a mild electrical charge if you got too close to it.

Some days Jo-Jo found that a pleasant antidote to his regular narcotic stupor. Mostly, though, he brooded at the wide end of his cell, which he kept darkened and sound-damped. He could still see into the other cells if they didn't have their privacy filters on.

The woman had it rough. When the guards were feeling narky or pervy they took the privacy controls away. Then you couldn't do your business without an audience. Seemed they liked to prey on her most.

Soon Jo-Jo knew the contours of her sagging thin arse and tiny odd-shaped breasts better than the back of his own hand. He reckoned that she was about the same age as him, or older and though she was permanently naked, she didn't attract him in the slightest.

Maybe that was why he asked the question. In a tiny space of emotional clarity that he managed to keep separate from his fugged and angry mind, he felt sorry for her.

'What's wrong, then?' Jo-Jo asked one day when he couldn't stand another moment of her sniffling misery.

Mercifully, she stopped her crying and crawled to the campfire. 'Do you even care?' she whispered.

Jo-Jo lightened his privacy filter so she could see him and crawled up to meet her. 'Care is a strong word . . .'

The woman gave him a watery smile. 'I'm Bethany.'

'Well, Bethany, let's just settle for mild interest.'

From the darkness of his cell filter, he heard Petalu Mau snort and laugh.

'Ignore him,' said Jo-Jo. 'So what's the score?'

'I made a mistake,' she whispered.

Jo-Jo gave a belly laugh, the first one in a long time.

Bethany raised her hand to protest. 'No . . . not just any mistake. Not a mistake you can be punished for and then forget. A moral mistake. A b-bad life choice. I had a man and a child – a daughter. He was different to me, a Mioloaquan.'

Jo-Jo pulled a face. 'You were flipping a scaly? How the hell did that happen?'

The woman shrugged. 'The way things do . . . I took work on a Mio explorer studying embryonic water fauna – not the Mios themselves, but more primitive species. Well . . . anyway, he was the pathologist on board. We conceived a child together . . . went to the amalgam clinic on Prospect . . . paid to have the genetic alterations so she would survive.' Some of the sadness dropped from her face. 'Ten years of a happy enough life. Work brought us here just a while ago. I noticed on our last trip that he was spending a lot of time with the Mios, less with me. Then I found him lying with one.' She trembled and the tears brimmed again. 'He told me that my humanesque habits had begun to repulse him. If I wanted to keep him our child must leave. He said she was an embarrassment to him now.' She gave Jo-Jo a swollen-eyed stare. 'Mios don't raise their children in family units. By the spawning age (we call it puberty) they are ready for mating. He told me it was unhealthy to have a spawn still under our care. To me, though, she is still a child.'

Jo-Jo stifled a yawn. Family hardships were only one step removed from politics on his personal measure of extreme boredom and avoidance. In his darkened cell even Petalu-Mau was snoring.

But Bethany's misery continued to tumble out. 'When we got here I booked a passage planetside. I put my child on it. I told her we were having a holiday but they had made a mistake with the seats and that I would be on the next shuttle down. I went to find Mio to tell him what I had done but the ship *shifted*. He left me. And I left my child.'

'Why didn't you just forget the fish-man and go after your kid?' Jo-Jo was quite proud of himself for having stayed with the story thus far.

'I had no lucre. It's impossible to get work on Dowl . . . if you're a woman. The Latinos don't have any regard for them . . . for us.'

'Oh, they have regard for women, all right,' said Jo-Jo. 'They like 'em plenty as long as they lie on their backs and kick their feet up in their air when they're told.' *Come to think of it, why have I never picked up a Latino woman?* He dismissed that idle thought with a shiver. *Friggin' aristos.*

But Bethany wasn't listening to him. Her eyes were brimming again. 'They put me in here rather than let me starve.'

'Then you've committed no crime?'

'Not exactly. Some places they would just call it vagrancy. But there isn't room on a res-shift station for people with no lucre. And Araldis won't have me. I tried that . . .'

Jo-Jo snorted. 'This place is the crud under the little

toenail of the galaxy. Even the judges are in and out of here quicker than an uuli's flange.'

'Flange?'

'Prick.'

Her watery eyes focused in on him. 'They say the judge had a personal vendetta against you.'

'You heard that?' He was surprised.

Bethany flushed a little. It gave her sallow skin an odd tinge. 'I know the court witness. He brings me extras sometimes.'

'In return for . . . ?'

She stiffened. 'I'm not a whore.'

Jo-Jo liked her primness. Stiff and proper seemed ridiculous in her naked state but she bore it like a shield.

'And *I'm* not a criminal.' He lowered his voice. 'I met an 'esque who called himself Jud, and a Balol soldier – a woman. The Balol distracted me and Jud planted an uuli on my ship. They got me for illegal importation. While I was in custody they stole my ship.' It felt good to talk to someone about it after months of stewing.

'How long is your sentence?'

'Three spins. Done most of one already.'

Bethany sighed. 'I'm sorry for you.'

'Don't be,' Jo-Jo said with infinite narcotic calm. 'I'll find them.'

They talked often after that and Jo-Jo turned his back out of respect when she had to piss. Petalu-Mau grudgingly joined in their tête-à-têtes, and they pretended not to hear him moan with hunger pains at night. Not that their Latino jailers didn't feed them but Petalu weighed more than Jo-Jo, Bethany and the three guards who rotated duty put together. He had an appetite that matched accordingly.

'Did they really slam you for selling aphrodisiacs?' Jo-Jo asked him.

'Mos' places want Petalu to sell stiff-makers. Here they lock you up. Can't figure them Latinos. What my woman gonna say when Petalu come home looking like this?' He slapped his loose skin folds like they were a musical instrument.

'You have a woman?' Bethany's eyes widened.

Jo-Jo could see her comparing her height and weight to his and wondering what she must be like.

'Mama Petalu Mau. That woman's strong like a Bangar buffalo. Mau has bred twenty-three 'uns from that girl.'

Jo-Jo's jaw dropped. 'You're shitting me. You have *twenty-three* children?'

Mau's eyes flicked upward while he thought. 'Last count 'em.'

'What are you doing out here, then?'

'Mama like it that way. Just cook up another 'un when Petalu home too long. She already wore out one womb.'

Jo-Jo and Bethany laughed.

'Bethany Ionil?' A guard's voice interrupted them. 'You have a visitor. Collect your clothes from the waiting cell.'

'A visitor, Beth?' said Jo-Jo, scowling. Protective feelings towards Beth had crept up on him over the weeks. He blamed it on boredom. She wasn't his kind of woman but she didn't annoy him either. Some people paid harder for their mistakes than others. 'Tell him I said to watch his hands.'

She gave Jo-Jo a mock-irritated look. 'How many times have I told you?'

'Yeah, yeah, you're not that sort.' Jo-Jo grinned.

Beth grinned back.

Her door scraped open and he watched her disappear from her cell.

'You want to make 'uns with Beth, maybe?' remarked Petalu.

Jo-Jo stared at him in shock. 'Never in a million, mate. Never met a woman yet who made me think in that direction and I can tell you right now, *I never will*.'

Petalu shook his head sadly. ''Uns are what gets a man to heaven. Petalu fear for your soul.'

'My soul is bright and shiny, mate.'

While Bethany was gone Jo-Jo drowsed on his bunk, enjoying some extreme revenge fantasies and contemplating jerking off. The fantasies flowered like fractals in his mind, fuelling his anger to such a pitch that he instructed his HealthWatch to increase his narcotic levels.

Instead of the expected wash of calm throughout his body, a message blinked up in front of his retina. *Your HealthWatch subscription will expire in six hours. Renewal may be made through a Gal Bank outlet or by farcast to any of the following relay stations . . .*

Crap! Jo-Jo let go of his balls and sat upright, heart pounding. Without HealthWatch he couldn't imagine how many past sins might catch up with him. Not to mention the claustrophobia of his cell. He had to get out of here.

He began to pace. Four steps before he hit the wall. He put his hands against it and hung his head, trying to swallow back the nausea that his panic had kick-started.

'Josef! Petalu!' Bethany's alarmed and excited tone got his attention. She was standing at the campfire, banging on the screen.

Jo-Jo switched off his privacy shade. 'What's wrong?'

Petalu was slower to respond, suggesting that his drowsing fantasies were more advanced than Jo-Jo's.

Bethany was sweating and panting as if she'd been running. 'Something's happening on the station. Lofario and I were talking in the visitors' room. Big Nose was watching us on screen. I heard a noise . . . like weapons. Big Nose ran out of the booth.'

'And?' urged Jo-Jo.

'Well, he never came back. The noise got louder and we could hear shouts. Lofario wanted me to come to his room for safety. I-I said no. I went to the observation booth and tried to work out the sequence for the containment release.'

Jo-Jo found that he was holding his breath. In the next cell, though, Petalu was breathing up a storm. 'And?' Jo-Jo repeated.

Bethany looked upwards. 'I think—'

The lights began to flicker and a faint fizzing sound followed. Jo-Jo suddenly realised he could not only hear Petalu but he could smell him: a heavy musk odour spiced with salt. He reached one hand towards Bethany and touched her. He held out the other to Petalu.

The giant man slapped it away and broke into a huge grin. 'Free,' he pronounced precisely.

Jo-Jo hugged Bethany tight. 'Lady Bethany,' he said in the most refined tone he could muster. 'You have impeccable timing.'

TEKTON

Godhead Ra has requested that you breakfast with him this morning, and Dicter Miranda has called seventeen times, Tekton's moud informed him when he awoke.

Both messages gave him immense satisfaction.

Tell my cousin that I should be delighted to dine with him. Do you wish to reply to Dicter Miranda?

Tekton stretched in his lotion sack. His repair nanites had begun gobbling the excess moisturiser away when he awoke. In a few more seconds he would be left with just the luxurious sense of softened skin. *Send her a message to say that I will attend her presently. After my breakfast with Ra.*

Yes, Godhead.

Tekton allowed himself a small smile. *That should make her hop.*

He gave his free-mind full rein to enjoy the moment. His small smile expanded into a chuckle and then a rather vigorous erection as he pictured a maddened Miranda bobbling up and down in a synchronicity of excessively undulating skin. There was nothing that put Tekton in a good mood like flopping flesh – except, perhaps, envy.

Oh, and competition – as long as he had the upper hand. And with Cousin Ra it appeared that he might now be a nose in front.

Tekton dressed in a traditional fitted soft robe that would accentuate his form and addressed the map on the wall. 'Transport to visit archiTect Ra.'

As the taxi mag-leved its way around the academic quarter of Belle-Monde, Tekton told his moud to convey his breakfast preferences ahead to Ra.

Quark eggs, plum quosh on carminga livers and pepper nuts. And champagne. Non-vintage will suffice if Ra cannot afford the other.

Yes, Godhead.

Godhead. Tekton so enjoyed the sound of the word.

Ra waited for him at the door, wearing only his ridiculous eye-mask and a sour expression. 'Cousin.' He gave a curt nod and indicated that Tekton should enter.

Tekton responded by opening his robe to display his well-lotioned body and the remainder of his erection.

Ra did not respond in kind but walked straight to the table. It was laid out with a selection of foods, none of which Tekton had requested. Vintage champagne, however, sparkled like a goddess in two glasses.

'A celebration?' said Tekton as he seated himself.

Ra waved towards the glass. 'Merely a welcome back, dear cousin. Did you have a pleasant trip?'

'Pleasant and fruitful.' Tekton's skin tightened. Something about Ra's demeanour prickled his comfort. His free-mind gave a warning snarl while his logic-mind ran through possibilities.

When Tekton had caught Dicter Miranda spying on him on Scolar she had freely admitted to being Ra's instrument. *'He promised me things to spy on you. Did you know he can see microwaves? Do you know what surgery I*

could perform with that ability? Bloodless, that's what!
Magical. Don't be cross, Tekton. I have not the faintest idea
what you were searching for in such an uninspiring slice of
the galaxy . . .'

The thought that Ra had sent Miranda to spy on him
had not unduly worried Tekton at the time. Spying was
perfectly comprehensible, given their situation. They
were competing for favours from God. The strange Sole
Entity that lurked just beyond the spin of their pseudo-
world had the power to alter any sentient and make
them much, much more than they were. Already it had
rewarded Ra by giving him the ability to see the full
electromagnetic spectrum. It was rumoured that one of
the uuli tyros could now alter DNA *in vitro*.

Tekton's free-mind had a sudden thought. *Did Sole*
find their mischief amusing?

Logic-mind snorted. *Why would a being with limitless*
power find anything amusing? Humour is a construct used
by lesser sentients. Transcendent beings don't 'laugh'!

Who says! Free-mind flounced off to sulk, leaving
Tekton feeling curiously detached.

'Cousin? Did you hear me?'

'Pardon?' Tekton flushed. He had not heard Ra
speaking.

Ra lifted his head in a faintly derogatory manner.
'Of course, you were talking to yourselves. Some take
longer to adjust to mind division than others. And of
course some just never do . . .'

Tekton ignored the jibe, scooped bitter-cheese potato
onto a plate and plopped a baby kidney into it. 'As I
was saying, my trip was fruitful. The women were
energetic . . .'

Ra curled his lip with distaste.

'. . . And I located the key to my project. I am optimistic that the Entity will find favour with my project. But then, I am talking too much. How goes the door?'

'You refer to my neo-brutalist aedicule?'

'A door is simply a door, Ra.'

'Not when it is in space, Tekton.'

'That rather depends on what is behind it. Or have you forgotten our creed? Structure, Purpose, and Delight.'

'*Your* creed. You are so mired in the earthly. Implied architecture was never your strength.'

'In my experience *implied* can be another word for unworkable.'

Ra shifted in his seat as though it had pinched him. 'I have begun a new task. The Entity likes to be surprised. It has an appetite for innovation.'

Aha! He has messed up! Logic-mind pounced on Ra's discomfiture. *I will check the astronemein bulletin boards.*

'How inspired of you . . . and how precocious. But then, you always were the latter.'

'I had hoped that your pettiness would subside when you were given this opportunity, Tekton. But I can see that you cling to it for comfort.'

'I doubt you would have any concept of what gives me comfort.' A flash of Miranda's thighs.

'Perhaps not, but I do recognise rivalry.'

Tekton did not shrink from the provocation. 'I will beat you, Ra.'

'The Entity has promised significant enrichment should we surprise it suitably. It is enough motivation for the biggest' – Ra sniffed and wrinkled the cracked skin of his brow – 'and the smallest of minds, don't you think?'

'*I* think that life has a splendid even flow to it, whether you are god or mollusc. Sole makes promises to you, you make promises to Miranda, Miranda makes promises to me . . .'

Ra removed his mask and blinked his oddly segmented eyes. Their Lostolian pink colour had been replaced by brilliant reds, lustrous black and vibrant blues. It was, Tekton thought, like looking into the deeply alien eyes of a jewel insect, and it made him slightly nervous.

'What on Mintaka do you mean by that, cousin?' Ra asked.

Tekton scraped his plate with deliberate and dramatic indelicacy. 'I mean that often when we start things, we cannot predict where they will end.'

Ra blinked again. 'Only a fool is sure of anything.'

THALES

Thales stormed from the apartment and caught the conduit back to the Temple, not knowing where else to go.

Young men need exercise? Rene was treating him like a maladroit: an uneducated common man with no discipline over his urges.

Thales controlled his desire to hit something, vowing to prove her wrong by finding his composure in prayer. Yet, as he exited the carriage he experienced an irresistible urge to vist Villon's statue instead of the upashraiya.

He hurried past the Jainist Temple, along the well-swept Avenue de Montaigne, and into the gracious sweep of Sextus Circe. The Circe was criss-crossed by streaming spotlights that roamed the neat garden borders and flashed across the colossal statues of the great philosophers – The Children of God. As Thales walked among them he found peace in their solidity; like the relief as a child of returning home after vacation, to a place where the world felt stable.

Villon's statue was on the northern side of the Circe, between his philosophic predecessors Shelaido and Averro. Thales sought it out and laid his forehead on the young Villon's feet, seeking solace. If his father was alive and here, he would, perhaps, have gone to him;

and his father would have pulled him into his embrace with warmth and humour and eternal optimism.

Why did he not carry that same optimism? Why was he so quick to become angry or excited over thwarted principles and ideas, and yet found little to care about in the common decisions that a man faces?

Lofty, the girls in his home town had called him, with a snide curl of their lips.

And then later, at the Noble Studium, *lofty* became *gifted*. And the girls had smiled – softly, invitingly. But all the while his father had loved him for those ideals, and encouraged and been proud of him.

Why aren't you *proud of me, Rene?*

Perhaps he was more like his mother than he cared to admit. But she had left them when he was so small that he had not known her well enough to make a truthful comparison. She was gephot, though, a member of an undeniably intellectual race who some thought had spawned the beginnings of transhumanism. Maybe his father's patience stemmed from recognising the gephot in him.

Thales finally lifted his head, and noted the fully darkened sky. The spotlights had steadied into a pattern. As he watched one full sequence, it occurred to him then how heavily Scolar was influenced by Cerulean philosophies. Other than Greatest Elder Muuluan, there were no uulis immortalised here, nor mios, nor skierans. Indeed, only one other non-Cerulean statue held its own in Sextus Circe – a huge flat, smooth jade block upon which rested a marble representation of a flame: the flame of the sentient spirit and a tribute to Exterus, the first true Extropist. The Flame had been placed in Sextus Circe over five hundred years ago to celebrate the vast difference in Sentients' beliefs.

Thales threaded his way over to Exterus and was surprised to find a small circle of candle-bearers kneeling at its base. He sank to the pavement beside them.

The one closest to him dropped her veil. The woman was of a similar age to Rene, and had a face that, surprisingly, he knew.

'Thales?' she whispered.

'Magdalen? May I join you?'

'What are you doing here?'

He forced a smile. 'Is it unreasonable for a native of Scolar to be sightseeing in his own city?'

'If that is all you were then I would welcome you to our remonstration. But you are part of the Pre-Eminence and that would serve neither us, nor you.' Her dark eyes were lined with kohl, which seemed to accentuate their hollowness. She and Rene had been friends until Magdalen had chosen to follow the doctrines of Eclecticism. Rene had found its system too unformed and open to perversion.

'I am not part of the Pre-Eminence,' Thales said hotly. 'I am me, Thales Berniere, Jainist.'

Magdalen smiled in a way that reminded him of his wife: patient and almost amused. 'When you married Rene Mianos you married the Pre-Eminence, Thales. To declare anything else is self-deception.'

Thales's anger returned in an instant, as if it had never really left him. He refused to have his life defined by his marriage or his relatives. The welling of his bitterness was so fierce and came from so deep within him that he could barely maintain a civil tone. 'I am not Pre-Eminence!' He did not shout, but the vehemence of his tone was meant as such.

'And neither are you Jainist, if you raise your voice in such a way,' Magdalen said coldly.

Her reaction stemmed Thales's moment of vitriol and he swallowed hard to moderate the harshness of his voice. 'Forgive me, Magdalen, but it has been a difficult day. Tell me, what remonstration is it that I am likely to disadvantage? Why are you here?'

'Haven't you heard?' Her surprise had a mocking note to it. 'Exterus is to be razed.' She touched the block base and the marble crumbled off in her hand. 'It has been injected with an industrial detrivore that will tunnel through it like a termite. In a matter of days it will fall. And it is only the first. Villon is next, then Averro.'

'But that is outrageous!' exclaimed Thales. 'The Children of God are sacred.' He glanced around the small group of candle-bearers, no more than ten of them. 'Where is everyone else? Where is your assemblage?'

Magadalen pulled her veil up to cover her face again and her reply was muffled but unmistakable. 'This is all there is.'

Thales left them and returned home, choosing to run up the stairs rather than take the lift. *They mustn't harm The Children*. The thought burned him. He must tell Rene. She would help extinguish the terrible heat in his chest.

The moud opened the front door but Rene's remained locked.

'Rene!' He hammered on it. 'Rene, we must talk. The Pre-Eminence is planning to desecrate The Childen.'

Rene's cool voice entered his head through the moud. *Be quiet, Thales. I can hear you.*

'Open the door so I can see you.'

Your tone suggests that you are not in control of yourself. I would prefer to see you when you have calmed down.

'Did you hear what I said? The Children—'

I know. My father has spoken of it.

'Your father?' Thales pushed his palms against his temples to suppress the building pressure. 'You knew?'

It is only selected statues, Thales. Villon was an agitator. It will not be a significant loss.

Not be a significant loss. Rene's last words shredded Thales's self-control.

In one quick movement he overturned the table, dislodging papers and Rene's favourite drinking cup. Then he tore the apartment's aspect cube from its mounting and threw it against the wall. As it shattered he looked for something else to break. Anything, *anything* to relieve the unbearable frustration. He lifted a chair and hoisted it at the window.

Alambra, call the politic, Rene instructed.

The moud set off the house alarm.

Thales threw the chair down and fell to his knees. 'Rene. Come out here,' he shouted. 'Moud, override that.'

The moud remained silent.

I am Alambra's priority, Thales. She will obey me. I think that you need appropriate reflection time.

I don't need reflection time. I need your appreciation.

I need your prescience. I am being marginalised, shelved because of my ideas. What does that say about Scolar, Rene? What does that say about your father and the precious Pre-Eminence? To Thales's chagrin his frustration turned to tears.

Behind him the outer door opened. He swung around to see the red sabres and brown robes of the politic guards as they swept into his view.

Rene, for Jain's sake . . .

MIRA

'Take us to the Rigel system,' Rast badgered Mira
again.

'If help does not come to Araldis quickly, it will be
too late. I must find an OLOSS representative first.'
Mira stayed resolute despite her churning stomach. *Rast
will not kill me. Not yet*, she told herself.

They sat, all four of them, in the ship's cucina, eating
diverse fare: a freeze-dried porcini risotto for Mira,
while Catchut was feeding Latourn soup between swallowing mouthfuls of rehydrated stew. Latourn had
recovered from the worst of his injuries but his strength
was slow in returning. He still could not walk without
help.

Rast played with her pistol as though it was a
favourite toy. But her expression was filled with suspicion. 'What else is going on, Baronessa, to put you in
such a hurry? Rigel is only two shifts away. A few extra
weeks and you would be rid of us.'

Mira hesitated. Rast had sensed her tension; she
could see no option but to tell the mercenary. 'The
biozoon's contract with my clan has nearly expired. It
may not choose to renew.'

Rast spat a mouthful of kranse back onto her plate.
'What in fucking Crux do you mean by that?'

'I mean . . . there was . . . an agreement between

Insignia and my ancestors. When the biozoon considers that agreement fulfilled, it may choose to do something else.'

'It?'

'I – I'm not sure of *Insignia*'s gender.'

'Thought you Inbreds were supposed to know everything about them?'

Mira wasn't in the mood for Rast's provocation. '*Innate.* You were in vein-sink as well as me – what do *you* think?'

Rast stabbed the half-chewed lump of kranse with her fork. 'I don't recall sensing any hard-ons, so I'd go with female.'

Catchut sniggered.

'You are wrong. They do not have a clear distinction between male and female,' said Mira.

'Self-fuckers?' said Catchut.

Mira winced at the crudity. 'Not hermaphrodites. No. They need several of their own kind to reproduce. Two are not enough.'

'Bonus.' Rast smirked. She slouched and slung her arm along the back of Mira's chair. 'We could learn something from that.'

Mira shifted forward to avoid any physical contact. The mercenary loved to goad her. 'Will it be so humorous if the biozoon decides not to allow us to stay aboard?'

'What's it going to do? Dump us?' Rast touched Mira's neck as if brushing away an insect.

She refused to flinch. 'That is possible.'

Rast stopped her teasing and returned to shovelling in the last mouthfuls of food. When she finished she pushed the disposable container away, belching. 'You're shittin' me. Right?'

'No.' *Would* Insignia *harm them?* Mira didn't know. Right now the biozoon murmured comfortingly, almost lovingly, in the background of her mind. '*Insignia* is a highly evolved tetrapodomorph, not a humanesque. I have no way to predict its actions.'

Rast exchanged looks with her companions. 'So what does the 'zoon want to renew the contract and not spit us into the vacuum?'

Mira hesitated again, not wanting to sound ridiculous. '*Insignia* was bored on Araldis. I think it seeks . . . stimulation.'

Rast guffawed. 'Now you are *definitely* shitting me.'

'It had not realised it would have such a long period of inactivity.'

'It's like living inside a cooked ribcage. Even smells like it.' Rast stared at the densely fleshed ceiling and ribbed walls of the cucina. 'Can it hear me?'

'If it so chooses.'

'Frickin' creepy,' muttered Catchut.

Latourn began to cough, his body racked by the effort. When the fit passed he laid his head on the table in exhaustion.

'Get him out of here, Catchut,' said Rast. 'He's hawking spit all over the place.'

Catchut hooked Latourn's arm over his shoulder and pulled him to his feet. He gave Rast an unreadable look and shuffled Latourn out.

The mercenary leader watched them leave, then turned to Mira. 'So when does this so-called *contract* run out?'

Mira suddenly wanted to slap Rast for her indifference to what they had left behind on Araldis. Surely even a mercenary had regrets for her own dead team.

And yet, in the same moment, Mira could not help but envy her. No male would ever force himself upon Rast. '*Insignia* has not said – other than that it is soon.'

'Ask it then.'

Mira listened for a moment to the background hum. 'It does not choose to answer.'

Rast made an impatient noise. 'Well, then, Baronessa, I suggest you get to know your tetrapodo-whatever a bit better so that you can bargain with it. Whatever its tastes are, I can probably get hold of it. Even the bizarre—'

'No!' Mira stared at Rast in disbelief. How could the mercenary think that way?

Rast saw her expression. 'What, then?'

'I will . . . see,' Mira said.

Rast dropped her hand onto Mira's shoulder and squeezed it hard. 'Thing is this, Baronessa. I don't fancy your exploding eyeballs being the last thing I ever see. But, one way the other, it will be, if you don't make a good deal with your ship.'

Rast kept away from Mira en route to Scolar after that, other than to check regularly on their progress. Catchut found a library of entertainment sims in one of *Insignia*'s many cabin spaces and the mercenaries spent their evenings drunk in one another's company.

Mira spent her time in the biozoon's buccal, enduring

her early-pregnancy nausea. Although she avoided total vein-sink, she let the Primo vein sucker adhere gently to her skin, massaging her body. The connection allowed the biozoon to help subdue her illness – mainly with distraction.

Insignia projected her own external views upon Mira's retina. Without the benefit of full immersion, *Insignia*'s version of space appeared as a translucent corduroy tapestry, ridged and furrowed, and impregnated with fiery pinpricks of light. Some of those lights passed in a blurred instant while others seemed to burn for ever. And all the while the biozoon rose and sank with the gigantic waves of the solar winds, leaving Mira hollow with awe.

'I had no idea it would be like this,' she said. 'No idea.'

But even her witness to the biozoon's marvellous abilities couldn't lighten her inner misery. And the misery made her angry. How could she allow Trin Pellegrini's act of violence to defeat her when so many Cipriano women had suffered as she had? *They* had not died inside from it. *They* had not been rendered impotent with resentment. *They* had accepted and moved through it.

Yet while the memory of hard male fingers on her body remained, Mira was caught on a pendulum of emotions.

She wondered how Cass was faring. And if it was Djeserit or she who was caring for Vito? Did he have enough to eat? Had Trin Pellegrini eluded the Saqr and led the survivors to the islands?

Insignia, *is there any news of Araldis?*

Constant reiteration, Mira Fedor, is a trait of the inferior mind. I would have told you had there been news.

When can you farcast to Scolar?

I have explained this already as well. My farcast relay is not functioning at optimum length. It will be possible after the next shift – perhaps.

Mira rolled unhappily onto her side in Primo vein. The biozoon could be so intractable when it chose. She must find a way to get closer to it.

What had you expected when you came to Araldis with my grandfather? She focused on the steady, unhurried rhythm of its biologics as she waited for an answer.

Learning. Although we were a nomadic race, our vanzoons knew that we must keep a reproductive core separate, to ensure the longevity of our species. I was born into this Core Mass. When it was my turn to be allowed to rove I dipped into our collective store of memories. That area of the galaxy is little known to us.

But you must have realised that our clan were destined to be planetbound?

It was my understanding that my Innate and I would be permitted to rove when the new world was settled. But the Latinos proved unreliable. When your father died, I lost my emissary to your Principe.

Mira wanted to speak more of her father but she sensed their conversation would be better served in another direction. *You enjoy wandering?*

'Wander' suggests lack of purpose and I have a deep purpose. We call our roving rafa.

Mira liked the sound of *rafa*. 'And what is your purpose when you . . . rafa?'

I don't share my purpose! it said in an offended tone.

Embarrassment further warmed Mira's skin. The biozoon reactions were so difficult to predict. *I apologise for my ignorance. It can make me seem . . . impertinent.*

Yes.

The vein temperature cooled abruptly and uncomfortable sensations prickled her skin.

Insignia?

The vein remoulded itself, forcing Mira into an upright position. The biozoon was forcing her out.

Reluctantly, she left the buccal to return to her cabin but Rast intercepted her in the high stratum. The mercenary was staggering, drunk or stoned.

'Haven't seen much of you lately, Baronessa. How are our contract negotiations coming along?'

Mira flattened herself against the stratum wall to avoid touching her. 'They are . . . progressing,' she lied.

'Progressing, huh? Well, we're getting bored and, let me tell you, that ain't a good thing.' Rast suddenly swayed across and leaned her body against Mira's. She dropped her head to Mira's neck, brushing her lips against the bare skin.

'No!' Mira cried out and pushed her away, running a couple of steps before Rast caught up with her.

'Whoa there!'

Mira wrenched her wrist free, shaking, and unable to calm herself. 'You have no right to—'

'Fuck it, woman, what's your problem?' Rast held her hands up in a placatory gesture. She glanced up and down the stratum, embarrassed.

Mira didn't answer; she fled to her cabin. When she reached it, she struck the pucker with her fist as if it were Rast. When it retracted she ran inside and fell onto the bed.

Mira? Insignia's thought was filled with concern. *Changes in your physiology show distress.*

I am . . . I do . . . not want the mercenary's attention. It is important that she understands this. Mira climbed off the bed to enter the washspace. *I wish to wash my face.*

Water flowed through a skin fold into a cavity on the wall.

You are angry? asked *Insignia.*

Mira was surprised. 'With you? No. Why?' she said aloud.

It is important that I understand your needs. I am in a position to protect you in some ways but I must know when it is necessary to do such a thing.

'O-oh,' Mira stammered, speaking aloud again. 'Thank you.'

She washed and returned to the bed. Lying on her back she stared at the silken canopy that disguised the lumpy flesh of the ceiling. 'The mercenary is no threat to me. At least . . . not if I comply with her wishes.'

But that is not how you behaved.

Perhaps, then, it is time that I shared this . . . Mira took a breath and let the painful memories break the surface of her mind. Somehow the biozoon's presence sharpened the images until she became lost in them again . . .

'Listen. We will retreat to Chalaine-Gema. If the Saqr are there we will cross the southern range to the Islands and wait for help,' Trin had said.

'What else do you want?' Mira had replied. *'What does that dogged face you present to me mean?'*

He'd hesitated then as if listening to an inner voice. *'There is no manner in which I can make this less brutal, Mira. I have thought it through. You can resist or you can accept.'*

'Accept what? To go to OLOSS?'

'No. That is decided already . . . I wish to make a bambino. Now. An heir.'

The fear had come to her then. *'Loco!'*

'I am truly,' he'd agreed. *'But there will be another Pellegrini and he will be Cipriano. You are the only patrician blood left.'*

She had tried to flee him but Seb and Vespa Malocchi had wrestled her to the ground and held her there. One of them had pushed the filthy hem of his fellalo into her mouth. It had tasted of iron and sweat.

Trin had forced her robe open and himself inside her. His tears, as they fell on her face, had meant nothing to her. Nothing at all . . .

That appears to be an unnatural violation. But we are very different from you humanesques. Respect for each other is intrinsic in us.

Insignia's voice jerked Mira roughly out of the past. She swallowed several times and licked her dry lips. Remembering had only made her misery grow. No peace came from reliving it; no amity. *Among my kind it is accepted that a man will decide when he will be fertile. This occurs between marriage partners, though, and is not forced upon acquaintances.* She wiped wetness from her eyes and rolled on her side, tucking her knees to her belly to relieve the ache that had settled there.

Insignia remained quiet for some moments. *And now you do not wish to be touched.*

'I do not wish to be vulnerable.'

What of the foetus? Do you care for it?

Mira huddled on the bed, wondering what the child inside her would be like: a Fedor or a Pellegrini? 'I do not know,' she whispered. 'I do not know.'

JO-JO RASTEROVICH

Jo-Jo found a farcaster in the node of banking and news booths that acted as a wall for one side of a small kafe. He entered his ID.

'What are you doing?' Bethany was a few steps behind him but ahead of Petalu.

While the 'caster processed Jo-Jo's request he turned and grabbed her arm. The public node-way was unnaturally quiet: only a few upturned stools and a puddle of spilled drink dotted with undissolved sugar crystals, as if there had been people there only minutes ago.

'Listen, I have to do something right now. You don't have to stay with me. Whatever the hell's happening here, I'd be grabbing the first ship in another direction.'

Bethany trembled, her face paler than the flickering cursor on the screen. 'But I don't have any lucre.'

Petalu lumbered up behind her. He was sweating from the short walk. 'Petalu skint too. Have to contact Mama-Petalu.' He looked hopefully at Jo-Jo.

Jo-Jo groaned and turned back to the 'caster. The HealthWatch update informed him that it would take several hours to process his application and that should he experience diminished health he should proceed to an infirmary or medi-centre until the update was approved.

He swore and kicked the booth in frustration. The screen flickered and died.

'Crap.'

A moment later the overhead lights dimmed. Then the whole area went dark.

'Josef?' Bethany's whisper was filled with terror.

Jo-Jo reached out and found her hand. 'Steady now.'

'Not good feeling,' Petalu muttered.

'Mau, you know any way off the station?'

'Petalu come in on Savvy.'

'One of the waste contractors?' Jo-Jo's stomach did a flip. Without his HealthWatch in order going near one of those things could be a risk. 'Where do they berth?'

'Topside port,' said Mau.

'But that's the farthest one,' said Bethany.

'Safety regs, in case there's a leak. Don't want to nuke the planet as well,' said Jo-Jo.

'Maybe ship's still there. Maybe not. Savvy don't like trouble much.'

A siren set up a belated whine and emergency floor lights flared. In the red lighting Mau's face looked puffy. Jo-Jo could barely see his eyes for folds of skin. He had no idea if he could trust the man. 'You know the way there, Mau?'

'Think yes.'

'But we don't even know what is happening. Maybe there's an organised evacuation and we are being left behind,' said Bethany.

'Smell smoke,' said Petalu.

'Yeah,' said Jo-Jo. But what concerned him more was another odour. Something sickeningly sweet and pungent. 'Which way to the top port? Central Truss Lift?'

Petalu nodded. 'Think there other ways. But that easiest one.'

Jo-Jo searched his memory for the station design. Most res-shift stations had the same basic layout. The jail/confinement modules were usually separated from the main station by a sequence of unity nodes. If there was a breakout, the stationmaster could slam the door on a node and pop it adrift. A quick blast of radiation and everything in the module would be fried. The main station was designed around the Central Truss Lift. Everything else spiralled off it. There were secondary lifts but each one only travelled through a couple of floors.

'Let's try the CTL first.' Jo-Jo ran a few steps and picked up the leg from a broken stool. 'Grab something,' he told the others.

Bethany retrieved a smaller part of the stool while Petalu wrenched a strut longer than himself from the wall.

Jo-Jo stared at him, astonished. 'I know where I'll be standing when the shit hits, mate – right behind you.'

'Strong,' Petalu informed him. 'Not quick.'

Jo-Jo headed towards the access-way exit. The unity node led into another and another. Each was as deserted as the last and had minor damage to the cablework. Some cables dangled loose from the ceiling while others had been gouged from their conduits along the sides of the passage. The air was tainted with gas, and puddles of oil and lubricants made the floor slippery.

'It's like something has attacked the walls,' whispered Bethany.

Jo-Jo had been thinking the same thing. 'Yeah. Well, maybe we'll find out soon. We should be nearly through to the bottom level of the trade court and the CTL. Through this last join.'

But the mating adapter that connected the final node to the main station began creaking ominously.

'Quick!' Jo-Jo flung himself over the lip of the join. If the passage integrity had somehow been breached, the station would lock each one.

He reached back and grabbed Bethany, hauling her through after him. She was lighter than he expected, or maybe gut fear was making him stronger, but she flew from his grasp, slamming into the bulkhead with a light *thunk*.

Petalu lumbered over next. He stumbled on the lip and fell; part of his body on one side, part on the other.

'Come on, man. This thing sounds like it's gonna snap.' Sweat ran from every pore on Jo-Jo's body.

Petalu's face was drenched as well. The big man tried to get up but his shirt snagged on the roughed-up plastic of the lip and he lost balance again. On either side of the join floor panels began to flash. An automated voice gave instructions that were lost beneath the noise of the sirens.

'GET OUT OF THERE!' bellowed Jo-Jo.

Petalu didn't bother trying to get upright; he just rolled his body over the lip like a giant worm and flopped onto the other side. As he hit the floor the join irised shut, tearing his shirt off, leaving Petalu bare-chested and shaking.

The whole node began to judder.

'Mama,' Petalu cried and scrambled to his knees.

Jo-Jo grabbed one of his huge flailing arms and helped him to his feet but the juddering threw them both against the wall. Bethany lay on the floor moaning.

The groaning noise got louder and louder until there was a crack, more deafening than any thunder.

The juddering stopped.

Jo-Jo squeezed out from underneath Petalu's sweat-slicked stomach folds and looked for somewhere to wipe himself clean. The big man had, unsurprisingly, pissed himself.

He staggered over to look through the peephole at the join. 'Fuck me,' he said. 'It's gone. The whole thing has broken off.'

Jo-Jo wanted to sit down then and collect himself. Take it in. No – he wanted to *lie* down, smoke some changlo hemp and go to sleep.

Instead, he shepherded the other two along the passage.

Bethany nursed her shoulder.

'Must be blessed, eh?' Jo-Jo said to her. 'A few minutes later and—'

But Beth's stare was fixed ahead to where the passage opened into the vast bottom level of the station's trade court. 'Maybe it would have been better if we'd been in it,' she whispered.

The trade court was under a light pall of smoke that didn't hide the wreckage: broken tables and chairs, booths that had been torn from their footings, racks of fellalos strewn across the floor and stained with the contents of an overturned Kafe Kart, a food warmer slammed through a glass-vendor's display shelves.

But there was worse than that.

Creatures, taller than Petalu Mau and encased in sticky insect-like carapaces, were moving slowly through the mess. Each had six clawed legs and a head but no visible eyes. A few of them grouped together, their long thin probosces extending downward under a table into a tangle of humanesque arms and legs. An overpoweringly sweet scent pervaded the entire court.

'What – are – they?' Beth whispered.

'A problem,' Jo-Jo whispered back. 'Don't move while I think for a moment.'

She began to sob.

'Stop!' He clamped his fingers around her wrist, jabbing his nails into her skin. 'Do nothing to attract their attention.'

She closed her eyes and bit her lip. 'What are they doing to those people?'

'Don't look at it, Beth. Just listen to what I have to say.' Jo-Jo scanned the thick central column that housed the CTL. The row of lift doors that normally flashed icons and blared music were blank and silent, their outlines dimly visible through the smoke. 'The emergency service lift should still be working. Mau?'

'Over there.' Petalu Mau nodded towards the farthest wall where a faint red light pulsed slowly.

'Had to be there,' muttered Jo-Jo under his breath. He released Bethany's wrist and slowly turned his mouth to her ear. 'We are going to crawl over to the emergency lift. You follow behind me. Understand?'

She turned her face to his. Her eyes were wide open with fear and so close to him that her eyelashes almost brushed his cheek. 'Don't let them do that to me. Will you?'

He nodded.

They crawled in a slow single file around the perimeter of the trade court. From floor level they could see humanesque bodies fallen everywhere under the tables. The creatures clustered near them.

As they reached the halfway point a creature broke from its group and crawled in their direction. Jo-Jo froze, feeling the thump as Bethany knocked into him and then a harder one as Petalu did the same.

The creature stopped at a dead body only two tables away from them and began to probe the flesh in a methodical manner. The corpse was partly disrobed, as if it had already been examined. It was male. Jo-Jo could see a beard and the side of a boot.

As the creature continued its search Jo-Jo saw that it had no definable face but that the feelers uncurled from a set of mouth lobes. Each feeler ended in bulbous tips that appeared to be *tasting* the body. When the tips reached the dead man's face they paused, hovering above the closed eyes. A needle-like probe shot out from one of them, directly into the man's eye socket.

Jo-Jo was overwhelmed by a putrid sweet scent that made him want to gag. Hot burning liquid climbed through his throat, causing such a sharp pain in his chest that he had to clamp his mouth shut to prevent a moan escaping. Bethany's fingers clawed at his foot.

Keep it together, Beth. Keep it to—

Then he heard a deep, distressed sob. Not Beth. Petalu Mau. But Jo-Jo didn't dare move his head to look.

The creature stopped its feeding and retracted its

feelers inside its mouth lobes. The upper part of its torso rotated in a semicircle as if it were straining to detect the source of the noise.

Jo-Jo wondered which its strongest senses were. Clearly it could hear – but how well could it see?

It crawled closer to them – only a table length away now – undulating as though it was caught in a strong wind. Extending its feelers again it ran them along the tabletop and down the closest legs.

Bethany let go of Jo-Jo's foot. She was going to run. He knew, because that was what he wanted to do himself. He felt his leg muscles bunching.

The creatures seemed slow-moving enough. Maybe they had a chance if they were.

He pressed his palms against the floor, ready to push up, when he caught a movement from the corner of his eye: a humanesque figure running straight towards the CTL column. The creature near them spun with freakish speed, bunched its body and sprang after it.

Jo-Jo raised his head.

In several agile bounds the creature covered half the distance to the column. But those closer to the column beat it there. One of them knocked the 'esque down with its raking mid-claws and the group fell on him, feelers intertwined and fighting for position.

Jo-Jo hugged the floor and began a furious belly-crawl towards the service lift, his adrenalin stoked by the victim's cries. He crawled over bodies, barely feeling the flesh beneath their clothes. He didn't look at their faces – didn't look anywhere but at the red light pulsing gently above the service lift.

When he was only a few body lengths away from it

he became aware of movement at his elbow. Bethany scrambled past him, blood spattered over her grimly set jaw.

She reached the lift first and hit the button to summon it.

Jo-Jo pulled her back down, but across the trade court the group feeding on the fallen 'esque retracted their feelers and started up an odd swaying motion.

They'd seen her.

'Be ready,' Jo-Jo rasped. He watched the lift icon pulsing downward as the lift itself descended from the top tier of the station.

One of the creatures bunched its body and sprang towards them.

As the lift icon hit the midpoint of its descent Jo-Jo jumped up and grabbed a chair, ready to swing.

Bethany threw herself at the lift door, pounding the summon button repeatedly. 'Please!' she cried. 'Please!'

Jo-Jo raised the chair. *Time,* he told himself. *Just buy some time.*

Then he felt a hand on his arm.

Petalu wrenched the chair from his hand. The big man's torso was heaving from exertion and sweat still poured from his plump face. But his earlier fear had gone. His eyes were quite calm. 'Me.'

Jo-Jo dropped back, looking for another weapon, but there was nothing within close reach. He backed up against the lift door next to Beth.

The creature bunched to spring as the door opened. Bethany fell inside with Jo-Jo after her.

Then Petalu took one almighty swing . . .

TRIN

They *felt* the water a long time before they saw it. It reached for them with fleeting salty touches on their skin and a stinging flavour at the back of their parched throats, giving heart to the misery of their flight. In the lightening sky Trin saw the outline of the high dunes and the hint of sea mist.

A few hours only.

He had ordered Juno Genarro and his scouts not to return this time unless trouble threatened but to save their strength to swim to the palazzo marina and bring back transport for the rest of them. He had held out against Cass Mulravey, insisting that the scouts retained their cooling robes.

Despite walking through the darkness of the night, those without suits or robes were dehydrated. Trin tried to keep Djeserit close to him but she insisted on helping those who struggled most. Her own skin was blistered and flaking from the searing nightwinds.

More of them had died during the night. Some were his men – those who had surrendered their robes on his orders. Trin's fury collected in a mental space reserved for Cass Mulravey. She nursed her women as though they were more precious. And her presence was a constant reminder that Mira Fedor had left carrying his child.

He fretted that Mira would not return with aid, that she would turn her back on her world. He held endless conversations with her in his mind, arguments that always ended in the same place, with the same look: him demanding and her accusing.

'Principe.' Djeserit was next to him.

'*Si*,' Trin said. 'We must cross them now.'

He knew that her gaze followed his to the towering shadows that were the last line of red dunes. 'They must be as high as Mount Pell,' Djeserit gasped. 'How can we climb them?'

'We will not if we wait for the daylight,' Trin said grimly. 'Ever.'

In the east the sky grew lighter. He did not need to explain himself to Djeserit. Her practical sense was greater than his, and her selflessness shamed and angered him. She had helped the weakest – man and woman – despite her own unhealed injury. And when they stopped to rest she always attended Trin, listening while he spoke with Joe Scali and the others, serving him a little food and water, soothing him with her presence.

'Tell me again,' Djeserit whispered. 'Tell me what is on the other side.'

'If our route is accurate we will see the Tourmaline Islands,' Trin said. 'And the holiday palazzo with its medi-facility. And food.'

She moved closer, not quite touching him. 'You have led us to safety, Principe.'

Gratification fluttered in his breast. Her respect never failed to lift his spirits. Djeserit was right: he had saved them.

Buoyed above his exhaustion by self-belief, Trin gave his order to Joe Scali and Vespa Malocchi.

'Everyone must climb. Now. We must not wait.'

Trin led them over the last line of dunes without once looking back, concentrating on the impossible task of moving his numb legs, thinking ahead to the sight of the palazzo, feeling the cool safety of its interior.

The world around him dwindled to a single dogged purpose, and he had only a dim recognition of the sounds that he could hear: a shout, and weak cries of despair that could have been people calling his name. But he thought the voices were part of his tortured inner world, or part of his past. The present was the hot sand into which his aching feet scraped transient hollows, and it was the slicing pain across his lower back from muscles pushed beyond their endurance. When his trembling legs threatened to collapse he fell to his knees and crawled.

Hand, knee, hand, knee . . .

Trin reached the crest that way. Then, as he came to the top of the dune, the slap of a cooler wind raised his energy, and he let momentum tumble him down the other side. It rolled him nearly to the edge. With rattling breaths he crawled the final distance and flopped himself into the water, tearing open his fellalo to let the tepid liquid flood inside it. He wallowed and gasped, his mind filled with the cooling feel of it on his skin and the irresistible desire to drink it in. Only the dragging sensation as his robe became waterlogged forced him to retreat to the sand.

'Principe!'

Trin dashed water from his eyes and sought the source of the voice. *Joe Scali*. He stared up at his friend. There was no relief in the man's ravaged face, no celebration of arrival. Joe's legs shook as if he would fall.

'Djeserit is not here—'

Trin stumbled to his feet, his heart thumping.

'And the palazzo—' said Joe hoarsely.

Trin turned seaward. The Tourmaline Islands were exactly where he had reckoned: a line of flat scrubby land dots so close together that they would have looked like another large land mass if each one had not been divided from its neighbours by narrow channels of foaming water.

He scanned north, seeking the palazzo's familiar outline. It too was where it should have been, its imposing column-edges pale against the dawn. Above it, though, flashed the lights of circling AiVs.

'They are there ahead of us.' Trin turned to Joe. 'Quickly. Call the men. We must get to the cover of the nearest island before the light is truly upon us.'

'Trinder.' Joe's tragic face again. 'See.'

With an effort Trin widened the scope of his view, as though his eyes had become a telescope through which he must alter magnifications scanning first along the beach line where he saw Cass Mulravey and her women in the water as he had been; saw Cass herself scooping water over the head of the bambino Vito. The infant hung limply in her arms. 'Where are the rest?' he demanded. 'Why are they taking so long?'

This time Joe Scali dragged at the front of Trin's robe, pulling him round to face the dunes. Bodies lay on the ridge and further down the side: men, all of them without robes, fallen from exposure in their final effort.

'Carabinere.'

'*Si*. Some did not make it that far, even.'

Trin struggled to remember something. Why was it so hard to think, and to see? Then it came back to him. 'Djes?'

'I saw her helping Seb Malocchi. I-I . . .'

Trin strained his eyes again to examine each fallen body, searching out the configuration of the limbs. On the furthest, half buried in the red sand, he thought he saw his pale ensign. He had bound Djes's leg with it when the Saqr had wounded her and now she wore it, hidden under her clothing. Wrenching free of Joe Scali's grasp he staggered along the beach, fuelled with emotion.

As he passed Cass Mulravey he stopped and waded out to her. 'See what you have done.' He punched his fist towards his dead Carabinere. 'See what you have cost me.'

She didn't flinch from his anger but held out her hand to the women. 'And see what you have saved. I'm sorry for your men, Trinder Pellegrini. But you have saved your future. Without these women you are nothing. You cannot even breed.'

Trin would have hit her then, slapped her down into the water and held her under until all the air left her limp body if he had not needed the last of his strength to reach Djes.

He left Mulravey and began first to climb, then to crawl up the almost sheer face of the dune, towards his ensign.

Djes was there, half buried as he had guessed, beside Seb Malocchi's body. Malocchi was gone, his tongue swollen, his cracked lips coloured with dried blood.

Trin dug for her underneath the corpse of the Carabinere, shuddering with the effort, unable to cry. He remembered the fire in Loisa. He had saved Seb from it, just so he could die with no less dignity.

Joe Scali joined him, and Vespa Malocchi, Vespa cradling his fratella's face while Joe helped Trin pull Djeserit free.

Trin put his face to her lips but felt no breath. 'Djes.'

'Principe.' Joe Scali brushed the sand from her neck. 'See.'

Her gills moved sluggishly as if her body was searching for another source of oxygen.

'Quickly. The water.'

Together they dragged Djeserit down the dune and laid her in the surf. Trin held her body against his, willing oxygen into her blood, muttering senseless words. The water sluiced off the worst of the dirt and the flaking skin, leaving her face hideously raw. But Trin saw only her failing gills.

The survivors gathered on the water's edge, watching in silent exhaustion.

Cass Mulravey pushed to the front of the group. 'She's part Mio. Move her through the water,' said Mulravey. 'In a circle – to get the water passing through.'

The cursed woman was right. Trin dug his feet into the sand and began to spin slowly around.

After a dozen spins Djeserit's gills started to open and close rhythmically and within a few moments her top eyelids slid open. She stared at Trin through the water and the milky aqua-membrane, orientating herself. She seemed so alien at that moment.

He continued to spin her until she tapped his arm to tell him to stop. When he let go of her she flipped over and swam in slow circles of her own. Finally she surfaced, taking in great gasps of air as water drained from her gills and they shut.

Trin wanted to hold her again to reassure himself of the life in her. Instead he moved stiffly away to the water's edge.

'Principe! The scouts!' shouted one of the men.

The lightening sky revealed three flat-yachts sailing in from the north. Trin recognised the type of vessels as those from the Palazzo's marina, and identified Juno Genarro at the bow of the lead one.

'There is cover amongst the thorn bushes on the closer islands. We must reach there before full light,' Trin told the survivors. They had clustered into their two distinct groups: Mulravey's women and the pitiful remainder of Trin's men.

'What about the palazzo?' Mulravey asked.

'You can see the AiVs as well as I,' said Trin.

'Perhaps they are survivors like us.'

'Then you should take your group and find out. Mine will take cover on the islands.' He swept his glance over her women and the couple of men with them. 'Those of you who would come with me will have my protection.'

'Protection?' Mulravey made a dry, disparaging sound.

Yet as she did so the familia women left her group to stand, heads bowed, among Trinder's men.

Mulravey's face crumpled with disappointment. 'You've brainwashed your women, Pellegrini, but when Mira Fedor returns things'll change. They'll listen to her.'

'Deserters do not earn respect.'

'Mira Fedor is no deserter. Careful whose reputation you dirty.'

Trin felt his anger rising again. 'What is your decision, woman? We have no time to waste.'

One of her group pushed forward to the front; a morose male wearing a cheap envirosuit, threaded at the knees and shoulders. 'Don' talk to my sister like that.'

'Lennie, stop!' hissed Mulravey.

Trin sneered openly at her. 'So you would take cooling robes from the backs of soldiers for your women, but leave your brother with one.'

'She wanted me to give it over,' said her brother. 'Not that it's good fer much.'

Mulravey held her head high but Trin sensed her chagrin. 'You have not given up yours either, Principe,' she countered.

Trin reached inside himself for self-assurance and righteousness. *Of course I must be protected. I am Principe.*

He turned to the flat-yachts rolling into shore on the breaking waves. 'Make your choice.'

Sole

*play'm play'm little creatures
scurry scurry in out 'round
scratch'm deep, bleed'm more
luscious luscious*

TEKTON

Tekton's free-mind remained in a bad mood for days after his breakfast with Ra. It shouldn't have been, really. Ra showed every sign of being rattled by Tekton's project. Yet Tekton knew that Ra and the others were not to be underestimated.

Show/beauty had been Sole's instruction.

It had taken Tekton so many months to settle on what God might find beautiful that he was not sure how advanced the other tyros' projects were.

In truth, *beauty* had been a puzzle that he'd been unable to unravel. The evening, though, when he had seen Miranda Seeward's thighs and arms rippling as she wrestled her lawmon colleague in the Melange bar, the answer had come to him: the archiTect's second creed, *beauty is in the eye of the builder*. Tekton would create beauty not for Sole, but for himself. And nothing – NOTHING – was more beautiful, more exciting, more ecstasy-beholden to his free-mind than the sight of undulating flesh.

Now that Tekton had located the exotic and rare mineral amalgam that would turn his vision into reality, he had just to keep it away from prying eyes while it was constructed.

To process the amalgam he would need a foundry of sorts and warehousing while it was sculpted. Logic-mind warned him that he would need to find a discreet workshop for the sculpting process. Manufacturing large quantities of quixite without OLOSS sanction would likely incur a great penalty, so fearful were they of any material that might be perverted to support the trans-humanesque cause.

But Tekton did not have time to wait for sanction. That would give Ra and the other tyros more time. He needed a facility now.

The Entity has requested your presence in the shafting room.

Now?

Yes, Godhead.

Not a little annoyed at the timing, Tekton hastened to the surface building. The Balol matron wasn't there this time. The attendant was a tall thin Pagoin who looked as if he might implode from sheer fragility.

Tekton entered the sheer-walled room and stared at the shafting cylinder, remembering his previous experiences with startling clarity.

'This will not be painful or nauseating like the initial procedure. Well . . . only *slightly* nauseating, so I'm told,' said the Pagoin.

'Why do I need to be here at all? I have had my . . . procedure as you call it.'

'The accentuation facility in this room gives you a more multidimensional and intimate communication experience with Sole. The Entity prefers to use this when it has something important to communicate. The auditory preceptors in your remodelled mind have limitations.' The attendant blinked several times. 'Do you mind me asking, Godhead, what is it like to have two separate minds?'

Tekton thought to ignore the question. Then he reconsidered. 'It is most . . . liberating,' he allowed.

The Pagoin smiled. 'That's what I thought.'

Tekton climbed into the cylinder field and braced himself. What did the Entity want to *show* him?

This time when space fell at him the transition was exhilarating. In an instant he had become an infinitesimal stitch in a majestic tapestry and yet he was also the central knot from which everything else would unravel. He hung in Sole's eye. In Sole's mind. In Sole's heart.

Humanesque concepts all.

<come>

And with that one powerful thought Tekton's humanesque framework fragmented. Him – the stitch, the mote, the minutest particle of matter – recomposed and he became a bounding, lightless energy shifting and expanding restlessly, thrusting against other equal forces.

Quintessence.

He [it] was a burgeoning intransigent, negative pulse. An energy rubbing and pulling. Sophisticated and raw in one cosmic breath. Time irrelevant.

He [it] was suffused with cold-warmth. And gradually he [it] became more than his [its] senses. A type of cognition formed. Not thinking but knowing. There was a difference. A billion mysteries unlocked and drenched his [its] cold-warmth with their knowledge.

Phantom Energy had its own sentience: giddy, infantile, wise and wily. Knowing offered everything and he [it] luxuriated in it. He [it] played and romped and fed greedily. Stirred. More answers than questions. A bath of answers.

But one single question.

He [it] gorged on answers to reach the question. But bloated knowledge slowed him [it], and he [it] lost purpose or meaning or momentum with the swollen greatness of himself [itself].

Many, many, many resided in that corpulent space/time: quarrelling and bargaining and gossiping in the manner of all-knowledgers. They had been there since the true for-ever. Unrelated, yet born of the same.

But he [it] alone retained memory of the question. And when the stirring came again, the itch that gave him [it] purpose, he [it] reached ... grasping, grasping ...

<context>

Imploding/explosion. Collapsing/expansion.

Separation.

A final glimpse. For-ever in a moment. Comprehension in emptiness. Ending in a beginning. Life in death, life in death, life in death ...

<context>

Tekton fell painfully back into humanesque thought, as if his body had been compressed into a tiny box.

He took time to orientate. A straw was forced to his lips. Blood wiped from his nostril. Lotion applied to his face.

Eventually he was able to focus on the Pagoin who ministered to him.

'Was that liberating?' the Pagoin asked.

Tekton shuddered, barely able to reply. 'No,' he whispered.

The Pagoin helped him to the taxi. 'Do you require medical assistance, Godhead?'

The Lostol archiTect waved him off and instructed the taxi to leave. Back in his rooms Tekton raised his privacy level and took to his bed. He stayed there for several days, imbibing only fluids while he attempted to assimilate his experience.

His minds remained quiet, both of them raw and unable to offer elucidation on the experience; bruised like fruit dropped from a crate. The 'all-knowing' sense fell quickly away, so incapable was either mind of sustaining the memory or comprehension of such a torrent.

What had Sole wished him to know?

When finally the shock subsided, one overriding thought prevailed. Tekton forced himself to get up and bathe. When he had eaten he sat himself at his bureau.

Moud, what do you know of Rho Junction?

That is an exponentially expanding subject, Godhead. Could you be more specific?

Moud, can the contents of our conversations be monitored in any way?

Not that I am aware of, Godhead. Not unless you allow it.

Then I wish you to provide a list of all the manufacturers on Rho Junction.

I am prohibited from actively searching for such information, the moud replied primly.

*And what, my incompetent little moud, does **actively searching** mean?* A thick tendril of anger began to uncurl in Tekton's breast. Had they deliberately engaged the stupidest, most spineless of assistants for him?

Some information is freely available on Studium Net. However, OLOSS has safeguards in place to prevent

*unverified information about dubious markets from being
accessed by just anyone.*

Just anyone! Are you implying that I fit that description?

That is their phraseology, Godhead, not mine.

Tekton made an audible clicking noise with his teeth.
Hibernate, he ordered the moud.

The faint buzzing sound that signified its presence
in his mind fell silent immediately.

Tekton paced the length of his sitting room several
times and then ordered honey, bread and mokka to be
sent to his quarters. In his present mood he didn't feel
like the company of the other tyros.

Instead he disrobed and climbed into his lotion sack
to try and relax while he waited for the light meal to
arrive. What he needed was someone outside OLOSS
influence to snoop for him. Jo-Jo Rasterovich would
have been the perfect solution but Tekton doubted
that he could get compliance from the vagabond mineral
scout after their previous encounter.

In fact, logic-mind urged again, perhaps he should
order his moud to add Rasterovich to his list of potentially dangerous personages whose whereabouts he
monitored.

Paranoia! sniffed free-mind. Rasterovich was far too
indolent and obtuse to be of any significant threat. And
there must be countless Rasterovich types in Orion.
Tekton just needed to locate one.

Logic-mind checked back in. He must verify the
Pellegrinis' delivery dates. While Tekton had enjoyed
his brief interlude with Marchella Pellegrini on Araldis,
he had no doubts about their efficacy when it came to
business. Patriarchal caste societies like the Latinos of

Araldis generally honoured their agreements, bound as they were by notions of honour and status.

What was it that the woman had negotiated for?

Logic-mind stamped upon his erotic memories and set about reviewing the contents of his negotiation.

Aaaah, yes. That's right. She wanted a tyro for one of her kind.

Never! squealed logic-mind. *Those Latinos are so socially primitive.*

Who cares? free-mind replied. *Just ask the question. Be seen to be upholding the agreement.*

Tekton saw the sense in free-mind's suggestion. He slid out of his sack and patted the excess of lotion from his body with an absorbent cloth.

Moud?

The hum returned. *Yes, Godhead?*

Make an appointment with the Chief Astronemein.

Balbao, the Balol scientific Chief-of-Station and Tekton did not share similar interests, ideals or biorhythms. In their previous two encounters the C-o-S had exhibited little concern for Tekton's complaints. This would work perfectly in his favour and Tekton approached the meeting confident that Balbao would deny his request instantaneously. He would then be able to relay the difficulties he was having to Marchella Pellegrini on Araldis and basically stall – indefinitely – for time.

On previous occasions he had met with the C-o-S in a laboratory but today the Balol assistant ushered Tekton into Balbao's private rooms.

Tekton took a moment to absorb the size and luxury

of them: the garish gold-plated fittings and pattern-switching floor covering.

The Balol sat perched in a swivel armchair with his feet on the ledge of a window facsimile. He sipped something frothy from a fluted glass and flexed his neck frill as if deep in thought.

Tekton ahem-ed politely to gain his attention.

'Yes, *Godhead*?'

Tekton detected Balbao's sarcasm. To the astronemeins the tyros were merely convenient study animals.

'I have a request.'

Balbao gargled the last sip of his drink before he answered. 'Let me guess. Longer opening times at the Melange bar? Pickled Ink Squid on the room-service menu? Lotion towels in the diner?'

'I'm sure you are well aware that I do not use towels. They are too abrasive. And while your humour is mild and inoffensive, it also suggests that you perceive us to be frivolous and superficial.'

'Superficial? You, Tekton? I would never think such a thing.'

Tekton fixed him with a cold stare. 'I wager, Balbao, that it will be our endeavours which uncover the truths about the Entity. Not your tedious measurements and excruciating empirical observations.'

Balbao frowned. His skin turned an unflattering shade of grey like the first puffs of a storm cloud.

Tekton assessed him as suitably enraged, and delivered his request. 'I wish to petition for a new tyro and I want you to support me to Higher Intelligence Affairs.'

The Balol's crest flattened into his thick neck and he made an odd choking splutter. 'You j-joke, of course?'

'Humour is not a strong Lostolian trait. I wish to petition for a female from the Latino races to join us here.'

'A Latino *female*?' Balbao flicked quickly through
some images until he got a representation. His absent
look suggested that his moud was enlightening him
about Latinos. After a few moments he let out an
unattractive hawking sound as though he had a throat
full of phlegm. 'Godhead, you do have a sense of
humour . . . a female tyro from a repressed, patriarchal
society.'

'Bigotry can achieve wonders,' stated Tekton loftily.
'Makes the mind hungry.'

Balbao snorted. 'Then you won't be surprised to hear
that not only will I not support your application, but I
will fight it to my last breath.'

Tekton conjured a look of annoyance. 'That is regret-
table,' he lamented. 'But I will not be denied.'

'Oh yes, you will,' growled Balbao.

Perfect, thought Tekton.

Tekton took a taxi to the Melange bar to celebrate his
easy manipulation of Balbao. To his disappointment
only Labile Connit was there. He had barely spoken
to the Geneer in his months on Belle-Monde. The man
appealed to him almost as little as Balbao did, although
his skin colour had a pleasant golden hue as opposed
to the grey pigmentation of the Balol. It seemed rather
unbalanced of nature, Tekton thought, to bestow such
a radiant skin on a Geneer: they were such dour and
imperative-bound types.

Yet you could not do without them, his logic-mind
piped in.

Not yet, countered free-mind.

In a far more expansive mood than earlier and contemplating the notion that with his Sole-gained enhancements he might never have to consult a Geneer again, Tekton engaged Labile Connit in conversation.

Connit was hunched over a table-screen that was blurred by the spills from his row of empty agave-beer glasses. Tekton could smell the sweetness of the beer's succulent base.

'Good morning, Connit. May I buy you a beverage?'

'Shure. Why not?' the Geneer slurred and waved his hand. 'After thish many I'll drink with anyone.'

Tekton ignored the insult and ordered drinks via his moud.

They sat in awkward silence until the waiter served them. That is, Tekton felt a trifle awkward. Connit seemed oblivious to anything other than the flicker of images running across the table-screen.

'The entertainment is tediously limited here, don't you think?' commented Tekton.

Connit shrugged. 'I hate this place.' Then, to Tekton's surprise, tears brimmed and trickled down the young Geneer's cheeks.

A crying drunk, said Tekton's free-mind. *Disgusting!*

But useful, countered logic-mind. *Drunker the better when it comes to secrets.*

Tekton ordered Connit another beer, this time with a shot of fatta extract. Fatta extract was expensive but as tasteless as vodka and was known for its numbing effect on the humanesque amygdala.

'It sounds as if you need a sabbatical. Or perhaps a visit with your family? That is . . . I don't know where you come from but it can't be too far. Orion is rather small.'

Connit slurped down the fatta-laced beer, none the wiser. 'No. No . . . Impossible!' He shook his head vehemently.

Why not? Tekton wondered. The tyros were free to go anywhere, anytime, unless their sponsors had set restrictions. Tekton's main sponsor was GOHI and his minor sponsor was his studium. He imagined the others had similar arrangements.

Moud, who is Labile Connit's sponsor?

The Group of Higher Intelligence.

And?

Tekton sipped his juice while he waited for the moud to answer. Really, it was bordering on the ineffectual as bio-ware went.

Godhead, there seems to be an anomaly in my information.

Yes?

Godhead Connit's co-sponsor is stated as being an industrial company called CGE.

And who in-a-Lostol's-fine-skin are they?

I have searched the Orion companies register and they do not appear to exist.

Aha! gloated logic-mind. *A secret!*

'What programme entertains you so, Labile?' Tekton enquired.

Connit scowled and turned the table-screen off abruptly. He drew shapes in the spilled beer and didn't bother to answer.

Moud?

The station AI informs me that Godhead Connit has been streaming Unbound *broadcasts.*

Unbound? Tekton had heard of Unbound – vaguely. *Where do they emanate from?*

There is no proven point of origin though it is commonly held that they originate from Consilience.

'How interesting,' Tekton murmured.

'Whassat?' slurred Connit.

Tekton realised that he'd spoken aloud and smiled blandly at the Geneer. 'What is what?'

'What'd you shay?'

'Perhaps you should get some sleep, my dear Connit, for I said nothing at all.' Tekton smiled again and excused himself.

On the taxi ride home he flipped things between his minds.

Why would one of Orion's top Geneers be watching streams originating from Consilience? And why would he not be able to visit his family?

Logic-mind was of the opinion that Connit was showing all the symptoms of dislocation syndrome.

Dislocation syndrome. Pah! said free-mind. *He's lonely and he's hiding something.*

When he got back to his quarters, Tekton told his moud to stream Unbound to his viewing screen. He spent impatient minutes while the moud ran lists of the programmes broadcast in the last hour through the myriad of sub-broadcasts that came through the Unbound node. The political propaganda from the countless groups uncensored by the OLOSS charter was at worst unintelligible and at best sinister.

Tekton felt a moment's relief that OLOSS had a powerful military force to suppress such anarchical tendencies among sentients. Those insufferable

Extropists perpetuated much of this lawless behaviour. He wondered if they realised that in their desire for post-humanesque evolution they had swayed danger-ously close to anti-humanesque. How peeved they must be by the appearance of Sole.

'Narrow the search. Reject "authentic war" and "combat injury".'

The feed dropped to a more manageable ten thou-sand channels. Tekton continued refining his search based on the glimpse he'd had across the viewing table in the Melange bar. With five hundred channels left he began to question the fruitfulness of what he was doing. What was he expecting to find? Why was he even bothering?

No good reason, said logic-mind.

Searching for a clue, said free-mind.

A clue to what? What had suddenly so intrigued him about the recalcitrant and graceless Geneer?

Tekton left the screen and went to his bed where he disrobed and ordered the room into complete dark-ness. There he let thoughts percolate in his mind for a time, letting them flower into possibilities in the way he let his designs mutate.

Moud, call Miranda Seeward.

Yes, Godhead.

When Miranda answered he climbed from his bed and returned to his living space. 'Good day, Miranda.'

'Indeed it must be, Tekton,' she said wryly, 'since you forgot to dress.'

He glanced down at his naked body and then back at his muse. 'Come now. Don't pretend to be shocked.'

'Shocked, pah! Now, what disturbs you enough to

call me stark naked? Something that obviously cannot wait until tonight.'

Tonight?

The tyros' weekly meeting, his moud reminded him.

Ah, yes . . . Now, how to say this so that she won't be too curious? 'I am concerned for Labile Connit. I spoke with him this morning and he seems beset by melancholy. Perhaps there is some way we could cheer him up. A surprise visit from his family, perhaps.'

Miranda's mouth dropped open, sending her chins into an outrageous wobble. 'Tekton, how thoughtful! I had noticed the same thing. You know, you really are a treasure under that brittle self-serving exterior.' She leaned closer to the screen. 'And I should know.' She winked. 'I have the fondest memories of our tryst on Scolar.'

Tekton felt his akula swamping his objectivity. Miranda seemed able to arouse him with the merest hint of her over-abundant pheromones. He made an effort to repress the rush. 'As do I, my dear. But it is Labile we should be thinking of at this moment . . .'

She frowned at having the conversation deflected from one of her favourite topics. 'Well, though your intentions are noble I think we would have little joy locating his kin. It is rumoured that he was incubated at an illegal birth-station.'

'Then he has no family?'

'Not a jot.'

'Oh.'

'Oh?'

'Then we must think of something else,' said Tekton.

Miranda gave him a sceptical look. 'I will put some thought into it. We can discuss it this evening.'

'I shall look forward to it.' Tekton ended the call and sat at his viewer for several moments, thinking of his conversation with Labile.

Moud, tell me what you can about Labile Connit's origins.

Godhead, Connit has a privacy lock on his biographical information.

Isn't there another way to access it?

No, Godhead.

If the moud had been corporeal Tekton would have kicked it. Really, it was next to useless.

He returned to his bed and resumed his darkened thinking. Geneers, he mused, were linear thinkers by and large. *Moud, search biographical details of Labile Connit's genetic parents.*

Tekton was rewarded with silence while it did as he bid, and he felt a little surge of triumph. Connit had placed a privacy screen on questions about himself. He had not thought to protect himself from a sideways query.

There is no record of such humanesques.

Was Miranda correct, then? Had Labile been incubated illegally? He sat up again and this time he dressed with purpose.

Moud, call me a taxi and then hibernate.

Yes, Godhead.

Tekton put on a comfortable day robe, moisturised his smooth skull and sat down to wait for the taxi. It looked like he would have to find out the old-fashioned way what he wanted to know.

Politic detention was in a grand Renaissance Redux building adorned with gold-impregnated pilasters and movement-activated uuli hums, and took up an entire block along Gorgias Boulevard. Each detainee – so Thales's guard informed him – was afforded a sleeping room and an antechamber with a desk and an aspect cube.

Though the surroundings were eminently comfortable, Thales felt the infringement of his liberty as painfully as a fresh scalding. Worse, when he realised that he would have to share his confinement.

As the Brown Robe thrust Thales to the floor and slammed the door, his room companion regarded him with interest.

'You *have* trodden on someone's toes. In fact, I would surmise, their fingers as well,' the man said.

Thales scowled and climbed to his feet. 'This is shameful. What sort of city is this where one cannot disagree with one's wife without being jailed?' He pounded on the door and continued pounding until his knuckles bled and his voice became hoarse. 'Release me! Rene. *Rene!*' he roared.

Then, finally, when it became apparent no one would come he slid to the floor and crouched in a trembling huddle.

The older man poured a glass of coloured water from a china pitcher and brought it to him.

Embarrassed and angry, Thales ignored him at first, but the man was gently insistent.

'Please. It will not serve you at all to be wretched. Perhaps a civil discussion might lift your spirits?'

Thales took a sip and held it in his mouth, letting the minerals soothe his throat. He stopped short of gargling for, at first glance, the other man seemed most refined and hence out of place in such an establishment. Not only were his manners and demeanour superior, but his bearded face bore the furrows of a man who thought much and had seen more. Not leathery or worn, but erudite. He did not affect the glamour allusions that many scholars favoured and his aquiline nose was untouched by the sculptor's rod.

Still, Thales was too upset to be gracious. 'What do you know of discourse? What do you know of me? Your presumption would suggest . . . very little.'

The older man did not sigh or take umbrage. He sat down and gestured across a small polished table at another plain leather armchair. 'You are quite right in that. I know very little other than that it will be more comfortable for you to sit here rather than on the floor.' He took a small sip from his own glass of stained water and waited.

Something about the man's mildness stung Thales into recognising his own childishness. He glanced down to his bleeding hand. 'I sh-should wash first.'

The gentleman nodded.

Thales climbed to his feet and found the washing cubicle next to the vacant bedroom. He hastily rinsed his hands and face and patted his hair into some order. It had come loose from its weave of plaits and fell loosely to his shoulders. The swing of it in the mirror reminded him of Rene and he clamped his lips together.

When he had dried himself he took his seat opposite the gentleman and attempted to adopt an air of reasonable composure.

'I am Thales Berniere, incarcerated by the Sophos for disagreeing with my wife.'

The man smiled sadly. 'Even in Scolar I would have thought that would be permitted.'

'Not when your wife is the daughter of a Sophos Pre-Eminent,' he said bitterly.

'Your disagreement was . . . philosophical in nature?'

Thales blew air from his cheeks. 'I suppose you could say that, though the nature of it was more encompassing than a simple point of dialogue.'

The man's eyes narrowed almost imperceptibly. 'How so, Thales? In a city of such wide and varied philosophy and learning.'

'Wide and varied Scolar may be, but it is also toothless. Here you may come to learn and preach almost anything but actual decisions are made only by the Sophos Pre-Eminence. And their doctrines are stale and limited. There are no challenges to their practice. Arguments between opposing doctrines are hypocrisy – no more than that.'

'Would you care to share your own beliefs with me?'

Again, the gentleman's mildness lulled Thales's antagonism. He settled back into his chair. Draining his glass, he nursed it against his chest. 'Currently I am investigating Jainism. I find the upashrayas serene and uncluttered with opulence. They are a fine place to think.'

The gentleman frowned in recall. 'Jainism? Aaah, yes . . . eternal, universal truths, spiritual independence and individual equality . . . non-violence: Ahisma, Satya, Asteya, Brahmacharva, Aparigraha.'

Thales blushed. 'As you can see, I am far from attaining Moksha. I am at the beginning of my journey but I would never, *never* use violence on another sentient.'

'What of the lower life-forms?'

Thales reddened, unsure how to answer.

They sat in silence for some time. When they spoke again it was of generalities, the gentleman enquiring at length about Thales's upbringing and pastimes.

Mira

The corduroy texture of *Insignia*'s outward vision showed the Intel Res-shift Station as a ball-and-flute construction, pirouetting midway between the third and fourth planet of the Tantine system.

You should be in Primo for this shift. I will protect the health of your baby, the biozoon advised.

'I don't care,' Mira said irritably from where she lay on the vein couch. She was constantly nauseous and her limbs felt heavier than they should. Sitting up had become a huge effort, walking almost unthinkable. *Insignia* said her body was flooded with large amounts of chemicals, which accounted for her symptoms. The knowledge did little to improve her mood.

'Don't care about what?' demanded Rast from the other side of the buccal where she was watching the station's vase-like structure loom closer. During the last few days the mercenary had taken to spending time in Autonomy where she could get a virtual representation of their position. Mostly she and Mira had ignored each other. 'You've been acting pretty weird, Fedor.'

'I was speaking to the . . .' Mira hesitated before finishing.

'Yeah, I know – the 'zoon. They say most of you Inbreds go whacko after a while. You got it coming already.'

Rast was deliberately baiting her. The mercenary was restless from inactivity and there were still a few weeks to Scolar before Mira would contemplate taking the mercenaries to the planet of their choice.

'Don't queue for a direct shift. We want to go station-side,' Rast said.

Mira sat up straighter. 'There is no time for that. Araldis—'

Rast cancelled the virtual feed, her eyes narrowing dangerously. 'To use your own words, Baronessa, "I don't care." I lost most of my team there and never got paid. I hope someone nukes the damn place.'

Mira clenched her fists. Tears of anger sprang to her eyes and blurred her vision. Her tolerance of Rast's taunting had been exhausted by her own misery. 'Is it possible that you are truly that shallow? Or perhaps you are not even humanesque?'

Rast's pale complexion suffused with colour. 'You calling me a ginko?'

'I am calling you inhumanesque. It is not the same. Do not assume that aliens do not have principles.'

'Principles!' Rast made a choking sound. She slammed her feet to the floor as if she might launch herself across the buccal.

Mira drew her knees to her chest and threw her hands up in defence.

Her reaction stopped Rast dead. 'Look, just give us a few hours there. We're used to ships that need to be worked. The boredom is killing us.'

Mira dropped her hands. 'Boredom does not kill people.'

Rast shot Mira a penetrating stare. 'Fedor, I need

some physical release. I'd hate to lose it completely and for you to be the only one around.'

Mira's mouth went dry. Did Rast know what had happened with Trin Pellegrini? Or was the mercenary simply being honest?

Mira, Intel station is requesting our shift plan, said *Insignia.*

Can I farcast yet?

Not from my relays. You could use the station relay. You will need to convince the stationmaster of your credibility . . . and need.

Would it be quicker simply to continue on?

Perhaps. However, I need to replenish unsustainable supplies. I was not stocked for this journey.

How will we pay for them?

Insignia paused. *Credit would automatically be extended to Latino nobility under flag, but once you have informed them of the invasion they may consider it unwise to allow you to incur a debt that may not be repaid.*

Surely they would understand our refugee situation?

Understand, yes. But it is my observation that humanesques are largely motivated by economic concerns.

Mira tried to recall the specifics of biozoon metabolism but the heaviness that dragged at her body had made her mind sluggish as well. *Your unsustainable supplies – can you survive until Scolar without them?*

Survive? Yes. But it may be uncomfortable.

How so?

I need over three hundred amino acids to avoid degradation of my body tissue. Without them I am unable to generate the normal level of comforts you are accustomed to. For instance, my core temperature may rise, thus affecting my ability to keep the climate suitable.

Anything else?

Should we encounter something unexpected, like unusually high magnetic streams, I may have to use energy reserves that will affect my ability to maintain a suitable atmosphere.

You mean we will not be able to breathe.

*While I am alive I can support **your** needs, as long as you remain in Primo. I can support Secondo for long periods as well. Other passengers, though, may not fare as well.*

What do you require?

Insignia began to rattle through a list.

After a few moments Mira interrupted. *Tell Intel that we request landing rights and request refugee status.*

I am pleased that you have made that choice.

The biozoon's relief surprised Mira. Had *Insignia* thought that she would run her deliberately into degradation? *You must explain your needs. I am unable to read your physiology in the way that you can read mine.*

Yes. I forget sometimes that you are so limited.

The biozoon's ingenuous manner did not offend Mira in the way that Rast's did.

The mercenary was standing now, staring at her. Hands on hips. 'Have you finished communing with the big whale?'

'Whale?'

Rast sighed. 'The 'zoon.'

Mira frowned. 'Biozoons are infinitely more sophisticated than most animals. I would hesitate before insulting them.'

'You clearly know shit about whales. What's your call, Fedor?'

'We will stop for supplies. That should give you long enough to . . . relieve yourself.'

Rast nodded. 'Dandy,' she said and spun on her heel.

The Intel Stationmaster kept Mira waiting in the chilled functional corridor outside his office. Though she welcomed the coolness on her overheated body, standing seemed to amplify her nausea. Her limbs felt bloodless and she wondered where she might run if the sickness became too great.

Finally, a small bow-legged humanesque dressed in smooth khaki overalls emerged. His hooked nose was like a hand-fashioned dividing line in his narrow face.

'Baronessa Fedor?'

'*Si.*'

'Master Landhurst.' He waved Mira through into an unadorned office but did not invite her to sit. 'Your reports of your planet are grave but I have not been able to verify them,' he said.

'Of course not, Signor Landhurst. Dowl station was overrun by the Saqr. There is no communication in or out,' she said.

'Yet you escaped?'

'The biozoon was well hidden and I am fortunate to have the Innate Talent.'

'Biozoons are rare enough and highly prized – but women do not have the Talent.'

'It is not usual, no. But I *do* have it.' Mira kept her face composed. Landhurst was trying to intimidate her. 'And if you are implying that I might have stolen *Insignia* then you do not understand the biozoon nature.'

'I assume it has an Autonomous function?'

'Yes. But I would never usurp that. Not unless . . .'

'You had to?' Landhurst gave a sharp deprecating laugh.

Mira stiffened. 'The Autonomy function is for protection of the biozoon and its crew. Should the biozoon be hurt or incapacitated in some way, a skilled pilot may take command. But the disabling itself is a cruel measure to be taken only in extreme situations. On Latino Crux the vaqueros liken it to a bosal.'

'Aaah, yes, I've heard that explanation – the bridle that tortures the nerves of the animal it controls. I gather, then, that your situation is not extreme?'

Landhurst twisted her words easily. 'I . . . yes . . . but the biozoon was in agreement that I did not need—'

'Why are you the only one of your clan on board? Where is your . . . what do you call your governor?'

'Our Principe was killed in the invasion. His son is the new Principe. Trinder Pellegrini recognised that I was the only one who could take the biozoon and bring news to OLOSS of this atrocity.'

'Yet he did not come with you?'

'He is loyal to his home. He wished to command the survivors, to keep them alive. They have withdrawn to the islands in the hope of evading the Saqr.'

Having to defend Trin to this unpleasant man cost Mira much precious energy. Shadows began to steal over the edge of her vision.

Landhurst noticed her swaying. 'Sit down, Baronessa. It is not usual for women to faint in my rooms.' He gave her a sly smile. 'At least, not in my *office*.'

Mira did not return his smile as she sank onto a hard chair.

Landhurst brushed past her to sit on the edge of his desk. 'How did you res-shift from the system if the station was overrun?'

'As you would know, signor, biozoons can calibrate their own shift, unlike ordinary craft which rely on the Station systems. Shifting was not an issue. Being damaged before we could shift was. Dowlspace was chaotic.'

He stared at her. 'I know a little of your culture, Baronessa. Women are not educated in the functional aspects of space vehicles.'

'I have degrees in Latino Studies, Orion Literature and Genera. The rest I learned by choice and . . . discreetly.'

Landhurst looked at her with more interest. 'Tell me about the Saqr.'

Mira attempted to put her tired thoughts into order. Why did he want so many details? 'They are tardigrades that have been adapted for land living.' She returned his intent look. 'They feed on fluids, Stationmaster. Body fluids. What more would you know about them?'

'Who brought them to your planet?'

'No one is sure. I understand your need for information but what I have told you is the truth. I am neither loco nor misguided.'

'You are travelling with known mercenaries. What would you call that?'

'They have told me that our Principe employed them. Perhaps he sensed danger for his people. Our own military force is . . . was limited. The mercenaries lost many of their own but they kept a town of people alive. I judge on what I see, not on what I am told.

Our travelling together is a coincidence based on mutual survival.'

Landhurst's expression hardened. 'I run one of the busiest shift-stations in Orion, Baronessa. I have heard every story imaginable. I need to be convinced that yours is authentic before I can provide you with the provisions you request and allow you to use our emergency 'cast. And, frankly, I don't know that I am.'

Besieged by tiredness, Mira found herself no longer caring about discretion or manners. 'My sorella is dead. While you search for your authenticity the last of my people are being hunted to death. I have a child there, Master Landhurst. *My child.*'

He wavered at that. 'You have left your child behind?' he asked.

She didn't attempt to hide her wretchedness. 'I had no choice.'

Landhurst watched her for a long moment. 'Very well, Baronessa. You may farcast on our emergency line and I will charge your consumables to OLOSS's refugee fund. But if it turns out that things are not how you say they are then I have my own methods of redress. I run a profitable business. I do not hold this position because of my compassionate nature.'

'I have found that compassion is a rare attribute, Master Landhurst,' said Mira. 'But decency will do.'

At that, he had the grace to blush.

When Mira had composed and sent her message to OLOSS, she returned to *Insignia*, sinking gratefully into the comfort of the Primo vein.

Where are the others?

I cannot locate them precisely but they left shortly after you.

Mira felt a mixture of relief and irritation. She was alone on *Insignia* – yet they would need to leave as soon as the supplies were loaded. *The stationmaster has agreed to provide our requisitions.*

Yes. Station Intel has contacted me.

How long before we can shift?

Two station hours if the loading is efficient.

Place us in the shift queue. Please. Mira entertained the idea of leaving without the mercenaries. The likelihood that they would ever meet again seemed slim. And yet they could corroborate her story. If OLOSS were as sceptical as Stationmaster Landhurst she might need their support.

Another wave of fatigue rolled over her.

I need to sleep for a few minutes. She relaxed back into the vein and felt the welcome relief as it moulded to her body. *Insignia*'s sensors skittered over her body like light, loving fingers soothing away the ever-present nausea. She felt safe, safe, safe until . . .

A stabbing sensation jolted her awake. The pain was in her stomach.

Insignia?

Humanesques are trying to enter my organ space.

Your compatible areas?

No.

What humanesques? Rast?

I allowed access to my absorption area for amino replenishment. Several humanesques accompanied the automon loaders. That is not uncommon when taking aboard provisions. But they have forced one of my sphincters open.

Mira experienced the slicing pain again.

While you are in Primo I cannot protect you from what I feel.

Can you repel them?

No. They have penetrated a vulnerable section of my body. I must concentrate my efforts on controlling my bleeding.

Mira felt sick. *Insignia* bleeding.

Who would do this? Mira's thoughts skittered over possibilities. *Insignia, ask Station Intel for assistance.*

Long moments passed.

Station Intel has been instructed not to respond to us. *Insignia*'s voice sounded fainter in her mind.

Landhurst! Mira knew it immediately. *What can I do? Don't leave me . . .*

Insignia? Insignia!

The biozoon's presence began to fade. Mira tried to pursue it into its darkening mindspace but their connection had narrowed to the width of a pulsing cord. She mind-grasped one end of the cord and focused her energy into it. Their combined thoughts brightened her awareness. She saw the six armed humanesques with cutting equipment burning *Insignia*, the trajectory of their approved shift queue position, Rast arguing with the marshals at the entrance to their berth.

Why won't they let her in?

Insignia did not – could not – reply. The biozoon's thoughts darkened again and the cord began to pull from Mira's mind-grasp.

She let go of it and ordered the vein to expel her. Its membranes shaped into an upright seat. She breathed deeply until the transition dizziness passed; swallowing the acid that fizzed in her throat.

Rast.

Mira ran along strata until she reached Rast's cabin. It was orderly, one wall lined with a selection of weapons from the Principe's armoury. Mira seized a pistol and ran to the egress scale that joined to the docking tube.

Insignia. Release.

The scale peeled back and Mira peered into the tube. At the far end she could see Rast, Catchut and Latourn. They'd exchanged their fellalos for casual garb. Rast had her hands jammed deep into her short-coat pockets and was talking to the tube marshal.

Mira hid the pistol in the folds of her fellalo. She walked slowly towards them, her head bowed as if she were hesitant and nervous. *Landhurst will not have* Insignia. *He will not.* She felt their stares on her.

'Halt!' said the marshal. 'Return to the biozoon.'

Mira's reply was to jerk the pistol from her robe. 'Let them board.'

The marshal froze – not from fear, she realised belatedly, but in concentration.

Suddenly the docking tube began to constrict around her. Mira ducked as the marshal drew a gun and fired at her but Rast spoiled his aim and Catchut leapt for his throat, gouging at it with a practised killing action.

The marshal flopped over and dropped his weapon.

The three mercenaries hastened towards Mira as the tube narrowed to half its inflated height. By the time they all reached *Insignia*'s egress scale they were crawling on their hands and knees.

They squeezed through in single file, Catchut last. As the scale sealed behind them, Rast grabbed Mira by the shoulders, giving her a shake. 'What in the shit is going on, Baronessa?'

Mira pressed the pistol against the mercenary's chest. 'There are people cutting their way inside *Insignia* from the payload cavity. I think it's the Stationmaster.'

'Landhurst? Why him?'

'I c-can't say for sure. He seemed more interested in *Insignia* than Araldis.'

The mercenary took a moment to weigh the likely accuracy of Mira's instinct. 'Where are they exactly?'

'Inside the high abdominal sphincter, cutting into her digestive system.'

Rast slid a small satchel from under her coat. 'Catchut, stash this in my cabin. Bring back some hardware.'

'On my way, Capo.'

'Lat?'

The injured man looked pale but steady. 'Time to climb back on, Capo.' He limped after Catchut.

Rast turned to Mira. 'Can we shift?'

'We are in the queue but *Insignia* is bleeding internally. I don't think she will be able to take her focus from it.'

'Then pull the plug on the 'zoon and fly us.'

Mira went numb with fear. 'Autonomy? I—'

'Do it. We'll take care of the rest.' Rast turned to follow Latourn and Cachut and then swivelled back. 'Where did you get this pistol?'

'From your cabin,' said Mira.

Rast shook her head. 'Never can tell with you. Now get movin'.'

* * *

Mira ran through the strata to her cabin and removed the royal lozenge from where she had hidden it. Grasping it tightly, she hurried back to the buccal and sank into the Primo vein. As the receptors settled into her skin, a searing pain cramped her abdomen and she was dimly of her knees pulling tight into her chest.

Dizzying perception took command of her mind. From somewhere inside the chaos, *Insignia* sensed her.

You must not . . . immerse with me now. Cannot . . . separate . . . pain . . .

Rast is coming to stop them. But we must leave here. Transfer to me.

You have . . . no experience to take us . . . to shift . . . *Insignia*'s mind-voice dwindled to a faint whisper.

Mira could barely hear the words but she could see/sense Rast, Latourn and Catchut. Feel *Insignia*'s pain. Weapon fire grazed her inner skin. Stinging. Burning. Yet insignificant compared to the excruciating, burning throb of the rip.

Rast fell upon a man, her hands at his throat. Determination. Sweat. Fingers taut and strained with the choking of him.

Mira forced her sight/sense away from the intimacy of murder to her outer skin. She saw/sensed the station umbilical reinflate and crowd with bodies and weapons. Shift-queue instructions streamed though her mind/view. Their shift-place hold had been deleted.

Insignia, I must. I'm sorry . . .

She struggled to free her arm from Primo's embrace position and flung herself across to the Autonomy sink. She pressed the lozenge into the interface dimple along the ridge of the artificial adjunct, holding it down hard, worried that *Insignia* might find a way to reject it. When the sink subsumed it, she allowed herself to fall back into the chair and wait. Her immersion in *Insignia*'s pain and mayhem subsided, leaving her head pounding and her tongue stuck to the roof of her mouth.

The flight manual's warning floated to the top of her thoughts. *Never exchange full immersion for Autonomy without an adequate adjustment period . . . failure to observe this caution will result in prolonged side effects. List of known side effects and treatments can be accessed in . . .* Mira thrust the memory away and concentrated on thinking past the headache.

Virtual add-ons unfolded around her. Her intuitive comprehension of the biozoon's functions had vanished and was replaced with a flood of schematics and a cue of pending decisions. She worked her way methodically through them, reviewing her procedure: uncouple from their berth, execute virtual-manual (V-M) prime for oscillation, measure for complex excitation.

'Fedor?' Rast was on the intercom in the payload cavity.

'*Si?*' Mira croaked.

'How's the 'zoon?'

'I don't know. I'm in Autonomy.'

'Well, get us the heck out of here before we have to spend the rest of our lives in confinement for nailing these guards.'

'There are shift tubercles in the cavity.'

'Right. Give us five. And Fedor . . .'

'*Si?*'

'You haven't freaked out on me yet. Now's not the time.'

No. Not the time. Mira's fingers spasmed uncontrollably and she gave authentication to the wrong movement sequence.

The biozoon convulsed and the mercenaries were thrown across the bay. Mira could see them on interface; could hear Rast swearing and Latourn moaning.

She forced herself to concentrate on shift preparation. When her trembling had abated, she began the tiny finger movements that would execute individual tasks.

She took *Insignia* out of her berth with minimum damage. The umbilical tore free and sealed automatically, wrapping up the guards inside.

Insignia drifted out into shiftspace and immediately incurred the wrath of the queuing ships. The shortcast hammered their complaints across, including those of Station Control who directed *Insignia* to return to her berth.

Mira's virtual sight showed six ships between her and shiftpoint: a couple of private cruisers, an OLOSS freighter, a Lostolian surveyor and two decommissioned Assailants. She triggered her emergency pulse but none of them were buying it. From stationside three more ships debarked, each one emblazoned with station-security colour sequences.

She doubted that they would fire upon her in the shift queue but they could force a boarding.

Trajectory?

Icons representing their route snapped into existence before her eyes, along with warnings that each pass would break interstellar proximity rules.

I know. I know, I know . . .

Mira twitched her index finger, overruling the default.

Stationmaster Landhurst came on open-frequency shortcast. 'Baronessa Fedor, your erratic conduct suggests you've taken Autonomy – a cruel act. You are also breaking every rule of shiftspace. Return or we will board you.'

Mira took a deep, slow breath. 'Sending your people to cut their way into my biozoon's intestines is what *I* would term a cruel act, Master Landhurst.' She made a stroking movement with the little finger on her right hand and *Insignia* increased speed.

'Change your course!' Landhurst barked.

All the other transmissions had stopped. Everyone was listening to the exchange.

Mira imagined Landhurst pacing his office, lips compressed into a wrinkle of fury.

It couldn't compare to hers. Her anger burned away all her hesitancy. 'My world desperately needs 'esque aid. You sought to take advantage of my vulnerability and steal my biozoon, preventing me from presenting my case to the OLOSS commission on Scolar. *You* are the criminal, Stationmaster Landhurst.'

Her virtual map began to vibrate warnings as *Insignia* got set to pass the outermost craft in the shift queue. Mira held her breath, waiting for any aggressive reaction. Landhurst might not attack them with so many witnesses but she had no idea what a privately owned decommed battleship might do.

It was an old P-class Assailant. They'd been used in the Stain Wars. From the thin nozzles running along its body Mira could see that it was still fitted with active depleted-uranium weaponry. Each DU projectile would be sealed in a mercury capsule and sheathed in copper wiring. What that could do to *Insignia* . . .

'Fedor, what's happening?' Rast was out of her tubercle and on the 'cast again.

'We are passing the first of the queuing ships. An Assailant.'

'Active?'

'No. Decommissioned.'

'DU weapons active?'

'*Si.*'

'Shit. Those decoms tend to be owned by our kind.'

As if to confirm Rast's suspicion, the Assailant altered its aspect, and rotated and elevated an array of weapons along its strake.

Mira held to a course that would bring them within millimesurs of the battleship's proximity buffer. If it was going to fire on them, it would be before they reached that point to avoid blowback damage.

As if anticipating a messy outcome several Savvies launched from the station, ready to clean up any debris.

'What now?' demanded Rast.

Mira didn't answer. Barely registered the question.

'Fedor, you sucked in a breath just then like it was your last. What did you see?'

'Savvies have been detached from the station,' she whispered.

'Crapshit. Can we repel fire?'

Mira felt she was floating, as though the pounding of her heart had flooded her brain with too much blood. 'Not from Autonomy and not that kind.'

'Find out who the captain is.'

Mira fired a shortcast query.

The reply came back short and sharp. 'Who wants to know?'

She relayed it to Rast. 'What should I say?'

'Tell them it's Rast Randall. First MI, Stain Wars.'

This time there was no quick answer.

Landhurst had also gone quiet, waiting.

The deep breath that Mira had taken minutes ago seemed to be still caught in her chest. Layers of required actions settled atop each other waiting for her decision. And all the while doubts assailed her. Had she made the right choice? Would *Insignia* survive? Would taking Autonomy harm her more?

Then there was a movement on her virtual map that caused everything to fade to the background: something unexpected and wonderful. Her seemingly long-held breath escaped, letting her take another, another.

'What is it? For fuck's sake, your heavy breathing is killing me!' Rast shouted into the intercom.

'The Assailant is dropping out of pattern. It is letting us pass.'

Rast whooped.

Tears spurted from Mira's eyes, blurring her view of the map. She dashed them away to clear her vision. 'Crux! Oh Crux!'

'FEDOR?'

'They are all dropping from shift pattern – *all of them* – they are letting us through.'

A general shortcast pinged from one of the P-classes. 'Dren from *Audacity* here. Let the biozoon shift, Landhurst.'

As the message was relayed the other Assailants casually orientated towards the station security vessels.

'We figure that'll be the least trouble. And we don't want trouble. Do we, Stationmaster?' added Dren.

Mira shifted her focus to the station security vessels. After an excruciating pause they began to withdraw.

She sent a private shortcast to Captain Dren. 'Thank you.'

'You should come by the Consilience sometime, Baronessa Fedor. We've always got a place for people with guts. And tell Randall she owes me.'

Mira sagged, all her energy drained. If she had been in full vein-sink, *Insignia* would have infused her with nutrients. But Autonomy had no such pilot nurture. And *Insignia* was—

'Fedor?'

Mira wished the mercenary would go away so that she could just sit quietly for a—

'Fedor!'

Mira jerked awake. How long asleep? A few seconds only but the centre of her virtual map was shimmering with a representation of the shift casement.

Two hundred millimesurs until maximum excitation.

Adrenalin shot through her. Her entire body tightened with anticipation – and dread. Could she navigate them through? ... *The result of an inexact res-shift is catastrophic and will have an irrevocable impact on humanesque tissue. Vibration calibration must be precise or molecules in the tissues will implode the flesh* ... Why did she have to remember that passage from the manual so exactly?

'Rast,' she whispered. 'Shift imminent.'

A fraction of her awareness saw Randall run for her tubercle, saw Catchut crossing himself again, saw Latourn curled up in a ball.

Then Mira stared straight into the face of both her deepest longing and her darkest fear – and wondered which one would say her name.

THALES

Thales slept heavily in the early part of the evening but woke from a dream before dawn. He realised, with a start, that he had not even asked the gentleman his name and yet the man knew much about him and his life.

He climbed out of bed and sat on the cool marble floor for his morning *samayik*, one small part of his mind tuned to sounds of stirring in the adjacent sleeping chamber. This morning, though, Thales found it hard to connect with *Atma*. His unchanging reality eluded him.

Discontented, he washed more thoroughly and retied his hair. Today Rene would rescind her complaint and he would be released, he told himself. A lesson in deprivation would not hurt him so much. He felt calmer now. More centred.

Not able to wait any longer for the gentleman to rise, Thales went out into the shared living room. A selection of breakfast foods awaited him – as did the man he had heard getting up.

'You slept well?' Thales halted, eyeing the food. 'At least one cannot complain of being starved. But one could complain about my poor manners. Forgive me for I did not even ask you your name yesterday. My *samayik* has helped me re-gather myself.' He sat in the same chair as he had the evening before and served himself a large helping of creamy eggs and bitter cheese.

The man gave a gracious smile. 'Amaury.'

'Well, Amaury. As, it would seem, we have time to kill, what shall we talk of today?'

Amaury placed his knife and fork on his plate without making any clatter, like a man who had long practised silence. 'I am out of touch with the outside world. Not just Scolar, but the worlds beyond. Do OLOSS and the Extropists still sniff each others' underbellies like cockstiff dogs?'

Thales laughed. The image was not one he would have expected from this gentleman's mouth. 'Well put, Amaury. I shall swap you. Orion's doings for your own story.'

'Of course. That would only be fair.' The gentleman nodded and settled back in his chair. 'Visitors first.'

Thales smiled and took several mouthfuls while he collected threads of thought. How long had Amaury been in here that he craved knowledge of the wider galaxy? What sin against the Pre-Eminence could such an amiable old man have committed?

Manners and grace, he thought sourly. *An interest in humanesque kind?* All crimes, no doubt, to the current Pre-Eminence.

As Amaury bit into a pastry, Thales became aware that he was waiting patiently for him to speak. 'My apologies again, Amaury. Meditation sometimes leaves me preoccupied. Rene, my wife, calls it my *introspection hangover*.' His laugh was intentionally bitter. 'Not only that, but I am somewhat uninformed about wider political topics. I have been so consumed by Scolar's own problems. Though it seems that little changes out there. OLOSS maintains its deep suspicion of the Extropists, and continues to hold to its ridiculous apartheid. Since the Stain Wars no one travels to the Extropist quarter of Orion.'

'You are not fearful of the transhumans, Thales?' asked Amaury.

Thales answered plainly. 'I am more fearful of my own demons.' He glanced up from his last mouthful of egg. 'Does it shock you to hear that?'

But the old man was still smiling. 'There is very little that would shock me and, in truth, I am of the same mind. If humanesques were more concerned with mastering their own "demons", as you called them, and less with mastering the demons of others, then harmony would not be merely one of our ideals.'

'Aren't ideals our vocation?'

'Ideals are our life force,' corrected the old man. '*Realising* those ideals is our vocation. Anything less is our failure.'

Thales detected something then: a conviction within the man that was as compelling and fervent as any he had known, but so delicately . . . so subtly veiled that it might have slipped past unnoticed. And yet the very quietness of it, the surety, stirred Thales's passion. 'Have you heard of the discovery near Mintaka? A godlike Entity, it is being called.'

Amaury leaned forward, his eyes alight and keen. 'Only scraps. Tell me what you know.'

'Precious little, other than that it is a manifestation of dark energy which has the means to communicate with regular sentients.'

'And how did this energy make itself known?'

'There is talk of it saving the life of a simple mineral scout, an average man who now goes by the title of *God Discoverer*. From that point a bevy of researchers have collected to study it. It is said to have intelligence far beyond anything we could imagine. Hence the title of God.'

'It is curious, our obsession with the concept of all-knowing and how so many of us cling to it as their vision of God. When, I wonder, will we be brave enough to cut our umbilical cord to the notion of something greater?'

'You sound like an atheist, Amaury.'

'It is not a word I acknowledge. For as you know, Thales, giving credence to one thing gives equal credence to its opposite. I would personally erase all religious concepts – including the naturalistic.'

'You mean God within nature?'

Amaury nodded. 'We lose autonomy each time we lend our thoughts to these beliefs.'

Thales felt a tingling in his body. The man's discourse was both stimulating and uncomfortable. 'You mean we refuse to grow up.'

Amaury nodded. 'You. Me. All of us, Thales.'

'But surely choice is more important than anything else. We should be free to choose what we believe.'

'Only when we can see the whole picture, Thales, not just our little corner of it.' Amaury's eyes sparkled. 'Surely you agree that informed choice is the best choice? And humanesques are eternally mired in their own limitations. Now tell me, is the Entity old by our measuring?'

Thales shrugged. 'One would expect so, although I have not seen any empirical reports.'

Amaury moved his fingers in the air as if flexing them, yet Thales knew it to be more of a mental stretching than a physical. 'Why would an ancient wisdom choose now to reveal itself? Has anyone thought to question its appearance?'

'OLOSS has sent Astronomeins to study it and has allowed Geneers, Lawmon, Dicters and archiTects into its tutelage – but no philosophers and no Extropists.'

Amaury shook his head slowly. 'Once we were the first to be thrown a challenge. Now it seems we are not to be challenged at all.'

'I pleaded with the Pre-Eminence to lobby OLOSS for a position with the Entity, but just yesterday I learned that they refused to do so.'

'Is that what precipitated your disagreement with your beloved?'

Beloved? Was she still that? Thales pushed back from his empty plate and stood. He walked a few paces and retraced them, aware that Amaury was watching him with the same calm patience.

'That amongst other things. Rene has changed; position and comfort have become more important to her than anything else.'

'One cannot dictate another's beliefs, Thales. Even those of one's chosen partner.'

'I don't believe it is just a matter of changed beliefs. It's as though an apathy sickness has taken her.'

Amaury nodded thoughtfully. 'Tell me what it is that you would learn from the Entity near Mintaka?'

Thales stopped his pacing. 'Infinite knowledge, of course.'

'And what would "infinite knowledge" give you?' Amaury prodded.

Thales thought for some time before he answered. 'Initially I would say knowledge is its own gain. But what lies beyond that?'

Amaury smiled. 'What lies beyond that . . . is what you really seek.'

JO-JO RASTEROVICH

Petalu, the chair, and the alien creature met at a speed that made a wet crunching sound that Jo-Jo knew he would remember for ever.

Petalu fell on his back but the creature only staggered, despite a crack in its exoskeleton, and recovered quickly. Its mouth lobes unfolded and long feelers extruded into the air. They wavered down towards Petalu's face.

'Pet!' shrieked Bethany.

But the big man was dazed, grabbing the back of his head and moaning.

'Crap.' Jo-Jo darted out and seized a shard of the chair leg.

The creature's feelers flickered in his direction and then back to Petalu as if confused by the choice.

Jo-Jo didn't wait for it to decide. He stabbed the shard into the crack in its exoskeleton with all his strength, jerking the piece from side to side. A large fracture opened along its abdomen and an opaque fluid began to leak out.

The creature doubled over as if surprised, and its feelers reached towards the fluid. The tiny maws on the end of each one began to swallow the fluid from the wound. It seemed to forget Jo-Jo and Mau altogether – but across the trade court others were beginning to move in their direction.

Jo-Jo tried to drag Petalu towards the lift. 'Beth!'

Bethany grabbed one of Petalu's massive arms and heaved with a strength that startled Jo-Jo. They dragged and rolled and pushed the big man into the lift and Bethany pinged the doors shut.

As the lift headed to the top of its shaft, Jo-Jo straddled Petalu's chest. 'Come on, man. No time for wimping.'

'We can't carry him any further,' said Bethany. She knelt near Petalu's head, rocking on her knees, hands clasped together.

'How did you get so strong?' Jo-Jo asked her.

She exhaled softly. 'Fear makes you strong. Isn't that what they say?' She turned wide serious eyes on him. 'And I have never been this scared, Joey.' There was no brave follow-up smile, no laugh.

No one had called him 'Joey' since his mum. She'd run off with a Galaxy Productions sales manager. Not that it ever stopped Jo-Jo from buying Galaxy sims. On the contrary, he felt compelled to do so. Just to make sure that his mother hadn't wound up on the screen. Something about Bethany reminded him of his mother. Except that Bethany had balls – and a sense of decorum.

'Me neither.' Jo-Jo sighed. 'I will live to regret this,' he muttered.

He slapped Petalu Mau across the face with enough force to get the man's attention. Then he leaned close to him. 'What am I gonna tell Mama Petalu? That you got knocked down and wouldn't get up? That you had your fat arse whipped by a slug?' Jo-Jo taunted. 'THAT YOU LAY DOWN AND DIED!'

Mau's eyes focused. 'Mama Petalu,' he said hoarsely. He edged up onto one elbow.

Thank Crux—

Then one huge fist knocked Jo-Jo sideways into the lift wall.

'No one tells Mama Petalu her man is a wimp.'

Bethany hugged his neck. 'You saved us, Pet.'

The man patted her gently and sent Jo-Jo a dirty look.

Jo-Jo righted himself and rubbed his jaw. It felt broken – dislocated at the very least.

'Which way is the Savvy?' he asked clumsily.

Mau pointed to his left. 'Long walk.'

'Along the flute?'

Mau nodded and sat up. Little bits of exoskeleton peppered the skin on his arms and face as if he'd rolled in liquid and been crumbed.

Bethany tore some cloth from her shirt and wiped off what she could. 'Might be toxic,' she said.

Mau sat still like a docile animal.

His submission to her ministrations baffled Jo-Jo. As though the pair of them had known each other for years. He shrugged off the notion and climbed to his feet. They were only a few levels from the top of the station now.

The lift halted and the doors pinged open. 'Keep it open for me, Beth.'

Jo-Jo felt his way to the door and peered around the edge. The little he could see to the right seemed impregnable: plastic conduits twisted around fallen metal joists and giving off a God-awful stinking gas where the fire had melted them. The left was clearer with enough room for single-file access.

'Let's go,' he told the others. 'Mau, show us the way.' He stepped out to let him pass.

The big man lumbered ahead. Bethany followed.

Jo-Jo found it impossible to see around Mau's bulk, so he fell to glancing nervously behind. Would the creatures follow them? Maybe he should have destroyed the lift panel – but what if they needed to get down again? What if the Savvy had already gone?

The titanium corridor of the flute section was tarnished with wear. Dark green oil had seeped along the floor from a ruptured hydraulic, and Jo-Jo and Bethany slipped every few steps. Mau was surprisingly steady on his feet, his bulk leaving little gap between either side of his body and the sloping walls.

Eventually the corridor opened on to a narrow mesh platform that hung above a huge scallop-shaped chamber filled with crusted tanks. A long pipe ran from one tank to the next, then joined another to make a thick conduit that disappeared through the chamber wall.

Mau pointed to one particular tank. 'Bad shit, that. Made Mau piss green stuff.'

Bethany took a spontaneous step away. Her reaction made Jo-Jo want to laugh. Right now pissing green stuff seemed more attractive than having his body fluids sucked out. Then he remembered that his HealthWatch had expired.

He took a step that put him even further away from the tank than Beth.

Mau pointed to where the pipes converged into one. 'Go through underneath there. You first.' He turned his finger to Jo-Jo and prodded him in the chest.

From his expression, and the jab of the finger,

Jo-Jo figured that Mau hadn't forgiven him for the bagging yet. It didn't seem like the right time to make up.

He squeezed past Beth and Mau to take the lead. The narrow gallery was joined to an even narrower ramp that spiralled down into the chamber in a looping slope. As Jo-Jo jogged ahead of the other two he noticed globs of dried uuli secretions on the ramp grating. He'd heard they had a high tolerance of heavy metals. Maybe that was why they smelled so bad.

When he reached the bottom he realised that Mau was walking sideways to fit the constricted passageway. Bethany was only a little way in front of him, making gestures of encouragement.

Her patience and consideration impressed Jo-Jo. His own mind was firing off a bunch of wild messages, including one that he should leave the others behind.

'Hurry!' he bellowed helpfully.

Bethany shot him an annoyed look.

Jo-Jo shrugged and ducked in under the convergence of pipes. In the recess behind them sat a docking hatch whose display strip flashed *unoccupied* above it.

The Savvy had gone.

Jo-Jo sagged back against the pipe, his mind racing even faster. They could return to the lift and search level by level for survivors. Or they could try to get through the trade hall to the main docking area. He discarded the second idea as a last option: the creatures must have come in that way.

How they got to Dowl in the first place was another thing. They didn't seem smart enough to transport themselves, which meant that someone else had brought them in. Araldis must be their target.

Jo-Jo suddenly felt exhausted. He hated all the crap that went with worlds. If he hadn't followed that manipulative little cunt Tekton here he would never have got slammed in confinement. No confinement – no wrong place, wrong time – no scrabbling around this toxic craphole looking for a way off. He spat on the filthy acid-scoured floor.

'Josef?'

Beth's anxious face appeared beneath the pipes.

He waved his hand at the display above the hatch. 'Savvy's gone.'

She made a despairing sound.

Mau squeezed under to join them. Sweat streamed from his face. His skin was as crimson as an Araldisian native's and his breath came in irregular grunting gasps.

'We'll have to go back,' said Jo-Jo.

But then a noise above them had them all craning their necks. Two of the aliens were on the high platform.

'They look like slugs,' said Jo-Jo.

'Not slugs,' said Bethany. 'Maybe arthropods of some type. They have an exoskeleton. And they can see.'

'Call 'em what you like, Beth. Mau? Ideas?'

'Go out onto dock.' Petalu Mau leaned past them and banged the hatch panel. It popped its seal with a sucking sound.

The noise carried high.

'They've seen us,' said Beth. 'Josef.' She grabbed his chin between her hands and forced him to look into her eyes. 'In case . . . promise me you'll find my daughter and tell her that I tried to come after her, that I didn't abandon her. Promise me.'

Jo-Jo pulled away, perturbed by the strength in her fingers and by her emotion. 'I don't do promises, Beth.'

Her head went up and she gave him a fierce look. 'Promise me or I'll—'

'Hatch stuck,' Mau interrupted.

'Shit!' Jo-Jo added his effort to the battle against the malfunctioning safety mechanism until the aperture was wide enough for Bethany to get through.

'Go down the tube,' Jo-Jo instructed her. 'There'll be a secondary hatch somewhere along it. Stick your head outside it and see what's there. There's got to be some other way off this piece of crap.'

She nodded and disappeared while he and Mau continued to push at the door. It opened wide enough for Jo-Jo but not for Mau.

Mau suddenly stopped pushing, exhausted, and fell back against the pipe. His face crumpled, looking as though he might cry. He pointed upward. 'You tell Mama Petalu that Mau died brave. Tell her not let my little Kia handfast with Toki Lomas. No good, that family.'

Jo-Jo groaned and glanced roofwards. The arthropods were over halfway down the ramp. Goading Mau again might work or . . . Mau just might kill him.

Short on options, he took a deep breath. 'Yeah, yeah, whatever. But I figured you could handle tough situations, man. Turns out you're green as that stuff you've been pissing. I'm reckoning Beth's got bigger balls than—'

The muscles in Mau's neck corded in fury. His big fists came up from where they had dropped by his sides. He charged at Jo-Jo who ducked to one side.

Mau caught the corner of the hatch at full tilt. His

momentum sprang the hatch – and cracked his collarbone. He doubled over, moaning, but Jo-Jo didn't give him a chance to suck in the pain. He pulled him through the door and into the docking tube.

Halfway along, Bethany was leaning out through a flexi-hatch. She heard them and turned awkwardly around in their direction. 'What's wrong with Mau?'

Jo-Jo didn't answer. He squashed down next to her and peered out of the hatch.

The dock was grime on grime. Rubbish filled every corner of the chamber and metal littered the floor space like a shower of food scraps.

From what he could see the berths at each of the four flexi-tubes were empty. The Savvies had most certainly gone.

Jo-Jo jumped down onto the floor and felt the crunch of crystallised corrosion under his feet. He skirted the perimeter of the chamber, praying that his soft detention bootees would survive whatever was eating away at the floor. He couldn't think of many worse places to die.

Soon his feet began to tingle. He lifted one. The fabric was dissolving.

Shit.

Along the farthest wall, though, he spied a dull glow above another hatch. He ran over to the hatch's spyhole and rubbed it clear. A tiny tubular lug with a one-operator cabin drifted on an external mooring. It wouldn't get them far but it would get them off Dowl. Hopefully, someone would pick them up. Hopefully, there were ships out there still . . .

'There's a lug left,' he bellowed.

Bethany stuck her head out of the flexi-hatch again and signalled that they were coming. She jumped down, naked to the waist. Mau followed, his shoulder strapped with her shirt.

Jo-Jo gaped at her as she approached.

She scowled. 'Stop acting like you've never seen me naked before. You know my butt better than I do.'

Jo-Jo gave her a grin and unhooked an EVA suit from the wall. 'Lug's got a one-person cab. Better be Mau because he won't fit into one of these.'

Beth took the suit and deftly folded her small body into it.

'Done this before?' said Jo-Jo as he struggled with his own.

'I'm a biologist, remember?' She grabbed the collar of Jo-Jo's suit and yanked it upward in one smooth movement. 'There.'

'*There!*' echoed Jo-Jo. Only now he was looking back at the flexi-tube. It was vibrating as if it had suddenly filled with a lot of shifting weight.

He turned to the lug controls and set them to wind it in. A few precious minutes passed while Jo-Jo and Bethany fumbled with their helmets and primed their airflow. Jo-Jo's suit had about a half-hour supply, Bethany's a bit more.

When the lug slotted into its bracket the hatch popped open for the driver.

'Pick us up at the first Savvy lock,' said Jo-Jo. 'If you miss us coming out of the chute . . .'

Mau gave a grimace that wasn't pain. 'Miss you, mebbe. Not her,' he said before he slammed the door shut.

Jo-Jo sealed his faceplate.

'Josef.' Bethany's voice sounded choked-up through the suit's transceiver. 'Hurry!'

An arthropod crawled out of the flexi-tube.

Jo-Jo grabbed Beth's hand and they stumbled, clumsy in their suits, to the larger external hatches.

Now the arthropods were piling over each other to get out.

Jo-Jo worked the chute levers and gave Beth the thumbs-up. 'Go!'

She climbed up the short ladder and into the mouth of the tube. Jo-Jo expected her to slide in and shut the two-way, but she rolled onto her stomach and bumped the top of her helmet against his. 'Her name is Djeserit. You come back here and find her.'

'I'll be the one who's dead if you don't shift your arse,' he barked and gave her a shove. She slid down to the bottom of the tube and he closed the first part of the lock. The distant 'pop' told him that she was out.

The lever icons blinked their changing sequence and the top hatch reopened. He began to climb the steps but a blow knocked him off onto his side. He crossed his arms automatically to deflect another hit but instead something long and wet slithered across his faceplate. The arthropod seemed confused by the EVA suit.

Jo-Jo tried to breathe but the air seemed to have gone out of his lungs and his suit.

Another set of feelers joined the first, then another.

His muscles turned watery. How long before they realised that his brain fluids were behind the shiny faceplate they were playing around with?

Slowly he brought his knees up to his chest so that he made a smaller target. But that seemed to agitate them. The arthropods unfolded to their full height and crowded in, their movements more aggressive. Claws scraped and rattled on his suit as they began to paw him. The maw of a proboscis opened above his left eye and a needle-thin hollow stalk protruded.

Fuck!

Jo-Jo's strength returned on a tidal wave of terror and he kicked at the middle section of the closest creature. It fell back, creating enough space for him to launch himself at the steps. He scrambled up them and dived into the chute where he floundered around for the hatch control.

The lock snapped shut, crushing the head section of the pursuing arthropod. Its slimy innards sprayed down the chute and coated his already blurred visor. Then came the pop of the outer hatch and he was out in the black: weightless and tumbling.

Jo-Jo scraped his hand across his visor, trying to clean it, but the movement left streaks. On each rotation he glimpsed the lug with Bethany tethered onto its flat back. It was moving away from him.

Beth will make him come back. She will.

Another swipe across his visor made things worse. He could see nothing now.

For long, long, long moments he tumbled sightlessly through space. His mind revisited the sequence of events. Had he made the right decisions? What should he have done differently? What would it be like to suffocate? What would he miss most? Who?

It was the last question that unravelled Jo-Jo

completely. There was no one he would miss. No one he cared for enough to grieve over. And worse than that – no one who would miss *him*. Not a single person to acknowledge his passing.

A sensation formed in his chest and forced its way up to the back of his throat. It would have been a relief to cry then: anything. But it vented itself in a sound that he had never made before: a whimpering animal noise that was part fear but more anguish, a noise that had no end: no intake of breath, no cathartic climax.

'Josef. Take the tether. We can't come any closer. You're going to collide with junk from the detention mod.' Bethany's voice was in his helmet, drowning out his own cries.

Why? he asked himself. *Why save myself?* An answer came that surprised him. *Tekton. Tekton, that's why. The prick will pay.*

'Josef!' Bethany cried again. 'Take it!'

Something thumped against his chest. Jo-Jo grasped it automatically with both hands and felt a soft jerk as his momentum changed. He was no longer tumbling away from Dowl but falling towards it. It took him time to steady his forward motion enough to pull himself along the length of the tether.

Finally he felt Bethany's gloved hand on his shoulder and the solid pressure as his thighs encountered the edge of the barge.

'Are you all right?' she asked.

'Can't see anything.'

'Just do as I say.' Beth sounded reassuringly composed now. 'Lift your right knee . . .'

As he followed her calm instructions, Jo-Jo's rational

mind reasserted itself. Shame over his moments of panic welled, and flowed, and subsided. Revenge might not be a noble or even a decent reason for living. But he'd take it.

THALES

The next few days passed in a pattern of conversation and meals which at another time, in other circumstances, would have nourished Thales's soul. Amaury was truly learned but was neither pompous nor dogmatic with it – in fact, his inquiring mind was so bright and fresh that Thales sometimes felt like the older of the two. Aside, that is, from the calm that Amaury exuded.

For once, Thales and Rene would have been in agreement – no *young* man could have hoped to have been so at peace with himself.

They enjoyed an undisturbed exploration of each other's minds, interrupted only by the arrival of meals that were brought in on a cart by a politic guard and left for them to arrange at the table however they wished.

Thales pursued his meditations rigorously, first upon awakening and then later in the middle of the day when Amaury was disposed to nap. He followed his contemplations with a bout of vigorous exercise – running on one spot and other calisthenics suitable for a small area – which he did in the confines of his room so as not to disturb Amaury's sleep. He then took a protracted bath and returned to their common area where Amaury would be transferring their evening meal from the cart to the table.

The old man seemed to enjoy this ritual, like a mother who was used to supervising mealtimes for her family.

Thales surveyed the present meal with some satisfaction: a choice of tender meats, gingered kumara and salt greens on silver platters, to be followed by a splendid cream pie perched on a crystal tier.

'A meal fit for the Sophos themselves,' said Thales as he seated himself.

Amaury did not reply. He seemed oddly distracted.

'Amaury, there is something I have been meaning to discuss with you. I took occasion to visit The Children of God after hearing that I had been denied my petition.'

'You were seeking comfort, no doubt.' It was a statement.

Thales flushed. 'I suppose that I have inadvertently proved your earlier argument with that comment.'

'I would never denigrate you for seeking comfort, Thales. But I would urge you to remove the root of your need.'

'It is something I will give thought to, Amaury. But, even so, it does not change the disturbing nature of what I learned . . . I joined a group at the base of Exterus. I spoke to one of them, a woman I know, an Eclectic called Magdalen. The Pre-Eminence have injected selected statues with an erosion substance which will cannibalise them within a short time.'

'Selected statues, Thales?'

'Yes. From what she said, only the statues of Exterus and Villon. I'm afraid it was then that my rational mind deserted me, Amaury. I became deeply, deeply . . .

incensed. When I returned to my wife for consolation she would not even see me. It appears that she already knew of this travesty. Her father, you see, is Sophos Mianos.'

Thales balled a fist into his palm. Recounting the event unbalanced his carefully created equanimity of the last few days. He forced his hands to his sides and waited for Amaury to speak.

But Amaury, for the first time, was neither listening to Thales nor watching him. And why, Thales wondered, was the old man trembling so . . .

Thales sought to distract him. 'So now, Amaury, tell me more about yourself. We have discussed ideas and values, but you have said little concerning where you were born, or your life.'

But Amaury continued to tremble, as if shocked. 'Who I am, my life, matters little now. Please excuse me, Thales. I have something for which I must prepare.'

'Of course. But may I ask for what you need to prepare?'

Amaury rose from the table and took shuffling steps towards his bedroom door. 'Today I will die and there are things to think about.' He said it simply and without dramatic pause. A quiet statement that invited no response.

'D-die?' Thales sprang up from his chair. 'And upon what do you found such information? A dream, perhaps? A portent?'

'I have long known that I would be executed. All the Sophos needed was enough time, and from what you have just told me that time has elapsed. This fare'

– he gestured to the meal before them – 'is significant in its splendour.'

Thales glanced across the magnificent silver and the succulent food. 'You mean a last meal?'

Amaury nodded.

Thales struggled to believe what he was hearing. The old man seemed so sane and rational and yet this was surely a flight of fancy. Had he been alone too long? Perhaps he could banish Amaury's fears with logic. 'For what crime would they execute you? What terrible offence could someone as temperate as you have perpetrated? And if it is, as I expect, not a crime at all, then why would they incarcerate us together? I am witness to anything unfair that happens to you,' said Thales.

Amaury ceased trembling and straightened as though infused with sudden new courage. He rested his hand on the handle of the bedroom door and looked at Thales with compassion in his gentle stare. 'Indeed.'

A crawling sensation stirred in Thales's stomach.

Amaury let go of the handle and returned to take Thales's hand. His skin was papery and cool, the way Thales's father's had been in his latter years.

'The Pre-Eminence seek to frighten you. You've spoken of many things these past days. Things that you have observed about our once-dynamic society. And your observations are correct. We *have* become stale and toothless. Our philosophising is nothing other than a way for us to justify our secure existence. We no longer have an impact on the worlds around us . . . on the future of the sentient species . . . but this malaise that you so accurately perceived is, I fear, not from the innate weakness of the humanesque mind, or lack of endeavour, but something much...much more sinister.'

Thales felt a light perspiration break out across his body. This was the longest speech that Amaury had yet made. He leaned closer to the old man, utterly enthralled by his sombre, smooth voice. 'Sinister? Are the clusters being held to ransom by the Sophos Pre-Eminence? Is Sophos Mianos behind this?'

Amaury's mouth twisted. A life-weary smile. 'Would that it were merely the harmless politicking of a few power-mongers! It is worse than that and more perva-sive. Scolar has been damaged in some way – our ability to think and debate has been compromised.'

Thales stepped away now, confused. He had been so captivated by the man's gently subdued manner and yet Amaury's latest suggestions bordered on paranoia.

'That is implausible!' And yet even as he said it Thales felt a growing empathy with Amaury's words.

The old man perceived the doubt in Thales's eyes and straightened his robe with infinite dignity. 'I cannot say what is happening here – Scolar knows I've had time enough to ponder it. But I am heartened by the knowledge that you are not blinded to it, and that somehow you have escaped it.' He gave a heartbreaking smile. 'They put you in with me, Thales, to frighten you and to destroy my hope. But they have in fact accomplished the opposite. I am overjoyed that I finally have a use for this.' Amaury reached inside his robe and produced a tiny container. Inside was a minute lump of a putty-like substance. He pressed the container into Thales's hand. 'This was smuggled to me by one of my advocates. It will dissolve most materials when wet. You will know when to use it.' He retied his waist sash as the tramp of boots sounded outside their door.

Thales held the object in his open palm. 'But why have you not—'

'It was not the way. They would have caught me. I am an old man. But you . . .' He did not finish. Instead, he closed Thales's fingers over the container and pushed his arm down.

A moment of silence passed between them, broken by the continuing trample of booted feet in the corridor. The door swung open and a group of Brown Robes entered. One of them crossed the room and knelt in front of the old gentleman.

'Eminence Villon,' said the guard and bowed his head.

Villon? Thales's insides were gripped by something painful. *Amaury Villon?*

'Forgive me.' The guard stood and held out a set of restraints.

Amaury shook his head sadly and placed his wrists in them. 'I am sorry – I cannot find it in myself to forgive you. But ultimately it is not my forgiveness that you need.'

Unhappily, the guard triggered the restraints and they wrapped around the old man's wrists.

The action broke Thales free from his state of shock. 'Where are you taking him?' he demanded.

But the Brown Robes ignored him.

He grabbed at one of them. 'Answer me! Where do you take him? Sophos Mianos will hear of this! The Pre-Eminence will know!'

'Thales, be calm now,' said Amaury as the Brown Robe thrust Thales away. 'The Pre-Eminence already know. It is their doing.' He let himself be shepherded to the door. 'Remember,' he said over his shoulder. 'Remember the things we talked about. Remember . . .'

Thales flung himself after Amaury but the guards blocked his way again, one of them clouting the side of his face with a baton as they took the old man from the room.

Thales fell heavily to the floor. He scrambled back to his feet and beat at the locked door. But, as before, nobody came.

TEKTON

Tekton knocked on Labile Connit's door rather than have his moud announce his visit in advance. In this case, he calculated, the unexpected might yield greater results.

Connit took some time to answer. He had clearly been sleeping off his hangover. 'Tekton?'

'I thought it seemed that you could do with some cheering.' Tekton brandished a bottle of lime-tinctured bubbly which he thrust upon Connit. Then from beneath his coat he produced – and popped the lid on – a dish of reconstituted pungent quark eggs. 'Here.' He wafted the dish under Connit's nose.

The Geneer swallowed several times and bolted inside, leaving the door ajar. As soon as Tekton heard the sounds of Connit's violent reaction to the eggs, he entered the rooms, placed the dish on a side table and began a quick, concise hunt through the Geneer's possessions. His rooms were similarly configured to Tekton's and with deft hands Tekton rifled through clothes and in drawers, finding nothing that might give away Connit's origins.

As the reassuring noises of illness had not abated, Tekton was encouraged to search the Geneer's sleeping quarters. The room was singularly uninspiring aside from one startling object. On the bedcovers lay a book.

Tekton knew it was a book because the Tan Andao Studium had one in its vacuum vault which was never removed for fear of deterioration.

Tekton pounced on it. The weight of it surprised him and the brittle outer cover pricked at his trembling thin-skinned fingers. Imagine a Geneer, of all 'esques, owning such a priceless thing and *using* it.

Horrifying, observed free-mind.

Insane, agreed logic-mind.

Their agreement left Tekton rather unnerved. He turned the pages with utmost care, wondering over the mess of hieroglyphics.

Moud?

A detectable delay as the moud brought itself out of hibernation. *I'm here, Godhead.*

Can you tell me what this means?

Another pause.

It appears to be the title of the work: 'Welding for Four Dimensions'.

And the other?

An inscription, I believe, Godhead.

Yessss . . .

'From your loving father, CF(C)'

Aaaah . . . copy this page to your memory. I wish to review it later.

Yes, Godhead.

Tekton heard the short blast of a sanitary jet and replaced the book in its original position on the covers. Several quick, soundless steps took him back into Connit's living room where he swiftly retrieved the dish of quark eggs.

Labile Connit returned, bleary and out of sorts.

'I can see,' said Tekton, with a bold lack of concern, 'that I have come at an inconvenient time. Please, have the quark eggs and champagne with my compliments. I will call again when you are feeling better.'

Connit stared fixedly at the dish of eggs that Tekton once more held out to him and pressed his hand to his mouth. Tekton dropped the dish onto a table and turned to leave. By the time he had reached the door he could hear the sanitary jet blasting again.

Back in his rooms Tekton reviewed the inscription. *From your loving father CF(C).*

For some reason those initials piqued his memory.

Is there any record of Labile Connit's planet of origin?

No, Godhead.

Tekton sucked a finger. To his annoyance the *ingre* membrane shed onto his tongue. He spat it out and made a note to increase the oil in his diet.

On what planet does the Yeungnam Studium reside? Tekton knew that he should remember such a detail but Geneering Studiums – even the famous Yeungnam – did not figure on his list of itinerant facts that were worthwhile retaining.

Yeung Lesser, Godhead.

I want you to collate the names of all the C. Connits – or variations on that name – alive or passed, living within several parsecs of Yeung Lesser.

I would have to employ the Vreal Studium's VI to gain such information, the moud informed him.

Tekton paused and thought for a moment.

Should I pursue this?

No, his logic-mind stated firmly. *Satisfying idle curiosity is not worth the computational allowance.*

Instinct is not merely idle curiosity, argued his free-mind. *Instinct is a most profound and valuable ally.*

Employ the VI, Tekton told his moud.

The list came back seconds later. It was lengthy but not interminable.

Now, see if you can connect someone on this list with your available known facts about Labile Connit, he told it.

Godhead?

For Lostol's sake, do I have to spell it out! Can't you think for yourself?

Of course, Godhead, in a restricted way. The moud sounded rather hurt.

Do any of them have a male offspring of Labile Connit's age? Are any of them engineers? Commonalities. I WANT COMMONALITIES! Tekton's mind-shout brought on the beginnings of a throbbing temple but when the moud reinserted a new list in his virtual eye the headache was swept away by a rush of akula.

Three Connits had commonalities but Tekton knew immediately that only one mattered. Lasper (Carnage) Farr-Connit: progeny – one male child, whereabouts unknown. Mother: Tekla Connit, deceased. Lasper Farr was currently reported as holding the ownership of the Savoire Refuse System.

Even Tekton had heard of Carnage Farr, the man who had thwarted OLOSS's plans to invade Extropy space by leading a small but effective force against League warships. The Stain Wars, the conflicts were called, and Farr had proclaimed himself keeper of the balance.

On some worlds he was considered a hero of peace, but Tekton's impression was that the man was a violent opportunist who railed against order, an anarchist who wanted indeterminate rules so that he could pursue his own shady ends.

If Labile Connit *was* his son then OLOSS were harbouring the ultimate viper in their bosom here on Belle-Monde.

Tekton's minds clamoured with opinions.

How titillating! declared free-mind.

Dangerous! proclaimed logic-mind. *But potentially useful.*

Informing OLOSS would cause a stir and possibly attract some type of commendation. But blackmailing Connit could mean some useful 'impartial' contacts.

Which did he want more? Applause for being a good citizen? Or to beat Ra and all the other tyros, and impress Sole?

A plan blossomed in Tekton's thoughts, as beautiful as a new design.

Moud, extend an invitation to Labile Connit to attend a soirée at my room tomorrow evening.

Yes, Godhead. Would you care to make arrangements for the event? Is there food to order? Are there others to be invited?

No. Tekton smiled. *None and no one.*

Connit arrived a little late, carrying a bottle of yellow liquid not dissimilar in its hue to that of his normally golden skin, which today looked sallow and dehydrated.

He glanced around the room. 'Late, am I? Or early?' His eyes lost focus for a moment as he consulted his moud.

'No, no,' said Tekton. He closed the door and stood between it and Connit. 'A little misunderstanding. The soirée is for another night. But I had some . . . personal business to discuss with you.'

Labile's eyes narrowed. 'Tekton? What trickery are you up to? You know I will record this.'

Tekton folded his arms in a mild but confident gesture. 'Actually, Labile – may I call you that? – while you are welcome to record our little talk it is most likely, I would think, that you would be disposed to erase it later.'

Labile's look of suspicion deepened into a frown. He took a step forward as if to brush past Tekton and leave.

But Tekton raised a hand. 'I also think it would be in your best interests to hear what I have to say. That is . . . better you hear it than OLOSS do.'

Connit froze. He reddened. For a professional and one of the foremost in his field, he was alarmingly ingenuous. 'Out with it, Tekton.'

'I know who your father is.'

'I do not have a father and I find your insinuation in poor taste.'

'The circumstances of your gestation and birth are not the issue here,' snapped Tekton. 'Your genetics are. So pray tell me: how is it that the son of the League's most infamous agitator is being educated at their expense?'

Connit looked, Tekton fancied, as if he might collapse. His body began to tremble in a way that suggested it might actually unglue.

'Are you in contact with Lasper Farr?'

Labile took a gasping breath at the sound of his father's name. 'What, Tekton? What is it that you want from me?'

'I require a neutral engineering facility on Rho Junction and I thought, my dear fellow, that you might be just the person to negotiate it.' Tekton slapped the Geneer on the back as one might an old friend.

Connit's shoulders squared and for one second Tekton thought that the younger man might hit him.

Duck, screamed logic-mind.

Hit him first, urged free-mind.

But Connit replied before Tekton had a chance to do either. 'And your silence is what I will get in return?'

'Precisely,' breathed Tekton. He loved this sort of bargaining. It was almost as sexy as conceiving a new model or overcoming a design flaw. Perhaps he should have been a Lawmon.

'What assurances do I have on that?'

'I'm choosing to consort with dubious types, my dear Connit. I will have just as much to lose as you.' Tekton paused and sniffed, allowing himself a small smirk. 'Well, not nearly as much, actually, but some, all the same. Our collusion itself will ensure my silence.'

Connit's fists clenched so tight that the golden skin of his knuckles turned a bright yellow.

Tekton took half a step back. It would not do to get the fellow overanxious. 'I understand discretion better than most,' he soothed. 'I have a need that you can help me fulfil and you have a secret that needs to be kept. It is quite simple.'

'No. It is *not* simple. Lasper and I do not have a close relationship. Fatherhood is not his strong suit.'

'What do you mean?'

'We are estranged.'

'But only for the purposes of distancing yourself from his nefarious activities, surely?'

'No.'

Tekton could see that Connit was recovering some composure.

'What of your mother, then?'

'She is dead. And she is the reason.'

Tekton felt the edge of frustration rising. He should have realised that the politics of such a family would be fraught – yet he would not lose his advantage. 'It would not matter to an OLOSS inquiry who speaks to who. You are Lasper Farr's biological son. You must have access to information outside OLOSS channels. Find me a place and this will be the end of it.'

Connit trembled again and the pair stared at each other for long moments.

'Very well,' said the Geneer. 'Send me a list of your basic needs and I will find you suitable premises.'

Tekton beamed. 'I've always admired your common sense.'

Connit took a deep, settling breath. 'There is NOTHING at all that I admire about you. Or your cousin!'

THALES

Thales counted the days of his imprisonment, five now, which he'd spent largely in meditation. In the moments between contemplations he pondered Amaury Villon's fate and the future of his own marriage. Did Villon's beliefs have some sound basis or were they simply the imaginings of a brilliant mind left alone for too long? And what of Rene? Thales was angry with her, sure enough. But more than that, for the first time in their life together he questioned the compatibility of their values, their ideological harmony. Rene had always – to him – been the most beautiful of minds.

'Msr Berniere?'

Thales relinquished his inner world slowly.

The door to his prison was ajar, and expressionless Brown Robes stood in front of him. One of them extended his hand to assist Thales from his meditative position on the floor.

He did not take it. 'Is my fate to be the same as Villon's?'

The guard dropped his hand. 'The Sophos Mianos wishes an audience with you.'

'He *wishes* an audience? And what if I refuse? It appears to be a fallacy that one is able to maintain a free mind and spirit on Scolar.'

The guard did not react.

Thales uncoiled and stood without assistance. He gave one sweeping glance around the prison apartment remembering all he could: remembering Amaury.

The guards escorted him, one before him and one behind, in a brisk march along narrow corridors and up dimly illuminated stairs. The stairs gave way to the high, elaborately-carved ceilings and diamond chandeliers of the Sophos assembly halls, and finally to the Eminence offices.

Sophos Mianos, Rene's father, had one of the more prestigious rooms. Thales had been there, once only, to ask for permission to wed the man's daughter. As he entered it now, he experienced the same impression of beauty and opulence.

An aquarium occupied one entire wall, while another was decorated with a huge Mioloaquan wall-hanging that reflected from its scales a soft rainbow of lights across an intricately pearl-inlaid escritoire. This time, though, Thales was not nervously seeking acceptance into a family.

'Berniere,' said Sophos Mianos without preamble. 'It is a grave occasion when I have to talk to you about the circumstances of several days ago.'

Anger rushed through Thales but he smothered it, knowing that Mianos needed little excuse to find fault with his son-in-law. 'Four days and six hours, Sophos, to be precise. I remember every second with great clarity, particularly my precious moments with the prophet Amaury Villon.'

'Aaah, he could not resist telling you who he was? Well, I had hoped you would learn something from the experience.'

'On the contrary, Sophos, it was your politic guards who informed me. And what I learned is that the Sophos are as autocratic as the most backward feudal planets, and that free thought is endangered on Scolar.'

The skin around the edge of Mianos's nostrils whitened. He stood and walked over to the aquarium wall. With a tap of a dispenser he loosed dried blood flakes into the water. A flotilla of tiny scalpel fish nibbled the disintegrating pieces. 'Your foolish impudence is divisive, young man. You have seen now what happens to those who choose the path of agitator. Our great world, indeed our species, needs harmony and unity, not—'

'Not what?' Thales interrupted. 'Challenging, inventive thought? Harmony does not mean that we must all agree. It means that we must be able to agree to disagree.'

'Are you lecturing me, young Thales?' Mianos returned to the escritoire and rubbed his fingers against the side of his aspect cube. 'Disguise your poor and irrational behaviour how you will, but know the consequences of your behaviour for yourself and your wife.'

'I want to see Rene.' *We must leave this place.*

'But she has no wish to see you.'

'Liar!' Thales accused.

But as he spoke a screen on the darkest wall of the office began to unfold. It blinked alive like a watching eye.

Rene appeared, standing against vast glazed windows – Thales could not place where – her thin figure outlined by filtered sunlight. She clutched the ruche of the curtains as though they were a support and Thales had a sudden fierce desire to take her in his arms and kiss her extreme pallor. She seemed agitated and distressed. 'Thales?'

'Why will you not see me, Rene?'

'I'm not sure that I can trust your reaction to . . . me. Father thought this way would be best.'

'You are a grown woman, my wife. Could you not make that decision for yourself? Could you not trust your heart?' Thales asked her softly. 'I would never hurt you.'

Rene turned to stare out of the window. 'My head is my heart, Thales. You know that.'

Thales sensed Mianos's satisfaction. It compelled him to provoke Rene.

'I met the prophet Villon. He was in the room in which they imprisoned me.'

She turned back sharply. 'Villon? What nonsense is this, Thales?'

'Nonsense, Rene? Why do you assume that I speak nonsense and your father speaks the truth?'

'Villon left Scolar many years ago when he discovered that his extreme propaganda left us unmoved. He took it to the Extropists. They have need of belief. Any belief.'

Thales was struck by the naivety of her perception. Did she really believe that the Extropists had no beliefs?

'Everyone has beliefs, Rene. I am saddened that ours have diverged so. But know the truth of this. I have seen Villon.'

'Your words are delusional, Thales. You must seek help.'

'I don't need help. I need someone to believe me.'

Why am I the one she can so easily deny? Anguish swamped him. She would not leave with him. Not now or ever. 'The Pre-Eminence had Villon—'

Mianos touched his aspect cube and the screen folded away, breaking Thales's link with his wife.

'Now remove yourself from my sight, Berniere. Your imprudence is dangerous. If you were not married to my daughter I would not have allowed you out of detention. She has pleaded for your release but you *will* stay away from her. And you will hold your tongue. Or you will lose it.'

The same politic guards took Thales to the foyer of the Eminence building and watched him walk across the marbled floor to the doors.

'Msr Berniere?'

Thales turned, his heart pounding.

It was not the guards, though, but the concierge. The humanesque extended a note-film to him on a glass salver.

Thales snatched it up and read it. Rene had rented him an apartment off the Eminence Boulevard. His possessions were already there, waiting for him. That was all.

He went straight there, bagged a selection of clothes and his personal aspect cube and crossed town where he checked into a boarding house in the Hume quarter. The boarding house's facade was differentiated from those of the many other buildings by the unsightly aubergine-striped awnings tacked onto the window frames, and a stand of large potted plants gathered around the entrance.

The location made his journey to the Jainist temple more arduous than he would have liked – he had to travel back across the city – but in truth he had little stomach for meditation right now. Restlessness had beset him.

For the next few weeks Thales sought company in the seamiest klatsches, hoping that carousing would crowd his thoughts enough to give him some peace. But was it peace he sought? Or was Rene right? Did he really seek conflict for its own sake?

He found himself drawn to a circle of Skeptics: young humanesques and aliens who followed the ancient philosophy that everything could, and should, be doubted. Thales hoped that they of all clusters would question the Sophos.

'Thales Berniere, Jainist,' he said, seating himself in the narrow corner section of the couch.

'Welcome, new face. I am Pascale,' said a tall, thin Pagoin fellow.

'Or is it new?' offered another from the group. This fellow was short and solid and had gill scars on his neck. A Mioloaquan, perhaps, who had had the change.

'Don't mind Lieffried,' said Pascale. 'It is our . . . joke.'

Thales bit his tongue. Did they really think that he would not understand their juvenile humour? He summoned an engaging smile. 'I would like to introduce a topic to your discourse. I apologise if it is not new but I am in need of some intelligent debate, having recently found such discourse to be lacking. Do you not think it contemptible that we are unrepresented to the new Entity? OLOSS really must be challenged on their selection process.'

'Which Entity?' a Balol/Lostol hybrid asked.

Thales searched the circle of faces. Could it be true that they did not know about the discovery of the godlike Entity?

'If you mean the energy anomaly out near Mintaka that we are calling God, then we have little interest in goblin tales, Thales Berniere,' said Pascale.

'Why so, Pascale?'

'We are bored with discussions of God. Even if the Entity's existence is well cited, we believe that our focus should be on the demonstrative.'

Thales did not disguise his incredulous tone. 'Demonstrative? You mean your belief is based only on what you can see before you? Here on Scolar?'

Lieffried stood up and stretched. 'Frankly, who cares what the southern sector busies itself about? Or if it is even there.'

The circle of listeners tittered.

'But your attitude is so ... exclusivist,' Thales protested.

'You sound like you are a probable-ist, Thales. Perhaps you would do well with the archiTects of Lostol,' said Pascal.

'One can see why you would make that judgement, Thales,' added Lieffried. 'But we are done with vastness and mystery. Concretism and pragmatics are our new muses. And they are so rewarding.' He added slyly: 'As is the Pre-Eminence when one adopts their beliefs – twenty thousand gals.'

'You are being *paid* to believe?' exclaimed Thales. 'That is outrageous. You stagger me.'

'Why do I think that you are not being complimentary?' said Pascal.

Thales stood and placed his drink on the table, unsure if inebriation or shock caused him to sway so. 'How can we inspire and lead our species with such a prosaic and self-centred ideology?'

'Inspire?' said Lieffried.

'Lead?' said the rest of the group in unison.

The tittering started again.

'What about Villon? What of his teachings?' asked Thales.

'Villon? Villon was of the past,' murmured Pascal. 'I heard he was dead.'

'No, no,' corrected Lieffried. 'He joined the Extropists. They are far more concerned with evolutionary possibilities than anyone else. It was best for all.'

Thales leapt to his feet. 'He did *not* join the Extropists,' he shouted. 'He is a victim of our own—'

The kafe's entire sea of faces turned upward to him, their owners as eager for rumour as the scalpel fish in Mianos's aquarium had been for blood flakes.

Thales felt their attention and thrust back from the table before his mouth betrayed him further. In doing so he collided with a *Mae ji* in a black kaftan and full veils. 'Careful, young Sophos,' the *Mae ji* murmured.

'I am not Sophos!' Thales cried. He grabbed her arm to emphasise his point, but the looseness of her clothing caused him to misjudge her shape. His hand grazed accidentally against the softness of her breast.

He withdrew his hand as if stung. 'I a-apologise—' he said.

The *Mae ji* froze but her companion gave an affronted cry.

The circle of Skeptics watched. Behind the bar the klatsch owners began whispering to each other. One of them disappeared.

'I-I meant nothing. That is, I did not mean to touch you in that way . . .' whispered Thales.

But the weight of the judgemental stares told him that his apology was wasted. The patrons were hungry for agitation. He edged towards an exit as a commotion of voices drew everyone's attention to the rear of the klatsch. Four robed guards entered with their batons loose in their hands. Their appearance sent a ripple of comment from one table to the next. Thales did not wait for the whispers to reach him.

He ran.

MIRA

Res-shift from Dowl had been shadowed by guilt and relief: relief to be clear of Araldis and its heartbreak, guilt for the fate of the ship that had crossed their wake, and for having left Vito and the korm and Cass and her children behind.

Res-shift from Intel was a thing beyond horror. Quanta streamed by Mira's virtual vision at shocking speeds, signals flared and flashed compelling her to make instant decisions. They backlogged so quickly that the virtual display became an aurora from which she had trouble distinguishing command prompts.

Assign default positions. Switch to audio only, she instructed.

Instantly her mind became invaded by noise.

Vibration calibration only.

Mira listened to the whispering of resonator read-outs. The tuition modules at the Studium on Araldis had said that most virtual-run craft could res-shift on Autonomy as long as the pilot primed the correct vibration, and allowed the V-I to operate a background safety default.

With the biozoon Mira was not sure how enmeshed the installed V-I was with the creature. Her tutor modules had not been able to be precise. The degree of Autonomy varied, dependent on what augmentations the individual biozoon allowed. Then there were those who had been hobbled and had had full V-I forced on them.

Like Sal.

An uneven hum started up as Mira began to prime the biozoon for shift.

That's not right. It should be steady.

She switched back to virtual vision and hunted for the anomalies in the shift field. The display showed nothing abnormal but the vibration still ran in shuddering bursts.

The biozoon's surface temperature fluctuated wildly and Mira heard a terrifying roar like the onset of a ferocious gale. She lost consciousness of everything save the shiftspace. What was causing the vibration irregularity? What had she forgotten? What had she overlooked?

Diagnostic reports crashed in waves of data. *Normal . . . normal . . . normal . . .*

It's not *normal!* she shrieked at no one.

Then she saw it. The biozoon's cephalic fins weren't at optimum span.

The roar geared to a higher pitch. Audio told her that she had 6.2 counts to even out vibration or . . . they would go into shift ripping apart.

Too late now. Is there pain with annihilation? Mira wondered.

6.1 counts: visual sweep. Station security gathered around the edge of shiftspace – ticks sucking a warm body. Their weapons primed. Waiting for her to abandon her course.

5.3 counts: *terminate shift – how much damage? – face Landhurst.*

3.8 counts: *or shift and die – certain.*

2.2 counts: nothing

1.4 counts: nothing

1.1 counts: ***untie me***

Insignia?

In a rush of adrenalin Mira found herself straining out of her seat as she frantically relinquished control of the vibration sets.

The hum steadied.

0.3: shift imminent

Mira clung to the add-ons as the Autonomy sink wrapped around her, supporting fragile flesh. After the suffocation it came . . . the exquisite, stabbing, devouring, mind-inverting pain of shift and then the release . . .

'Fedor.'

The voice was a welcome intrusion into Mira's dark, swirling, unhinged thoughts.

'You did it, Fedor!'

Somewhere among the tendrils of requests and screeds of location data Mira knew Rast's twang.

You may relinquish everything now, Mira. I am healed enough.

Insignia sounded disappointed and just faintly amused, Mira thought, like a parent who had watched their child try and fail. She detached herself from the add-ons and plucked the lozenge from the sink. Blinking brought the rest of the buccal into focus. She coughed and manoeuvred her body to the edge of the sink where she sat with her head in her hands.

'Fedor.'

Rast again. This time, though, the woman stood in front of her, swaying. Her hair was slick with tubercle secretions, her face shiny.

'Are . . . are you well?' Mira enquired politely.

'Am I well?' Rast gave a snorting laugh. 'You've just taken us through res-shift and you're asking if *I'm* well?'

'No, I—' Mira stopped. Perhaps it was safer for her if Rast believed it. 'Yes, I mean . . . I guess so,' she finished limply.

'I *guess* so?' Rast laughed again but this one was belly-deep and tinged with relief. 'You're even beginning to sound like one of us. We've got some bodies to get rid of and then we'll be up in the mess celebrating. Join us when you've got your head straight. How is the 'zoon doing, by the way? Things were messy down there. Those bastards took a blowtorch to her.'

Mira shuddered. '*Insignia* is stable. I will be along in a while.'

The last flicker of concern left Rast's face and she managed to saunter out.

Mira sighed. The mercenary seemed to thrive on danger. *Why can't I be like that? Why does each hurdle make me more tired?*

She placed her hands on her abdomen and prodded at the lower area. Had the baby been harmed? And why now, when she so craved only solitude, did her body demand food? She could not face the others yet.

Insignia, *how are your wounds?*

I am depleted of fluids but Scolar is close. I have time to replenish.

What would have happened to us if you hadn't recovered sufficiently?

Insignia hesitated. *It is deeply instinctive for me to survive resonance shift. Even wounded.*

So I was wrong to use Autonomy.

Silence.

But Mira could not let it rest. *If I had maintained Autonomy would I have killed us?*

Yes. You are inexpert.

A longer silence this time while Mira fretted over her choices. *Why would Landhurst cripple you?*

It is the nature of some to destroy what they can't have. But more, he did not think that you would have the courage to attempt an Autonomous shift. He did not count on your resolve.

Mira felt warmth soak from the vein into her aching, weak muscles. *You are comforting me. Can I do anything for you?*

You can sleep and recover. Then we will discuss my Autonomy component. It is time you had some proper tuition.

Instead, Mira dragged herself to the cucina.

The cellar shelves stood unfolded and bare. The mercenaries were drinking straight from demijohns – the last of the Araldisian wines.

'Saved you one, Baronessa.' Rast swung a full bottle up from beside her. 'Figured you, out of all of us, deserved it.'

Mira accepted the bottle and searched for a flute. She found one in a cabinet full of Pellegrini-crested utensils. Rubbing the stem of the glass gently between her fingers she took a seat on the side of the table opposite the mercenaries.

The first sip tasted harsh, not only because of the

acidic wine but because of the memory it evoked. Her last drink had been with Faja. Tears pricked the rims of her eyes.

'When you came tottering down that docking tube and pulled out a pistol, Fedor, I nearly pissed my pants,' Rast pronounced. 'Thought you were going to shoot *me*. You better watch out or I'll start counting you as one of ours.'

Mira stiffened at the good-natured comment. 'I would never kill for a living.'

'See, Capo, you throw her a bone and she gets all hoity,' observed Catchut, with a belch.

But Rast ignored him. She lifted her blood-spattered boots up on the table and rocked back on her chair. 'Do you think your farcast got sent to OLOSS?'

Mira turned away from the disgusting sight of the mercenary's boot and shrugged. 'I will try again now that we are in better range.'

'So you think Landhurst was after the 'zoon?'

'*Si.*'

Rast steepled her fingers. 'I knew him for a businessman but I didn't know he was dangerous.'

'What about Captain Dren from *Audacity*? How do you know him?' Mira asked.

The mercenaries exchanged glances. Latourn, whose complexion had turned as white as Rast's hair, rested his head on his arms on the table.

'Why do you ask?'

'He said that "you owed him now".'

'What else did he say, Baronessa?'

'That I should join Consilience; that there was room for people like me.'

The mercenaries all exploded into laughter. Latourn

hammered the table with his fist and Rast rocked back and forth on her chair until tears streaked down her filthy cheeks.

Mira took a large swallow of wine. It was beginning to lift the edge from her fatigue. She let them spend their mirth, not caring one way or the other what they found amusing.

'Have you heard of Consilience?' Rast asked finally.

Mira sipped deeply again –

Mira, your body chemistry is changing. It might not help your foetus if you ingest drink—

– and refilled her glass before she replied.

'*Si* and no. You hear things on Araldis but there was no way to prove their veracity. Our farcast links were always unstable and our Studium texts were . . .'

'Bullshit?'

'Parochial,' Mira finished.

'Consilience is the third side,' said Rast.

'The right side,' added Catchut.

Mira regarded Rast with a steady stare. If the mercenaries wished to talk more she would listen but she would not play a guessing game with them.

'OLOSS brought order and rules and accountability to most of Orion but not everyone wants that.'

'Criminals do not, I should imagine,' Mira said.

'That's where you show your ignorance, Fedor. It's not as simple as that. Not everyone wants to be safe and constrained. OLOSS is seen as a protector by most, but as a dictator by some.'

'The Extropists?'

'Them, yeah. And others.'

Mira found Rast's ability to switch between crude

and eloquent baffling. For the first time she wondered about the mercenary's background. 'Where do you fit in this web?' Mira asked.

'I fit where I please. I take people as I please. But Consilience believes in something that OLOSS doesn't, and that's loyalty. Loyalty can keep you alive.'

'*You* believe in loyalty?'

Rast took several noisy swigs from her demijohn. Her cheeks flushed and her eyes shone with an unnatural sparkle. She ran her tongue over the neck of the bottle, licking the runaway drops. 'I could teach you something about loyalty, Baronessa. In fact, I could teach you . . . a lot.'

Mira's throat tightened. She put her flute down so that they would not see her hand trembling. She let her glance slide to Rast's filthy boots. 'You should wash yourself,' she said.

They all laughed again at that, as if she'd meant to be funny, not acerbic.

Catchut yawned and stood. 'I'm heading to kip down, Capo. And, like the Baronessa says, to wash. Feel like I've been poking my shaft in a jam roll.' He moved his thighs apart in an exaggerated fashion as if they were stuck together.

Latourn climbed unsteadily to his feet as well. 'Me too, Cap. This 'zoon goo crusts up your crap-hole.'

They left together, still laughing.

'I knew Dren in the war,' Rast announced when the pucker settled shut. She sprawled sideways out of her chair, taking quick swigs. 'He fought for Consilience too, but he wasn't just on the payroll, he was . . . *is* one of them.'

Mira saw her guard dropping with each swallow. 'We didn't hear much news of the war – until it was over, at least.'

'If you take the history downloads they'll tell you that the Extros started it but it was OLOSS.'

'What do you mean? OLOSS retaliated after one of our worlds was attacked.' Mira searched her memory. 'Longthrow, wasn't it?'

'The Extros need raw materials; they exist in one small corner of Orion and there's not enough minerals there to support their needs. They bought Longthrow from its OLOSS owners. The owners were broke and it was a shitty, slimy place overrun by amphibians. OLOSS panicked and sent in a bunch of hired meat to spoil the sale. They expected to send the half-heads packing but it turned out that the Extros had been sitting on some advanced-tech weapons. They didn't crawl back into their hole like OLOSS expected.'

Mira frowned in disbelief. 'How do you know all this?'

'Because I was the hired meat. That's how I met Ludjer Jancz. He was my Capo.' Rast gave a short laugh. 'He said it would be short and sweet and lucrative. But things got out of control. The Extros only had a small force but they were close to home and, as I said, their weapon tech was classy. I mean, you'd expect that, I guess, but it seemed to take OLOSS by surprise.' Rast's stare fixed on the last measure of wine in the demijohn. She swirled it around. 'I'll sure never forget it.' She drained the demijohn and tossed it onto the table. 'Don't ever underestimate Extros, Fedor. They don't think like any humanesque or alien I've ever met. Damn near impossible to predict and not given to fits of compassion.'

Rast rocked her chair back to the floor and closed her eyes. A moment later she was asleep.

Mira was astounded that the mercenary could relax so instantly, bolt upright and in company: just another disparity between them.

She sat for a while, watching Rast's face. The mercenary seemed more feminine in sleep, her skin smooth and her lips soft. But the shadows under her eyes and the bruise along one cheekbone kept the picture real. Rast was as unpredictable and pitiless as the Extropists she had fought against and yet Mira felt envy again at the woman's freedom. Was it as easy as that? Could you just grasp it? Or did you have to be able to kill and fight and view life through a sieve of cynicism?

Would she swap her life with Rast?

Even with the weight of tradition and her enslavement by her altered biology she would not. But she could transform herself with knowledge.

Mira dragged herself to her feet and went to her cabin where she removed her fellalo and laid it onto the steam couch. While it was cleaned she examined herself in the small mirror. It reflected a person vastly different from the one who had looked back at her on Araldis.

This person was thinner and had lost much of her vibrant crimson colouring. As with Rast, there were exhaustion shadows under her eyes and her skin had developed a waxen texture. It was the kind of fatigue, she knew, that did not quit easily: the fatigue of a person living in constant dread and uncertainty.

It gnawed at her that she had not been able to say goodbye to Cass Mulravey, nor give her a word of explanation.

'*Don't let her return to the mine,*' Trin had told his Carabinere. Then he had driven away.

The muzzles of their rifles had stabbed into her back as they forced her inside the cabin of the AiV. They'd shared Trin's righteousness, the imperative that his line should continue, that a woman should be accepting of everything.

But nothing in Mira accepted Trinder Pellegrini's act.

The memories began to well up but she clamped down on them. What had Trin told the women about her, she wondered? That she had stolen an AiV and run away? He would have been careful to ensure that she did not become more than him to them; more of a hero. And now she carried his child.

My child, not his! My child. My child. Mira intoned the words as she crawled into bed and let oblivion finally claim her.

Insignia woke her.

There is a farcast from Scolar, Mira.

She surfaced instantly, as if her sleep had been only a breath below wakefulness.

Si. Si. What does it say?

You have been granted an emergency meeting with Sophos Mianos, the OLOSS delegate for Orion Edge. The meeting will occur in twelve hours.

How can that be? We are days out still.

Insignia hesitated. *I enhanced the length of your sleep cycle and nourished you.*

Mira jerked up out of bed. *You sedated me!*

It was for the best – for the baby. Your blood pressure was elevated and your liver function had degraded. You are refreshed now. Your organs are coping better.

Anger flared hot through her body. *Do not do that again. Never do that.* She thrust her feet onto the floor. *Insignia!*

The only reply was the biozoon's whispering rhythm.

Mira dressed and hurried to the buccal.

Rast was there, lounging in Autonomy, dressed in a strange combination of amber Latino brocade robe and grey mercenary garb.

'What are you doing?' Mira demanded.

Rast's eyes focused on her slowly as she came out of virtual sight. 'Baronessa. We tried to wake you up but short of breaking into your cabin . . .' She shrugged. 'Figured maybe you'd died in there and I should start working out how to fly this thing.'

Mira stared at the mercenary. Was Rast joking?

'I found the shift phase extremely . . . exhausting. Now I have had contact from the OLOSS delegate on Scolar. I will meet with him in twelve hours.'

'Then you'll be taking us where we want to go?'

'I . . .' Mira dropped her head. She had given her word to return Rast to their planet of choice yet she wanted to go with OLOSS to Araldis. She *had* to go back. 'I will do what I can.'

'We had a deal, Fedor. You don't ever want to break a deal with someone like me,' Rast added softly.

'But I must go back there with OLOSS – quickly.'

Rast lifted her hands from the conductivity pads and leaned forward. 'I thought you aristos cut your teeth on politics.'

Mira sat on the edge of Primo. 'What do you mean?'

'Do you really think OLOSS will go running off to Araldis to save a bunch of Latino idiots from their self-inflicted fate?'

'The Saqr are not self-inflicted,' said Mira stiffly.

'What makes you so sure about that? You're smart, Fedor. Think it over. You know that the Principe hired me for added protection.'

'You have alluded to that, but you haven't been specific.'

'He wanted us to protect a woman and her property – a mine.'

Mira suddenly remembered the data sponge that Trin had pressed upon her. She had slipped it into the inner pockets of her fellalo and forgotten about it. 'Do you mean the mine where Cass Mulravey lost her husband?'

Rast nodded. 'I lost two of my crew in there.'

'What was the woman's name?'

'Lancia or something.'

'Silvio?'

'No . . . wait . . . Luna something.'

'Luna Il Longa?'

'Yes. What do you know about her?'

That name. Trinder had spoken of her in their last conversation. 'She is . . . *was* the Principe's concubine. The name Il Longa is an Eccentric name.'

'Eccentric?'

'Not full-blooded Latino. Like me.'

'Eccentric, eh?' Rast ran the word over her tongue, exaggerating the last 'c'. 'That fits you well. Eccentric and erratic.'

Mira did not want to continue the conversation. 'I will return to my cabin for a while. Do not touch the Autonomy controls. *Insignia* is well enough now to manage herself.'

Once out of the buccal she grasped the folds of her robe and ran her fingers along them. Her fellala was badly worn now but she could not bring herself to wear another; she wanted the reminder of what she had left. There were many luxurious royal robes stored in *Insignia*'s cabins but they belonged to the Pellegrini familia. Although the child she carried made her part of their clan, she would not wear their colours. *Not ever.*

The data sponge had worked its way into a side seam. She felt the unevenness as she squeezed along the hem.

'Problem, lady?'

Mira glanced up, dropping the end of her robe. Latourn was leaning against the stratum wall. He was taller than Rast and dark: dark eyes, dark hair, but a different swarthiness to the Latino kind. Thickset enough, too, though his frame had thinned with fatigue and injury, as if his health had not properly recovered. She had not spoken to him really, and his closeness made her nervous.

'No.' She moved to pass him but he stopped her with a hand on her sleeve.

'Jus' wanta say . . . that . . . you getting us on board here . . . saved me. I was gone fo' sure. I'm wantin' you to know that I'll keep that with me. Knowin' you did that. Capo was right about loyalty.'

'It was your . . . captain who saved you. And your friend Catchut.'

Latourn blinked. 'But you got us through shift. Never met one woman who could do that before. Maybe 'cos you're one those . . .'

'Innate,' said Mira. She stepped away from him and he dropped his hand, rebuffed by her cool reaction.

'Well, whatever, I figure to be evening it up one time. Showing you what I can do,' he said.

Mira shook her head. Latourn's intense manner and the idea that he thought he owed her something, made her uneasy. 'There is nothing. No debt. Please, I must go to my cabin.'

His look was part longing, part annoyance but he leaned back for her to pass.

She hurried on, knowing that she had handled the interchange poorly. But he reminded her of Trin and Innis – damaged somehow. Rast, at least, was not like that.

Once inside her cabin Mira worked the sponge along the seam of her fellala to a worn patch. Then she tore a tiny hole in the robe to remove it and reached for the virtual-sight add-on attached to the wall by the bed.

Mira pushed the sponge into the insertion port and slipped the mask on. When her eyes had adjusted she began to wiggle her fingers along the conductivity pad.

Icons cascaded into her v-sight and a burst of nausea hit her. It was still too soon after the strain of res-shift to be back.

Audio sotto, she told it.

The speed and luminosity of the icons immediately diminished and a stream of murmuring took its space in her mind.

Mira let it saturate her, waiting for her senses to attune. As before, it seemed a better way to manage the clamour. She began to distinguish noises: the wave booms of their movement and the faint glub of *Insignia*'s organs processing amino fluids.

Then a small thing took her attention away from finding the data: a high-pitched whine that she intuited to be the farcaster.

'*Focus on farcast*,' she told the v-sight.

All other sounds diminished.

'*Decode*.'

Rast's voice came through as intimately as if the mercenary was speaking in her ear. '. . . on Scolar. Who is it?'

The answering burst was on relay from the Scolar hub.

'*Retrace*.' But the stream split and disintegrated.

'Half payment at pickup,' said Rast.

Another burst.

'Agreed.' Rast gave a dry, deprecating laugh. 'She won't be a problem.'

Mira's heartbeat quickened. Was the mercenary talking about her? What arrangement was Rast making?

The farcaster fell silent, the whine disappearing from the v-sight's sound spectrum.

Mira sat for a few moments just listening and thinking. As long as Rast did not hamper her meeting with OLOSS, what harm could the mercenary do? And yet she continued to worry over it as she restarted her data search.

'Reconstitute data from tertiary source.'

Mira listened intently.

Though the quality of the recording had deteriorated, the reason for the meeting between Marchella Pellegrini and the unknown purchaser remained clear enough. In return for the exclusive rights to a mineral alloy called quixite, the purchaser had agreed to pay a large sum of money *and* secure an apprenticeship to the godlike entity discovered near Mintaka.

Replay.

As she listened a second time Mira was struck by how different Marchella sounded. There was no hard edge to her voice, no mock-plains accent, and yet the determination was still there. Marchella had secured the deal she wanted.

Her final words to Mira flooded back. *'There is a name you must remember. It is Tekton. Say it. Say the name. He owes me a debt. He owes this world a debt . . .'*

Tekton had promised the God-apprenticeship. But why did Marchella want that so much?

Mira slipped the mask from her face. She pressed against her forehead and summoned the scraps of her various conversations with Marchella. Everything had been about the women of Araldis; her whole purpose had been to save them . . .

No, not that . . . to *free* them.

But why did she battle so? What did she hope to gain? They could never be free while their fertility was held to ransom – and worse, most did not even desire it.

Mira?

Si? she said automatically. *Insignia* had not spoken in her mind since their earlier disagreement.

OLOSS have sent a craft out to meet you.

W-what?

They wish a representative to come aboard – once we have been secured.

Mira felt the taut edge in *Insignia*'s tone as clearly as if bands had tightened around her own body and clamped across her head. Was it usual, she wondered, to experience such a sympathetic physiological reaction? *Is Rast still in the buccal?*

Yes.

I am coming.

This time Mira ran. *Women should never move quickly or with visible purpose . . .* Yet at this moment, she wished that her robes were less cumbersome and her body more accustomed to action. Though her muscles were firm from youth they did not respond now when she demanded more from them. Did the baby hamper her as well?

Hamper. She must not think so. *Otherwise how could she care for it? How could she care for it, anyway?*

Rast was still seated in Autonomy, murmuring. Catchut was there as well; standing beside her, watching over her.

The mercenary's eyes flickered open. 'Don't let them on board,' said Rast aloud. 'Don't let those OLOSS fuckers in.'

It was more than belligerence. She was hiding something, Mira thought, the way her fingers gripped the armrest.

'Why?'

'You've arrived here squealing trouble. They will want to be sure you are who you say.'

'Then why should I deny them? My plight is genuine.'

Rast grunted and slapped the armrest. 'You are so damn naive. *Now don't let them on.*' She ground the last words out.

Mira stiffened at her intimidating tone. She took a side step towards the safety of Primo – an instinctive reaction. 'I have no wish to antagonise them.'

'I would be more concerned, Baronessa, about antagonising *me*,' said Rast softly.

And there it was: the open threat, and the switch to hardened mercenary. Gone was the humour, the amused admiration and the begrudging gratitude.

'What are you hiding from them?'

'What you don't know can't be tortured out of you,' Rast replied matter-of-factly.

Catchut laughed at that.

Mira frowned, glancing between them. 'You brought something on board, onto *Insignia* at Intel. I saw a satchel. What was it?'

Rast stood slowly, loosening her muscles in a way that made Mira's throat go dry. 'What makes you think that, clever Baronessa?'

'It explains your behaviour.' *And the conversation I heard.* 'It also explains . . .' She had a flash of intuition. A day for it – as if her mind had only just begun to work again after the events on Araldis. 'It explains why Stationmaster Landhurst was so eager to stop us and more importantly' – she gambled on the last bit – 'why Captain Dren and the other warships backed us.'

Rast slipped her hands into her pocket. Did she have a weapon in there? She always carried a weapon. 'Like I said: clever little Baronessa.'

Mira swallowed to ease her dry throat but she did not retreat. She had learned with Rast that you did not show weakness. 'Do not patronise me, mercenary. I think the scale of favours between us is currently balanced. Even you should respect that, if indeed you believe your own propaganda.'

Catchut's sharp intake of breath sent a pang of fear shooting through her chest. *Don't weaken. Don't . . .*

But Rast surprised her again by giving a belly laugh. She withdrew her hand from her pocket and rubbed her chin.

Mira felt a flutter of relief but she did not relax her guard. *What had Rast brought onto* Insignia*?* She moistened her lips. 'What would happen if they were to search *Insignia*?'

'Have you ever been in prison, Baronessa?'

'Prison is not simply walls or containment fields,' Mira replied.

'Yes. But when it is you understand what freedom means.'

'Then why do you risk yours?'

'You of all people should understand that. Didn't you run from your Principe because he wanted to steal your Inbred talent?'

'Innate,' corrected Mira automatically. 'How did you know that?'

'I've been working around injustices all my life,' Rast replied. 'I don't like dictators.'

Mira saw something then, behind the callousness

and the bravado that Rast wore closer than her own skin – a tiny, tiny glimpse of the real woman. She tried to vanquish the flicker of perception. Rast was governed by no set of rules that Mira understood. Yet the flicker persisted, an illumination, a hope. 'What have you brought aboard *Insignia*?' she breathed.

Rast's gaze did not waver for an instant. 'Cryoprotectants.'

THALES

Thales took a roundabout route to his apartment to be sure that the Brown Robes had not followed him, staying off the boulevards of the Hume quarter, hugging the crowd-laden alleys jammed with bok-kafes and barsomas.

Scolar's skies were crisp with cold and busy enough with air traffic, the precision lights of Orbit-To-Earth vehicles flashing in regular landing sequences. It made it hard to see the stars from Scolar's denser locations. But Thales had grown up in the thin strip of farming land on the far northern reaches of the planet and he still remembered the blazing star showers and his father's enthralling tales of distant planets with moons circling around them.

'In many places the moon is as heavily populated as the planet it circles,' his father had told him.

Afterwards Thales had spent many hours wondering how it would feel to have a large object in the night sky and how much it would impede his view of the galaxy. He also wondered what it would be like, knowing millions of moon-based dwellers stared back at your planet, night after night.

He decided, then and there, that Scolar was the most special and beautiful world in Orion because it was free from prying eyes.

Suddenly he longed to feel that way again: exultant and free. Instead, the last week weighed on him as if Scolar had a moon, and a million prying eyes were bearing down on him.

He longed for the comfort of Rene's soft, thin body and the fall of her long hair across his skin. *How could she . . . how could . . .*

As Thales turned the corner to his boarding house something jolted him from his thoughts; a difference in the air or the night sounds. The awnings cast deep shadows on the imitation cobblestones, causing the stand of potted plants to seem more like an army of men lying in silent wait.

He braced himself to cross the road, knowing that he'd become fanciful and paranoid. He could not, however, stop himself from climbing the stairs as quickly and silently as he was able.

With relief he shut the door behind him and leaned against it in the dark, catching his breath. He had not been followed. The bar episode was merely a mis-understanding: no one would have given it another thought. He reviewed the evening with logic and a calmer mind.

'Thales?'

The anxious whisper came from the couch against the window. He glimpsed a shadowy profile against the curtainless window and knew at once who was there.

'Rene.' He stayed where he was, not sure whether to throw himself at her feet or throw the door wide open and order her out.

'Don't turn the light on. I have been watching the street.'

'How did you get—'

'I am the daughter of a Pre-Eminent, Thales. You are as naive as a child sometimes.' There was no sting in her voice, no criticism, just a sad fondness. It hurt him more than cutting words. Had she always treated him like a child?

'If we are to speak of naivety, Rene, then perhaps I am not alone in that fault.'

'You are speaking of my father.'

'Not just your father, dearest. The entire Sophos.'

Rene did not reply to that and Thales had a sudden desire to shake her from her silence. Couldn't she see?

He rushed on. 'They had Villon murdered. He never went to join the Extropists. The Sophos incarcerated him until he was forgotten and then they quietly took him away and executed him.'

'How can you know such a thing?'

'I told you that. I was imprisoned with him.'

Rene gave a faintly derisive laugh. 'Why would they do that, Thales?'

'To frighten me, to show me what would happen to me if I challenged them.'

'If only you could hear yourself. You sound like a million other young men, brimming with conspiracy theories and paranoia.'

Thales made a noise of frustration. 'You dismiss me so easily. Doesn't your conscience prick you just a little? Can't you see how little our world has become?'

She glanced back to the window. 'Where are your facts? If you were incarcerated with him as you said, how could you know where he was taken, or that he was not an impostor?'

Thales stepped towards her, closing the gap in two strides. 'It was him, Rene, I swear. If you could have heard him speak, felt his presence. A man does not acquire such a presence from practising fraud. And the guards – they knelt before him, asking for forgiveness.'

Rene turned back to him, her hair slipping around her shoulders, releasing wafts of her personal scent. 'There are politic police on the street!' She reached out for him, their argument suddenly dismissed.

But Thales avoided her embrace and brushed past her to locate the uniformed bodies and purposeful gait. 'Something happened in a kafe klatsch in Kantz: a misunderstanding. Now they have found me but I will explain it—'

Rene clutched his wrist. 'I fear they will not listen to anything you say. That is why I am here. Trouble has nested in you and laid its eggs. They will not let go.'

Thales felt the sharp edge of an object against his skin, pressing into his palm. A Gal identity clip.

'Leave Scolar. This will assure that you have money wherever you are.'

'You want me to leave!' His heart folded in pain. 'You want rid of me.'

She pulled his hand to her mouth and kissed it.

He felt the wetness of her spilling tears but shock prevented him from moving. *Leave Scolar without her.*

'I wish many things, dearest Thales, but the most desperate of those is that you are alive . . . have a chance to live. I-I am not sure what I believe now but I know that the Sophos do not trust you and that I cannot protect you.'

Thales wanted to return her kiss then, finally. To take her shaking hands and clamp them tight against him. 'Rene, I . . .'

'Please, Thales.' Her voice was hoarse beyond emotion – it was an order. 'Leave now. Find your truths.'

He took the identity clip and jammed it in his pocket. 'What good is the truth,' he said harshly, 'when you and I will not share it?'

Rene raised her head, her tears and emotion in check now. She reached down to a small pack resting against her legs. 'There will be someone . . . I have packed you some things. You must leave the rest and go.' She handed it to him, then turned away and peered through the window. 'They are at the entrance. You will need to leave by another route.'

Thales pushed open the window. The street was empty now. The Brown Robes were already in the building. He climbed out onto the slated roof and slid down to the guttering. He looked back at Rene one last time before he jumped – but already she had become indistinguishable from the shadows.

Thales ran to the closest conduit and entered a busy carriage on the up-station line, using Rene's clip to pay. The press of bodies was comfortingly familiar. If he concentrated on them he could pretend for a few moments that he was on his way to the upashraya and that Rene was at home, working on her treatise. He clung to the self-deception, but as quickly as it had settled on him it evaporated.

He was running from the politic: running from Amaury Villon's murderers. The prophet's words were like a bleeding cut in his hindbrain. He used them to try and form a plan. He needed a destination.

But Thales was not used to making decisions. Rene had always been his guide. She had told him to leave. But to go where? To do what?

Fool! He chastised himself. *Fool of fools for not knowing myself! What should I do?*

As the conduit disgorged its passengers into the sprawling terminal, Thales let himself drift amid the throng. He searched the outbound displays for something that resonated but every destination was somewhere too far from Rene.

He wandered further, past the elevator walks and gleaming shopfronts that lined the exit gates, along the less salubrious rows of moneylender booths, finally settling at a drab kafe where he ordered a chocola drink and lard-chips.

The boost of sweet nutrition raised his spirits a little.

When he had finished he gave the attendant his clip to pay.

The despondent fellow shook his head. 'Not here, Msr. Damn things cost more to process than it's worth. You give me lucre.'

'But I have none,' admitted Thales. 'Can I offer you some service to pay for my drink and food?'

The attendant shook his head. He reached for his 'cast. 'Politic'll deal with you.'

'No!' Thales leapt towards him, grabbing the man's hand.

The attendant tore his hand away and produced a jolt weapon from under the counter. Before he could use it on Thales, a third man intervened.

'Let me pay for the gentleman's drink and offer him another,' said the intervener, a man with soft wavy hair and a high forehead. His wide-spaced eyes were full of sympathy.

The attendant glanced between them, caught between an urge to redeem his lucre and an offended ego.

Lucre won. He snatched up the cash.

Thales's rescuer ushered him to his table and took a seat next to him.

'I-I th-thank you, sir,' said Thales. 'An awkward position I found myself in.'

The man held out his hand. 'Gutnee Paraburd.'

'Thales.' He did not offer more than that.

'A man of your calibre at this end of the station is likely game. I would recommend that you should not flash a Gal clip around. You could maybe get rolled for such a thing.'

Thales coloured. 'Of course. How naive of me – but I have been somewhat out of sorts today. Not thinking, perhaps.'

'Down on your luck, poor fellow?'

Thales felt a quiver of pride. 'No. Not at all. Affairs of the heart.'

'Aaah. I understand completely. Then you are not in need of lucre. My mistake. Let us enjoy our drink, then, and forget our woes.'

'Agreed,' said Thales with relief. The man was clearly a kind enough fellow and he must make an effort to reward that. 'And what pastime is your pleasure, Mr Paraburd?'

'Import and export – of the medical kind. Not an

easy life, pandering to the whims of laboratories. And it's hard to find reliable employees.' Paraburd smiled in a confiding kind of way that made his eyes seem wider. It was an ingenuous face and friendly. 'But you must know the sort of problem,' he added.

Thales sighed. 'Not really. As you may have guessed I am a philosopher. But I am considering embarking on a change of lifestyle. I am truly interested in what you say.' *At least to distract me from my own troubles.*

Paraburd settled comfortably in his chair and Thales marvelled at the man's familiar, easy way. 'Today, for instance, an employee of mine was supposed to leave to collect a naked DNA sample from a mesa-world laboratory in Saiph. He was to return with it so that our own medical facilities can begin the process of upgrading our HealthWatch against the next year's influenza. The DNA, as you can guess, will prevent many deaths. But just a moment before I met you, my office notified me that the man has failed to appear. Thousands of lives are at risk for a single man's folly.'

Thales was shocked. 'Without a hint of warning. Is there no one else who can go in his stead?'

'It is not so easy to find biological couriers, philosopher Thales, at a few hours' notice. It is the job for only a special few who wish to serve their community. We have become such a selfish and inert world. Even money will not entice them.'

'Y-you pay?' Thales stammered.

'Most handsomely, Thales. A million lucre for little more than a leisurely trip abroad.'

Thales felt a rush of heat in his body. A million lucre

could finance a trip to Belle-Monde and he would not have to rely on Rene's charity. With that amount he could be independent. 'A m-million lucre? That is indeed generous. Are there risks?'

Paraburd waved his hand and squeezed his eyebrows together in disdain. 'Tiny, tiny risks.'

'Wouldn't an animal suffice as host? An alpacania or even a rodent?'

'Lesser animal hosts do not provide the most efficacious response. Besides, it is quite safe for humanesques. No, Thales, altruism is the key here. And there are so few altruists in Scolar any more.' Paraburd stared sadly into the distance.

An idea formed in Thales's mind as he sipped his chocola. It was a particularly delicious drink, and relaxing. He must have it again soon, he thought. With a million lucre he could enjoy many more of them. 'Where must your courier go?'

'To a laboratory on Rho Junction.'

'And then?'

'The courier will receive the naked DNA and return with it to our own facilities here on Scolar where we can harvest it and begin the transfection process.'

'Will the courier need travel finance and so forth?'

Gutnee Paraburd clicked his tongue. 'No, no, no. My company covers all such things, of course.' He rubbed his temples with frustration, then stared at Thales with a hopeful expression. 'Why do you ask?'

Thales cleared his throat, took another sip of chocola, then cleared his throat again. 'I would offer myself. My services, that is, if you would have me.'

Paraburd's mouth fell open in undisguised delight.

'Indeed. Would you, sir? A distinguished philosopher working for me! Well, I'm smitten shivery with shock.'

'I am just a man like you, Mr Paraburd. You have done me a favour, now I can return it . . . Does that mean you accept my offer?'

The man bowed in his seat. 'I accept with most humble gratitude. Let us hasten to my office.'

Thales returned Paraburd's smile with less enthusiasm but a lighter heart. He had made a decision and done a good turn. 'One thing I would ask. I would not care to run into the politic.'

His new employer nodded in complete understanding.

Gutnee Paraburd led Thales through a door in the cato-plasma wall and into the rear corridors of the station. The filthy halls were piled with disused tubing and other unrecognisable items, and smelled of sour chemicals.

'I did not realise there were parallel passages in the landing port.'

'All large transit stations have service areas,' Thales's new boss explained. 'It wouldn't do for travellers to see the less glamorous end of things. Now, Msr, when we reach my office I will provide you with a courier uniform. Then we will hasten to the ship. Loading has already begun.'

Thales felt a sharp twist in his stomach, a pang of anxiety, followed by a thrill of anticipation. He was going into space – something he had not had occasion to do before, certainly not as a paid personage. It gave him a sense of purpose. Rene would be surprised if she knew and he liked that notion.

Paraburd turned along a narrow, dim corridor and

opened a door at the very end. His office was crowded with shelves of receptacles and chilled by a draught from an adjacent cool room. A balol hunched over a desk in the middle of it all, dwarfed by the stacks of laboratory objects. He scowled at Paraburd who ignored him and ushered Thales into a small ablution cubicle.

'I will hand a uniform in to you.'

Thales squeezed past a crate of tube syringes and waited behind the door. After a few long moments, in which he became acutely aware of the dark stains in the ceiling and an unpleasant smell coming from the toilet, Paraburd tapped on the door and passed a uniform in.

Thales emerged in ill-fitting pants and jacket. 'There is a tear under one arm,' he said.

Paraburd shook his fist at the balol. 'Tell me what it is that I pay you for?'

The balol's scowl didn't alter. Nor did he proffer an explanation.

Paraburd took Thales's arm. 'Keep your arm at your side and no one will notice. You see, your position on this ship will be a dual role. For the duration of the trip you will assist as an escort for a travelling diplomat. It is a way of managing costs, you understand. Now for the DNA barrier.' He went into the refrigerated compartment and returned with a fluid-filled, sleeve-shaped object. He pushed the uniform up to Thales's elbow and slipped the sleeve over his wrist.

Thales felt a series of tiny pricks.

When he tried to remove the sleeve Gutnee Paraburd held it fast with a surprising show of strength. 'Do not move until the sleeve has drained.'

The pricks continued for a few more seconds until Paraburd relaxed his grip and removed the empty sleeve.

'You are now protected from the disease. But please remember, Msr Thales, that the barrier substance has a finite lifespan. You must deliver the naked DNA to me in order to have it harvested. If not, transfection will occur in your genome.'

Thales felt a twinge of uncertainty. 'Mr Paraburd, this DNA I am to receive . . . is it that important?'

Gutnee Paraburd appeared hurt and shocked. 'Mr Berniere, all my work is important—'

'But what do I know of escorting dignitaries?' Thales interjected.

'Pfft!' said Paraburd. 'It requires nothing more than trailing around after a diplomat. This type of cross-utilisation of labour is a common and accepted practice. But then, as an esteemed scholar you would have seen such things. I am a reputable businessman and if you do not wish to make honest lucre, then—' Gutnee Paraburd made a show of returning his purse to his pocket.

Thales forestalled any further negative pronouncement by taking the purse. 'I apologise. Of course you are.'

'Indeed,' said Paraburd, mollified. 'The purse contains an instalment of the lucre. You shall have the balance when you return. It is not safe for a man to walk around with a million lucre in his pocket, Msr Berniere. Now let us go.'

Their final words were exchanged a short time later at the entrance to a docking tube. Thales could not see the craft but a deep whine emanated through the tube and it shuddered periodically.

Gutnee Paraburd pressed a document film into his hand. 'Your instructions are all here.' He gave Thales a wide-eyed look. 'Safe travelling, Msr Thales – may fortune bring you back to me quickly.'

Thales could not think of a suitable reply and settled for 'I will do my best, sir.' He climbed the small rubber gradient to the entrance of the tube but when he turned to give Paraburd a final farewell the man had already gone.

A humanesque dressed in the same kind of uniform as Thales waited at the ship's entrance.

'You Paraburd's man?'

Thales nodded, not sure that he liked the fellow's curt tone and thick features.

'Here,' said the guard, slapping a mask against Thales's chest. 'Get this on. The diplomat will be here in a moment. Make sure you stand at the back.'

'Is my uniform too unkempt?' asked Thales, anxiously prodding the rip.

The man gave him an odd look. 'Yeah. Sure enough. But that's it.'

As Thales pulled the visor down over his face, more uniformed personnel appeared in the lock, assembling themselves into two lines. He dutifully lined up in the second row.

A few moments later two Brown Robes entered through the shuddering docking tube.

Thales held his breath, grateful that he'd been instructed to stand back. The politic guards scanned the group of assembled personnel and exchanged a few

words with the man who had greeted Thales. Satisfied
that all was in order, one of them spoke into a personal
'cast.

The tube rattled again and the diplomat entered.

Thales found himself unable to let go of the breath
that he was holding in. Sophos Mianos stood a mere
body's length away.

'Cryoprotectants?'

'Surely even on your backward planet you've heard of them?'

'I-I . . .'

'Who opposes OLOSS, Baronessa?'

'The Extropists, of course—'

'OLOSS has been trying to destabilise them for years because they won't sign the charter. One of the ways they've done that is to make the cryoprotectants that the Extros use in their transformation processes illegal – outside approved consignments for OLOSS use.'

'They are illegal?' Mira's heart thundered.

'Not just illegal, Fedor. Do you know what they do to 'esques caught trafficking them?' Rast's eyes were so narrow that Mira wasn't sure if they were even open. 'They don't bother to put them in jail. They just box them up and cremate them,' she said.

'OLOSS would not be so barbaric.'

'Would be and are,' Rast said flatly. 'Crux, Fedor, you've just had a close-up view of what humanesques can do to each other. Why would OLOSS be any different?'

'But the charter—'

'Prevents lawlessness but doesn't stop cruelty.'

Rast impatiently tapped her fingers on the conductor pad while Mira digested what she had learned.

'But if you knew I was going to an OLOSS planet – why would you risk such a thing?' Mira said slowly.

Rast's glance flicked to Catchut – so quickly that Mira wasn't sure whether of not she'd imagined it. 'You were going. Not us. We – ah – intended to . . . stay aboard. Didn't figure the suspicious bastards would come out and search us.'

Is that the truth, Rast? Mira wondered. She examined the mercenary's face but Rast's expression showed nothing, neither guilt nor discomfort nor fear.

Insignia, *how long until the OLOSS ship reaches us? Exactly?*

Approximately.

Less time than it takes you to dress.

'They are too close now. We cannot avoid them boarding – you must hide it,' said Mira decisively.

Rast reared up out of her seat and grabbed Mira's arm. 'No, we must run.'

'We cannot run,' Mira cried. 'I have to tell them about Araldis.'

'They won't believe you—'

Mira stood impassively in Rast's grasp and summoned her most imperious tone. 'Hide it. And send Latourn to attend me at the egress scale.'

'A-attend you!' Catchut spluttered. 'Why, y-you—'

But Rast cut him off with a decisive hand movement. 'Play your game well, Baronessa. Your life depends on it.'

Mira took that warning back to her cabin where she hurriedly changed into a Pellegrini ceremonial robe.

The bodice and skirt were too large for her thin body but the headdress fitted well enough. She bundled her hair behind the wimple and tucked away a couple of stray wisps. The mirror showed her strained eyes and faded skin colour. She turned sideways and stretched the fabric across her belly. There was no hint of her secret in this voluminous dress.

Insignia, contact the OLOSS ship and explain that they are welcome aboard but that one of the survivors has a quarantine-level illness. And—

Mira?

—Why did you not tell me that Rast had brought cryoprotectants on board?

I am not interested in the minor activities of your species.

You mean . . . only when it suits you.

There was a long pause before *Insignia* replied.

The OLOSS ship has requested that your delegate comes to their quarantine area.

Mira let out a relieved breath.

Latourn was waiting for Mira at the egress scale. His dark hair was slicked flat and he wore an ochre-coloured everyday fellalo over his grey garb. The robe was a little short but he looked well enough in it – as though he could be Latino.

Mira felt the force of his stare. 'I do not need you to speak, merely to act as my attendant. Stay behind me,' she said.

Latourn nodded, and smiled in a way that made her uneasy. There was no warmth in it, only a strange kind of hunger. It was a risk taking him to the meeting but preferable to the others.

She heard a dull thud.

'That's them,' said Latourn, turning to face the rough, thickened flesh of the egress scale. 'Lemme go first. Might be that someone's nervous in there.'

Mira shook her head. She would let no one risk themself on her behalf. 'No. Stay behind me,' she repeated.

He shrugged and gave a mock bow. 'Whatever m'lady wants.'

The docking connection is complete, Mira.
Let's proceed.

The OLOSS ship's entry chamber was as grey and functional as the corridors of Intel station. Mira was forced to sit on a bench close to Latourn as they were screened for contamination. Finally, a strong astringent scent filled their nostrils.

'Anti-bac spray. It cakes your pores. Gives you a rash,' Latourn muttered. Then he added, 'Let me know if you need a hand to wash it off.'

A masked guard in an olive OLOSS uniform entered before Mira could react to Latourn's suggestion. Two more joined him a moment later, carrying a chair and a fold-up table. When the table and chair had been set in front of Latourn and Mira, all three guards took up positions on either side of the door.

Latourn mimicked their action, settling himself against the wall opposite. Mira clasped her fingers together to keep them still and sat stiffly, waiting.

Finally, an affluently robed male with thin patrician features and soft skin entered. Something in his manner reminded Mira of the Principe Franco: confidence born of authority. And not just authority, she sensed; self-belief as well.

He held out his hand in greeting. 'Sophos Mianos, OLOSS designate on Scolar.'

Mira half rose from her seat and returned the soft-fingered touch. 'I am Baronessa Mira Fedor of the Cipriano clan on Araldis.'

The man stumbled over her use of her title, she thought, but he quickly arranged his expression into sympathetic lines. 'Now, Baronessa Fedor, tell me quickly of this tragedy that brings you in such haste across Orion.'

Mira began hesitantly but found momentum in the reliving of her story and the presence of a sympathetic ear. She told Mianos most things – except for Marchella's part in the events and Trin's final act. When she had finally exhausted herself she sat, hunched and miserable, wishing for sleep or any type of oblivion.

Sophos Mianos took her hand and patted it for long moments until she grew uncomfortable and withdrew it.

'Would you care for refreshments, my dear?' he asked gently.

'Th-thank you,' Mira stammered. His refined manner was almost jarring after so long with the mercenaries.

They sat in an awkward silence until a menial bought a jug of iced water. Mira drank hers quickly but Latourn refused, frowning at her.

When the menial had removed the tray, another one appeared with a plate of meats and pastries which he

placed in front of the Sophos. With a sigh and an innocent smile, Mianos tucked a serviette over his robe and
began to eat. Between mouthfuls he began to ask
questions.

Mira could not concentrate due to the smell of the
marinated meats and the look of the honeyed cakes.

Her exhausted mind struggled to answer Mianos, for
his questions seemed designed to trip up her logic and
confuse her recollection.

She began to realise that though his skin was soft
and his eyes gentle, Sophos Mianos was neither of those
things. He continued to eat with a fastidiousness that
could only have been intentional – fussing over the
tiny scraps of fat and drips of meat juice, never once
offering food to Mira or Latourn.

'Tell me again, Baronessa, why the Principe's heir
provided you with transport to escape, while he stayed
on?' he asked.

Behind the Sophos one of the masked soldiers
moved restlessly as though he too was impatient with
proceedings.

Mianos turned and scowled at him: a fierce, quelling
look.

Mira forced herself to speak. 'I have explained,
Sophos Mianos. The young Principe Pellegrini chose
to stay to lead the survivors to a safe place. Our fleet
had been destroyed – only the biozoon remained. He
told me where it had been hidden. He knew—'

'He knew *what*, Baronessa?'

She hesitated before continuing. 'He knew that I
was the only one who could fly her.'

Sophos Mianos put his fork down on his plate and

blinked. 'Are you telling me that you – a woman – have the Innate gene?'

Mira clung to her erect posture despite the dreadful fatigue flooding her body. '*Sí*.'

'But you cannot—'

'*Sí*, Sophos. But it has happened – a freak of nature, perhaps, but undeniable.'

Mianos threw his napkin down on his meat scraps and stood. He paced a few steps as if the knowledge of Mira's talent had somehow changed things.

He turned to her. 'What is it that you expect OLOSS to do?'

'Trinder Pellegrini said that you would lend humanesquetarian aid. That the OLOSS charter meant that you would intervene on behalf of the Ciprianos.'

Mianos paused, plucking at his soft hairless chin. 'Indeed, our accord protects worlds from such atrocities – but these things are never simple matters. An investigation and recommendation will need to be made to the OLOSS secretariat before any intervention can occur.'

'But how long will that take?' Mira cried.

'I cannot answer that precisely. You will be notified when a decision has been reached. In the meantime, OLOSS will need to isolate and examine the biozoon. We will of course provide supervised accommodation for you on Scolar while the decision is pending.'

Isolate the biozoon. Supervised accommodation . . . Blood thundered in Mira's ears. 'No!' She rose hastily from her seat and stepped back towards the connecting matrix. Latourn did the same.

'Politic!' snapped Mianos at the three guards.

Two of them reacted immediately, bringing their weapons to bear on Mira and Latourn. The other, though, pulled his weapon from its holster and threw it towards his fellow guards. The impact when it hit the ground caused it to discharge and one of them fell to the floor, wounded.

The now-unarmed guard cried aloud – a childish, frightened noise. Then he rushed at the standing soldier, knocking his weapon from his hand.

'Flee!' he shouted at Mira.

But she was riveted by his clumsy movements and obvious desperation. She saw his ill-fitting torn uniform. *Who is he? Why does he help us?*

'Please go!' he cried again. 'Do not trust him.'

As Latourn dragged Mira into the connection matrix, the uninjured guard grappled with the inept dissident and ripped the visor from his face.

Mianos gasped. 'Thales! What in Kant's name are you doing—'

'You would imprison this woman as you did Villon? As you did me?' The young man's voice was impassioned. Wild.

The guard caught the dissident's arm and jerked it hard behind his shoulder, twisting it to dislocation point.

The dissident roared with fury rather than with pain. His shouted words became incoherent angry sobs.

Mira's heart beat harder at his distress, but Latourn showed no such concern. He was pounding at the egress scale.

Mira stayed where she was in the centre of the connection matrix. 'Help him,' she said.

Latourn stared back at her, incredulous. 'No,' he barked.

'*Insignia* will not open the egress scale until I tell her,' Mira told him.

'What do you mean?'

'Help the dissident and I will instruct *Insignia* to open it.'

Latourn's eyes widened. 'Capo said not to go with you – she said you were loco.'

Rast had said that? Mira kept her expression impassive. Perhaps she was. 'You are a fighter. So fight for me.'

Latourn made an infuriated noise. He unbuckled the belt around his fellalo and plunged back through the matrix into the other ship's link chamber.

Mira followed him.

The uninjured guard thrust the dissident aside roughly, bent swiftly to retrieve his weapon from the floor and turned it on Latourn. But the dissident threw himself against him, spoiling his aim before he fell sprawling.

In a deft, quick move Latourn looped his belt around the guard's throat and twisted hard, snapping the man's neck. He pulled the dissident upright and tossed him from the link chamber into the matrix. He landed almost at Mira's feet.

Mira ran to the egress scale. *Open for us*, she instructed the biozoon.

The scale peeled back and she scrambled through first. A moment later the dissident followed with Latourn behind him.

Insignia's presence filled her. She felt stronger and lighter. *Thank you*.

Then Rast had her, pulling her to her feet by her throat, shaking her into the present.

'Whatisit!' The mercenary demanded. 'What's happening? And who the fuck is this?'

Mira peeled Rast's fingers from around her neck. Pushing back her disordered wimple she glanced down and saw the dissident's face clearly for the first time. She did not think she had ever seen a more beautiful man.

Insignia, *break away from the other ship*. She looked back at Rast. 'I really do not know.'

JO-JO RASTEROVICH

'You're the God-Discoverer.'

'Some call me that,' said Jo-Jo.

'I'm Loker.' The round, sweaty man shot out his hand. 'My H-M picked up your heat signature.'

Jo-Jo shook Loker's hand. Then he turned in the tight confines of the small cluttered bridge and nodded his thanks to the scruffy glassy-eyed kid seated in the immersion sink.

'Tell me, what was the God-Discoverer doing floating around tethered to a station lug? Shouldn't you be toastin' your naked backside on a beach somewhere?'

'Bad Timing's got no manners,' said Jo-Jo in a noncommittal manner. 'Am obliged to you for picking us up, though, seeing as you've already got a fair load.' They'd climbed over the bodies of 'esques and aliens in the corridors of the Savvy's ventilated section.

'Yeah. Too many. We're thinking of going for a scrapshift. Get these people off my ship as soon as I can.'

'Scrapshift?'

'Can't see much in the way of alternatives. Maglev is working to the outstations but there ain't nothing out there but a bunch of satellites and some demounts on one of the moons. If we don't go while scrapshift is still working we might get stuck here. I only got a week's food left, and that's for a crew of ten. No knowing what those ginkos will do, either. Or how long until help comes.'

Jo-Jo realised why they'd been brought to the bridge. Scrapshift was a shitty experience. Sometimes people died from it. The Captain needed a second opinion – or someone else to blame. Jo-Jo had done it once before but he'd been in a half-decent can and unconscious drunk to boot. Afterwards he'd still felt like he'd been shredded. 'You got extra vibration cans?'

'Yeah. But not enough for everyone. We got a ton of bodies sardined into a Savvy rated for thirty. My ventilators are crapping themselves while we stand here flapping our gums suckin' air.' The Captain sounded cool enough but tension played around his mouth.

Jo-Jo thought about it. He couldn't see many options either. 'Tough call, though, Loker. Might lose some.'

The Captain shrugged. 'I figured you'd seen a bit. You got anything better?'

'Can you distribute people onto the other craft?' asked Bethany.

Loker ran his fingers along his com-sleeve and a low-resolution image of Dowl res-space flickered into life in front of them. It reminded Jo-Jo of acid hour at the Vega swap meet. 'Each ship is in the same situation, only they can't do a scrapshift – their ships aren't built for it.'

'Maybe we could take a vote. Those who don't want to risk it can get off,' suggested Beth.

Loker's face seemed to expand with annoyance. 'This ain't a frikkin' election, lady. I'm betting we've got an hour before life-support craps itself completely, which will at least spare us death by starvation. Every damn ship out there is in the same situation. Either we put down on Araldis or we risk an unattended scrap-shift.'

Beth blushed but she didn't back down. 'I see the dilemma, Captain, but you're making a decision that might kill people. I wouldn't want that on my conscience.'

'So it's better if we all die, then?' said Loker hotly.

Yet Jo-Jo could see that Beth had rattled him. He was a Savvy captain. Life-and-death responsibility didn't come in the job description.

'I think we should put down on Araldis,' Beth insisted.

The Captain gave her an incredulous stare. 'The place is burning. We can see it from our sats.' He tapped the sleeve again and a primitive slide-show of images replaced the shift-space representation.

Beth sagged when she saw the grainy pictures of billowing smoke. 'Araldis has a high oxygen quotient. The fires will take a long time to burn out,' she whispered.

'What's not burned is desert,' said Loker.

Mau put his arm around Beth's shoulder and squeezed her gently. 'Scrapshift best.'

Jo-Jo nodded agreement. 'Where's the nearest station?'

'Jandowae.'

Loker lifted his sleeve and spoke into it. 'Get everyone into the buffer cans.'

'Captain?' replied a crew member from somewhere on the ship. 'There ain't enough roo—'

'I know. We're scrapping in eight minutes.'

The virtual representation of their position vanished and reappeared in the air above the H-M's sink, flashing between schematic and sectioned real-time views.

Loker muttered into his sleeve, his eyes half-closed as he became absorbed in interface. The H-M was slack-jawed as well; spit bubbling at the corner of his mouth.

Jo-Jo felt a tightening hand on his guts. Could the kid handle this?

A third crew member entered the bridge and grudg-ingly handed out antispasmodics. 'Scrapshift is rougher than most – even in the cans. Need two of these normally but there ain't enough to go around. Should save you from the worst, though,' he said.

Jo-Jo slipped his into Beth's hand. She frowned at him and shook her head.

'Mothershit!' cried the H-M.

Jo-Jo didn't have to ask what was wrong. The schematic showed another ship crossing ahead of their shiftspace trajectory. Not a Savvy. Something bigger, creating an uncommon energy signature.

'Where are they going?' cried Jo-Jo. 'I thought normal res-shift was buggered.'

'H-M?' Loker's voice quavered.

'Must have entered at the same time as us, Captain. It's an organic. A 'zoon or a biobe,' said the young kid. 'They don't need working res. They just need the—'

'Coordinates. I know,' finished Jo-Jo. *Was it* Salacious?

'They're going to squirt.' Loker lifted his sleeve. 'We're in their slipstream. Secure the vibration cans. *NOW!*' he screamed.

'Josef,' Bethany wailed.

Mau grabbed her hand – the one that held the anti-spas – and twisted it. She opened her mouth to protest but he forced her palm to her lips and made her swallow the caps.

'Loker,' said Jo-Jo sharply. 'We go in on their tail and we'll pixelate.'

'Not if we stay close enough.'

'Close enough? We'd have to be fucking 'em!' Jo-Jo roared.

Loker was staring over the edge of his own indecision: shaking; eyes blank.

Calmer, thought Jo-Jo. *Be calmer.* 'Loker, pull out and we'll go again.'

'He's right, Captain,' said the H-M. The kid was shaking worse than Loker but he was still thinking.

'No, too much damage,' insisted Loker. 'We tuck in tight. Don't argue, Len.'

The Savvy started to groan as though the long-married seams were planning a separation. Jo-Jo felt the start of a tooth-rattling, bone-deep vibration where there should be none.

'Cans are malfunctioning, Captain.'

'Why?' demanded Loker.

'Slipstream's causing a vacuum. Can program's getting the wrong data.'

'Change the parameters.'

'Take too long,' said the kid.

Mau looked at Jo-Jo.

Jo-Jo nodded at him, then slung his arm through one of the grips that hung from the ceiling. 'Don't damage the sleeve,' he said softly.

Mau made a deep-throated noise and pushed

Bethany down into a wall cavity. Then he launched at Loker with his undamaged shoulder, knocking the Savvy captain out of his crib onto the floor.

'H-M, peel out,' shouted Jo-Jo. 'NOW!'

The kid looked at Loker. The Captain was unconscious.

He punched his fist into his palm and nodded.

For as long as Jo-Jo could stay upright and keep watching the schematic he didn't think they would make it. Then he lost his handgrip and flew across the cabin to crash into Mau and Loker.

Sound replaced sight: Mau's swearing, the H-M grunting as though lifting something heavy, and the distant but persistent screams.

Jo-Jo lost his grip on Mau's leg and juddered across the floor, whacking the side of his face against the bulkhead. The pain was nothing compared to the agony that had overtaken his body: cramps in every conceivable muscle – legs, arms, stomach and, worse, his lips and cheeks sucking inward as though he was trying to swallow his own mouth.

Then the Savvy broke out of the slipstream with an unforgettable jolt.

The vibration stilled.

The H-M stopped grunting and took in dry gulps of air. So did Bethany.

'H-M?' Jo-Jo rasped when he could speak. 'Report?'

Young Len gave a lunatic's high-pitched laugh. 'I think we're good to go again.'

They re-entered scrapshift thirty minutes later. Jo-Jo felt the relief of comparative stillness as they reached the optimum speed and the vibration buffers kicked in.

Even so, his bones felt as though they'd been compressed and mixed into a paste. Mau lay atop Loker, swearing still, and Beth was curled into a ball. Only Len seemed to be functioning.

Tough kid.

'We're calm,' Len pronounced wearily a few moments later. 'Jandowae.'

None of them moved or spoke for a long while.

Loker surfaced from unconsciousness. Pressing the back of his head with one hand, he kicked free of Mau and checked his sleeve.

'Jandowae,' he said, and smiled. 'We slipstreamed it.'

Jo-Jo waited. It was the H-M's call; the kid had to work with Loker.

But Len stayed silent.

The Savvy captain bestowed a sneer upon all of them, then climbed to his feet and stumbled from the bridge.

Jo-Jo helped Beth to her feet. She was trembling but composed enough. He couldn't see any signs of bruising on her.

He touched his own cheekbone and winced. *Better than me.*

'I want to go back to Araldis,' said Beth.

Jo-Jo stared, not sure if he had heard her right.

'I want to get help and go back.' Her expression had a weird kind of intensity about it that he'd only seen once before. 'My daughter is there,' she whispered.

'Help? You go to OLOSS for help and they'll tie you up for years asking questions. And mercenaries cost lucre that you haven't got.'

Beth nodded dismissively and turned to Len the H-M. 'When do you drop your load at Akouedo?'

'We were on our way there when this shit happened. I guess that's where we'll go when the Captain clears things.'

She nodded again. 'I want to go with you.'

Len tried to sit up straight and rub the exhaustion from his eyes. 'Captain might take you.' He looked at Mau. 'Then again, he might not. Depends on the lucre.' He crawled up out of his sink, his legs shaky. 'Better go see if I can help out.'

'Why there?' Jo-Jo asked Beth when the kid had gone.

She hesitated. 'I know someone who can help. Not OLOSS.'

'A mercenary?'

'Not exactly.'

There was silence again. Jo-Jo's face throbbed and he felt a sudden powerful hunger, making it hard to concentrate. 'Well, Beth, I'm sorry about your girl but I got no need to go back to Araldis.'

'What *do* you need to do?' she asked curiously.

'I need to find someone.' *And then what?*

'You'll want your own ship to do that, won't you?'

He thought of *Salacious* and felt a surge of anger.

But Beth wasn't giving up. 'I can get you one on Akouedo if . . .'

'If what?'

'If you can convince Captain Loker to take us there.'

'Us?'

Mau was sitting on the edge of Loker's platform, looking like he wanted to say something but was waiting for permission.

'It's OK, Pet,' Beth said.

Jo-Jo didn't like the feeling he was getting. The one that meant he'd been left out of a secret.

'Petalu is my guardian. My brother insists I have one,' said Beth.

'So all that Mama Petalu and Savvy stuff was crap?' Jo-Jo turned on Beth. 'Why do you need a guardian? And who's your brother?'

She glanced at Mau again.

Jo-Jo realised what an idiot he'd been by not picking up on the protectiveness.

'I c-can't explain yet. When we get to Akouedo, Josef,' she said. 'Please can you convince Loker to take us there? He won't listen to me.'

Please? She'd lied to him, yet she was also the reason he was still alive and feeling belligerent – he owed her this favour at least. 'I'll talk to Loker,' he said.

Jo-Jo stepped out of the tiny bridge and straight into the slippery stink of blood and urine. People were spilling from the vibration cans into the corridors.

He forced his way along to where Captain Loker knelt over an injured woman. 'Loker!'

The Captain glanced up at him, annoyed.

But Jo-Jo wouldn't be deterred. 'I don't want to get off here.'

'Station security is about to come aboard. Everyone's off then.'

'I want to go to Akouedo. I'll pay,' said Jo-Jo. 'Me and my two friends.'

But Loker's attention was drawn away from him to an eruption of shouts as the hatches opened.

Jo-Jo knelt down next to him 'Loker!'

The man swung Jo-Jo another look. 'Fee is ten thousand gals. Now get out of my hair unless you know something about this . . .' He lifted his hand from the woman's thigh and blood seeped down onto the floor. She moaned in a way that made Jo-Jo want to crap himself.

Loker clamped his hand over the wound again. 'Crux, where are the fucking medics?'

Jo-Jo returned to the bridge and warned Beth and Mau not to leave. They crouched on the floor space around Loker's platform, saying little to each other.

After a while Len appeared, looking haggard. He went straight into his sink without a word.

When the station security guards finally shouldered their way into the cramped bridge space Jo-Jo was first on his feet. Loker swayed in the door, well past exhausted. He pointed. 'That's my H-M and these ones are paying customers on their way to Akouedo,' he said.

'Smells like they're going to the right place,' said the station-sec guard closest to Petalu Mau.

'Stand against the wall,' ordered another.

'Loker?' said Jo-Jo sharply.

'Station sec thinks some of the refugees might not be genuine.' Loker's stare met Jo-Jo's. 'Are you working for the nasties, Rasterovich?'

'What's your business in Akouedo?' said the sec guard with the most stripes.

'My ship was stolen from a berth on Dowl. I need a short-term replacement. Thought it might be the place to pick one up cheap.'

'And these two?'

'My crew,' said Jo-Jo without hesitation.

The sec guard checked them all with his recog-ware.

'So, you're the God-Discoverer. Figured you'd be bigger, somehow. Smarter-looking.'

Jo-Jo ignored the insult, thankful, for once, for his reputation.

'Well, God-Discoverer, according to our recog your HealthWatch has expired,' said the sec guard helpfully. 'Better get that fixed.'

'Yeah,' said Jo-Jo. 'Well, I've been a bit busy.'

The sec guard turned his attention to Beth.

'Bethany Ionil, biologist,' said Beth calmly. 'Recently on the *Miofarr*.'

'The *Miofarr*. She's been here plenty,' said the guard.

They stood and waited while the recog confirmed Beth's story. 'You left the *Miofarr* at Dowl. Why?' he asked.

'My relationship broke down. He was a Mio.' Beth let a small waver creep into her voice. Jo-Jo couldn't tell if it was real or acting.

The guard made a disgusted noise. 'Always found those Mios slimy sons-of-fishes.' He smirked and turned finally to Mau.

'Petalu Mau?'

'Work on Savvies. Now work for Mr Rasterovich.'

Mister Rasterovich. Jo-Jo sucked on his lip to keep his mouth shut.

Loker was doing the same, his instinct for paying

customers warring with his desire to see them off his ship.

The sec guard ran the same checks on Len the H-M and then nodded at Loker. 'Let's move on, Captain.'

Loker dragged himself upright. 'Yeah. Riveting stuff,' he said dryly.

They disappeared down the corridor.

Len hauled his weary body out of his sink. 'Going to catch some sleep before we shift again. We got no spare cabins but there's a crawlspace above the maglevs. You might want to stretch out.'

'Thank you. Yes,' breathed Beth.

They followed Len to a narrow floor space that vibrated and stank of burned oils. Mau lay down and rolled onto his side, facing away from them. In a few moments he was snoring.

Jo-Jo lay down and watched as Beth removed her outer layer of clothes.

'You going to tell me what's going on with you, Beth?'

She sat cross-legged between him and Mau: the floor space was just large enough for the three of them to lie side by side. 'How much do you know about Orion politics, Josef?'

He shrugged. 'As much as the next person, I guess. There's OLOSS. And they spend their time worrying about the Extropists taking over. In between the two there is Consilience, who like to keep everyone off balance.' Jo-Jo settled his hands under his head and stared at the low bulkhead. It was coated with a thin but percept- ible layer of oil. 'I never really understood why the Extropists are such a threat to OLOSS. Guess I've spent too much time on my own – away from it all.'

Beth slid down now, head to toe with him. She propped her head on her folded clothes. Her colour was drained by fatigue and she looked suddenly much, much older. 'Who knows really? I mean at the most practical level. But I've always thought it was about God. OLOSS want to protect their notion of evolution. They want it to be a "natural" thing. The Extropists have forced evolution in a direction that they don't like. They see the Extros as non-spiritual. Although I'm not so sure that's really the case . . .'

Jo-Jo thought about Sole. From the beginning many had called the strange entity God. *What do the Extros think of that?* he wondered. The Sole voice had been absent from his head since before Dowl and his mind seemed almost like it used to be. 'What about the Entity? What do you make of that?'

Beth yawned and rolled towards Mau's back. 'You're the expert on that, Josef. What do *you* think?'

For the first time Jo-Jo tried to put his experience into context, thinking back over the moment when his propulsion had died. His impression had been of a bloated energy-shaped leech overwhelming him and his ship. He remembered dying. At least, that was what he had thought. But something eluded his memory, a shadow around the corner that disappeared every time he turned to catch it.

Afterwards, his mind had altered. The tyros of Belle-Monde referred to it as 'shafting'. Sole had required them to undergo the transformation to make it easier to communicate. But no one knew that Jo-Jo had been *shafted*. No one knew that Sole could reach out to him, wherever he was.

Then, as if he had somehow summoned it with his thoughts, Jo-Jo felt Sole's presence return. A tug; a gentle, insistent pull forward – as if his life, his volition was not his own.

He lay next to Beth, with Mau's snores forming a background lullaby chorus, and wondered where the pull would take him.

Sole

bring'm closer
bring'm tight
get'm messy messy messy
luscious

TEKTON

'My cousin Ra? What has he to do with this?'

Connit acquired a cunning expression. The words had slipped out.

'Both of you are ambitious beyond calculation,' Connit declared.

'*Beyond calculation* is rather histrionic, don't you think?'

Connit shoved Tekton through the door. 'You have what you want, Lostol. Now get out of my sight.'

Tekton stumbled backwards, grabbing the corridor rail to prevent a fall.

His free-mind seethed at the assault on his person, and, though his logic-mind rushed to reinstate his *witness* option, it was not quick enough to capture the actual push.

Tekton left Connit's rooms with two things on his two minds. What had Ra used Connit for? And how could he best repay the shove?

The Ra topic caused his minds to argue all the way back to his apartment. Logic-mind determined that though Ra was a person to be watched, Tekton's time would be better served making arrangements for his Sole project. Free-mind thought that its counterpart was obsessed with arrangements, and encouraged Tekton to follow his interest in Ra – or to plan a suitable payback for Labile Connit.

By the time Tekton had reached his rooms, the tension in his head was akin to severe dehydration. He drank several glasses of viliri juice which gave him heartburn and an uncomfortably loose sensation in his lower belly.

When his moud chimed, it was a welcome distraction.

You have received a farcast from Araldis. The first shipment of quixite has arrived at the holding facility.

Excellent! His minds spoke in accord.

And you have a call from Dicter Miranda Seeward.

Yes, yes, put her on.

'Tekton, you dirty devil. How did you get on with Labile? My moud tells me you've been to visit him.'

Tekton took a slow breath before replying. Miranda was astute and intuitive. 'He seems well enough. A false alarm, perhaps – must have caught him in a mawkish moment. We've all been known to fall into the grips of the maudlin from time to time.'

'Indeed we have. You rescued me from my own bout not so long ago and whisked me off on a romantic trip to Scolar.'

'Now, now, my dear, are you trying to make Lawmon Jise jealous? You know as well as I that the trip was purely work-related.'

Miranda chortled, sending her famous chins into a wobble. 'It's hard to know, between us, who the bigger tease is, Tekton.' She fluttered her eyelids. 'Or who has the bigger appetite.'

Tekton's free mind leapt to partake in her flirtation, but his logic-mind had other concerns. *I will need craftsmen skilled in mineral processes.* 'Miranda, how truly thoughtful of you to call. I will no doubt see you soon.'

Tekton ended the call without ceremony and turned his attention to perusing the master craftsmen's register.

He had worked with many fine trade professionals but there was one who had always eluded him, a brilliant eccentric who chose his work – it seemed – solely on whim. He had thrice refused Tekton – on the floating palaces, a synthetic-reed balustrade and, more recently, on the majestic Latour-moons bridges. It was said that he preferred boutique projects; projects inspired by love and beauty, not gal credits.

I will have you this time, Manrubin. Even you cannot resist the lure of quixite.

Tekton farcasted to the master craftsman's last known point of contact.

Within the shortest ping time, Manrubin's moud returned a vulgar out-of-office response. 'Manrubin is out fucking, so fuck off.'

Ignoring the rebuff, Tekton pinged back a lucrative contract shell which also specified the materials that he would be supplying for use in the sculpt.

Then he peeled off his clothes and treated himself to a well-deserved lotion rub.

Several days later Manrubin's moud responded again; Manrubin had agreed to the contract. Gleefully, Tekton closed his farcast connection and clapped his hands.

Labile Connit is outside, Godhead, his own moud informed him.

Tekton left his 'cast node and opened the door. He stepped outside tentatively, the memory of the younger man's assault still fresh.

Labile held out a small bead. 'I have a location for

you for the business we discussed. Here are the details. It is the only record of them. The hire cost of the premises will be waived by my . . . contacts.'

Tekton fitted the bead to his ear and listened to the content. When he was satisfied, he removed it.

Moud. Send a farcast to my holding facility to begin shipment of the alloy to a workshop on Rho Junction. And book my passage. I will meet both the master craftsman and the consignment there.

TRIN

Djeserit swam beside the flat-yacht as it sailed through the dawn to the closest island. Occasionally she flipped to the surface, sending small splashes of brown seawater onto the crowded deck where Trin sat. Mostly, though, she was just a shadow among others, moving beneath waves.

Trin gave up trying to track her and turned his attention to the two remaining yachts on the shoreline. What would Cass Mulravey do? Would she follow him, or would she risk going to the holiday palazzo?

His own feelings on the matter were torn. The woman was divisive and proud but without her group, his band of survivors numbered less than sixty – so many had been lost on the journey.

Too many.

As the last few refugees crammed on board the Mulravey yachts Trin's own craft reached the breakers. Soon it would roll down onto the beach and they could seek out shade under the low scrub until nightfall.

'She is a fool not to stay with you, Trinder.' Jo Scali hunched next to him, his feet trailing into the water from the laden deck.

Trin waited a moment before he answered, watching the last yacht push off the beach. Its plax sails glided up the mast and rotated.

'She is no fool,' he said. Mulravey was following them.

Trin relaxed into a moment of satisfaction. Mulravey had been forced to follow his lead and that would add weight to his authority. Perhaps the two groups could yet assimilate – if the Saqr did not find them first.

'Juno?'

The scout had given the rudder over to Joe's cousin, Tivi Scali, and lay curled on a small patch of deck behind Trin. '*Sì*, Principe,' he said hoarsely.

'Was the marina guarded?'

Genarro rolled his head from side to side. 'Too busy around the palazzo to take much notice. No Saqr near the shore, only an 'esque and a balol. I left some other boats adrift as though the nightwinds had loosened their moorings. Doubt they will even know they are gone.'

'Your reasoning is good,' said Trin. 'What else did you notice?'

Genarro shifted position, wincing from the pain in his weary joints. 'I didn't go close, Principe – we did not want you to be waiting for us. But the hangar roof was open.'

'That is not so unusual.'

'Pardon, Principe. I am not being clear. The hangar was open to its limit as though they were expecting a large SGV.'

A Space-to-Ground-Vehicle? What could that mean? More Saqr? More 'esques? Whichever the case, it was imperative that they moved south quickly.

Trin turned to the island ahead. Even in the last moments before dawn there was already a heat shimmer making it seem larger and shadier than it was – the black thorn bushes clumped together in the centre as though gathering strength from each other's endurance.

To the south the islands were bigger and spaced further apart. Would the yachts withstand the stresses of more open water?

Djeserit was ahead of them, on her knees in the shallows, tossing small objects high onto the beach.

'She's got fish,' shouted someone at the front of the yacht.

'The ginko girl's fishing for us,' said another.

A small cheer went up but Trinder didn't join in. They had called her a ginko and the sound of the word made him feel sick.

'Principe?' Joe Scali put an anxious hand on his shoulder.

He shrugged it off. 'Collect the fish and gut them straight away. We will eat as we rest.' He turned from the sight of Djeserit then and clung to the deck as they wallowed over the last of the waves and down onto the beach.

Djeserit didn't join Trin on the island but fished throughout the day, returning more food to shore.

'You must tell her to stop, Trinder. She is exhausted,' said Joe Scali. 'She will not listen.'

But Trin remained distant from her. Instead, he ordered that the strongest refugees should scoop out hollows under the thorn bushes to reach the wet, cool sand beneath, while the weakest were charged with cutting up the fish, using the few knives they had pooled or the edges of broken shells.

When it was done, they crowded away from the rising

sun into the shade and ate the fish raw. Those too list-less to chew sucked at the pink flesh for moisture and for the salve of oils on their burned lips and throats.

Gusts of moist salt wind tempered the unbearable heat but Trin worried about their lack of fresh water. He dozed fitfully in his hollow, unable to sleep properly because of thirst and the press of the exhausted bodies packed in around him.

At suns set he walked alone to the water, opening his fellalo, to lie in the shallows. Even the stinging of sea lice couldn't deny the refugees the balm of the sea. But could they live off it until help came?

Trin looked along the darkening beach line to the clumps of survivors. Vespa Malocchi sat crying between Juno Genarro and another. He had wanted to bring his fratella's body but Trin had forbidden it. The yacht had barely been able to carry the weight of the living. So Vespa had scraped the burning sand over Seb's body and left him.

Trin sat recalling the fire in Loisa and how he had risked his life then to help Seb Malocchi. The futility of it made him want to laugh but he had no heart for such things.

Then a movement in the water made him shift uneasily. The shallow seas of the coastal islands harboured few predators but occasionally a xoc would find its way in from the deep. He had seen one at the holiday palazzo; speared by the Cavaliere and left on the beach to die. When he had dug Djeserit from under Seb Malocchi, the sluggishness of her gills had reminded him of that xoc – gasping as it expired.

'Principe?'

It was her. She had surfaced alongside him and was lying with her face raised from the water. Her voice was thick as if she had already forgotten how to use it. Her skin was no longer flaking, though, and the burns had faded, leaving her gleaming like the wet flesh he had eaten during the day.

'You provided food for us. *Grazi*,' Trin said stiffly. 'Another night and we must move south to the bigger islands. There will be more shade and the Saqr will not bother to search for us there.'

'Yes,' Djeserit agreed. 'The sea will care for us.'

'For you,' he said with a tinge of bitterness.

She heard it in his voice and moved closer. 'It is better if I stay in the water. I can fish for us and my skin – my body – will heal.'

'Until when?' Trin asked.

'Until we are safe, Principe. I will rest for a while now and then I will swim to the Palazzo for fresh water.'

Trin's heartbeat quickened. 'That is too dangerous. I forbid—'

'You did not forbid Juno Genarro,' Djeserit said softly.

Trin hesitated. She was right. Their water supplies had dwindled to almost nothing and he had not thought ahead clearly. 'There are several huts around the back of the palazzo that are used for storing leisure equipment. One of them will have a desalinator.'

He waded back to the hard wet sand above where the waves lapped and drew for her a rough diagram of a small machine that consisted of tubes and cylinders.

Djeserit rolled in the shallows like a seal, watching. 'I will need something to float it back.'

'They may be guarding the marina now.' Trin thought

for a moment. 'But there is an inlet on the northern side, a tidal tributary. There is a pinnace for fishing trips moored in there.'

He sank to his knees and slid into the water alongside her again. 'Please, Djes . . .'

Her hand grasped his and pushed sharp round buttons into his fist. 'I have saved these for you. Pipis will give you strength.'

Then she dipped under the water and was gone.

THALES

The two women faced each other across a ribbed, odorous cavern that they called the buccal: one was lean and muscular, her face rigid with fury, the other, the Latino aristocrat, was fragile-looking and trembling with emotion. At her shoulder stood the man who had accompanied her to the meeting with Sophos Mianos.

Another man stood behind the muscular woman. All of them, aside from the Baronessa, were of a type that Thales had not previously encountered, and their manner alarmed him in a way that the OLOSS guards had not.

'What have you done?' said the muscular woman. 'Who is *this*?' A hiss as she jerked a finger at Thales.

'OLOSS wanted to impound *Insignia* while they conducted an investigation – and hold me.' A glance at Thales. 'He . . . he gave us a chance to get away.'

'And so you saw fit to tear the 'zoon from the docking matrix and send us running from an OLOSS envoy.' The hard-looking woman folded her arms, some of the heat going out of her expression. 'And you call *me* fool-hardy, Baronessa.'

'I thought that was what you wanted – to run.'

'With a distance between us, yes. Not while we're almost in bed with them.'

'My action was motivated by survival, not avarice.' The

aristocrat held her head high and Thales watched the emotions play across her face. She seemed at once sane and unbalanced. What situation had he brought himself to? Yet while he'd been standing behind Mianos, listening to her story about her world had been like a spear to his heart. She had been forced to leave her child behind, maybe leaving it to its death.

'So you think I am motivated by greed?' said the muscular woman.

The Baronessa didn't flinch. There seemed to be a weight of feeling between them. 'What do *you* call it, then, Rast Randall?'

The woman, Rast, balled her fists in anger and turned to Thales. 'Your story: quick and to the point.'

Thales licked dry, nervous lips. 'I am indebted to the Baronessa and her . . . servant for—' He nodded at the one whom Mira had called Latourn.

'Yes. Yes,' said Rast. 'But why did you help her?'

'It is not a simple tale. I am not who I appear to be. I am a philosopher who has been wronged. I took work as a courier to help a friend; to help myself. Life had become difficult for me on Scolar.' Thales swallowed several times before continuing. 'My misfortune continued, though. When I boarded the OLOSS craft, my nemesis was destined for the same trip.'

'Sophos Mianos?' asked the Baronessa.

'Yes. He had me wrongfully imprisoned on Scolar and more. He kept me from my . . . my wife. When he spoke of imprisoning you and your organic craft, I . . . I . . . became rash . . . I would admit . . . impulsive. My wife tells me it is my biggest failing. I am recovered now and regret any inconvenience.'

'Regret any inconvenience, eh?' Rast Randall sucked in her cheeks as though she might be on the verge of exploding.

The Baronessa nodded her head politely at Thales. 'I am indebted to you . . .'

'Thales Berniere,' said Thales.

'Msr Berniere, I have, I am afraid, put you at further risk.'

He returned her nod. Despite her fragile appearance the woman had fine manners and strength of mind. 'I have a work obligation to fulfil. Would it be too much trouble to ask you to convey me as far as Scol station?'

The Baronessa smiled at him: a beautiful shy smile that warmed his numb senses.

Rast frowned at them both. 'Catchut,' she said to the man at her shoulder, 'find him a cabin and show him the cucina.' She then gave Thales a hard look. 'We'll take you to Scol station. In the meantime you are in one of those two places unless you are with one of us. Understood? Nowhere else. If I find you roaming around the 'zoon, I'll spit you out into the black.'

Mira

Rast eyed Mira unpleasantly when Catchut Latourn and Berniere left the buccal. 'I can only think that you are missing your own ilk, Baronessa? Why else would your risk your own and Latourn's life for *him*.'

Mira? said *Insignia*.

Just a moment.

'It happened quickly. I-I made a decision.' Mira braced herself for further ridicule but it didn't come.

Instead Rast slumped down into Autonomy. 'At least you *made* a decision, Fedor. Now what do you propose?'

Mira sank opposite her into Primo. The warmth of the vein pulsed around her and she could feel *Insignia*'s receptors flirting across her skin, gently pricking places to allow the transmission of fluids and sugars. Within moments she began to revitalise but with the energy came a welling of tears. She turned her face to the vein wall, letting it absorb the trickle of moisture.

'I am at a loss. OLOSS will not help Araldis, at least not quickly. Perhaps not at all, now that I have done this. I-I am failing.'

They stayed in silence while Mira let Primo subsume her. When the process was complete she immersed herself in *Insignia*'s propulsion and self-repair of the egress scale.

The OLOSS craft was still becalmed. Had Mianos

and his guards survived the tear? Had her decision killed more people?

'There is an alternative.'

It took Mira a while to realise that Rast had spoken. She dragged herself from her immersion, enough to speak. Rast was still in Autonomy.

'What is that?'

'You could raise your own intervention.'

Mira waited.

'Consilience, Fedor?'

'What? An organisation that opposes everything!'

'That perception is nearly as outdated as your society, Baronessa. Consilience is not an organisation – it's an assemblage.'

'Why would an *assemblage* wish to help my world? I have no money to pay them.'

Rast sat up straighter and ran her fingers through her short white hair. 'Don't you understand? OLOSS was a coming together of races and species that shared common beliefs about law; but more than that, common beliefs about evolution. They believe that it is a natural process that should not be interfered with.'

'And so?'

'On the other side are the Extropists – a multi-species group that opposes those beliefs. They believe that they are in charge – destined to control and shape their own evolution. They don't give a crap about moral and ethical debate. They'll do anything to advance themselves. Their genetic manipulation is extreme.'

'*Si*. Monsters and so on,' Mira murmured.

'It sounds childish but it is scientific and utterly ruthless.'

'And so?'

'So Consilience sits between them. It wants neither body to have the upper hand and believes that diversity is the key to sentient survival.'

Mira was silenced by Rast's eloquence. The woman was such a contradiction.

Rast guessed her thoughts. 'Mercenary does not equate with stupid *or* uneducated, Baronessa. That's where your blinkers go right back on.'

'But you are mostly so crude. You speak in a way—'

'I speak in a way that will get me understood and I need you to understand.'

Mira withdrew from her immersion and felt her 'external' mind reawaken properly. 'The cryoprotectants you brought on board are for the Extropists. Are you one of them?'

'I brought cryoprotectants to trade with the Extropists. They struggle to get what they need. Without that stuff their society will degrade.'

'You are helping to keep the balance of power,' said Mira slowly, making the connections. 'You work for Consilience.'

Rast merely stared at her. 'I can help you meet the people who might mount an intervention. But you have to tell me what you know.'

Mira hedged. 'What do you mean?'

'You know something about the invasion. You've viewed something you brought from Araldis. I checked your add-on history. I want to know what you learned.'

Fear twisted up her stomach. Rast had been spying on her. 'Why would you care to help me?'

'Because it may suit me to. Now tell me.'

Mira closed her eyes. The mercenary was impossible to predict. *What else does she want? Should I trust her?*

She is a potential ally when you have no other. You must rest again now. Your baby needs it, Insignia responded unasked.

Mira opened her eyes and climbed stiffly out of Primo. She felt the sting, and the loss, as the last of the vein's receptors withdrew.

'I was given an audio recording of a meeting between one of the Cipriano nobles and a Lostolian visitor. He was purchasing minerals from a certain mine on Araldis. It produces quixite, a naturally occurring alloy that is normally only found in minute quantities. I think that the invasion was a way of securing this substance. Yet that seems ridiculous. Why would anyone commit genocide for a mineral alloy?'

Rast's face went whiter than her hair. Her eyes glittered. 'Shape-metal alloy. Are you sure?' she whispered.

'It is called quixite. That is all I know.'

Rast took one large step across to Mira and gripped her shoulders. 'Who was the buyer?'

Mira hesitated again. Her senses warned her against divulging all, yet she needed Rast's strength, her pragmatism and, perhaps, her contacts. 'His name was Tekton. She – the negotiator – referred to him as an archiTect. He is currently a tyro to the newly discovered Entity.'

Rast began to tremble.

'An OLOSS member.'

Mira nodded. 'I suppose so. Lostolians in general are.'

'What does he want quixite for?'

'I cannot imagine. You called it a shape-metal alloy. What does that mean?'

'An alloy is a mixture of minerals—'

'I am not a fool, mercenary. I know what an alloy is but what is special about *this* one?'

'It remembers its shape. That is more than useful for some of the evolved Extros.'

Mira?

Si?

There are some things you should know.

Si?

We have just joined the Scol shift queue. However, the OLOSS craft has made its repairs and has gained significantly on us. It is faster than I am at sub-light speed.

How close is it?

It will be in shift queue within an hour.

Proceed with haste, then.

Station security is requesting that we dock.

Can we ignore them and go straight to shift?

Yes. Although the situation will be the same as Intel. They could fire upon us.

Mira took a deep breath. *I will speak to Rast.*

There is one more thing.

Si? Her concern translated as impatience.

My contract has just expired.

Mira's entire body went cold. She swayed in Rast's grip.

'What now?' Rast's question sliced through the air between them.

'The OLOSS craft has caught us. We are about to enter the shift queue but station security is insisting that we dock. Sophos Mianos has 'casted a complaint.'

Mira's knees gave and she sagged back towards Primo, but Rast held her up, refusing to let her sit.

'And?'

'*Insignia*'s contract has expired.'

Rast's sudden alertness shifted to intense focus. 'Time for more hard choices, Fedor. Sit and wait for OLOSS to catch up with you. Or run.'

'To your Consilience assembly?'

'Theirs, not mine, but it seems to me like your best chance. I mean, if they catch you now with cryoprotectants on board, your Araldis story won't hold up.'

Rast was right in that. They might even think that Mira was the instigator of the invasion. Rast would certainly not claim responsibility for the purchase of the illegal substance.

Reluctantly, Mira nodded.

'You've got a few minutes to strike a bargain with your 'zoon, then, Fedor. Make it good,' said Rast.

Mira stared at her. 'I need some quiet.'

The mercenary let go of Mira's shoulders, easing her gently down into Primo. 'I'll be right here.' She gestured to Secondo. 'You make the deal and I'll get us a clear path through shift.'

'How will you do that? You have no friends in the shift queue this time.'

'Just do your bit. I'll do mine.'

Mira sank back and waited for immersion. As the receptors crawled under her clothes and penetrated her skin her link with the biozoon heightened.

Insignia?

Yes, Mira.

We are in a delicate position.

I think that you mean you *are in a delicate position. I am free to do as I please.*

But OLOSS wish to impound you also.

It is you they wish to question.

But you they wish to examine. And they must stop you to get me.

Not if I withdraw my humanesque life-support and expel your bodies into space.

Mira's breath seemed to run out. *You would do that?*

I'm not sure. It is a possibility, I suppose.

But I thought we had . . . a bond.

We do, Mira Fedor. As I had with your father. You are my Innate. But that does not prevent me making decisions that concern my well-being. My culture is not the same as yours. Humanesques make that mistake. One of their greatest failings is that they suppose other sentients to be and to think the same way.

Mira gasped in some air. *Insignia* was neither angry nor vindictive; simply pragmatic and she must approach this the same way. *What is it that you wish for, then? What would rebind you to me?*

I have told you of my desire for 'rafa'.

You wish to travel to Orion?

Yes. And further.

But I must return to Araldis. I have to find Vito. And the korm child . . .

I am prepared to wait some time for you to deal with immediate concerns. But then . . .

Mira thought through the consequences of such an agreement. It was not something to be made lightly. With it she committed to the life of a ship-bound wanderer. She had thought that to be her deepest desire but now, faced with it, she was not sure. *I n-need time to think. This is a decision . . . I cannot make it quickly.*

Indifferent amusement. *But I do not think that you have much time.*

Are you threatening me?

No. But understand. If there is no accord between us I will act without thought of you or your company. That is how it is.

Will you take us through shift now?

It is unlikely. Scol station security is maintaining an aggressive stance. They wish me to withdraw from the shift queue and dock. I do not wish for injury. My scales are already damaged. Self-repair is tiring.

Mira felt a pang of guilt. She had ordered *Insignia* to such an act without real thought of the effect.

Rast/Secondo: *Tick-tock, Fedor!*

Possibilities whirled through Mira's mind and yet each led back to the same place: survival. Marchella Pellegrini had taught her that.

She ignored Rast and spoke to *Insignia*. *If I agree to your desire for 'rafa' can I bring those I deem to be my familia with me?*

Indeed. Your choice of family will be mine.

Will our contract be enduring?

Yes. Until you die.

Or you?

It is unlikely to be me.

One last, long silence. *Agreed.*

Mira felt luscious warmth spreading through her limbs, a cocktail of endorphins that were her reward for her agreement. Then *Insignia* made her ultimate demand.

I will need some assurance of your commitment until such time as you have retrieved the child Vito from Araldis.

The flow of endorphins thinned.

What is that?

Once your child is born it will stay with me. It must not leave me.

Mira gasped. *No! But a baby needs to be fed, to be cared for by his mother . . .*

I have the facilty to do that. I can grow any tissue, replicate any nutrients. The babe will be cared for more adequately than if it is in your care . . .

A spinning, sickening feeling consumed Mira.

Rast/Secondo: *Fedor – now or never.*

Mira/Primo: *What, Rast?*

Rast/Secondo: *We're at a point where we can scrapshift from the refuse loop. But if we move any further in the queue we are stuck. Sec is already stationed on the final lip. Make the deal work, Mira. Now. NOW!*

Insignia. I agree.

Prepare!

The biozoon's visual shift-schema flickered and altered. Mira sensed adrenalin building through the biozoon like the bunching of muscles in an animal preparing to leap.

Rast/Secondo to the rest: 'Find a nub.'

Impressions flared and extinguished: Latourn hauling the screaming philosopher to a tubercle, Catchut praying again, Rast fighting her desire to urinate, Mira's own uncontrolled panting.

They were all caught in the building energy, helpless to affect it in any way.

At your mercy. The words stung. Then they began to

blaze. Then every micro-measure of Mira's body and mind caught fire. Not a hot white sizzling but a core-deep burning pain, as if holes were being drilled in her nerves while she lived and breathed and watched.

Rast/Secondo screamed. Latourn and Catchut and the philosopher too. Screaming . . . screaming.

But Mira did not join them. She folded the pain inward and clasped it close, smothering it with her own brand of coping.

It bucked inside her, contorted and fought her, building to a peak of pain-energy where she knew it would rend her open: disperse her.

But then its final rush came and a silhouette engulfed her, deluging her vibrating pain with stillness. The meeting of sensations trampolined Mira's molecular structure high and wide, and as it fell back into an arrangement that felt more or less like her own she became aware of *Insignia*'s long and heartfelt *Aaahhhhhhhh . . .*

When Mira could think again, a question waited in the forecourt of her mind. *Insignia? The sentients who work on the Savvies. How do they survive this experience repeatedly?*

She sensed approval of her questioning from the biozoon.

They have ways to soften the experience. My own biological adaptation makes it possible but not comfortable. I would not choose to do this under normal circumstances.

Mira wondered how the mercenary felt. *Rast?*

Yeah, Fedor. Everyone should experience this once.

Only a sadist would believe so, Mira thought back.

Your protected upbringing is showing again, Baronessa.
Mira did not bother to disguise her annoyance.
Where do we shift to now? Where do we find your Consilience?
We have found them, Rast answered.
Here? Insignia, virtual representation, per favore.
A stimulus passed through Mira's occipital cortex. She sensed the mercenary's brain pattern altering as she interpreted the same images. They both saw the biozoon's unique representation of an ancient white-dwarf star in its dying phase, and the cool light it cast across a dozen AUs, and as many planets. The star system was unremarkable, even dismal, compared to Leah's blue-hot brilliance.
An unbearably cold place, thought Mira.
Rast's reaction was different. Mira sensed her satisfaction. Almost . . . pleasure.
She also felt an incongruity that she could not understand flowing from the 'zoon's data collectors.
How fascinating! Insignia's excitement cut into her thoughts.
The map began to fill with detail: colourful representations of planet densities and a scattering of moving colours between them.
The moving lights are the Savvies, came Rast's thought.
They are different sizes.
The smaller ones are the tugs. They tow things around.
What things?
Wait . . .
And there it was – the map overlaid its final detail, bringing the freezing barren system to bizarre awe-inspiring life.

Insignia: *Akouedo.*

Rast: *Home.*

Mira: *Crux! What are they?*

Rast: *The things we once valued.*

Huge glittering rings circled each of the twelve planets: moving bands of objects caught in an endless spin. Tugs darted in and out of them like firebugs braving the surf spray along the beaches of the Tourmaline Islands. Some reappeared towing a glittering mote to another location. Occasionally a gap in the ring would afford a better view of the planet beneath. Through it Mira saw swirls of brilliant colours: magenta, lime and burning gold.

How beautiful.

Rast: *Poisonous gases. And refuse.*

Mira: *Ohhh—*

Rast: *Where else did you think it went?*

I didn't—

Rast: *No.*

Insignia: *I have heard of this system but had not imagined it would be so beautiful. It is not recommended to my kind.*

Rast: *It was beautiful once.* Wistful.

You are a native? Mira felt the mercenary's nod: a small, sombre gesture. Almost vulnerable.

There are many of us now. That call Akouedo home.

Rast? Where do we go?

Rast's energy shot to the seventh planet from the dying star. *There. Take us there.*

JO-JO RASTEROVICH

Mau, Bethany and Jo-Jo watched their approach to Akouedo's seventh planet, Edo, on a tiny banged-up screen in an operator's cabin next to the maglev gens.

Shift had been more comfortable this time – apart from the imitation Oort whisky. Loker kept his distance but the crew were keen for God-Discoverer stories over an evening of cards. To oblige, Jo-Jo told the story of his flight from the woman with the suffocating thighs. That tale alone – and his method of escape – got some of the crew refilling his cup for the duration, while the rest slipped off to their cabins for 'private' contemplation. What had seemed most agreeable at the time had turned into a gigantic hangover.

'How does anyone navigate through this circle of junk?' he demanded tetchily.

Mau shrugged.

But Bethany watched the screen with glittering eyes. 'Each planet has a designated "chute" area for entry. Ingenious, really, but it's disturbing to think that we produced all this rubbish.'

'Who are we going to see down there, anyway? The garbage chief?'

Mau glowered at him. He pointed to a spot on the screen. 'Here.'

The Savvy catapulted toward that very spot, a gap into

a narrow channel kept clear by an elaborate cable-net system that reminded Jo-Jo of the shark nets on the beaches of Cerulea. It twisted inelegantly through the thick band of floating rubbish, leaving Jo-Jo with fleeting impressions of damaged solar arrays, discarded twirling metal stairways from space habitats, and endless torn sheets of reflectives drifting like glitter motes in water.

The view became brighter and brighter until the screen dimmed to compensate. Jo-Jo felt the Savvy straining against the acute angle of its dive and he found himself taking shallow breaths.

Bethany seemed to be doing the same, punctuating hers with little grunts each time she exhaled.

Apart from the thin sheen of perspiration on his cheeks and forehead Mau seemed unperturbed.

Only when they broke free from the ring of rubbish did Jo-Jo begin to breathe normally. He closed his eyes then, waiting impatiently for the Savvy's chorus of docking noises.

When it finally happened he was deep in reverie.

'Mr Rasterovich?'

Jo-Jo opened his eyes. Len the kid H-M was at his elbow. 'Yeah.'

'Captain Loker says for you to leave through the cargo hatch. Someone will be waiting for you.'

That was it? No fond farewell?

Jo-Jo nodded. The sentiment was the same from his side.

He held out his hand to the kid. 'Find yourself a decent Captain.'

Len blushed and hurried away.

*   *   *

The three disembarked into a huge hangar that looked like a group of superseded docking modules that didn't quite fit together. Everything overlapped and some things seemed to be duplicated. Jo-Jo could hear air blowing in from above but couldn't see the vents in the dimly lit ceiling.

'Ahem.' A smartly attired Lamin stepped from the shadows to address them. Its tri-part nose quivered while it documented their scents and it pushed back a section of stiff black immaculately sectioned hair with fingernails that appeared to join straight to its wrist. Ridiculously cruel high heels attempted to flatter its stumpy shapeless legs.

Lamins usually worked as highly paid PAs for OLOSS politicians. This thought-caster was a long way out of the loop. 'Step this way.' It gestured towards a booth with plax walls.

As if to reinforce its demand two black-uniformed soldiers stepped forward. Each carried a lightweight firearm and wore a complicated blade kit around their waists.

Mau shepherded Beth inside the booth and Jo-Jo followed them. He stopped to watch through the plax as a small tug hooked onto the Savvy and towed it deeper into the hangar.

'What a beauty!' exclaimed Bethany. She was standing next to him but looking in the opposite direction at a large flat-winged ship floating against its dock.

Jo-Jo's heart skipped: a biozoon like *Salacious*. 'How much do you think?' he murmured.

Bethany gave him a fierce stare. 'You don't *buy* that

kind of creature. If you are lucky, it might pick you as a pilot. It's not a hybrid that's been hobbled.'

Jo-Jo looked back to the glistening scaled animal. 'You mean it has an Innate?'

'Yes, I would imagine so,' said Bethany. 'How lucky they are.'

The Lamin cleared its throat to gain their attention. 'Edo is a closed port. While Mistress Bethany and Petalu Mau are welcomed home, we are not yet satisfied with the reasons for your presence, Mr Rasterovich.'

Home? Jo-Jo stared at Beth.

'Lamin, he is here at my invitation,' said Bethany.

Part of the creature's nose twitched towards her. 'I am sorry, Mistress, but it is required that he be questioned.'

She sighed and shrugged.

The Lamin continued. 'What is the nature of your visit? Please be precise and accurate or you will be considered an intruder and isolated.'

Jo-Jo hesitated but the soldiers were inside the office as well now, gripping their weapons a little tighter. He could see little harm in the truth – in fact, he might be able to garner information from it. 'Bethany wanted to come here. I helped her do that because she helped me. I don't have business here as such. I am seeking a Lostolian named Tekton, an archiTect. We have some – err – business.'

A delay again. 'You were involved in a Hera contract with this 'esque.'

Jo-Jo took a breath, sensing Beth's curious glance at him. Lamins made it their business to know everything. 'Yes.'

But to his surprise the Lamin pursued it no further. Instead it asked them to follow. With the soldiers bringing up the rear it led them through a labyrinth of corridors. Each one was made of a different kind of material: foul-smelling singed plastics, extruded metal, synthetic tissue and wood. All were patterned by spreading fungi.

Jo-Jo realised after a while that the constant change was due to the nature of the building. The rooms along the corridors were actually giant packing crates cobbled together to simulate one mass.

The Lamin opened a hatch on a seemingly random crate and pointed inside with its long fingernails. 'Sit and wait,' it said.

It disappeared, leaving the soldiers guarding the door.

Jo-Jo crossed the interior of the bare crate and sat on a low shelf. Glancing upward he noticed that the light was coming in from under the unattached roof. Then the wall moved under his back, sending him straight to his feet again.

Beth came over and prodded it. 'Cartilage. It was a popular building material for a while but was prone to bacterial infections. Modelled on the biozoon idea. People started to get sick from it, though. It was banned on OLOSS planets.'

'Brilliant,' said Jo-Jo between gritted teeth. The place had him on edge. He was already hungry and he needed to pee. It didn't seem like the kind of place where you could do either of those things without a map and a day's food supply, so he dug his hands into the pockets of his poker-won Savvy jacket and fell to thinking about recent events.

Their escape from Dowl still made him want to crap all the time; the closest he'd ever been to death and his bowels wouldn't let him forget it. The terror of drifting in the black and the thoughts he'd had . . . they were with him still in the moments – like this one – when he let himself remember.

He looked across at Beth. She'd hauled him in on that tether, kept on talking to him, urging him to stay alive.

Did that make her a friend? Did he want her to be?

He wasn't sure. He'd always thought himself perfectly happy without close company but she had put a tiny nick on the hard edge of his beliefs and now the whole damn thing had begun to tear. Nothing seemed as solid as it had.

The door opened again and the soldiers beckoned them back into the corridor. They were forced to walk between them this time, twisting and turning down the makeshift corridors again until they stopped in front of another crate. The walls on this one looked organic as well – but catoplasma this time, grown and modified.

Inside the crate/room a group of 'esques sat around a low table. The 'esque at the table end was flanked by more soldiers. Jo-Jo thought him unremarkable at first – an older man despite obvious rejuve, with cropped silver hair and a lean body.

Then he got close enough to see the man's eyes. They were overly large for his face, and grey: dispassionate, intelligent eyes.

'Beth?' said the man softly. He did not stand or make any other change in his casual posture.

Beth blushed but met his gaze.

'Lasper,' she said.

Jo-Jo identified two of the other four people at the table as mercenaries. That left a soft-faced pretty young man who plucked at his sleeve with nervous fingers, and, lastly, a young woman. She was a small slender type like Bethany but dark-haired and fine-featured with vibrant crimson skin. She sat stiffly in a formal robe.

'Are you going to introduce your friend, Beth?' asked the grey-eyed man.

Jo-Jo didn't much like his attitude. 'Josef Rasterovich.'

'I know who you are, God-Discoverer, but I don't tolerate poor manners. My sister seems to have forgotten that.'

'Yeah, well, it's possible that *your sister*'s got things on her mind,' said Jo-Jo curtly. 'Things shitty enough to bring her to you looking for help.'

Bethany froze. The robed woman stared at him. In fact, everyone in the room seemed suddenly on edge as if he'd crossed an invisble line of protocol.

The grey-eyed man leaned his elbows on the table and clasped his hands together. 'Seems like you've found a champion, little sister.'

'A friend,' Beth corrected him. She balanced on one foot like an awkward kid. 'You've always said I don't have enough.'

Her brother's mouth twisted into something that should have been a smile but wasn't. He settled back in his seat. 'Sit, please.'

It was not a request.

'Mr Rasterovich, meet Baronessa Fedor and her

companions. She is one of the last remaining royals from the planet Araldis – or so she would have me believe.'

The young Baronessa held out her hand to Jo-Jo. 'I am pleased to make your acquaintance, sir.'

Jo-Jo couldn't think of anything else to do, so he walked over and shook it.

Something appalling happened when his skin touched hers. The worst of things. Perhaps it was the incredible softness of her hand. Or the way her erect posture seemed to be a brace against the hard life she led. Or maybe it was the deep, deep look of desperation in her eyes. But in that moment, the *something* that had glued Jo-Jo together for his entire life came unstuck. He found himself stranded between diffident and nervous – a place he had never been before. 'J-josef,' was all he managed to stammer.

'Now, Baronessa, continue your story,' said Bethany's brother.

'But it is not the business or the interest of these people,' replied the Baronessa.

'*I* think it is. Now *continue*.'

The woman glanced at the soldiers. There was no mistaking the grey-eyed man's imperative.

She took a breath. 'My planet, Araldis, has been invaded by a tardigrade species known as the Saqr. A mercenary by the name of Ludjer Jancz, we think, is responsible for it. Mia sorella was killed in an explosion set by him. All the bambinos that she gave shelter to died as well: babies, barely able to suckle. The invasion is widespread with only a few survivors, who are in hiding. We did not bring this upon ourselves, nor are they likely to survive much longer if I do not bring help.' She drew another shaking breath. 'My bambino, Vito, is still there.'

Her bambino? Jo-Jo looked at her fingers and ears. She wore none of the traditional emblems of legal marriage.

'Tell me about the survivors. Did you see a young girl alone anywhere? A part-Mio. She's my daughter,' Beth implored the woman.

The Baronessa frowned. 'I don't know how many are left alive in all. But there are some. The young Principe led them into hiding. That is why I am here. I must find a way to get help to them.'

'Fedor is right. It's a crap shoot down there. We only got out because she could fly the 'zoon,' added one of the mercenaries.

Jo-Jo took a sharp breath. 'You're an Innate?'

The Baronessa gave a faint nod.

'Rare and intriguing,' said Beth's brother. 'The Baronessa is a very special woman.'

Bethany took a step closer to her brother. 'Lasper, we were there too – at any rate on Dowl station – when the creatures came. We missed the evacuation and tried to escape on a Savvy but the Saqr followed us to the dock. We had to go EVA on a lug. A Savvy picked us up.' She shuddered.

'You say your girl is on this planet, Beth. What of her father?' asked Lasper.

'He'd already gone with his ship. Left us there. I would have joined her on the planet but . . .' This time she stared straight at her brother. 'You were right. And I was wrong, Lasper. And I need your help.'

His grey eyes filled with an intense look of satisfaction. He stared at the crimson-skinned young woman. 'And you, Baronessa?'

'I went to OLOSS first. They wanted to impound both myself and the biozoon while they investigated the matter. They gave no indication that they would give aid. My . . . companion indicated that you might be sympathetic to our plight.'

The white-haired mercenary seated next to the Baronessa let out a sudden hoarse laugh. 'Sympathetic was *not* the word I used, Lasper.'

'Indeed, Rast Randall. I would not imagine it.'

'Rast?' said Petalu Mau suddenly. He had not sat with Bethany and Jo-Jo but had positioned himself at the wall alongside the soldiers. 'It's Petalu.'

The mercenary twisted around in her seat to stare at him. She held out a hand which Mau stretched across to slap.

'Mau? I didn't recognise you under all that fat.' Rast gave a laugh, and then offered Lasper an explanation. 'We grew up next door to each other on Edo Lesser. Went our separate ways. I went to work for myself, and he . . . came to work for you.'

He came to work for you. Jo-Jo ransacked his memory. Who was this man? He'd been in enough bars, heard enough rumours, enough crap talked, to work it out. But the Baronessa's proximity seemed to have numbed his mind.

'There is always an opening in my ranks for someone like you, Rast Randall,' said Lasper. 'You were with us in the war. Did a good job, I heard. Dren speaks highly of you.'

The mercenary with the stark white hair nodded her thanks. "Preciate the offer, Carnage. But I don't like to lock myself into things. You know.'

Carnage? Carnage Farr! Jo-Jo's balls jerked up inside him and refused to come down: the Commander of the Stain Wars? Even in the direst *farouche* bars Farr's name inspired fear talk.

'Ahem . . . my name is Thales Berniere.' All attention shifted to the nervous young man who had finally summoned enough courage to speak. 'I do not want your help. I have been brought here against my free will and I wish only to leave.'

The Baronessa sent the young Thales an imploring look that caused Jo-Jo an irrational stab of jealousy.

'Let me guess, Mr Berniere. You are from Scolar, perhaps? A Jainist or Buddhist?' asked Carnage Farr.

Thales's shocked look made Rast Randall laugh again.

'The Baronessa had agreed to take me to Scol station after I—' Thales began.

'After you assaulted an OLOSS dignitary and jumped ship,' finished Rast. 'You're lucky to have your skin on.'

'W-what do you m-mean?' stammered the scholar.

'I mean that you should be grateful we hijacked your plans. If Scol security had caught up with you and the set of "instructions" you are carrying, you would have been imprisoned without trial. Maybe executed. I haven't met a sanctioned bio courier yet. Whatever you're collecting's gotta be illegal, no matter what they told you.'

Thales swallowed hard. 'You've been through my room!'

But Jo-Jo's curiosity wasn't piqued. His thoughts

were racing ahead. *Why are we all here – together? What is Carnage Farr planning?*

As if sensing Jo-Jo's paranoia, Orion's most infamous man stood. He placed his fists, knuckles forward, on the table, displaying the faint scars from old military augmentations. 'While I am neither a Jainist nor a philosopher of any one doctrine, I am *a believer*. And this is what I believe. There is a pattern in everything and a reason for it. I have on one side of the table a woman desperate to raise an army, and two mercenaries who will work for her if the price is right.

'I have on the other side my own sister whose child is lost on the very planet the Baronessa wishes to save, and an entrepreneur – a God-Discoverer – who has unfinished business with a Lostolian academic under the new god's tutelage – an 'esque, as it turns out, who had recently visited the Baronessa's planet.'

Farr clapped his hands: a short, emphatic noise that made everyone jump. 'You have much in common and you arrive on my doorstep at the same time. A pattern is emerging from seemingly random events. Someone has begun something that has had consequences for you all. And I . . . I am another part of it.'

Glances intersected all around the table but the Baronessa spoke first. 'Then you will help us?'

Jo-Jo's heart pounded just to hear her voice again.

'Please, Lasper. You can't ignore this,' added Beth softly. 'There is more than territorialism going on here.'

'I think your sorella is right, Mr Farr. I have in my possession some . . . some information that would suggest a precious mineral is the reason for the invasion on my planet,' said the Baronessa.

Farr stiffened as though he'd been unexpectedly shot. 'How interesting, Baronessa. What mineral would that be?'

'It is called quixite.'

'And you say your planet has an abundance of quixite?'

'I am not sure. There is a single mine, I'm sure, in which the alloy can be found.'

'Quixite is only ever found in small quantities. Are you sure your information is correct?'

Mira reviewed what she had heard in her mind. '*Si*,' she said simply.

Farr closed his eyes for a moment. When he opened them again, Jo-Jo noticed that they had changed colour. No longer grey but darker, almost black.

'I have some things to consider. Randall, take your people back to your biozoon. You are free to move around the city and enjoy the biannual Trade Fest as long as you respond immediately to my next summons for a meeting. Bethany and Mr Rasterovich may use our guest facility as you have no current transport. Petalu Mau, you may return home.'

Mau's lip quivered in appreciation and Jo-Jo felt relieved for the big man – and for himself.

He and Bethany walked to the door.

'For the record, too, Farr,' said Jo-Jo, 'when we tried to shift here, a ship cut into shiftspace ahead of us. We had to loop out and go again. The H-M on the Savvy saved our skins by being smart. The Captain . . . he would have got us all dead.'

Carnage Farr nodded. 'I will investigate it.'

To his right the Baronessa suddenly sagged as if

punched. Rast Randall moved to her side and jerked her upright. 'We've been through a rough shift too,' said the mercenary. ''Zoon's had some injuries. Think maybe the lady needs to rest.'

Jo-Jo sensed the undercurrent between the women.

So did Carnage. The famous warman's gaze flicked around the group. 'Later,' he said. 'We will continue this later.'

THALES

Gutnee Paraburd lied to me. That thought obsessed Thales. *I could have been imprisoned. If I hadn't lost my temper at Sophos Mianos . . . if the Baronessa hadn't sent her man back to help me . . .*

He found it impossible to reconcile the notion that his aggression, his loss of composure, had been the thing that had saved his life. Jain taught that self-control was the only way to attain *moksha* – true realisation of the soul.

Thales nursed his revelation all the way back to the biozoon and into the ribbed space that the Baronessa called the cucina.

The five of them convened around a table over a variety of recomposed meals. The Baronessa sprang up and took a container from the unfolded shelves.

She handed it to Thales. 'Risotto without meat,' she said. 'I hope this is suitable.'

He smiled and thanked her.

She looked weak with fatigue.

'Sit and eat,' Rast ordered her.

The Baronessa resumed her seat near the mercenary. She broke off a tiny amount of bread and put some to her lips. 'It was them,' she whispered.

Rast shovelled in large mouthfuls of beans. 'Too late for conscience now, Fedor. We survived. Most of them survived. Coulda been worse.'

Thales didn't understand the meaning of their exchange and knew it pointless to ask. He'd become caught up, unwittingly, amongst fugitives, and in truth he did feel some sympathy for the plight of the Baronessa's world. But he had too many of his own concerns.

His shaken faith, for instance; Paraburd's DNA, the state of his own world, and Rene, of course. What must he do to win her back?

He knew that the people he sat eating with thought him to be naive and senseless. But naivety was a phase soon passed, and senseless he was not – although it seemed useful for now that they thought of him as such. Their tongues would be less guarded if they did. They would take less notice of him.

The God-Discoverer Jo-Jo Rasterovich interested Thales the most. Though obnoxious and uncouth, the man had knowledge of Belle-Monde and the Entity. Tonight, at the Trade Fest, he would seek out his company . . .

'Will Lasper Farr support me?' Mira Fedor asked Randall.

The mercenary scraped a fork moodily across her empty plate. 'Carnage won't do anything that doesn't suit him. Course, there's one thing in your favour.' She shot Mira a look. 'His niece is on Araldis. That might be enough.'

Latourn, the one who had brought Thales from the OLOSS ship, stood up and belched. He had not been with them. 'I hear we're goin' to the Fest, Capo?'

'Reckon we might be due some downtime, Lat. Not much work around for a team of three.'

Latourn nodded. Then he gave the Baronessa a lingering look. 'Reckon I'll go rest up, then, ready for the show. Never know what Luck might bring me.'

Rast and Catchut laughed at that. Leaving their plates and cups piled at random, they followed Latourn from the cucina.

In the silence that followed Thales was surprised to find the Baronessa staring at him.

'Will you go out this evening, Thales?' she asked after the others had gone.

He shrugged. 'Perhaps, Baronessa. It seems there is little else to do.'

'I am sorry for the way things have happened. And I have had little time to thank you for what you did. I fear Sophos Mianos would have imprisoned me.'

Thales was unsure how much he should tell this woman. She seemed educated enough, but something irrational lurked within her, something stronger than she could control. She lacked the centred calm of the truly sane. 'Sophos Mianos has a habit of doing such things.'

'You seem unsuited to the job you have undertaken.'

'Bio-courier?'

'*Si.*'

Embarrassment warmed Thales's cheeks but he decided to continue. He badly needed to unburden himself a little. 'M-my circumstances changed. I was wrongfully accused of sedition. My world has become a reactionary, oppressive place.'

The Baronessa nodded thoughtfully. 'I am distressed to hear that, Msr Berniere. At my Studium we were taught that Scolar was Orion's ethical and ideological centre – her soul.'

Thales felt the passion rising in his breast, loosing his tongue. 'It is no longer what it should be. It is like a malaise that has crept unheard and unseen upon us. My colleagues have embraced Pragmatism and, worse, I fear that the Sophos have ceased to encourage honest discourse.' He thought of The Children of God and Villon. *More than that, they have murdered it.*

The Baronessa watched him with an intent expression on her face.

He stopped. 'My apologies – I am speaking of things that mean nothing to you.'

'No, no,' she said. 'Please continue. Although I am not a philosopher I am educated and I have a love of learning. It is . . . invigorating to listen to a man with such meaningful comprehensions.'

Thales blushed again. He had not been called a man before – not by a woman.

'I had heard that your culture did not encourage women to be . . .' he searched for words that would not be offensive '. . . reflective or informed.'

The Baronessa smiled and her face lost the tiny age lines that should not have been there. 'You have a most refined manner . . . may I call you Thales?'

Thales nodded. 'Of course, and should I continue to address you as Baronessa?'

'Mira,' she said. 'And you are partially correct. The women of higher castes in my culture are educated in a certain way. It is expected that we should have a full comprehension of Latino history and we are encouraged to be familiar with literature and art and with alien genera. I am unusual in that I have acquired learning in aerospace technologies.'

Thales put a mouthful of the recomposed potato to his lips and sucked at it. 'This is part of your Innate Talent, I suppose?'

Mira's smile faded and he saw bleakness replace it. 'In part, I suppose. But much was from my own initiative. Women are not supposed to possess an Innate Talent. It has not been that way before.'

'It was difficult for you, then – in a patriarchy.'

Her face took on a gaunt appearance. 'They sought to take my Talent from me.'

'How so? I am not trained as a biologist but I imagine it would need something akin to gene transference.'

She bowed her head. '*Sì*. And afterwards . . . what would be left?'

They sat in silence then for a while.

'Would you accompany me this evening? I am uncomfortable with the mercenaries,' Mira asked.

Thales thought of Rene and felt a pang of guilt. 'I – er – of course, though you may be safer in their company.'

The Baronessa shivered. 'I do not think so.'

Thales escorted Mira from the biozoon a little before the Edo bells heralded star-set. He wore a robe called a fellalo that the Baronessa had found him in one of the myriad of cabin spaces.

She had also changed from her simple shapeless dress into something ornate but equally as shapeless. Thales wondered that Latino men could find attraction in their women under such voluminous garb.

Still, he felt a slight stirring as she placed her arm in his. He was unused to being so long without physical contact with a woman and the Baronessa's crimson colouring was not unattractive but exotic in a way. Scolar was home to a variety of humanesques, but he had not previously known a race with such vivid skin tones.

The Lamin creature was waiting for them on the docks. 'Commander Farr has sent me as your guide.'

'But how did—'

The Lamin clacked its fingernails together as if pinching something. 'It is customary for us to know our guests' movements.'

Customary? Thales suppressed a bitter laugh. Words could not disguise hegemony in any place or time. Was this Lasper Farr no better than Sophos Mianos?

The Lamin hustled them into a preprogrammed taxi which transported them up and away from the docks across an arched viaduct. The biozoon became a miniature of itself as they arced high, and then down again towards a complete wall of darkness.

Thales was astounded to see the gloom separate into compacted metals thousands of mesurs high. The viaduct connected directly with a tunnel that passed through the metal wall, much like the chute they had navigated through to land. As the taxi slid purposefully onwards, Thales glimpsed tunnels branching off in many directions. Some were lit while others appeared disused; easy to become lost in, he imagined.

After a time the vehicle entered a huge shaft, the diameter of which extended well beyond their line of sight. The Lamin instructed the vehicle to halt alongside a block of a dozen airlifts.

'Please leave the vehicle and enter the closest available lift,' it said, flicking its tongue across its lips.

Mira Fedor had spoken few words since leaving the biozoon but Thales could see her escalating curiosity.

'What are the proportions of this metal wall?' she asked.

The Lamin appeared to ponder over an answer.

'The wall, as you call it, is one of Edo's wings, and it stretches three thousand mesurs high and a thousand mesurs wide.'

'A wing?' The Baronessa frowned. 'Planets do not have wings.'

The Lamin laughed: a moist, wheezing noise. Tiny droplets of spit sprayed from its mouth, causing it great embarrassment. It snapped a handkerchief from the pocket of its sleeveless suit and dabbed at its face. When it was satisfied with the result it continued. 'Edo is not a planet, Baronessa Fedor. Edo is a Self-Made Object comprised entirely of amalgamated refuse.'

Mira's mouth opened. 'But how—'

'The core is magnetised.'

Thales had a sudden and overwhelming sense of unease, his imagination firing in many directions. 'Why would anyone make a planet of refuse?'

'The core of Edo is a disbanded mega-space station. One of the first large objects to be brought here. As you may have noticed on your arrival, Akouedo is a hazardous system through which to navigate. The Savoires sometimes spill contents in the disgorging process. Over time the magnetised core of the station began to attract much of this loose material. And, of course, gravity makes its own.' It cleared its throat. 'As the process was entirely random, and influenced by the strength of the core, more accumulated in certain locations. Think of Edo as a unique diminutive spiral galaxy surrounded by an outer halo,' said the Lamin. It lifted an arm in a dramatic fashion and then proceeded to groom the long, fine hair of its armpits.

Thales wondered if the creature was anxious or merely had no sense of delicacy. When, a moment later, it began to lick the same area, he decided it was the latter and turned back to his observation of the scenery.

As they descended in the airlift the Baronessa remained quite animated, pointing out and listing things. What had seemed to be merely a grotesque and ugly mass now began to take on more recognisable shapes.

By the time they reached their destination, Thales could make out the gigantic trusses bedecked with barrel-shaped habitation modules. He saw innumerable sheets of broken solar arrays sandwiched between broken-backed service modules, and unit nodes speared through by abandoned robotic arms and bristling antennae.

The airlift stopped along the route and their capsule rotated inside another shaft before continuing downward until it reached a cavernous space illuminated by banks of light arrays. Mira Fedor pointed out the arms of the original space station branching out from the bottom.

The sight of the bones of such an ancient object thrilled Thales more than he would have thought possible. Thousands of years old, at the very least. Stations had been artificial spheres for that long at least – not these gangling elongated things.

'Beautiful,' breathed the Baronessa. 'Like a starfish.'

The Lamin hustled them to another vehicle which transported them into and along one of the arms.

'Are the airlifts part of the original station?' asked the Baronessa.

'Only the lower section,' the Lamin said. 'The lift well has grown as Edo has grown.'

The station arm was wide enough to allow several lanes of medium-sized transport in either direction, each one separated by islands filled with racks that the Baronessa told Thales would have housed payloads and experimental equipment. Periodically they passed small central parking nodes that had been converted into kafes. 'Esques sat at tables eating and drinking, oblivious to the traffic.

Some way along the arm the vehicle veered into a side bay.

'We must walk from here,' said the Lamin.

They followed the creature through a series of medium-sized compartments, jostling alongside other pedestrians, until they reached the entry to a grand bulb-shaped chamber.

'This must have been the recreation module. Each arm had one,' the Baronessa panted. She was breathing heavily for the light exercise they were engaged in. 'It is larger than the Principe's palazzo.'

Thales had no idea of a palazzo's dimensions but the chamber could easily have accommodated several of the Pre-Eminence buildings.

This was not, however, aesthetically manicured like the boulevards of Scolar. In this chamber, silvery chaos reigned: mesurs and mesurs of foil streamers and balloons hung from the roof. Beneath the decorations, liquid-metal fountains interspersed the hundreds of lots where the bartering of recycled refuse was conducted.

On a circular dais in the middle of the chamber an array of weird and spectacular sculptures teetered.

Thales pointed. 'What in Scolar are they?'

'Installation art. Many of Orion's most famous sculptors sell their products at trade time,' said the Lamin.

'Artists? Here?' Mira Fedor sounded shocked.

'Commander Farr is an entrepreneurial genius. He has requested that you join him on the dais for refreshments.'

The Lamin proceeded to thread a path for them towards the bizarre towering displays, its head constantly turning to make sure they were close behind.

Soldiers ringed the dais, and a sombre tattooed Balol scanned the three of them before they were permitted to take the escalator to the top of the dais.

'We have a few moments before we meet the Commander. You are welcome to observe the art but I would ask you to stay together. I cannot protect you if you are separated.'

'Protect us?' said Thales.

The Lamin showed a row of barbed teeth. 'Everyone has enemies, Msr Berniere, most usually without knowing it.'

'But I know *no one* here other than the Baronessa and her companions,' Thales protested.

The Lamin closed his painted lips over his teeth. 'Indeed.'

Thales's insides twisted. What did the creature mean? He looked to the Baronessa for reassurance but she had drifted away and was not listening.

'I have never seen such things,' she marvelled as he joined her.

Thales regarded the nearest sculpture. 'That is a dragonbee and those are sea membranes. I'm not sure what that is, though.' He pointed to a moving shape in a large frame that seemed to be constantly folding in on itself like a whirlpool of living tissue.

'Crux!' exclaimed Mira.

Thales's gaze followed hers to the centre of the dais where a huge shard of green glass thrust up towards the ceiling. Tiny lights glowed along the myriad cracks that it contained, some appearing to be moving up and down along the fissures. The whole sculpture shone with both reflected and internal light. Though scarred and irregular it was the most beautiful thing Thales had ever seen.

'Spectacular indeed,' agreed the Lamin. 'This monolith of glass was damaged during the construction of the Floating Palaces of the Armina-Pulchra Raj. The artist transported it to his home where he continued to place the material under duress. It is said that he dropped it repeatedly. He then lowered it onto a deep ice-well and left it there for several years. When he retrieved it a silica symbiote had taken up residence in the fissures. It is now the most valuable recycled sculpture in Orion. Although shortlived. The symbiotes will eventually swell the fissures and then one day it will explode.'

'But before that it will glow brighter and brighter,' said the Baronessa.

The Lamin nodded. 'The artist is already selling tickets to the final event.'

'And what is that alongside it?' Thales pointed to a small naked humanesque form reclining on a pedestal, unmistakably an aroused male. The sculpture's expression alternated between lascivious and haughty. The height and strength of its erection also changed as the sculpture appeared to liquefy and re-form.

'It is one of our few quixite sculptures.'

'Few?' asked Mira Fedor.

'Quixite is a rare and expensive naturally occurring metal alloy which has many applications. Many think that using it for art is immoral.' The Lamin bared its teeth. 'It is certainly a sign of wealth and status. Only our most successful artists can afford it. This is called "The Travelling Companion" and is quite new, I believe.'

'Quixite?' said the Baronessa in a sharp voice. 'Who is the artist?'

'I am unsure. Now we must meet Commander Farr for refreshments.'

Commander Lasper Farr was seated in an armchair under a foil marquee decorated with small bouquets made from iron, brass and aluminium swarfs. The God-Discoverer, Josef Rasterovich, was on his right, and on his left an obese shapeless creature took up an entire couch.

'Everything is so bright, so clean,' said the Baronessa. 'How is that possible?'

'Commander Farr has very high standards.' The Lamin nodded as he spoke, as if to emphasise that statement. 'Edo laboratories have patented a rust-eating parasite. It is effective, but over-colonisation by the parasite can also weaken the material. It is a fine and lucrative balancing act.'

Farr stood when he saw them approach. He gave the Baronessa a brief bow. 'I see you were admiring the Fest's centrepiece. Please let me introduce you to the artist, Fenralia.' He waved a hand at the large jelly-like creature with trailing tendrils and a rudimentary face. 'And of course you have already met Josef.'

Fenralia's body shivered as if it was preparing to move.

The Baronessa forestalled it with a curtsy and a series of quiet glubbing noises.

Fenralia stopped shivering and responded in kind.

The Baronessa rose. 'I am hoping that you speak 'esque as well, Fenralia. My Uralian is very basic and learned only from Studium simulations.'

The artist emitted an odorous liquid from underneath its body, which pooled on the couch and began to drip onto the floor of the marquee. 'Well-enough-so.'

Thales could not discern the origin of the mechanism that Fenralia used to speak.

'You are educated, Baronessa,' said Lasper Farr. 'And you will find Fenralia to be so as well.'

'Flatter-Carnage-me-more.' Fenralia's 'voice' was high-pitched and unformed like that of a very young child.

'May I say that your sculpture is magnificent,' said Thales. 'I have never seen the like of it. So powerful.'

The artist's skin changed colour with pleasure. 'Thank you, skin-pretty-hung-with-ugly-danglings.'

Shock and embarrassment burned in Thales's face and the Baronessa averted her head, biting at her lip.

'Now, Fenralia, do not tease the young ones. Not all are as liberated as you,' said Farr. He pointed to a deepening queue beyond the dais. 'Your fans are waiting for a chance to imprint themselves with your juices. Perhaps it is time to bestow reward on them.'

A guard rolled a small trolley over to the couch. Fenralia undulated onto it with practised ease.

'What in Scolar is that?' Thales whispered as the artist was transported across the dais.

'An uuli-skierin hybrid. They are quite rare and not long-lived. Most have brilliant creative minds,' replied Mira.

'You have met one before?'

'I have studied species genera at the Araldis Studium. The skierin culture was one of my preferred choices.'

'Wet, sticky place, Skiera,' said Josef Rasterovich. He had left his seat and was standing behind Mira Fedor. His eyes were fixed on her face with a hungry expression that made Thales want to look away. The Baronessa, however, did not seem to notice.

'I should be interested to hear of your impressions, Mr Rasterovich. If time will allow us,' she said.

'The time would seem perfect for that,' said Lasper Farr. 'Mr Rasterovich, could you entertain the Baronessa while Msr Berniere and I . . . discuss some things?'

Rasterovich paled, then frantically scanned the crowd. He was unable to hide his relief when he saw Farr's sister, Bethany.

'Beth,' he called out. 'Here!'

Not an invitation but a demand, thought Thales. The God-Discoverer did not wish to be left alone with Baronessa Fedor.

'Msr Berniere?' Farr was standing waiting for Thales.

'What is it that you wish to discuss with me, Commander Farr?' said Thales nervously.

Farr took his arm. 'A matter of some delicacy,' he murmured in Thales's ear, 'that would be best served up in private.'

Thales hesitated. It seemed impolite to refuse and yet he did not entirely trust the man. Gutnee Paraburd had been a liar. Was Lasper Farr any different?

'Please,' Farr said. 'I will be brief.'

Thales allowed Farr to steer him through the crowd to a private but plain room some distance from the main chamber. It was pleasantly quiet after the cacophony of the Trade Fest but Farr did not invite him to sit.

'I am not a man to waste time, Msr Berniere, so I will come straight to my point. Why do you have a barrier substance in your blood?'

'P-pardon?' Thales stuttered.

Farr lost some of his mild demeanour. 'We have scanned your biologics. Your blood contains a barrier substance commonly used by bio-carriers. We cannot detect the DNA itself so we assume you are on your way to receive it, or have just delivered it. DNA warfare is still one of the most dangerous threats to sentient species, Msr Berniere. I do not like carriers on my world – unless they belong to me.'

'I do not have to put up with an interrogation, Commander Farr. I mean you no harm. I am here on your planet through no fault of my own but because of a conspiracy of circumstance.' Thales raised his chin stubbornly.

'Do all philosophers have such a shallow grasp of life?'

'I may not be worldly, sir, but I am intelligent.'

'Intelligence is admirable. But can you handle yourself?'

'Handle?'

Without warning Farr tucked his head under Thales's arm and spun. With the weight of his shoulder he threw Thales against the wall.

Pain radiated across Thales's skull and down his spine. Dazed, he took some moments to climb to his feet.

The Commander faced him, arms dangling loose against his sides, his expression quite relaxed.

Thales glanced at the door but a balol guard was still there, its neck frill stiff with aggression.

'H-h . . . d-d.' Thales couldn't make the words come unstuck.

Farr lunged at him and struck him again with a series of harsh blows to the soft parts of his body.

Thales retaliated, as he had aboard the OLOSS ship, lashing out with all his energy and strength. But this man was very different from a scant-trained OLOSS guard. The veteran warman hurt him in ways that made him gasp for breath until he slumped back to the floor, his hands raised, cowering.

Farr kicked his arms away. 'Look at me!'

Thales obeyed, unable to think of what else to do. *Let this be over.*

Farr was neither perspiring nor out of breath; he was smiling, though, as if he was party to an amusing conversation. 'There are many, many ways I can find out the truth, Msr Berniere, of which this is the most straight-forward and the most civilised.'

Tears collected in Thales's eyes. He let words tumble out instead. 'I w-was employed to retrieve the DNA for a businessman on Scolar. A good deed in part to assist HealthWatch upgrades against influenza.'

'HealthWatch upgrades on Scolar?' Farr roared with laughter. 'The planet cannot even organise its own refuse system. What was this man's name?'

'Paraburd. Gutnee Paraburd.'

'And why would you be such a philanthropist?'

Thales told him haltingly about Rene, and her father, and his own imprisonment.

Farr's expression became solemn. He withdrew a film from inside his suit jacket and spent some time staring at it. Finally, he held it in front of Thales. 'Is this the man?'

Thales blinked several times and nodded. It was Gutnee Paraburd with less hair and smaller ears. 'Do you know him?'

'You are worse than a fool,' said Farr. 'Scolar has a dire future if they are breeding more like you. Gutnee Paraburd is Gutnee Fressian, a bio-merchant of the most immoral kind. Did you really believe that the DNA you were to collect was legal? That Paraburd was an honest businessman?'

'He seemed so.' Thales tried to suppress his memory of the torn uniform and the peculiar travel arrangements, and find a way to salvage his pride. 'I might have been naive to trust him, but at least there are some of us left who would do a thing for the good of it.'

'For the good? Or to improve your kudos with your wife?'

Thales fell silent at that; demoralised by the truth.

But Lasper Farr was not finished with him. 'Where were you were to receive the DNA?'

'On a place called Rho Junction.'

'Where are your instructions?' said Farr.

Thales took the packet from the vest under his borrowed robe and handed it over.

The Commander left the room for a time but the balol remained, guarding the door. Thales stayed on the floor, nursing his physical hurts and his shame at his mistakes. He sought the peace of a meditative state but his Jainist learnings and beliefs seemed to belong to another person, from another place and time.

When Farr returned Thales was unable to rouse himself from his morose state of mind. So mired was he in his troubles that Farr's simple statement took some time to register.

'Do you wish to die?' the Commander asked.

When the meaning sank past the layers of self-pity Thales sat up straighter, his heart thudding.

Farr continued. 'It is my assumption that you do not. If that is the case then you will continue to your rendezvous on Rho Junction and receive the DNA but instead of returning to Gutnee Fressian on Scolar you will return here. My laboratories will decant it and you will be cleared of any penalty and will be free to go.'

Thales felt a flicker of outrage. 'I have committed no crime. I deserve no penalty. My life is not yours to govern.'

Farr produced a small tube from his pocket. He did

not call for the balol guard but simply took Thales into his arms and held him as an adult would a small struggling child. He squeezed the contents of the tube into the corner of Thales's eye.

'I have introduced a bacterium into your body that will break down Gutnee Fressian's barrier substance within a matter of months and kill you. If you return here in a timely manner with Fressian's DNA in your system, I will administer the vaccine and all will be well. The choice, Msr Berniere, is entirely yours.' Farr released Thales and gave a pleasant smile. 'Now, please, feel free to enjoy the rest of the Trade Fest while I arrange your transportation to Rho Junction.'

Mira

Mira found Josef Rasterovich both repellent and fascinating. Repellent because of his coarse and presumptuous manner, yet fascinating because he had been to places that she longed to hear about. The contrary emotions left her tongue-tied in his presence – and inclined to take refuge in aloofness.

He seemed equally lost for social conversation. Fortunately, Farr's sister, the woman Bethany, joined them as soon as Farr and Thales Berniere left them. The three of them stood in the entrance of Farr's foil marquee, just out of the reach of the mêlée.

Mira had warmed to Bethany. The older female reminded her of Cass Mulravey. Bethany seemed well studied, though, where hard experience had been Cass's educator.

Bethany frowned as she watched Lasper Farr and the young scholar disappear together. 'What is my brother doing?'

'He wished to speak with Thales alone. He seems a courteous man,' Mira said cautiously.

Bethany gave her a keen look. That penetrating gaze was the single resemblance that she and Lasper Farr appeared to share, though Mira imagined there were other, deeper things.

'You know who he is, don't you? Who it is you are bargaining with?' asked Bethany.

'I understand that he led the Consilience force in the Stain Wars. Now he is the owner of a very lucrative business. I would suppose he is an entrepreneur and a very clever one.'

Bethany trembled at that. 'He is much more than an opportunist, Baronessa. He is most single-minded and he allows nothing to interfere with his ambitions. No one. Not even family.'

'And what *are* his ambitions, Beth?' asked Josef Rasterovich.

'Impossible, ridiculous things.' Bethany looked away, into the heart of the Fest. 'Those things make him so dangerous.'

Mira thought that Farr seemed sane and reasonable, yet his sister's words hinted at fanaticism – imbalance, even. What did that mean, she wondered, if a sister disparaged her brother so openly? Was Bethany motivated by jealousy? Or did she have good cause to speak that way? Faja and she had never been jealous of one another. But then Faja had been more of a mother than a sister, and Mira missed that love with every step she took, every turn of her head.

But it is still there. It will always be there. Both ways.

Bethany looked back at Mira. 'Please, can you tell me more about Araldis? I am sick with worry for my child.'

With that question the diversions that the Fest had provided vanished, and Mira felt all her tensions return. What could she say to this woman? That the place was burning? That her daughter was probably dead like the bambinos she had buried on the plains?

'Baronessa? Are you unwell?' Bethany touched Mira's arm, concerned.

Mira realised that she had doubled over and pressed her hands to her stomach as if in pain. She straightened and forced composure onto her face. 'I am a little nauseous. Resonance shift has left me with some after-affects.'

Bethany made a hand signal to Josef Rasterovich. 'How inconsiderate of us . . . shall we find somewhere to eat and sit?'

Mira nodded gratefully. '*Si.*'

Josef found them a kafekart on one corner of the dais and while he purchased drinks Mira talked with Bethany. 'You said your daughter was part Miolaquan. Where did she reside?' she asked.

Bethany flushed. 'I'm not sure. It's not a story I'm proud of . . .'

Mira listened intently as Beth told her how she had sent her child to the planet alone. With each detail, dread and excitement fought each other to create a nervous mix in Mira's stomach. 'Her name – you called her Jess before – was it Djeserit?'

Bethany grabbed Mira's hands. 'Yes. Yes. Do you know her?'

'Does she have certain Mio characteristics? The webbed fingers—' Mira prised her own from the older woman's grip.

'Yes, and gills, here and here.' Bethany touched her own neck. 'And beautiful. She is young and beautiful. Please, please tell me that she is alive.'

'I c-cannot be sure now, but she was with the survivors when I left. She saved me when I was in deep shock. She is determined.' *But vulnerable.* Mira told Beth then of Faja and the Villa Fedor – as much as she could bear to recount, at least.

Josef Rasterovich had rejoined them with two frothed mokkas and a small tumbler filled with a burned liquid: Oort whisky or an Edo brandy. He sat and sipped, picking up the threads of the conversation.

'Jess,' whispered Bethany brokenly when Mira had finished. 'Oh, my Jess. How could I have left you alone?'

Mira thought of Vito and the korm. 'Choice does not always provide right and wrong.'

'You couldn't have known the shit that was gonna happen on Araldis, Beth,' said Rasterovich. 'And if she's anything like you she'll be surviving just fine.'

But Bethany was too submerged in her guilt to heed them. 'So she is with the young Principe?'

Mira forced herself to find some comforting words. '*Si.* The young Principe is . . . clever. He will outwit the Saqr.'

She would never tell Bethany the rest of it – how Trinder Pellegrini was a treacherous, selfish man who had seduced her Jess.

But Josef Rasterovich was watching Mira intently, as if he guessed there was more.

'Has your discovery of the Entity given you unpleasant choices, Mr Rasterovich?' she asked him by way of distraction.

The quick change in focus caused the man to swallow most of his drink in one gulp. He coughed to clear his throat. 'Yeah. Well, uh, I guess so.'

Josef's laconic reply puzzled Mira. One moment he appeared perceptive, the next almost dim-witted.

'When Araldis is – when my world is restored to my clan, I would like to visit Belle-Monde. Is that possible?' she asked.

'That depends, Baronessa.' His voice was husky from the alcohol and the coughing. 'You can't go sightseeing, if that's what you mean. Nor would you want to. Place is overrun with arrogant pricks – smarts and scientists.'

Mira ignored his bald description in the same way that she ignored Rast's rough talk. 'I wish to be tested by the Entity.'

'To become a . . . a tyro?' Josef stammered. His eyes widened, and surprise dropped some of the lines from his face.

She saw then that he could be perceived as handsome by some. Not in the pure, aesthetic way of Thales the scholar, but his face displayed a damaged kind of strength, an unkempt confidence. '*Si.*'

'For what damn reason would you want that?'

And Mira knew then, before she spoke, what it was that Marchella had wanted of her. 'I must unbind our women, Mr Rasterovich.'

'You don't need the Entity for that – you just need a revolution.'

'There are things about us – our culture – that you don't understand.' She heard the formality slipping from her voice and no longer cared. 'I need to be greater . . . better than I am . . . to bring them that change. Impotence is cruel. I will not let it hold me.'

'You're telling me that you want to save your culture, and then you want to change it?' Josef slapped his thighs and laughed. 'Well, there's a god complex if I've ever heard one.'

Mira felt the twist of bitter anger; a man such as this could never comprehend oppression. She wanted to walk away from him and never see his face again.

'Baronessa?' It was Thales Berniere, pale and shaking, standing beside her.

'Msr Berniere? Please . . .' She indicated the spare seat.

He sank into it automatically, rubbing his arm in a distracted manner.

Mira leaned towards him. 'You are distressed,' she said softly.

The scholar looked then as if he might weep, and her heart constricted. Concern for him vanquished her anger at the God-Discoverer.

'I-I am tired and somewhat dislocated, that is all,' Thales said. But his young face had a grim set to it which stole the soft curve from his lips and the glow from his skin. Something had shaken him badly.

Mira wanted to press him further but the Lamin was back with three soldiers. 'Excuse me, Baronessa, but Commander Farr requires you all to return to his marquee.'

Thales reddened and stood. 'I am not interested in meetings. I will return to the ship.'

The Lamin made no attempt to stop him and Mira watched him disappear into the crowd. What had happened between him and Lasper Farr?

Inside the marquee Farr was pouring amber wine into long bulb-ended glasses. 'Sit, please,' he instructed.

Mira perched on the edge of one of the armchairs while Josef Rasterovich lounged across an entire couch.

Bethany chose to lean against a high-backed lacquered stool.

Farr appeared almost convivial as he handed them each a glass.

Josef Rasterovich drank with one prolonged swallow and held the empty glass toward Farr.

The Commander ignored him, sipping his own drink delicately. 'I have had time to consider your situations. Baronessa Fedor, I may be prepared to assist in the reinstating of the Cipriano Clan on your world. And, Bethany, in doing that I could put some resources into finding Jess.'

Bethany sagged against the stool with relief but Mira kept her back straight, apprehensive of Farr's motives. *What does he want in return?*

'In order for me to do that, I would need something from you,' Farr went on.

'Lasper?' demanded Bethany in a shrill voice.

'I want you to accompany your biozoon to Rho Junction in the Saiph system, where Thales Berniere will collect something for me. You will then return here. When this is done, I will undertake to restore control to the rightful owners of Araldis.'

'Saiph is part of Extropy space,' said Rasterovich. He'd let his empty glass fall to the floor and was eyeing it angrily, as if he might crush it underfoot.

His demeanour was not lost on Lasper Farr. 'But Rho Junction is not. That is where you come into it, Mr Rasterovich. Your reputation as God-Discoverer can gain you entrance and acceptance anywhere. I'm sure The Alliance of Free Thinkers on Rho Junction would be entranced by your God stories. I've heard they are entertaining.'

Rasterovich frowned. 'Why would I want to do that? Too many damn Extros around Rho Junction for my liking. The Entity shoves a whole fist up their basic belief system. Don't you think they might want to do the same to me for finding it?'

'Not before they have examined you from the inside out,' said Farr, smiling. 'Which would give Msr Berniere plenty of time to complete his errand.'

Rasterovich clenched his fists. Mira saw him struggling to control his anger; to appear as calm as Farr. 'And which of your pet delusions tells you I'd be stupid enough to make that kind of sacrifice?'

'But Mr Rasterovich, the Baronessa needs your help.'

Josef seemed winded by that.

'But this will take too long, Lasper. Jess's life is at stake while you bargain,' protested Bethany.

'Jess's life is at stake because you abandoned her for your lover. No other reason. As for what you call my "bargaining" – it is what will ensure the safety of our futures,' said Farr. 'I can't pull together a force of this nature without some planning and preparation. Araldis is an OLOSS world. This will have to be managed with subtlety.'

Josef Rasterovich cleared his throat. 'I ain't convinced, Farr. And even if I was I sure ain't available to act in your version of the future.' He got up off the couch and walked towards the marquee's entrance.

Farr flicked a glance at the soldiers and they stepped directly in front of Rasterovich.

'Even if I can tell you the whereabouts of Tekton the archiTect and bestow a ship upon you?' asked Farr. 'Bethany tells me you are in need of one.'

Josef turned and walked back to the couch, grasping its back edge. 'I know where to find Tekton. He is on Belle-Monde. And yes, I need a ship, but only if I can cut through the strings that come with it.'

'Tekton *was* on Belle-Monde,' corrected Farr. 'You followed him to Dowl some time ago and due to your imprudence wound up in the detention facility with my foolish sister. Tekton returned to the study station, but has since moved on.'

'Big deal! I can find him myself,' Rasterovich said coolly.

Mira's heart fluttered. She could not help but admire Josef's stubbornness in the face of Farr's threats and bribes.

'Can you? Your ship has been stolen. On board was your entire resource network. You have access to money but information takes time to acquire. Even if you locate Tekton then you may well pass him in transit. I foresee many possible frustrations for you. However, if you assist the Baronessa and Berniere with this errand then I can provide you with resources to find Tekton, and my blessings.'

'Your blessings?' Rasterovich gave a strident laugh that was almost a shout.

Mira held her breath, unsure what he would do next.

But Lasper Farr had settled back in his chair. 'No need for dramatics, God-Discoverer. My proposal is an arrangement for mutual benefit. Simple – and elegant . . .'

JO-JO RASTEROVICH

Jo-Jo wanted to murder Carnage Farr right then; strangle the hero of the Stain Wars until his tongue protruded and his eyelids fell still in death.

From the moment Jo-Jo's feet had touched this rotating scrap heap he'd felt uneasy. Now, staring across at Farr, he knew that he'd give a testicle to be back on Jandowae station.

Right now he wanted to stuff his fist so far down Farr's throat that he could squeeze the man's balls with his fingers.

Even more compelling, though, was his desire to agree to Farr's demands. Not because of Carnage's promise to find Tekton, or because he was frightened of the lunatic, but because Mira Fedor needed protection.

How fucking ridiculous! He'd met her only a few hours ago.

The intensity of his emotion sent Jo-Jo's mind sliding apart like two pieces of slippery sliced fruit. Not sure what else to do, he listened to the discussion that started up between his inner voices.

The loudmouth of the two had a plan: *Pretend to go along with Farr's wishes and then bail out at the first res station. Catch a ride to Belle-Monde and track down Tekton. It's the logical course to take and the safest. Carnage Farr is insane and best avoided—*

No! cried the other voice. *You will never see her again.*

Jo-Jo's mouth opened and words came out. 'Prove that you can help me locate Tekton and you've got a deal.'

Lasper Farr drained his drink and leaned forward. 'I'm not in the habit of proving myself to anyone, Mr Rasterovich. But for the sake of expediency I will make an exception.' He took a small tubal inhaler from his pocket. 'Breathe deeply.'

Jo-Jo took the object and clipped the tube to the skin that separated his nostrils. He squeezed one end and the inhaler discharged its contents into his nose.

His transition into a virtual space was sharp: instantaneous, in fact. Farr was in the same chair but the marquee had disappeared, leaving a darkened space. Jo-Jo's viewpoint had also altered. He was alongside Farr instead of opposite him.

A sprinkle of lights began to grow in the darkness around them: a beautiful intricate patterning of colours that pulsed and flickered and wound around each other as if connected by an infinite number of lines.

As Jo-Jo studied the delicate knots and loops he noticed tiny colourful explosions occurring among them: miniature supernovas. Some became subsumed by what was already there; others thinned and extruded into new webs.

'A small window will open in the corner of your vision. It will isolate one of the tiny eruptions you can see. Concentrate on it for a few seconds.'

Jo-Jo did as Farr instructed. He felt himself drawn forward towards the eruption which grew in magnitude until the brightness became a pure white brilliance that blinded him. His eyes burned and mucus trickled down onto his upper lip. He wanted to wipe it but he didn't dare move.

The whiteness suddenly resolved into shapes that he recognised. A ship's bridge.

Salacious?

Jo-Jo knew his ship immediately – but not the 'esque with the cold blank stare who lounged on the captain's platform. Then it faded. More images followed in a sequence that made no sense to him: a water-planet panorama, small aqua-creatures, one of the same creatures being dissected, and, finally, night combat in a jungle. Three shadowy figures crawling on their bellies – a balol and two humanesques – leaving mines for their enemy to trip. There was something familiar about them all . . .

'Closer.' He spoke the word without thinking.

The virtual progression threw him forward again.

Suddenly he was *lying on the jungle floor, his fingers deep in slimy moss, his foot tangled in vines. The air was so damp that he could barely breathe. An insect crawled between his shoulder blades, biting him.*

The figures on either side of him were panting hard, glancing back over their shoulders. Their way forward was lit by the dim glow-bands across their foreheads, illuminating thick tree roots underpinned by leaf-rotted soil.

He turned one way. Saw a male face streaked in 'flage and filth.

'Randall? How many left?' the male asked.

Jo-Jo turned the other way.

'Three fully charged.' This face was female. Rast Randall.

'I'll save one for us, Capo,' Rast added grimly.

Jo-Jo turned back.

The male 'esque gave a cold stare that froze Jo-Jo. 'Save it for yourself, Rast,' he said. 'I ain't dyin' out here for no ginks.'

Randall laughed. 'Don't tell her that.' She jerked her head.

Jo-Jo twisted, looking around again. Who? There. Behind them. A balol soldier. A female.

Ilke? From Dowl.

There was a small popping noise in front of them.

'Shit! Grenade!' barked Rast. She rolled frantically towards a gully. The man scrambled to his knees and flung himself behind a tree.

Jo-Jo's heart pounded. He didn't know which way to move. Too slow! I'm too slow—

'End.'

Farr's sharp command brought Jo-Jo back to his chair. The light web had vanished. Only Farr and he occupied the darkness.

Jo-Jo tried to quieten his heartbeat while he sorted realities. The balol was Ilke, the one he'd been dallying with when *Salacious* had called about intruders. What was Ilke doing in an adventure sim with Rast Randall? And the male – who was he?

'No. Not a simulation, Mr Rasterovich. Random recordings. What you have just witnessed is my own personal soothsayer. I procure records of events and my Organic analyses them, looking for patterns.'

'Record?'

'*Eges* – eyes. I have them all over Orion. The last event, the one you chose to look more closely at, was a record from combat implants used during the Stain Wars.' If I can't observe it with my own eges, I buy it or appropriate it from another source. In extreme cases

I will rebuild visual scenes from audio records or eye-witness accounts.'

'Re-enactments?'

'Re-animation is a better description, using DNA behavioural projections, audio patterning, semantic decoders and other classifiers.'

'What for? You trying to predict the future?'

Farr's expression remained neutral. 'It could be perceived as that. Many of the patterns are only established in retrospect. The tiny explosions you witnessed are signals that a link has been established. Determining where to look for what you need to know, however, is the key . . .'

Jo-Jo's heartbeat speeded up again. Not in fear this time but in awe. 'You've got a Dynamic System device.'

'Device is such a carnival word and this is something far more sophisticated, God-Discoverer. Prediction is merely one of its uses.'

'What did those images mean? The ones I saw.'

'I'm honouring you with proof that I can find the archiTect for you, Mr Rasterovich, by showing you who has taken your ship.'

'Randall?'

'No. But Rast has known them. In time you will be able to determine the nature of the connection for yourself. Now, you are of course welcome to leave, Mr Rasterovich, although I do believe your personal HealthWatch has expired. You really should be careful what you inhale in strange places . . .'

The darkness turned grainy and then fell away completely. Jo-Jo was back in the marquee – on the floor of the marquee, to be precise – face down.

Acutely aware of the Baronessa, and of Farr's last words, he flicked the inhaler away from his nose. A small auto-cleaner scurried over and gobbled it up. It took all his self-control not to smash it with his fist.

'Josef?' said Beth in a reproving tone. 'You've been drooling.'

Summoning the remnants of some dignity, Jo-Jo wiped his mouth with the back of his hand and climbed to his feet.

MIRA

'What is happening to them?'

Both Lasper Farr and Josef Rasterovich had fallen silent. Josef's eyes were closed but Lasper Farr maintained an eerie half-open-lidded look.

'The inhaler is full of VR nanites. Lasper is showing Josef something within his virtual world. I imagine it's like the way you communicate with your biozoon,' said Bethany.

Mira looked at the men's slack mouths and twitching fingers. 'I would hope I do not look like that.'

Bethany smiled, her face relaxing into a more natural expression. 'I'm sure you don't.'

Mira stared down at the floor. They had been thrown together and now, suddenly without a purpose, the moment became awkward.

Bethany covered it with a question. 'Do you think the Entity will accept you into its tutelage?'

'I know little of the procedure for being tested but I will find a way to convince it. Somehow . . .' Mira tried to sound confident.

'It may not be the Entity that you have to convince, Baronessa. I expect the OLOSS politics would be enough to shrivel your skin off.'

'I'm afraid I'm naive about such things, although every society has its manners.'

'Academics have more than a *manner*, especially with so much at stake. I would think it might be dangerous to go there unprepared.'

'You are quietly warning me?'

Bethany gave a short laugh. 'More than quietly, Baronessa Mira. With a very loud shout. You are used to a particular kind of etiquette and certain rules. Academics have etiquette but only one rule: the rule of competition. Their world can be more ruthless than a battleground.'

'You speak from experience? And please call me Mira. Baronessa seems an unnecessary encumbrance in the wider worlds, but I confess I am used to it.'

'Thanks, Mira. But don't be too quick to dismiss your title. Anything that gives you an edge in the respect stakes is worth hanging on to.'

'Do you think it does?'

'Maybe. And yes, I studied for a year – an abridged grading in embryology at the Fuentes-Morales studium. Lasper paid for it. It was an accelerated course so we were treated badly by the purists who refuse compressed learning and ignored by the technocrats who believe in complete immersion with no abridgement.' She sighed.

'Humanesque embryology?' asked Mira.

'Not only. But it was a large part of what I learned.'

'Can you detect if a foetus is healthy?'

Bethany's curious stare made Mira immediately regret her question. She had given away too much.

'Why do you ask? You're not . . . you couldn't be . . . pregnant? Are you, Mira?'

Mira glanced around for a reason to deflect the

question; anything to prevent her having to answer. And it came to her like a gift from a munificent god.

Jo-Jo Rasterovich gave an almighty twitch and fell to the floor where he continued to spasm, a puddle of saliva collecting near his mouth. His eyes flickered open and with uncoordinated fingers he inserted his fingers into his nostrils to pick out the remnants of the inhaler.

Mira wanted to embrace him.

Josef Rasterovich accompanied them back to *Insignia*, forestalling any more probing questions from Bethany. To Mira's relief the conversation steered in another direction: a back-and-forth between Josef and Bethany that sustained the same jolting rhythm as their taxi.

'Time you told me about your brother.'

'What do you want to know?' asked Beth.

Mira thought she sounded defensive.

'Start with how long since you've seen him and fill in the blanks around it.' Rasterovich was peevish and kept scratching his nose. 'I don't like being manipulated – *by anyone.*' Josef gave Bethany a level stare.

She reacted immediately. 'I'm not manipulating you, Josef. But I want Djes back. I'm desperate. Even you must understand that. I thought I was going to die back on Dowl. It makes you sort through things.'

He took a deep breath as though he was unsuccessfully seeking patience. 'Your brother is a power-broker, Beth. I've got an allergy to those sorts of people, but when I have to get involved with them I like to know what's going on. *So start talking.*'

It was the first time that Mira had heard Josef

Rasterovich be curt with Bethany, and the older woman's face regained its worried expression.

'I haven't seen him since a while before I joined the Mio ship. Lasper paid for my education but he wanted me to work in his labs here. I didn't like some of the things he was playing around with—'

Rasterovich raised his eyebrows but Bethany wouldn't be stopped now that she'd started. Mira sympathised with her need to unburden herself.

'I'm an embryologist, Josef. Lasper had some . . . disturbing ideas. I figured if I got far enough away he'd find someone else to do those things, and would leave me alone. It's hard when you owe a debt to someone whose beliefs oppose your own. Worse when it's family.'

'What did he want you to do for him?'

'I-I can't tell you that but you need to understand. Akouedo was only a poor, struggling economy here when Lasper purchased Edo. He's brought wealth and employment and hope to all the planets in the system. When someone does that, word spreads. People actually move here to live now. Imagine that. Moving to a system full of rubbish for a better lifestyle.'

Rasterovich shrugged. 'Makes for an interesting tourist brochure and I guess it beats starving somewhere else.'

'Everyone in this system owes Lasper something and he knows how to collect on debts. He hooks them in, one generation to the next. And that was before the Stain Wars. He's a hero now as well.'

Rasterovich looked unimpressed. 'You're still telling me stuff that I already know. Were you with him in the war?'

Bethany shook her head. 'But the Mios hate the Extropists more than OLOSS. The ship I was on was research-based but during the war we were diverted out near Saiph to give some expertise to Consilience.'

'What kind of expertise?'

'Ionil, m-my . . . man, he's a molecular pathologist. They wanted someone out there who could examine the captured Extros.'

'He did the autopsies?'

'Yes. We were ordered there by the Mio Assembly. Ionil thought it was a great honour but I think Lasper was behind it. He wanted to draw me back in.'

'So what does he want from this?'

Beth rubbed her hands over her eyes. It should have been a simple gesture of tiredness but seemed to be more an ordering of her mind. 'I don't know exactly. You saw into his virtual world. What did he show you? Maybe you can guess.'

Jo-Jo Rasterovich stared out of the taxi window. They were almost back at the huge lift well. 'He's got hold of something that he shouldn't have. No one should have.'

'That sounds like Lasper,' whispered Bethany.

TRIN

At twilight Trin roamed the perimeter of the tiny island, waiting for Djes to return. He was not alone. Food had revived the spirits of some and they stayed all night down at the beach line, talking and cooling their skin in the tepid water.

Trin pondered a strategy while he waited. He had flown over the island belt twice in his life, and could still picture the jigsaw puzzle of islands, beginning with a sprinkling of dots that gradually turned into clumps and then decent tracts of land. The shape of them was what had intrigued him most: bizarre scribbles that at one time had fitted together as a solid land mass. There were caves in some, he was sure – he had seen the dark-holed cliffs. And there was thick vegetation; creepers strung in veils over what he imagined were clusters of trees – not the stunted spiny-leaved bushes under which they had passed the day.

They could live in caves. But how long would it take them to find these islands without navigation aids? They would need method and determination. And faith.

He would send Djes ahead of them during daylight to scout directions and any perils. The rest would wait until twilight. The flat-yachts were stable enough at night but sluggish in their rudder response and slow.

They had to be certain of reaching the next island before each sunrise.

'Pellegrini?'

It was Cass Mulravey. Trin did not answer or even look at her – he was not yet ready for her questions.

But Mulravey was not one to be put off. 'The women have voted to stay with you, but we want to know what you are planning.'

'The women? Does that include you, Signora?'

'Frankly, I'm not con—'

A low cry and splashing – louder than the gentle breakers – from further along the beach interrupted her.

Djeserit!

Trin ran as quickly as he could to the huddle of shadows. To his annoyance, Cass Mulravey kept pace with him.

'What is it?' he demanded when he stopped.

'Out there, Principe,' said one of his men.

Trin strained to see. In the wane of Semantic he saw a boat's outline as it bobbed over the break towards the beach; a small pinnace without oars.

'Looks like it's gonna roll,' Mulravey warned Trin. 'You'll need swimmers to help those aboard.'

Those aboard? Trin peered harder. Mulravey was right: two figures clung to the bow. 'What if we don't want them with us?'

'You'd let them drown?'

'What if they are with the Saqr?'

'They have no sail, no oars – what are the chances?'

She was right, Trin knew, but he detested her arrogant manner.

'Where is Juno Genarro?'

'Here, Principe,' said a voice behind him. 'I heard the boat and came.'

His best scout was puffing slightly from running, and Trin knew that if he could see Juno's face in better light it would be thin and lined with utter exhaustion. But Genarro was tough – maybe the toughest of them all.

'There's a rope in the water,' called one of the men standing out in the shallows. *Tivi Scali*, Trin thought, *Joe's cousin*.

'Boat's over!' called someone else, a woman standing further along the beach.

'Juno!' said Trin.

Juno waded straight into the water, calling for Vespa and Joe Scali. Trin watched them swim towards the capsized boat, their heads just black dots in the grey swell.

'Principe? It's Djeserit! Here!' cried Tivi.

A quiet cheer went up from the group. Nearly all the surviviors were there now, crowding around to see.

Trin shouldered through them and strode into the shallows. He dropped to his knees and scooped Djes close. 'Are you hurt?'

'No,' she gasped. 'But – I have – two with – me. They – cannot swim.'

He lifted her higher, wanting to pull her right out of the sea. But she protested. 'Let me – rest – tired – couldn't row – towed – them . . .'

She'd towed them from the palazzo. Trin felt a surge of anger. How could she risk herself like that? And for who? Who had she found there?

He let go of her and Djeserit submerged, staying near his legs. He let his hand stray under the water so that it contacted her. She grasped it and he forced himself not to recoil. The webbing on her fingers had grown thicker and longer, almost down to her finger tips; the Mio part of her was overtaking the 'esque. Soon she would be lost to him altogether. Was she choosing to become incompatible with him?

'Principe!' Again.

Juno Genarro was only a small mesur out now, towing someone in the crook of his arm. Behind him Vespa and Joe Scali struggled with another figure between them.

Trin waded towards them and pulled the figure from Genarro's trembling grasp. A young girl, he thought, and a face he might have known had the light not been so dim. He handed her to Tivi who had followed him. 'Take her out.'

Then he waited for the roll of the waves to bring in Vespa and Joe. The person he took from them was much older and frail. She clung to him, sobbing and sobbing; a pathetic, trembling bundle of saturated flesh that he did not need light to recognise.

'Trinder,' she choked out. 'Caro . . . caro . . .'

'Jilda,' he replied. 'Madre.'

JO-JO RASTEROVICH

Jo-Jo filled the time it took to reach the Saif system by stewing over his situation and quizzing Bethany more about her brother. They had taken cabin space next to each other with Mira Fedor on the other side of Beth and the mercenaries and the scholar, Thales Berniere, a stratum below.

Jo-Jo managed to extract two pleasures from his current situation. First was the sense of familiarity. The *Insignia* craft was larger than *Salacious* but with less interior cartilage and flesh on show, although each stratum was lined with tubercles that puckered and shrank dependent on the 'zoon's biorhythms. He wandered the strata, enjoying the whisper of the 'zoon's life force around him, trying to ignore his second pleasure – his closeness to Mira Fedor.

Every moment in her presence seemed to intensify his longing. Between trying to fathom Carnage Farr's plan, and his own bitter thoughts about Tekton, Jo-Jo dissected his reaction to the Latino woman. It made no sense. He detested aristocrats and had a preference for confident women (although not as confident as that crazed academic who used her suffocation techniques on him). Mira Fedor was reserved, uptight and had obviously been damaged by her experiences.

For some unfathomable reason, the combination

aroused Jo-Jo to the point of obsession. He wrestled constantly with a desire to follow her around the ship, or to do something stupid and heroic so that she would look at him with more interest.

Instead, he avoided her company, and when they were together, he tried to ignore the fact that she only noticed him when he spoke to the others of the places where he had travelled. In those moments, and only those, he earned her full attention.

But it did not stop him fantasising like a hormonal adolescent. And hoping.

So he took refuge in exercise.

The crew fell into a pattern where each attended their tasks for the first part of the shipboard day. Mid-cycle each of them drifted to his or her individual pursuits; and in the evenings they assembled for a meal.

Although Mira Fedor attended the evening gatherings she drank little and seldom contributed to the conversation unless goaded by the mercenary, Rast Randall. The tension between the women, Jo-Jo guessed, was born of their experiences escaping Araldis. He envied their bond, just as he envied the gentle, almost shy glances that the Baronessa bestowed on the scholar, Thales Berniere.

Jo-Jo would have cheerfully vacced the useless prick but that would have deprived the mercenaries of their sport. The three whiled away the hours of boredom playing childish tricks on Thales: locking him in obscure sections of the biozoon, stealing his clothes and spiking his drinks with disinhibitors.

Jo-Jo enjoyed the pranks. He found the mercenaries better diversionary therapy than the cheap wine that

Lasper Farr had provided for them – especially Randall. She was tough, not easily offended, and could laugh at most things.

Most days he joined her on her daily run through the 'zoon. Inevitably, when the gradients got too steep, or their legs became too fatigued, they fell to a walk and conversation. Rast showed him all the biozoon's inner chambers, including the scarred lower walls near its intestinal system.

Jo-Jo gave a low whistle when he saw the ugly ridges of discoloured tissue. 'Even a 'zoon can bleed to death from those kinds of cuts.'

'You know Landhurst at Intel station?'

Jo-Jo nodded. 'By reputation, at least.'

'She went to him for help. He figured a lone woman in a 'zoon would be easy pickings.' Rast laughed. 'Didn't figure on her passengers, though.'

'Wouldn't be the first time Landhurst's seen an opportunity and stepped outside the rules.'

'Yeah,' Randall agreed. 'But Carnage Farr makes him look giddy and soft.'

Jo-Jo felt a sudden urge to hit something. He'd spent his lifetime avoiding these kinds of involvements. 'What does Farr want, anyway? Why's he sending that soft cock Berniere to do business in Extro territory?'

Rast's eyes narrowed. 'He wants him to pick up DNA.'

'What sort of idiot would accept a bio-courier's job?'

The mercenary threw him a look. 'Carnage must figure it's worth it. He's been keeping the balance between OLOSS and the half-heads since the war. Guess he's got plenty to gain if neither gets the upper hand. Trade mostly. To both sides.'

Jo-Jo reached to the wall and ran his fingers along a length of raised scar. It was slightly sticky and warm. 'Beth says much the same. Are you sure he's keeping things on balance, though? Might be that's what he wants everyone to think . . .' He tapered off.

Rast laughed. 'You're a paranoid bastard. Waste of time trying to second guess Farr, though.' Randall walked ahead, bored or uncomfortable with the conversation. Jo-Jo couldn't decide.

'You one of his people?' Jo-Jo wasn't sure if he'd get a straight answer but it was worth a try. The mercenary seemed direct enough when it suited her.

Rast stopped and turned back to face him. 'Yes and no. He's paying me well for this job and I mostly like what he stands for – but I'm not partial to being anyone's bitch. I like to pick where and when I work – and when I leave.'

Jo-Jo saw the opening and took it. 'Stain Wars vet?'

'Yeah.' The white-haired woman shot him a sharp look. 'Why?'

'You got that manner about you. Good crew?'

'Yeah. Mostly dead now, though. I was in the first wave on Longthrow. Not many survived that.'

'Aaah,' said Jo-Jo. 'You were the meat that OLOSS were prepared to waste.'

'You know the real story, then.'

Jo-Jo nodded. 'If there was a real story. I heard a few versions. One that sounded most likely reckoned that OLOSS started it on Longthrow by sending in a bunch of mercs to spoil a kosher deal. Things went cone-shaped.'

'Glad to see not everyone believes the history

fastloads. That was pretty much how it was. When Longthrow got going skirmishes broke out around about the Saif system. If you could draw lines from one to another you'd say that the Extros were poised and waiting for a chance.'

'What do you think?'

'Could be they were. Could be there would never have been any trouble if OLOSS hadn't provoked things on Longthrow. Thing about Extros is that you can't always pick them out from normal aliens or 'esques. Depends on what body they've snatched. On Longthrow they *were* their weapons. You shoot one down and it just slides across into another machine.'

Rast stabbed the toe of her boot into the stratum wall and twisted it as if she was gouging a hole.

'Oww!' She pulled her foot away and shook it. 'Damn thing stung me.'

Jo-Jo laughed. 'What did you expect? It's alive.' He wanted to ask her then who her Capo had been, but he didn't want to make her suspicious. He tried coming at it from another angle. 'So how did you come by this line of work?'

She gave him a narrow look. 'You really interested or you pissing into the black?'

Jo-Jo shrugged. Following Rast's lead he started to stretch. He wasn't one for regular exercise but right now it was the only thing that kept him from making an idiot of himself in front of Mira Fedor. 'Take it how you want.'

Rast bent down and touched her toes, pressing on her boot to ease the pain. 'I grew up on Edo Lesser. Not much of a place. Cold and boring. We lived underground most of the year in something not much better than a rut in the ground. Petalu Mau was next door. He had sixteen brothers. They taught me how to fight. Seemed I was better at that than anything else.'

Jo-Jo eyed her lean frame. She was built like most mercenaries he'd encountered, strong without too much bulk. Her hands though, were bigger than they should have been, the knuckles more scarred. He wondered how many people she'd killed.

'Pet wanted to work for Farr right from the start. Everyone on Edo Lesser did. Farr's more than a hero on our world. He's our economist. Our standard of living got way better when he purchased Edo and began to dump Orion's shit on it. People'll do anything for you if you keep their bellies full and their living comfortable. Crux, he even paid for education.'

'Lasper Farr?'

Rast nodded. 'Yeah. Not directly. But he paid a bonus to our government for every person who joined his corps or his other forces. Our govs put that into a fund to educate the ones who were interested, or smart enough.'

'What happened to the rest?'

'Everyone got accelerated-learning basics but that didn't teach you much more than how to work the different tech tools. You were supposed to do the rest yourself. Course, no one did.'

'So why didn't you want to work for Farr?'

'I got the education. I guess it changed things. I began to look for more but I was still only good at one thing.' Rast blushed. 'My ma was a gov.'

Jo-Jo couldn't suppress a grin. 'A gov's girl, eh? What's she think about your line of work?'

Rast pinned him with a flat, unemotional look. 'She died in the war, representing Akouedo on peace talks. Wrong place, wrong time. It could have been me – should have been. Ma had ideals. I've just got grudges. Nowadays I don't get caught up in the games of supremacists. Not unless they pay me what I want.'

Jo-Jo didn't offer any sentiment about her mother. Rast wasn't the kind to take it. 'Yeah. That's why I took to my line of work. I don't like complications. In fact, I don't like people. One thing about mineral scouting; you can do it solo.'

'Must get kinda lonely,' she said.

'I'm good at lonely,' Jo-Jo replied.

'Yeah, you've got that manner about you.' Rast mimicked his earlier statement. 'Word to the wise, though – wouldn't waste all that precious-earned bachelor-hood on the Baronessa. She's dragging more than her share of baggage around. Doesn't take to men much, either; prefers my type.'

Jo-Jo's fingers clenched on the biozoon's thick scar ridge. 'You warning me off?'

Rast rolled her shoulders in a relaxed gesture that Jo-Jo didn't buy. 'Just saving you some grief.'

Their moments of camaraderie faded, along with Jo-Jo's opportunity to find out who she had served with in the war.

He faked his own kind of indifference. 'So what happened between you two back there on Araldis?'

'When the Saqr hit Ipo, the town we were holding out in, we split. Few days later she pulled us out of a firefight. Lucky all round, I guess. Only been a few days since I'd seen her – maybe a week. But something happened to her in that time. When she picked us up in the AiV she was frozen, like shock. Never really been the same since then. Not that those Latino women are friendly at best. Especially the crown aristos.'

Jo-Jo nodded agreement at that. 'What's your figuring of how we get to Rho Junction without being blown to the crapper?'

Rast chewed on her upper lip. 'Only been there once; just before the war. Funny kinda place – supposed to be OLOSS territory but Extros are creeping around all over the shop. You need to do your "God" thing, get us landing rights. Berniere's got a validation document for the DNA pickup but he's not coming in on the prearranged connections. We got to convince the supplier that the bio-courier's just an idiot who messed up and missed his designated ride and hope they haven't already found another slab for the job.'

Jo-Jo sneered. 'Convince the buyer that Berniere's an idiot? Shouldn't be too hard.'

Sole

work'm work'm
round round
prickle prickle
find'm secret not'long

TEKTON

Tekton arrived at Rho Junction by way of three trouble-free res-shifts and two interminably long sub-light legs. On the trip he spent much of his time sketching designs for sculpting the alloy, beginning first with simple wave effects and then moving on to the more complex forms.

On the first leg from Belle-Monde to Mintaka he had the pleasure of meeting the famous skieran sculptor, Fenralia. The two whiled away their leisure time imbibing some of the artist's exceptional hallucinogenic hoard while they swapped ideas. He found Fenralia's gelatinous body and trailing tendrils almost as inspiring as Miranda's flesh, though – due to their odour – not at all sexually appealing.

Despite that, Fenralia persuaded him to pose naked one evening after they'd imbibed a range of ineffably awful Uralian beverages.

Towards the end of his posing session Tekton became aware that Fenralia's sexual organs had unfolded from within her/his bell-shaped body and were creeping across the floor to him, rather like pieces of meat escaping a frigerator.

At that point he instructed his travelling moud to fabricate an urgent call from the ship's Captain, and he hurriedly robed and left.

Fortunately, Fenralia disembarked a few days later

on her way to an Exhibition Trade Fest in some obscure location.

After that Tetkon kept mostly to himself.

On the day of disembarkation at Rho Junction he reviewed Labile Connit's instructions and integrated a map of the station into his supplementary memory.

Rho Junction, the map told him, was actually six pseudo-worlds joined by long cylindrical sections based on a molecular design. It was also one of the earliest mega-stations, commissioned by a wealthy entrepreneur who preferred to spend their money on purchasing a slice of orbit rather than a planet. But rejuve programmes had been less effective back then and did not keep Li Ti Rho-san alive long enough to ensure the condition of her legacy.

The autonomous station fell into the hands of her less than commercially astute descendants. Over time the Rho-san family were forced to allow a gamut of seedy businesses to flourish on the station in order to survive. Its reputation as a haven became tarnished as it evolved into something more tawdry.

Tekton's excitement at seeing the curious construction was dampened when he enquired about accommodation. He was told that due to the unusually high visitor traffic the available rooms provided only modest luxury. They were, however, located quite near the restaurant district on Rho One which, the visitor information gushed, was *'famous for its eclectic eateries which cater for all tastes'*. Followed closely by a warning: *'It is recommended that all visitors to Rho Junction employ maximum HealthWatch and – at the minimum – mobile security.'* It went on to advertise various security suites, as well as indemnity certificates against death or injury of another party through self-defence.

Never one to skimp on his own safety, a precaution somewhat justified by his enforced stay in inferior digs, Tekton chose top-of-the-line security and insurance. The Heedless Shadow floater weapon counted in its large specification list a Local Positioning System, a Magnetic Anomaly Detector, a miniature javelin missile, ordnance disposal and a kinetic rifle/pistol combo all neatly contained in a hat-sized floater. The floater could be carried in a light knapsack arrangement when not in use.

Satisfied that his personal safety was accounted for, Tekton donned his new bodyguard and took a taxi to the Flin Flon Flo Bath and Breakfast, staying just long enough to check in and ascertain that he would need to purchase a strong antibacterial spray if he were to reside there. He then ordered the taxi to transport him to the industrial area on Rho One which his map optimistically called the *Heijunka*.

As the taxi glided along the tiers and tiers of spiralling mag-rails, Tekton thought dreamily of a continual production flow and the exquisite moving structures that it would yield.

Heijunka, indeed . . .

But his dreams evaporated somewhere between the slug-shaped catoplasma warehousing and the grimy pop-cap workshop doors.

Tekton's unease grew when he found Lot FF, tucked behind a small odorous bio-separation plant and next to an unobtrusive but tatty medi-clinic. He wrenched the door ajar on Lot GG to reveal a medium-sized cold-floor space with poly-sheeted walls. The copper-inlaid catoplasma ceiling was coated in a gangrenous green fungus.

In one corner stood a longish benching arrangement boasting a metals lathe. Beside it was a simple pouring system and stacks of empty moulds. Next to that was an antiquated laser kiln.

Tekton drew the mask of his cloak tighter around his face as a figure detached itself from the kiln and shambled over.

The figure appeared to be wearing several layers of clothes, none of them clean. The face, when it was close enough to be seen, was aged beyond current health permissions and the eyes were bloodshot. Humanesque. But barely.

'Jus' keeping warm by the kiln,' the being pronounced in thick Gal. 'She hain't fired in weeks but she keeps her heat like a true hoarder.'

'Who are you?' demanded Tekton.

'Manruben,' said the disgraceful-looking creature.

'*You* are Manruben?'

'And you be the one from God's stadium on Belle-Monde? Figured so.'

'Studium,' corrected Tekton. 'You may address me as Godhead Tekton.'

'Belle-Monde used to be the pickins' of all the whore's palaces. So I bin tellin' all that's interested.'

Tekton drew a calming breath. How was it possible that this rotting piece of flesh had such a vaunted reputation? Should he ask for proof of identity?

'Kin see your thinkin', Godhead Tekkie. Reckon I don't look fit for workin'. Jus'... jus...' Manruben took a rattling, liquidish breath. '... Don' believe in rejuve and all tha' pretty-pretty. When you ain't got for ever, you live it better.' Despite the bleeding eyes, he managed a piercing look.

Tekton wondered just how long Manruben had left; his laboured breath and shivering, the archiTect's moud informed him, fitted all the symptoms of advanced lung disease.

'When does ma darlin' get 'ere?'

'Darling?' *Is this rubbish heap delirious?*

'Darlin' quixite, Tekkie; gotta hankering for it so deep I caint sleep nights. It's singin' to me already. Teasin' me like a young whore.'

Before Tekton could react Manruben tore aside the archiTect's veil and cupped his cheek with an over-familiar filthy hand. 'Betcha you know what tha's like. Betcha you c'n afford some pricey cunt.'

Tekton thought in that instant that he might faint, but he pulled himself together. *Moud, run DNA check.*

While his moud ran a DNA analysis of the sample that Manruben had left on his cheek and searched Rho Junction's image archives, Tekton's HealthWatch hastily neutralised the dangerous bacteria.

Tekton played for time by strolling around the workshop. The space was large enough to stockpile a reasonable quantity of quixite and the equipment looked worn but functional. *Lucky for you, Labile Connit!* But this disgusting creature following him around was an impostor, he was sure.

Godhead?

Yes?

I am able to verify that this humanesque is Manruben the metal craftsman.

Great Sole! thought Tekton. *How appalling!* He cleared his throat. 'Ahem. It would be pertinent for you to examine my preliminary sketches. I shall have them sent to your lodgings.'

'Loj – loj—.' Manruben made several tries at repeating the word and gave up. Instead he pointed to a pile of textiles near the far end of the kiln. 'I be kippin' right next to her. Like to live wi' it. You know.'

'Very well. Do you have a personal moud?'

'Them ones wot's in yer head? Don't trust them buggers.' He wagged his finger in the air, then broke into a broad lecherous grin.

'Manny? You got it ready?'

Tekton swivelled. A voluptuous female 'esque dressed in fine-mesh lace and with a velvet purse hanging at her throat teetered into the workshop on preposterous high heels.

'Lookee,' said Manruben. He produced a tiny bracelet of delicately interwoven metals from inside his layers of rags.

'Show me,' the female squealed, baring a row of perfect teeth. She wobbled straight past Tekton and flung her arms around Manruben's neck.

The scrawny old 'esque swayed and nearly fell. 'Careful, pretty-pretty,' he said.

She let go of him and teetered back, prayer-clasping her hands together. 'Can I see it work?'

Manruben reached out and slipped it on her wrist. The interwoven metals slid across each other like writhing snakes. She gave them a gentle touch and they clamped shut like a handcuff.

'What about the other one?'

Manruben squeezed her breast. 'Payment first, pretty-pretty.'

She frowned. 'But Manny, I have a client soon—'

Manruben folded his arms and shook his head.

'All right,' she said, pouting. 'Do you want the usual?'

He nodded and licked his lips like a child anticipating sweets.

Before Tekton could imagine what the 'usual' might be, the female knelt down and popped her front eight teeth out into her palm. She dropped them into the little velvet purse hanging around her neck and pressed the seal shut. Then she pulled down Manruben's grimy pants and buried her face in his groin, making indelicate sucking noises.

Tekton was caught between utter revulsion and complete fascination. Manruben's bloodshot eyes rolled backward beneath his eyelids in rapid ecstasy.

Tekton's instincts told him to leave the warehouse, this grubby artisan and his whore, and never return – but he had come too far and risked too much to let Manruben's sexploits deter him.

So he sat it out, lips pursed, arms folded, toe tapping on the filthy floor. Manruben reached his climax by way of a series of unathletic grunts. But the female was not finished. On his final groan she smeared something between the crease of his slack-skinned buttocks.

To Tekton's dismay, Manruben gave several further violent thrusts of his pelvis and collapsed backwards, clutching his chest. The whore shrieked and pounced on him, ratting about under the craftsman's clothes. Finding the precious second bracelet that she sought, she scrambled to her feet and tottered out.

Moud?

The craftsman has no HealthWatch. I would surmise that if he does not receive medical assistance within three to six minutes then the cerebral damage will be irreparable.

Where in Sole's name can I get that?! shrieked Tekton.

Next door, said the moud calmly.

MIRA

Your abdomen is enlarged.

Mira lifted the folds of her night robe and stood in front of the mirror in her bathing cubicle to examine her belly. The bulge was still slight but was unmistakable now on her thin frame. Her robe would not hide it for much longer. Already she was taking care not to brush the material against herself for fear it would show her pregnancy. How would the men react? How would she explain it?

Mira felt a sharp pang for the loss of her beloved sister. Faja would have known how to deal with things. But Faja could not rescue her this time.

Not ever again.

Mira felt worn out with the burden of her secret. She longed for a familiar face from her life on Araldis. Estelle. Poor, dear Estelle. Even Marchella. Or Cass Mulravey. Cass would not be shocked by Mira's pregnancy. She would be angry at the act that had produced it and then she would set about making preparations.

But those women were beyond reach – and Cass was the only one still living and breathing.

Did she dare trust Bethany Farr with her worries? Would the woman even care? Beth had her own concerns. And her brother, Lasper? How deep did the bond between brother and sister really go? How inbred was their need to manipulate others?

No. For the moment she would keep her secret close. Time enough for Thales Berniere to be appalled. For Rast to sneer. For Josef Rasterovich to lose his fascination with her. An unwed woman with child was a burden and an ill omen across most cultures and species. A woman who had been raped was worse.

You are pensive.

Mira sighed. *Insignia* had become increasingly skilled at reading her moods. *Si. This errand for Lasper Farr wastes time. I don't know if the little ones I left behind are alive. What has happened to the last of the survivors?*

Perhaps there is no need to return – if they are dead? The biozoon had no empathy for her world. It had been eager to leave for Saif space.

'No!' Mira cried aloud. 'Vito is alive and Commander Farr has promised to help Araldis.'

And these other humanesques? Soon the baby will hamper you. Will they help you as well?

They mustn't know about the child. I must keep it from them at least until we return from Rho Junction . . .

Simple enough, Insignia conceded. *Humanesques are imperceptive and self-absorbed.*

Mira reflected on the irony. *Insignia* did not think greatly of humanesques and yet she had tied herself to one for her own reasons; her own needs. Which one of them did that make self-absorbed, she wondered?

What is your defence capacity? she asked the biozoon.

Without the Assailants, I am limited to the kinetic energy produced from my tail spine.

What is its range?

Far enough.

Mira did not pursue the matter. She had learned that the biozoon would only tell what she would tell. Persistence had little effect.

Instead, she smoothed the night robe down over her stomach and left the cabin to make her way to the cucina. The extra demands of the baby had begun to make her constantly hungry. Particularly, it seemed, during the ship's designated sleep hours.

Insignia's rhythms changed when the crew were asleep, as if the biozoon herself enjoyed a more relaxed state, the crackle of her biologics dampening to a whisper.

Mira didn't need lighting to find her way along the strata. The ship's channels were as familiar to her as the corridors of the Villa Fedor had been.

No more. She suppressed the pang. *No more.*

Lasper Farr had not skimped on replenishing their provisions. The cucina's compactus was so crammed with foodstocks that it ran heavy on its tracks and Mira needed all her strength to roll the shelves apart.

She found the crisp dried-meat sticks between layers of compressed fruit and a large pail of nuts and slipped some into her sleeve, deciding she would eat in the privacy of her cabin.

As Mira left the cucina she glimpsed someone from a diverging channel entering the medi-facility. Thales Berniere, she thought, since the figure was not as lean as the mercenaries, nor as hulking as Josef Rasterovich.

Concerned, she followed him. Was he ill?

But she hesitated, one hand holding open the pucker,

suddenly shy to be coming upon him in this unexpected manner. They had not been alone often. Perhaps she should leave him to his business. Or perhaps she could give him advice or comfort.

Tentatively she stepped inside.

Thales did not hear her. He had a finger pressed to an assay pad and was staring, engrossed in the audio of a blood analysis.

When he had finished listening to the report he slumped across the analyser.

What does it say? Mira asked *Insignia*.

The male humanesque has a bacterial infection, the biozoom answered in a distracted manner.

You mean a barrier organism?

Yes. The biozoom sounded impatient. *But he also has an infection which is breaking down the barrier organism.*

Is he contagious?

Unlikely. Not to me at least, or to you, without exchanging fluids. It is curious, though, that the infection markers indicate that the humanesque has only recently contracted the bacterium.

How recently?

On Edo, I would surmise.

What is his prognosis?

Untreated he is likely to expire within weeks. Those with strong immune systems have been known to last months.

Can our medi-facility provide a treatment?

No.

Mira recalled Thales's distracted anger after his meeting with Lasper Farr, his unwillingness to go near the Commander again. What had Bethany's brother done to Thales? What had he done to all of them?

Hurry, Insignia. This task had to be completed quickly – for all their sakes. Mira removed her hand from the pucker and slipped away to her cabin.

Mira sought out Rast Randall after a restless night. Her dreams had been filled with urgency and frustration and she awoke with an ache under her breast that made it painful to breathe.

Insignia located Rast up in the designated armoury, a cavity in the upper body of the biozoon directly under its uppermost fin.

Mira watched the woman as she bent over a weapon. Rast was still slick with sweat from her morning run with Josef Rasterovich. The muscles in her forearms were taut as wire and the veins on the backs of her hands stood out like bulging tributaries.

Rast didn't bother to look up but, unlike Thales Berniere on the previous night, she sensed Mira's presence immediately.

'No wonder Franco hired us. These weapons couldn't stop a puff of wind.' She slapped her hand against her thigh in exasperation. 'What's up?'

'Do you believe that Lasper Farr will honour his promise to aid Araldis?'

Rast straightened, putting down the rifle and sliding her hands to her hips in her usual aggressive stance. Finally, she looked at Mira. 'Figured you already decided he would, otherwise you wouldn't have agreed.'

'I know why I am here – but why are you?'

'Pretty simple. He's paying me to watch after Berniere and his sister. And you, by default.'

'And?'

The mercenary folded her arms. 'Reckon you're getting a bit of a handle on me at last, eh, Baronessa?'

'Perhaps I am not as naive as I was,' Mira allowed.

'Well, that's a damn relief.' Rast wiped sweat from her temple with a finger and flicked it from the tip. 'You may recall that I did a little buying on Intel station.'

Mira's eyes widened. She had almost forgotten about the existence of the cryoprotectants.

'Can't think of a better place to sell 'em than Rho Junction,' said Rast.

'And then?'

'Well . . . you owe me a trip to Rigel but I'm kinda thinking the lucre might be elsewhere. Could be Lasper has some more work. Maybe I'll let you off the hook.'

'You would go back to Araldis with Commander Farr?'

Rast leaned towards her, close enough so that their cheeks brushed. 'If it's worthwhile.'

Mira recoiled from the bare, moist, heated flesh. 'How would I know what is "worthwhile" to you?'

'I didn't know you cared,' Rast teased.

But Mira saw no humour in it. She pressed her fingers to her face as shaking overtook her body. 'I care about the bambino I left on Araldis. I care that the women are starving. I worry that they are forced to rely on a cruel, selfish man for their safety,' she said.

Rast rocked back on her heels and let out a long breath. 'If you want me on the same film as you, Baronessa, then maybe it's time you told me what happened to you – after Ipo.'

There was no teasing in the mercenary's manner now, only an intense scrutiny that drew the poison in

Mira's mind-wounds to the surface. 'Why is that necessary?'

'Because I work for who I frikking please, *because* I please. I'm not some custom-bound Carabinere who'll jump when the Baronessa sniffs. I need reasons and background, or I won't play in your puddle.'

Rast's blunt honesty crumbled Mira's barriers. She needed the mercenary on her side, even if it meant being vulnerable. There was no one else.

Still, the words came haltingly as she told Rast of their flight in the TerV: the deaths, her fingers dipping into the child's skull-wound, burying the child, pulling her mother from the grave, the korm starving and trying to eat the flesh of the dead humanesques. And then the dark fear in the Pablo mines.

Mira meant to stop at that, but Rast probed with more simple, direct questions, and with each word that Mira released the pain under her breastbone eased.

Finally, the last of it came out – how they had held her down for Trinder, and why; his fertility chant and his sickening remorse.

After she had finished, the vacuum of spent words made room for quiet, grieving, relieved tears.

'Women get raped,' said Rast harshly, her pale skin flushed with emotion. 'Sometimes in war, sometimes just for the hell of it. That's what happens.' She gripped Mira's wrist and pulled her close. Then she hugged her tightly for a long moment.

'We'll get your world back for you, Baronessa. But tell me something: are you sure you really want it?'

THALES

As Thales listened to the medi-log's immune-system analysis his hope disintegrated. A tiny part of him had held out for the possibility that Lasper Farr had bluffed him. But the proof was in front of him now: an irrefutable auditory confirmation of Farr's criminal act – of his own helplessness.

He wished desperately that he could reverse things; that he had never left Scolar; or at the very least that Rene was with him.

There was no comfort. No hope.

Idealism and principles had been desirable – laudable, in fact – when he was safe. Now they had begun to seem both futile and dangerous.

Anger and fear came in alternate waves. From the moment Thales had adopted a dissident's position and met Villon, his life had begun to unravel.

Did he care about which philosophy was observed when moment by moment his body was being destroyed?

Panic ringed his anger and he fought down a desire to cry out. He must calm himself. He must think . . . he must . . .

. . . But the calm would not come and he flung himself out of the medi-facility and ran randomly through the ship's strata.

But was it random? For when his legs would no longer carry him and he could no longer catch his breath, Thales found himself at the egress scale. If somehow he could force the scale open then Farr would be denied what he wanted and Rene would be freed from the guilty burden of her husband.

How long before she would find out that he was dead? How would she feel then? Relieved? Annoyed? Would she hold a requiem? Would Sophos Mianos play the part of a grieving father-in-law?

Thales tugged at the fleshy inside of the egress scale, one thought bothering him – he would never have a child. Somehow that seemed more important than anything else; more meaningful than the people of Scolar's indifference, and his revenge on the insufferable Sophos Mianos.

Thales sobbed as he tugged, hearing or seeing nothing until a hand gripped his shoulder. Even then he did not take his hands from their task.

'Msr Thales? What is it? What has happened?'

But he continued to tear at the scale until the heat of his intention diminished. Then he crouched down, unable to speak.

After a while, arms slipped around him and a warm body moulded itself lightly against his back. Two small hands patted his arms and soft whispers soothed him. When his tears were spent he turned into Bethany's embrace and stayed there.

Later, she took Thales back to her cabin. She was not much taller than him and yet he leaned on her shoulder as if he was injured. She helped him onto her bed and disappeared, returning a short time later with a cool, sweet drink.

She watched him drink it from the edge of the bed, her eyes serious. 'I went to the medi-facility for my headache. I saw you leave. I knew you were upset but it took me a while to find you. You ran so quickly.'

Thales huddled into her pillows like a sick child. 'Why would you bother? You barely know me.'

She frowned, and the lines made her face older: a worried mother's face. 'I know my brother,' she whispered. 'He's found a way to force you to do this. Lasper has seen some opportunity in you and he will exploit it – as he exploits everyone.'

Bethany's voice trailed off and they sat in silence.

'He has infected me with a bacterium that will alter my genome. If I bring him the DNA that I was meant to receive, he will nullify the infection,' said Thales abruptly.

'He could be bluffing.'

Thales shook his head. 'The infirmary gave me an analysis of my immune activity. I'm fighting a bacterium – and losing.'

Bethany paled. She sprang up, her fists clenched. 'Crux!' She paced the length of the cabin. 'Msr Thales, I am deeply sorry. I-I . . . I loathe him in so many ways but you have to understand.' She turned back to him, her eyes burning. 'He can accomplish anything. Anything. He will save my daughter.'

Thales's anger waned in the face of her honesty. He understood this woman's motives, at least: her desperation for her child.

'I will collect the DNA and return it to Edo,' he said. 'And then I will be free of him. When he has retaken Araldis, maybe you will be free of him as well.'

Beth hugged herself tightly. 'I believe that *you* will be, Thales. Despite everything, he is a man who keeps his bargains. But for what *I* ask from him, I will never be free.'

Thales saw into her then, to the heart of her guilt and her weaknesses. They mirrored his own so perfectly that he could not stop himself climbing from the bed to stand next to her.

'Comfort me,' he said simply.

JO-JO RASTEROVICH

Rast called a meeting in the cucina after the biozoon calmed near Rho station. With the exception of Jo-Jo, they all gathered together around the table. He stood near the door, watching.

Randall sat next to Mira Fedor, a slight protectiveness that was new apparent in her manner. Latourn stood behind her, equally attentive. The scholar, Thales, leaned close to Bethany, his knee touching hers.

Jo-Jo had heard their muffled passion on the previous nights and found it hard to begrudge Bethany her pleasure even though he thought her taste in men was atrocious. Necessity changed perspectives – Jo-Jo knew that better than most. But the sounds of their ardour had only sharpened his own desire and it had plucked at his nerve ends. His craving for Mira Fedor had grown so powerful that he could not bear others to be close to her.

Get control of it, he ordered himself.

Only Catchut seemed detached from everything. Rast's second in command rocked his chair back against the food compactus so that it made an annoying repetitive clunk.

Rast scowled at him and hooked her foot under his seat, toppling it over. 'Desist!'

Catchut climbed to his feet and righted the chair without a word.

'We need you to get us landing permission.' Rast addressed Jo-Jo.

Jo-Jo nodded. 'I'll request a speaking tour.'

'Catchut will go with you, in case there's trouble. Once we're docked Berniere will make his contact. Latourn will go with him to collect. I will stay on the 'zoon with Beth and the Baronessa.'

Her last statement triggered a wave of suspicion in Jo-Jo. Rast Randall wasn't the type to stay behind anywhere. Was she manufacturing time alone with Mira Fedor? *No!* He wrestled his paranoia down. There must be something else on Randall's agenda.

'I will go with Thales,' said Bethany.

They all stared at her.

'I suppose so. But stay with Latourn out of the way. I don't reckon they would be expecting him to bring *his woman*.' Rast ladled sarcasm onto the last two words.

Thales blushed and stared down at the table.

Jo-Jo clenched his fists. Did the young idiot think he was too good for Bethany?

'All settled, then?' said Rast.

'Might be best if *you* went with Berniere,' said Jo-Jo.

The mercenary's expression became cool. 'Might be best if I make that decision.'

'Yeah,' said Jo-Jo softly. 'As long as you make the right one.'

His challenge was mild but unmistakable. The mercenary was running more than one job here, Jo-Jo was sure of it.

'Just get on with your god-speaking, Rasterovich. Leave the protection to us.'

Jo-Jo shrugged. He didn't need to say any more. They'd all heard him.

'I need to use the shortcast.' He gave a half-serious bow. 'Baronessa?'

Mira Fedor stood up immediately. 'Of course.'

As she moved behind Bethany and Thales her robe caught on the corner of Thales's seat. It pulled tight for a brief moment and she wrenched it loose with quick, nervous hands. Her belly seemed unnaturally round on her slim frame.

Jo-Jo's heart contracted. *No. Surely not . . .*

According to the visitor information, Rho Junction didn't have a studium or any other such pretensions to learned institutions – but it did harbour a body called The Alliance of Free Thinkers. The TAFTers welcomed Jo-Jo Rasterovich with open arms.

'It is timely,' said their spokesperson, 'that you should contact us just as we are about to hold convocation.'

'Timing,' Jo-Jo replied, 'is one of my many talents.' *Like crap.*

His bold approach had been rewarded and *Insignia* was granted landing rights along with priority docking. But the TAFTers' enthusiasm and the proximity to Extropy space had made Jo-Jo jumpy.

The half-heads were unpredictable. Look at the Stain Wars. Just as Orion had looked set to be dragged into a protracted battle, Commander Lasper Farr had led an intervention backed by his own mercenary force, and the Extros had withdrawn. Just like that. *Just like that.*

Although Jo-Jo was pissed off with Rast, she was his best sounding-board. He sought her out again before he left the ship. She was in the armoury, counting ammunition, and halted only to give him a scowl.

Jo-Jo wasn't going to be put off. 'Why do you think the Extros pulled out so quickly when Farr entered the war?'

She logged a number in her filmtab and crossed her arms. 'Funny time for a history lesson.'

'Not a lesson,' said Jo-Jo. 'I'm about to go and hang my arse on the line about a few things. I want to know if it might get shot.'

'Didn't think you were the kind to worry about what others thought.' Rast was being deliberately obtuse and Jo-Jo knew it. 'Loner like you.'

'I'm not and you know it. I'm also not stupid. This is too close to Extro space for my liking. Hell, just look at the station log-in – the place is teeming with them. Come on, Randall, you've seen them up closer than I have. What's the deal?'

Rast counted and logged another shelf of ammo before she answered him. 'Like I said to the Baronessa, they don't think like us – or like any alien I've known. Maybe it's something to do with the cryo process or the chemicals they use but it's hard to get a grab on their logic. Maybe they don't have any.'

'What about Farr, then?'

'There're a million theories about why Farr had the juice to stop them. Most 'esques don't care, though – they just know he did and that's enough.'

'You're not most, Randall. You make your living out of this kind of thing.'

'You shoulda asked Lasper when you had the chance.'

This time Jo-Jo scowled. 'Yeah, well, I'll remember that next time we're having beers together.'

He left Rast to it but continued to brood over what might await him as *Insignia* was directed to Bell Six of the mega-station: a huge, grey dome with multiple docking shelves affixed to its fluted outer shell.

When the Baronessa confirmed their arrival, he collected Catchut from the cucina and went to the egress scale.

On the outside, a long uuli escort draped in a scent-and-colour translator waited in the docking tube for them. Without turning, it undulated back along the tunnel and out into Bell Six, stopping next to a taxi.

As they followed, Jo-Jo noticed flakes of dried uuli excreta, like dry snow, swirling in the air. His skin started to itch and his throat thickened. What if he lost his voice? No voice, no God-lecture, no distraction for the idiot Berniere.

'Convocation convenes in the Orb Chamber in Bell Four,' said the translator in pompous Gal. Its lofty tone seemed ridiculous in contrast to the uuli's soft, quivering movements.

Jo-Jo got into the taxi and peeled off one of the complimentary filter masks from the back of the headrest.

Catchut climbed in next to him. 'Stink, don't they? Why do they have to shit everywhere?'

'It's not shit,' said Jo-Jo. He coughed. His eyes were beginning to water. ''S mucus. Reduces friction when they move. Ever seen a mollusc?'

'Eaten plenty,' Catchut conceded.

'Think of molluscs.'

Catchut laughed and licked his lips as the uuli slid onto the front seat of the taxi. 'Probably best not.'

The trip to Bell Four nearly had Jo-Jo forgetting why they were there. Where Edo had been almost colourless in its meld of grey and silver parasite-polished metal refuse, Rho Junction was a riot of colour and movement and scents that forced their way past Jo-Jo's mask and fizzed in the back of his throat like a scoop of sour sherbet.

While his mind tried to sort out the assaults on his senses, the taxi veered from the designated road and drove straight up the nearest wall. With a loud click it ejected a slide from a side panel which magnetised to the silver tracks snaking along the walls. Suspended there above the mêlée of foot traffic, Jo-Jo and Catchut were free to gape.

Jo-Jo had travelled more than most, first as scout and then as God-Discoverer, but *nothing* compared to the Arrivals Bell at Rho Junction.

'What the shit is that?' said Catchut.

He pointed to a group of transparent fluid-filled figures with large oval heads from which odd flaps protruded. The flaps resembled ears but seemed to be used for propulsion.

'Extros, I'd guess,' said Jo-Jo. 'Heard they like to hang out in different bodies.'

The uuli translator spoke. 'Msr Rasterovich is correct. Those are Extropists who have adapted siphonophores as their means of transport. The corporeal part of the Extropist takes many different forms. The forms designate rank and intelligence. It is a complex society that is difficult to decipher from the outside.'

'Whassat mean?' said Catchut.

The uuli paused as if retranslating the question. 'Many of their forays into the post-humanesque form are neither successful nor aesthetic. We see many variations here, and each is a product of a particular faction or trend within Extropy culture.'

'So they aren't all super-brains swimming around in lumps of jelly like these,' said Jo-Jo. Immediately the words came out he regretted them. The uuli's skin flared crimson as if the creature was blushing. Or angry.

'The siphonophore is one of their more common and successful forms. It is modelled on my own species.'

Fortunately the taxi swerved under an archway and then took a fierce upward trajectory to enter the Bell proper – bringing their conversation to a halt.

The pedestrians were now far enough away to seem insect-like in size. Above them, however, the Bell's dome was busy with traffic: lightweight fragile flyers and butterflies, creatures without abdomens.

'The wings you can see are another of their more successful forms,' it said.

'But they're just flappers,' said Catchut. 'Can't see no body.'

The uuli's body twisted its elongated torso into a knot as if it had suddenly been tied by an invisible hand. Jo-Jo got the impression that it was laughing. 'Their post-human mind is impregnated into the large spots on each wing,' it said.

Jo-Jo was intrigued. 'How do they land, then? There's nothing to attach their legs to.'

'They don't require legs,' said the uuli. 'Observe above them.'

Jo-Jo and Catchut craned their necks to view the dangling vegetation that grew from the apex of the dome. Broad leaves floated gently on stems that were attached to a network of vines and creepers. The Wings hovered above them and occasionally dropped onto them like slowly settling dust.

'But how do they move around once they've landed?'

'They don't,' said the translated uuli voice. 'They spend their time hovering and settling. When they wish to take off, the vibration of their wings creates momentum. The leaf bounces.'

'They're pretty vulnerable, then,' observed Catchut.

The uulu knotted up again. 'Don't ever assume a transhuman is unprotected, no matter how delicate or vulnerable its *corp* is.'

A sinister sensation crept up the back of Jo-Jo's neck, making the roots of his hair stiff. Despite the marvels around him, he wanted to hurry back to the biozoon and get the hell off Rho Junction.

Besides, the place was clogging up his airways. He glanced at Catchut whose expression remained bland and untroubled, though he noticed the mercenary's hand was resting against his pocket. There were no weapon restrictions for those entering Rho Junction, although Jo-Jo knew that he would be searched before he entered the convocation chamber.

'How much longer?' he asked.

'Longer,' the uuli answered.

Jo-Jo tried to fix his mind on the speech he was about to give, but other thoughts intruded. He shouldn't have agreed to this. He should have got off the Savvy at Jandowae with the rest of the refugees. And something else was *really* bothering him. Something Jasper Farr had said. '*Prediction is one of its uses.*' The lunatic had a sophisticated device that correlated huge amounts of information. If he wasn't using it to predict outcomes, what was he using it for? And where the hell did he get the design for it? Even the most advanced spintronics hadn't produced anything like Lasper Farr's Dynamic System device.

The sinister sensation began to spread out across his body until his skin was crawling with unnamed fear.

'You're weeks late.' Gutnee Paraburd's contact had his privacy screen on, but even with voice distortion he sounded suspicious. 'Figured Gutnee stiffed me on this one. You got the guarantee? 'Cos if not, I got another buyer comin' in soon. Mebbe I'll use them anyways. I prefer reliable.'

Thales attempted to keep his face calm. The mercenary, Rast, had told him that they would run identity checks and reaction analysis – skin colour, pupil dilation – from the shortcast. If that checked out, he'd be given a meeting place and time.

'If you get it right,' Rast added.

The mercenary scared him: her stark white hair and the mouth that switched between maliciousness and laughter in an instant. Mira Fedor was at least the type of woman he could comprehend. Mira Fedor had manners and breeding.

He sighed. Not so Bethany.

She held his hand now, out of sight of the shortcast viewer, leaning against one of the many tubercles in the biozoon's buccal. He'd never met a woman like her. Despite her toughness she seemed so willing to do things for him, to listen. The respect she gave him was intoxicating. She loved the way he spoke, and his ideas. And her lovemaking was so natural. It made him forget that her flesh had lost its tautness and that her hair was thin and lacking lustre.

Rene's hair rippled like poured water.

He pushed away that memory and concentrated on the 'cast. 'I ran into some trouble travelling. I had to pick up an alternative route.'

'What kinda trouble?'

Rast had prepared him for this. 'There's a rogue stationmaster hijacking cargo.'

'Where and what name?'

'Landhurst at Intel.'

'You came through Intel?'

Thales regurgitated Rast's ready-made story. 'I got diverted there from Scolar station. Seems there are some problems on a planet in one of the outer systems. Refugees are choking the shift queues.'

'How come your 'zoon's showing high traces of mercury?'

Thales resisted a panicked glance at Bethany. He tried to give the impression of bewilderment. 'We had an encounter with a refuse ship. It tried to shift out of sequence, right into our space. It must have left us with some – er – residue.'

'Damn Savvy bastards. That Carnage Farr thinks he's got free run of everthin'.'

The voice fell silent.

Thales maintained a steady forward glance. He could think of nothing else to say, so he sought the space between his fear and his anger.

'Well, your visuals check out, Thales Berniere. Get yourself over to Heijunka section on Rho One. Find bay GG. Wait in the reception area. And a word to it

– don't be squiddin' me. My supplier's got more pull than a gravity well. She'll slice you up and use your DNA for paste.'

She?

The shortcast finished abruptly. Thales pulled his moist palm from Bethany's and shook the feeling back into his fingers. 'You'd better stay behind. They mentioned your brother.'

'He's right,' said Rast from the sink of thick biozoon tissue she called *Secondo*. 'Good catch on the mercury traces, scholar. *Residue*. Hah! Maybe you did learn something from all that studium time.'

Thales clenched his teeth. 'Education doesn't equate to idiocy,' he said stiffly.

'Does in my worlds,' Rast guffawed.

Thales tried to relax his jaw. The mercenary was an expert in the art of belittling and she wasn't particular who she practised it on.

'Perhaps you're right,' agreed Bethany. 'It is possible that I might be recognised, or linked to Lasper. My brother has more enemies than friends.'

Thales gave her a warm look. 'It would be safer.'

Bethany stood and moved behind him where she rested her hands on his shoulders. He was sitting in what Randall had called *Autonomy*, a larger nub with recognisable add-ons that moulded to fit its occupant. With the virtual display pushed aside he could view the entire buccal with a glance.

Rast had closed her eyes. 'Better move, then. Don't know how long Rasterovich can keep most of the attention his way. We'll all leave together. I'll take Bethany and the Baronessa sightseeing. Act like you're doing the same. According to the tourist map, Heijunka section is right next to The Hocs in Bell One. Take a detour through The Hocs like you're after some distraction – anybody that's watching will lose interest the moment you get there,' she said.

'What are The Hocs?' asked Thales.

Rast opened her eyes abruptly.

He felt Bethany's lips at his ear. 'The Hocs is another name for the sex parlours,' she whispered.

Thales's whole body flushed with heat. Scolar did not have such places. Carnal pleasures were NOT something philosophers paid for . . . though nothing would surprise him about those Pragmatists. But even they would not be tawdry about it. There was no sex industry on his planet. He imagined Rene's repulsion at the very notion.

Mira Fedor entered the buccal and frowned over at Randall. 'The port authority has finished their scan of the ship. We have been given permission to disembark.'

Rast leapt from her prone position with an agility that caused Thales a stab of envy. The woman was more of a man than he was in so many ways. And though bigoted and coarse, she was not a fool either.

Thales felt a sudden desire to shirk off his upbringing – his beliefs – and become someone else. A person of action – not a piece of flesh manipulated against its will by a Lasper Farr or a Sophos Mianos and especially not by a Gutnee Paraburd. A strange coagulation of certainty occurred deep inside his chest.

He could change.

*   *   *

Thales and Latourn parted from Rast, Mira and Bethany at the market stalls that lined the docks near their berth and took the suspended fast-trak to Bell One. The wavering overhanging tube only afforded brief glimpses of Rho Junction when it stopped and the doors flashed open and shut. There were no windows on the fast-trak, only bright dancing icons that recorded their journey with meticulous precision.

Thales sat opposite Latourn, who kept his eyes on their route marker. He tried to find his meditation space again, to keep out lurking fears about the disease with which Lasper Farr had infected him and the new biological cocktail that he was about to receive, but it eluded him still . . .

'Scholar?'

Thales glanced around.

Latourn stood in the doorway of the fast-trak forcing the sensors to keep it open. 'You comin'?'

Thales scrambled to his feet and joined the man.

The fast-trak sped off, leaving them to ride a steep conveyor down to the floorspace of Bell One.

The descent gave them a broad view of the layout. The conveyor led straight into an area of rooftops that resembled an ocean of rust-coloured waves, peaking but never quite breaking. They were divided periodically by large and bawdy sculptures.

On the distant side of the Bell another city of high-rise factory buildings loomed through light haze.

Thales sniffed the air. An acrid taste like pepper caught at the back of his throat, sending him into a coughing spasm.

Latourn surveyed the vista with a curled lip.

'Ventilation ain't too good in this one. Extractors must be cheap. Or old.'

'They sh-should be able to get rid of s-smoke at least,' coughed Thales.

''Taint smoke, scholar. It's flakes.' Latourn held out his hand and Thales watched tiny particles settle on his skin.

'W-what f-from?'

Latourn nodded at the uuli ahead of them on the conveyor. 'Them, mebbe.'

'Y-you mean their skin?' Thales swallowed. 'But we do not have that p-problem on Scolar.'

Latourn jerked his head to indicate behind him. 'Yeah, well, guess you don't get so many. Or them, either.'

Thales turned to the group overtaking them: transparent round-bodied creatures with strange flaps tagged in an irregular pattern across their skin. They balanced on long suckered feet that exuded unpleasant odours with each quick-flowing step. Within moments he and Latourn were left behind in a swirl of floating wet skin flakes.

Both coughed violently.

Latourn spat when he caught his breath. 'Extros. Filthy skin-shedding Extros.'

Thales couldn't rid himself of their smell. It besieged his senses and he rushed to the edge of the conveyor to vomit. The hot liquid splashed onto his robe and splattered across the girders below.

When he dragged himself back to Latourn he expected the man to taunt him, but the mercenary was already staring ahead at The Hocs. Thales appreciated, for once, a mercenary's lack of finer feelings.

They left the conveyor and walked into the first row. At the forecourt of each building was an exhibitor's bubble where humanesques and aliens performed samples of the pleasures on offer within. Buyers crowded to each bubble.

Thales wanted to vomit again when he saw the enactments. Latourn was wiping his hands against his side and swallowing, repeatedly.

A humanesque female approached them wearing a stiff rainbow-thread robe not unlike the one that Mira Fedor had worn to greet Sophos Mianos. Her hair was secured under a silver-wire headdress and her face had been lightly sprayed with heavy silver paint that disguised any real expression.

The woman spun slowly around. The back of her body was entirely bare, the edges of the fine clothing sutured to the skin at her sides. A belt slung around her waist carried a sheathed dagger that fitted snugly against the line of her backbone. Her bare flesh was a ghastly mess of raised scars and newly crusted cuts and the backs of her thighs were grazed raw.

She pulled the dagger from its sheath with a practised hand and offered it to Latourn. He took it and fingered the blade.

'We mustn't stop,' whispered Thales, terrified.

But the mercenary was transfixed. 'Go ahead, then, scholar. I'll catch you up. Stick to this route,' he said hoarsely. He unhooked the map from his ear and pushed it against Thales's chest, shoving him away.

Thales opened his mouth to protest but the words never formed; he was better without the surly man. Instead, he turned and kept walking. Confining his gaze to the view directly ahead, he held the bud to his ear and let the map navigate him through the centre of The Hocs. He did not need protection, he told himself. He had changed.

Whether through luck or destiny no other trader approached him, though he felt the weight of their curious stares.

At the edge of The Hocs the architecture changed with no space or allowance for the transition; wave buildings turned into a layered hive.

The smells were different, too; the spicy musks and florals were replaced by something less salubrious, less hearty. The factories of the Hiejunka were made from *grown* technology; dirty catoplasma tubes squeezed on top of each other like the inner workings of an insect mound.

The map steered him to bay GG and Thales found himself in front of a modest narrow *popped* doorfront bearing a medi-lab symbol.

He hesitated before entering, glancing around. None of the factory units had windows. *Are they all interconnected?* he wondered. *A hive of darkness.*

The factory unit on one side was much, much larger. A balol lounged against the wall of the other side, picking under its neck frill and inhaling from a small tube. It seemed oblivious to Thales's presence.

He reached for the door and pushed inward.

A cooling chill and polycoated grey rubber greeted him. He walked to the desk and pressed on the reception pad.

For a long time nothing happened.

Thoughts streamed through his head. *Wait for*

Latourn/press for attendance again/call out/leave/no! He had to get the DNA and return to Edo.

As Thales reached for the pad again, a four-legged figure in mask and overalls scampered out from a doorway behind the desk. He propped his prehensile paws up on the counter and did not offer any introduction.

'Your DNA profile correlates with our visual scan. Welcome to Junction, Msr Berniere. I have sent a farcast to our associate on Scolar to let him know our deal is in progress.'

Gutnee Paraburd. Thales felt a stab of anger. 'Yes,' he said. 'It would be good for Mr Paraburd to know that I have received the DNA.'

The lab-rat pressed a paw on the corner of the counter. It sprang open to reveal a small, cold-storage space full of vials and instruments. He selected a capsule and slotted it deftly into a gene gun.

'Please hold out your arm.'

Thales licked dry lips. What if the naked DNA combined with the bacterium to break down the barrier substance more quickly? What if he did not have as much time as Farr had predicted? Would there be a warning?

He wanted to ask the lab-rat but any questions would arouse suspicion.

I can change.

He pushed up the sleeve of his robe and held his arm out.

'The other side,' said the lab-rat.

Before he could proffer the other arm a commotion broke out.

A moment later the door burst open and a thin well-dressed Lostolian male staggered in supporting a filthy old 'esque who was naked from the waist down and gasping for breath.

'I need urgent medical help,' cried the Lostolian in a commanding tone. 'This man MUST NOT DIE!'

TEKTON

'Do you understand? He must not die!' Tekton repeated himself slowly and with unmistakable vehemence.

A lab-rat in a laboratory uniform of mask and frock coat edged out from behind the counter and hopped around as Tekton dropped Manruben on a chair. The old craftsman's colouring had turned from chemical-ruddy to an unhealthy shade of white.

'What is it?' hissed the lab-rat.

'Heart failure, I would surmise,' said Tekton. 'I believe he has no HealthWatch.'

'I have a temporary patch,' said the lab-rat. 'You want it?'

Tekton stamped his foot and gave him a fierce glare. 'Are you mentally impaired? Of course I want it!'

The lab-rat blinked and twitched but it didn't move.

An oddly dressed young man stepped from the corner of the counter into the ensuing silence. 'I think . . . what he means is . . . well . . . who will pay.'

'Lucre? Of course!' Tekton tossed a credit clip at the lab-rat.

The 'rat ran behind the counter. When the clip verified itself he scuttled back and stickered a HealthWatch patch on Manruben's chest. 'Nanites will take a little while. Maybe it's too late, even. Have some business to attend to now. You should wait outside.'

'Wait outside?' Tekton frowned and mustered his most imperious demeanour. 'Most unlikely.' He turned on his heel and began to pace the length of the office.

'Sir, may I say,' said the young man, keeping his eyes carefully averted from Manruben's exposed and shrunken manhood, 'that it is surprising to meet such a cultured gentleman in this . . . establishment.'

Tekton stopped and looked properly at the young man. Despite the voluminous robe, he was refined in looks and educated in manner. 'I should say the same to you, young man.'

To Tekton's astonishment, tears filled the young man's eyes and he cast the lab-rat a desperate look. 'I-I c-can't d-do i-it without knowing!' he said between chattering teeth.

'Knowing what?' Tekton glanced back and forth between them. Then a sense of prescience tingled across his scrotum. What dealings had he interrupted?

Words spurted from the young man's mouth. 'Whether the DNA will interact with the bact—'

'You gotta go,' insisted the lab-rat, hopping from paw to paw. 'We got business. Now see! Now!'

Moud, who is this impertinent creature?

The door opened and a scarred balol entered, brandishing a Micro Tavor.

Tekton initiated his Heedless Shadow which shot up from his shoulders like a tossed hat, arming itself as it unfolded. Its kinetic pistol blew the Tavor and the balol's hand back out the door. The balol went howling after both.

'I have paid for this temporary HealthWatch and I *shall* remain here until it works,' said Tekton calmly.

According to station records, Godhead, this laboratory is a bio-merchant's distribution office for an OLOSS company. The 'creature' is simply a local employee.

Tekton's scrotum stopped tingling and tightened.

Which company? The top of the chain, moud, not some insignificant subsidiary.

That information will need to be retrieved from the Vreal Studium Byways. It will be charged to your allowance.

Yes, yes, I know that. Just hurry up!

Manruben gave a cough and began to breathe more evenly. Some of his colour had returned and his belly rumbled. He reached down between his legs and scratched.

. . . There are several inexpert attempts to conceal the connections but the original company is called Jis-Ward Inc . . .

Tekton's prickling testicular prescience spread into a full-scale body quiver. *Who is the Principal?*

While the moud continued to hunt records in the Vreal Byways, Manruben began to hawk and spit and then mutter. Finally he sat up. When his eyes were able to focus, he seemed neither surprised nor concerned. 'Where's that girlie gone?' he demanded. 'I haven't finished wi' her.'

'Sit still, you disgusting bag of bones. I have just paid exorbitantly for temporary HealthWatch which has brought you back from the dead. *You* will now keep away from women until our business is complete.'

Manruben's jaw sagged in dismay. 'You're a harsh one, Tekkie Godhead.'

'Godhead?' said the young man. 'Does that . . . mean you are a tyro – from Belle-Monde?'

Tekton inclined his head. 'I am.'

Good Sole, said Tekton's moud, *it's Dicter Miranda Seeward*.

Aha! Tekton's minds crowed. *Gotcha!*

Instructing the Heedless Shadow to target the agitated lab-rat, Tekton drew the young man by the elbow over to the door, out of earshot. 'And I sense that somehow you have been forced into unfortunate circumstances. Can I be of assistance, perhaps? I have access to the foremost expertise in microbiology.'

The young man held out his hand. 'Thales Berniere from Scolar. I have been tricked into accepting a job as a bio-courier.' He lowered his voice. 'My life has been further complicated by a chance meeting with a man who sought to further exploit my situation.'

'May I enquire who engaged your services on Scolar?'

'A man named Gutnee Paraburd from my homeworld. His real name, I have since learned, is Gutnee Fressian and he is a known criminal. He led me to believe that I was bringing back DNA that would be used in the vaccination of influenza. I am not at all sure that is the truth.'

Tekton's stomach fluttered with excitement. *What is dear Miranda up to in her effort to impress Sole?* 'Perhaps it is time for you to find out.' He reached to the door and flipped the lock. Then he turned purposefully back to the lab-rat who was gnawing the end of the counter in aggravation.

'What is the true nature of the package that Msr Berniere is about to receive?'

The lab-rat made a high-pitched sound. 'I've 'casted for station sec. Your arse is about to be dragged out of here.'

Tekton did not quaver. 'You may have noticed my security float. Not even the OLOSS elite forces would interfere with a gentleman wearing the Heedless Shadow.'

The lab-rat's whiskers quivered. 'That's a Shadow?'

'Indeed. Would you like another display, or is it safe to assume that your job as a wretched laboratory hack is not worth the risk of a mishap?'

'Mishap?'

Tekton instructed the pistol to shoot the leg off Manruben's chair.

The craftsman crashed heavily to the ground, rolling into the middle of the room. 'Oi! Oi!' he cried. 'You be trying to kill a man with fright?'

'If necessary,' said Tekton. He was enjoying himself immensely. More so, even, than during his blackmailing of Labile Connit.

The lab-rat had crouched down behind the counter. Tekton could hear him gnawing the catoplasma.

'Stand and speak,' he ordered. 'Or . . .'

'Steady, steady,' the 'rat said. It popped its head around the corner. 'You said it. I'm the hack. I just gun the couriers with their payload and go home. Don't get involved past that.'

Tekton told The Shadow to target the middle of the counter.

The lab-rat spied the pistol realigning and a few moments later Tekton smelled the pungent aroma of urine.

'I jus' know the disease targets the orbitofrontal cortex,' it squeaked.

'To what purpose?' Tekton could barely keep the shrill excitement out of his voice.

The lab-rat peeped up and gave him a deprecating look. 'To affect decision-making, of course. There are some subtleties to it that I don't get. Haven't seen it at work yet. Clever, though.'

'Why would she want to affect decision-making on Scolar?' mused Tekton aloud.

Thales reached a hand out to the wall to steady himself. His face had drained of all colour. 'I think I know. But you said "she". Who is "she"?'

The lab-rat, Thales and Manruben all stared expectantly at Tekton.

TRIN

He should have been relieved, even pleased, that Jilda was alive. Yet each evening as they boarded the flat-yachts to sail to the next island Trin's irritation grew. At first he had tolerated her joy, was even able to endure her obsessive embraces and fondling. But within days her prattle and her moaning and her needs became the burden they had always been.

She wept too long at the news that Franco was dead.

'He gave you neither respect nor love and yet you grieve for him?' Trin dug angrily into the sand, preparing a daytime hollow for them both. This island was larger than previous ones and had a shadowy spread of stunted bushes. Under Semantic's indifferent glow he had chosen his shade bush furthest from the others. They were curious about his reunion with the Principessa. Too quick to listen and talk among themselves.

'It would be the same if you had died, *mio figlio*. You have not always treated me respectfully but a woman loves with her heart, not her mind. Franco was a strong man, Trinder.'

'And I am not?'

Jilda clasped his hand and patted it in a way that made his stomach churn. 'You have saved these people. You are destined to be like your father – a leader. But it was hard for you to become that in the shadow of his greatness. It was the right decision to send you to Loisa. He would be proud of you.'

'Franco would never have been proud of me, madre. I am your child.'

His barb stung her to silence and she huddled disconsolately in the grey dark, a frail, unkempt woman in the tatters of a grand fellalo.

Trin continued to scoop out sand. Dawn was close now and Djeserit still hadn't returned to the shallows. He had seen little of her during the past few days, as if she was hesitant to come near him since rescuing Jilda.

It was Jilda and her Galiotto servant who recounted their escape from the Palazzo Island. They told Trin how they had been hiding in a backhouse since the Saqr had landed at the Palazzo, living on sea vegetables and molluscs that the Galiotto collected from the tide line under the cover of dark.

When they were alone the Galiotto also told Trin of her meeting with Mira Fedor, and how the mercenaries had killed her brother before her eyes. The girl wept as she remembered the chore of burying him, using shells to dig deep enough into the sand. Her voice became so thick with emotion that Trin could barely understand her. But finally, when she had unburdened the worst of her memories, she sat up straighter and managed a tremulous smile. 'The Baronessa entrusted a message to me. She said that you must go further south to the Galgos, that the Saqr would not follow you into the water. And scuzzi, Principe. Felicitazione for your bambino!'

Trin was stunned for a moment. 'How do you know this?'

'Baronessa Fedor spoke of it. She wanted your madre to know.'

'How kind of the Baronessa,' he said softly. 'And did you pass this news to the Principessa?'

The girl bowed her head. 'I-I have not. It seemed—'

'How did it seem, Tina?' Trin urged.

'I was not sure if it was true. The Baronessa was distraught. Not in a calm mind.' The servant trembled, fearing that she had given offence.

Trin put a comforting, collusive hand on her shoulder. 'You must not speak of this to anyone, Tina. Mira Fedor deserted us and escaped with the mercenaries. It has caused much upset among those who are left.'

Tina Galiotto's face registered shock. 'But I thought that the Baronessa had left to bring help for our world.'

'No!' said Trinder quickly, barely controlling his impulse to shake the girl. 'That is not so, Tina Galiotto, and do not let me catch you speaking of such things.'

'*Si*, Principe.' She bowed her head. '*Si*.'

Trin returned to the beach after he had fashioned day-hollows for Jilda and himself, leaving her to be tended by her servant. Djeserit had left them only a small amount of fish and Juno Genarro had taken help to search the lightening shoreline for weed and edible sponges. Trin could see the group now, bent to their task, shaking sand from weed and piling it into makeshift slings.

A small group lingered around Joe Scali as he fussed over the tiny desalinator that Djeserit had brought from the Palazzo. Lack of fresh water was their biggest single fear. If the desalinator broke they would perish.

Trin turned his gaze back the way they had come. The islands were like dark stones on the lighter sea and behind them was the long, unending shadow of the mainland. How he longed for the taste of cooked meat and the mellow flavour of Araldisian wine on his palate. They were simple cravings but profound and they brought with them a surge of disproportionate rage. How long could they keep up this ridiculous flight of bare survival? And Djeserit – she could not continue the gruelling duty of providing food for so many.

He kicked out angrily against the gently slapping water, repeating the action until his legs shook with fatigue and the pain of fury weighed deeply in his chest.

Trin threw himself down then, his face barely clear of the water, his hands gripping deep into the sand against the pull of the tide. It would be easy to drift out of his depth. It would not take long to drown – like all the Ciprianos he was a poor swimmer. Perhaps he should have left with Mira Fedor and taken his child to another place.

'Trinder?'

Djeserit was there, surfacing alongside him, blowing a gentle exhalation spray from her gills.

Trin rolled on his side to face her. 'How did you know?' he said hoarsely. 'How did you know that I needed you?'

She gave a low chuckle, a sound rusty from lack of use. 'I heard you, Principe. You cannot thump at the water in such a way without deafening us.'

Us? The word caught in his chest. 'You have been avoiding me.'

Djes buckled onto her knees and cupped Trin's face

in her hands with her thick webbed fingers. Her face was changing, her skin glistening like that of the fish she pulled fresh from the sea for them to eat.

'Not avoiding you. I've been exploring as far ahead as I could and I've got news. There are two islands between us and a deep channel. On the other side of the channel there's a bigger place where I think we can stay – high cliffs and thick vegetation. Never seen it like that before on Araldis.'

Trin sat up, pulled her onto his lap and kissed her. They sank down into the water together, flattening their profile to the curious watchers. Her arms felt cool and prickly around him as if scales were forming on them, and her mouth had the briny taste of the seaweed that they had all been eating. He was losing her to the sea and yet he could not make her stop. Her special physiology was all that kept them alive.

'You are sure?'

Djes nodded. 'I left the water and walked as far as I could before I had to turn back to still be here before dawn. The island is huge. Fifty times the size of this one.' She sounded excited now.

'The channel must be the Galgos Straits. Will the flat-yachts be able to navigate it?'

'I think the crossing will take more than a day. It's rough and I had to swim deeper than I wanted to, to avoid a family of xoc.'

She said it quickly, with no great emphasis, but Trin's heart contracted. 'Xoc! Then you must not go out again. It is too dangerous.'

Djes patted her webbed hand against Trin's cheek and breathed salty flavours into his nose and mouth.

'You'll need me in the water for the crossing. It's not like these gentle passages. There're reefs that you won't see until you run across them.'

'But—'

Her hand pressed to his mouth. 'I will come aboard to rest.'

Trin could think of no argument to deter her. Her devotion to him somehow neutralised the offensiveness of her independent manner. Or perhaps it was simply that she made such simple, logical decisions. Unlike Cass Mulravey whose abrasive way and ready prejudices were like oxygen to his fire.

'When we reach the new island, we will be able to fish for ourselves. You will come back to the land,' he said.

But the mounting light showed Trin the uncertainty in Djes's expression, and he pulled her tightly to him. 'You will,' he repeated.

The uuli guide led Jo-Jo and Catchut through a series of smaller compartments into a large darkened space. The dim lighting revealed the convocation chamber to be a catoplasma balloon ridged with concentric seating – and stinking of an unreasonable fusion of odours.

Jo-Jo's throat began to close again. He massaged it from the outside and told himself that he couldn't be allergic to sweat.

They were shown to armchairs at the bottom of the chamber.

'When you are ready to convene, make contact with the conductive strip in the curve of your headrest. I will return to you afterwards,' said the uuli.

Catchut poked the strip with suspicion. 'Like my virtuals to be somethin' I can put on and take off,' he grumbled. 'Never know what they're stealin' from you otherwise.'

Jo-Jo had an urge to laugh. He hadn't reckoned Catchut for a Luddite.

'Why don't you just sit and watch me breathe, then?'

Catchut growled and banged his head back against the sensor. A few seconds later his face relaxed.

Jo-Jo leaned into the strip more carefully. But the transition was smooth enough and he found himself in a perfect representation of the same chamber surrounded by tiers of bodies engaged in the type of squabbling behaviour that Jo-Jo had spent most of his life avoiding.

He glanced across at Catchut. The mercenary had chosen a female avatar with long, sensuous legs: a suitable companion for a God-Discoverer.

Suppressing his desire to laugh, Jo-Jo let the clash of the surrounding arguments sink into his mind, sorting one thread from another. One section of the convocation was bickering over trade agreements with OLOSS, while a smaller, less vocal core were analysing the reason for the unusually large presence of Extropists on Rho Six. Beneath those layers of discussion were individual conversations. He skimmed across them until one blew all other thoughts from his mind: a report of a shooting incident in the Heijunka section of Bell One between a hired balol security guard and a visiting Lostolian archiTect.

Lostolian archiTect?

'Convocation has the privilege of an unexpected visit from one of Orion's most notable speakers, Josef Rasterovich the Third, frequently referred to as the God-Discoverer. Welcome, Msr Rasterovich,' announced the speaker.

No. But . . .

Jo-Jo was forced to launch into his patter, which he delivered while he tried to follow the sub-channelling. Annoyingly, most of it had stopped or had dropped below his auditory level. The Convocation, it seemed, were captivated by his story.

To his relief the speaker called for a break before question time.

Jo-Jo leapt from his chair. Nausea from the rapid

reality switch burned its way up his oesophagus. He burped it out and called for the uuli escort.

'What is it?' Catchut was standing behind him, blinking and clutching his stomach. 'What happened?'

'Msr?' The uuli escort appeared from inside the chamber.

'There is talk of a shooting in the Heijunka district. Where can I find out more about it?'

The uuli took some time to reply. 'There is a public viewer outside the chamber should you wish to access public news.'

'Show me.'

The uuli slid ahead of them, back through the small antechambers and out into a heavily trafficked section.

Jo-Jo ran past it to the closest 'cast node but the queues wound back for half a mesur into the CBD.

Catchut was breathing in his ear. 'What in fuckin' cruxsakes are you—'

'Another one. I need another 'cast.'

'There is another one behind the water tower,' volunteered the uuli. It had caught up with them and was contorting in and out of shape, as if agitated.

Jo-Jo, followed by Catchut, ran the short distance to the node behind a large cylindrical tank. He thumbed the shortcast into action and began searching the feeds. The story was logged in Gal, between unverified reports that the Arrivals Bell was being closed while The Families investigated the flood of Extropists onto the mesa-worlds, and a notice that the TAFTers' Convocation was in progress.

Jo-Jo opted for audio only and peeled an earpiece

from the dispenser. He listened carefully to the report and then placed a query.

The reply was quick. 'The identity of the archiTect is not public information at this time.'

Jo-Jo cued up the unverified sources. 'Potential identification?' he asked.

They all returned the same educated guess. 'Tekton of Lostol.'

Jo-Jo reeled back. 'Well, fuck me, Carnage Farr. Did your System Device predict that?'

Then a thought slapped him across the head. He blanked out the feed and stepped away from the 'caster. Farr hadn't shown him a tool for forecasting at all – he didn't want to predict the future, he wanted to shape it. It was a Bifurcation Device. And where in Crux had he got the technology for that?

Realisation became a throb in his temple. There was only one possible answer—

'Rasterovich!'

It was Catchut, with Rast Randall standing beside him.

'Saw the Capo on the other side of the node.'

Jo-Jo glanced around. 'Where are Beth and the Baronessa?'

Rast hesitated. There was a shifty look in her eyes that could have been guilt. 'I got called away to do some business. Sent 'em back straight back to the 'zoon. Only . . .'

'Only what?' Jo-Jo demanded.

'Only I just tried to 'cast them. Can't get a reply.'

MIRA

According to the tourist guide in Mira's ear, the markets that populated the Rho Six docks never closed. Vendors replenished their stocks from flat-backed automons which meandered down the rows with arrogant lack of concern for the passing foot traffic.

Mira was overwhelmed by the collision of pungent smells and the colours and shapes of the myriad sentient forms. She found herself wanting to reach for Bethany's hand like a child afraid of losing its mother in a crowd. She had craved to see such a place but now, confronted by it, she was terrified.

'Siphonophores. Incredible,' breathed Bethany as a group of nearly transparent creatures passed by them. 'Their feet are so fluid it's as though they are floating.'

Mira glanced at the pale suckered rippling flaps of skin that flowed across the floorspace. 'They look amphibious.'

'Probably were,' said Rast Randall. 'The Extros would have modified them when they stole their bodies.'

'Then it is true?' exclaimed Mira.

The mercenary stood aside from them a little, watching. 'What? That they are body stealers? Yep. They poach bodies like we change clothes.' She looked down at the borrowed Cipriano robe that she had worn over her grey garb almost constantly since Araldis. 'Well, most of the time, anyway. And they don't care too much about the organism they've used up, either.'

'In their defence, they normally pick a sub-sentient species,' said Bethany.

'"In their defence"?' Rast didn't attempt to hide a sneer. 'Why would you be defending them?'

Bethany flushed and shrugged. 'Just a comment.'

Rast had been restless and antagonistic ever since they had left *Insignia*. As if the mercenary was pre-empting trouble.

'How long do you think Thales will be?' asked Mira.

'Shouldn't take long to give him the shot. Might be Rasterovich that takes the time.' Rast frowned. 'Seems like a lot of Extros on the docks and up there.' She pointed to the high part of the dome where extraordinary butterfly-like creatures glided about.

'They are Extropists.'

'I'm guessing,' said Rast.

'I've seen them like that in the war, only far less innocent. Those ones were carrying lots of military fruit.'

Mira was entranced by the grace and shining transparency of their wings. 'It's hard to imagine.'

'I've tried to tell you this before, Fedor. Never underestimate an Extro in any form.'

They moved on slowly. 'What are those?' Mira pointed to large once-white catoplasma tubes stacked alongside each other like bits of a flattened hive.

'Cheap sleeper units,' said Bethany. 'Not everyone can afford proper accommodation in these places.'

'But there must be barely enough room to roll over in them,' said Mira.

'Space comes at a price in these places, Baronessa. You planet people never really get that.'

'Why? Were you born in one of these?' asked Mira innocently.

Rast guffawed and for a moment Mira was almost enjoying herself.

Then a thickset ordinary male humanesque detached himself from the milling crowd of buyers and touched Rast's elbow.

The mercenary twisted his fingers backward in a cruel and deft move.

Mira stepped back at the look of pain on the 'esque's face. With her other hand Rast patted the weapon under her robe.

She spoke a couple of quiet words in the man's ear and let him go. He hastened back to the throng.

Rast glanced across at Mira and Bethany. 'You know which docking tunnel we came through?'

'*Si.*' Mira pivoted and pointed to the Tau Crux symbol above one of the many tube ends.

'Berniere should be well on his way to his errand now. When it's done we need to dust this place. Finish up your gawking and get back to the 'zoon. Don't let anyone other than us on board.'

'Why? Where are you going?' Bethany asked anxiously.

Mira's stomach knotted. Rast was leaving them alone. She had foolishly expected the mercenary to be dependable. Since that moment aboard *Insignia* when she had bared her soul Rast had been different. So she had thought.

'Got some business to attend to that can't wait,' said

Rast. She strode away towards the fast-trak without another word.

'So much for our protection,' said Bethany. She looked less composed now, her face a sheen of perspiration. 'What is she up to, I wonder?'

Mira guessed what it was. She had seen the satchel outlined beneath her robe beside the mercenary's weapon – but she did not share her knowledge with Bethany. She was Lasper Farr's sister. Like Trinder and Franco Pellegrini, familia traits often ran deeper than appearance. Even Rast didn't deserve that kind of betrayal.

'I think we should return to *Insignia*. I am not sure that we are altogether safe alone,' Mira said. Her imagination was already at work. The crowd seemed to have closed in on them without Rast there, as though the mercenary exuded some sort of personal power that demanded space.

'Yes,' Bethany agreed.

They began to retrace their route to *Insignia* but within a few steps of joining the main stream of traffic they were engulfed by a group of the towering transparent jelly creatures. Bethany and Mira were separated. Mira reached through the gelatinous wall for Bethany's hand but what had appeared to be fluid flesh was now as rigid and impenetrable as steel. She let their motion propel her along, fighting off the sensation of suffocation. *They will pass me by and I will be free of them. They will pass . . .*

But a few steps later black ink squirted through the siphonophores' bodies and they lost all transparency.

Mira tried to call out to Bethany but her voice was dry with fear.

Then she felt her body lifted up by their momentum and the light faded to something terribly, terribly dark.

JO-JO RASTEROVICH

'You what!?' Jo-Jo's fists balled in anger and fear lodged in his throat. If Rast had endangered Mira Fedor he would rip the mercenary apart.

Rast saw his expression and squared her shoulders. She stuck out her jaw. 'They were a few hundred mesurs from the docking tube. They've probably gone off sightseeing. Never seen such a pair of gawkers.'

'Msr Rasterovich. You're required to return to the Convocation.' It was the uuli. It stayed outside their tense huddle, twisting its torso nervously.

Jo-Jo swore in every way he could. He had to finish the Convocation discussion to keep trouble away from Berniere – but right now there were only two things he *wanted* to do, and he wanted to do them at the same time. Find Mira and hunt down Tekton. He cut his losses and turned to the uuli.

'Show's over, mate. A friend's in trouble.'

The uuli's skin flushed a rainbow of colours, which Jo-Jo expected meant that it was pissed off. 'It is not appropriate to leave Convocation before dismissal—'

'Tell Convocation that they've got more things to worry about than my interrupted story. This place is crawling with Extros and I don't think it's for the sightseeing. I'd say you've got problems. Jo-Jo turned his back on the uuli then and faced Rast. 'You'd better go and find her, hadn't you?'

For a moment Rast looked like she might argue but Jo-Jo let his expression become ugly. Rast might be an experienced fighter but he had reason. Reason was worth shitloads. So was a 'nothing to lose' attitude.

Rast read all that there and nodded. 'I'll take Catchut. And you?'

'Where is Berniere?'

'Heijunka section near The Hocs. Factory unit is in FF. Will be a medi-lab, I would reckon.'

Heijunka was where Tekton had been reported. Jo-Jo pictured the tourist map. 'Bell One. I'll find Berniere and get him out of there. I've got a bad feeling about these Extros. They're everywhere.'

Rast nodded. 'That's why I was looking for you. I think we should pull out.'

'Agreed. See you back at the 'zoon. And Randall – it better be good news.'

The two exchanged looks and walked away.

The fast-trak to Bell One only increased Jo-Jo's agitation. It was crowded with strange Extro-inhabited creatures, many of the floating gelatinous kind but others as well, including a group of small, almost humanesque-shaped bodies who had what looked like bones protruding through their skin. The rattling as the bones clattered against each other was the most reassuring of their attributes. They bore no facial characteristics on the segment of their body that should have been their head but Jo-Jo noticed a bulbous pod under each arm that was coated in several layers of translucent tissue and was ringed by fine spines. They kept their arms permanently lifted, as if airing their sides but Jo-Jo wondered if it was to allow them to see. They were utterly silent and utterly alien.

By the time he reached the exit conveyor for Bell One, Jo-Jo was drenched in sweat and strung out with worry about the various possibilities. What if Tekton had left the area? What if he was still there? What if he couldn't find Latourn and Berniere? What if Mira Fedor was in trouble? What if Mira Fedor—

'Rasterovich!'

Jo-Jo jumped at the sound of his name. Latourn was standing in the up-queue waiting to get on the fast-trak. He glanced around for Berniere but couldn't see the scholar. He threw up his hands in a questioning gesture.

Latourn dug his hands into his pockets and narrowed his eyes in a mirror of Rast's action. Jo-Jo took one stride to the dividing barrier and punched him in the solar plexus. Latourn howled and doubled over.

Jo-Jo hauled the bigger man over the barricade, barely feeling the weight. On either side of them 'esques and aliens scattered to give them room but he shoved Latourn down the conveyor and out of the main stream of pedestrians until he had him backed up against a structural pylon. 'What fucking game are you and your boss playing? You're supposed to be with Berniere.'

Latourn pulled a sullen face.

It was then that Jo-Jo noticed the cuts on him: a fine network of them at the base of his throat and on his forearms where his shirtsleeves were pulled up. He grabbed

Latourn's shirt at the waist and jerked it up to expose his stomach. The mercenary cringed and tried to wrest the material from Jo-Jo's grasp.

Jo-Jo let it go in disgust. The cuts on Latourn's stomach were deeper than those on his arms and were neatly connected with stitching like a child's joining game, excepting where Jo-Jo had punched him. There they were torn and bleeding.

'If you've been in The Hocs then where's the idiot?'

Latourn fumbled to tuck his shirt in and Jo-Jo noted the glassy eyes. He was stoned as well.

Just as well. Or I— Jo-Jo's thought stopped there.

Latourn had pulled a blood-sticky knife from his pocket. He swung it in an unsteady arc. 'Get out of my face, God-man,' Latourn hissed. 'Everyone deserves a little downtime.'

Jo-Jo didn't flinch. 'Your boss took a little downtime and and now Mira Fedor is missing. What's yours cost us?'

'She's gone?' Latourn's knife hand dropped to his side.

'Maybe. Randall's looking for her. This place is Extro soup, so we're pulling out.'

Some of the glassiness left Latourn's eyes. 'Berniere went ahead of me to a factory in Heijunka. When I got there, I found a dead balol and a lab-rat that had shitted up its lab gear.'

Jo-Jo's adrenalin spiked so hard that his temples hurt. 'A dead balol? How long ago?'

'Less than an hour, maybe. No police but the rat had called them so I pissed off. Took the scenic route back here, to stay low.'

'Did the lab-rat say where Berniere had gone?'

'It was jabbering stupid about a Shadow.' Latourn shrugged. 'Didn't think Berniere had the balls to shoot a balol.'

'He doesn't. Sounds like he's got company of some kind,' said Jo-Jo flatly. Was it Tekton? The news feed fitted too closely for it to be anyone else. But why would Tekton shoot a balol? Smarts didn't usually get their hands dirty on anything – Jo-Jo knew that from experience. He wanted to go and talk to the lab-rat but that was too risky from how Latourn had described things. Where would Berniere go if he'd got caught in some crossfire? He would run home – to the biozoon and the protection of the mercenaries.

Jo-Jo turned and began to walk away.

'Hey!' shouted Latourn. 'Where are you going?'

Jo-Jo didn't care to waste his breath on an answer.

TRIN

'We will have to make part of the trip in daylight, Principe,' said Juno Genarro.

He crouched near Trin in the wet sand of the last bay island, peering across the Galgos Straits. Tiesha was high but Semantic was on the wane, yet even the softness of their light could not disguise the rough chop of the waves.

'How far do you think?'

'Maybe fifteen mesurs. A day and a night on the water.'

'It took me half of that to get there and back,' said Djeserit. She had come out of the water and sat next to Juno. Her legs were too weak to stand and he could hear the breathiness in her voice. 'But I was able to swim the currents.'

'The yachts are like sinkers in the water,' said Joe Scali, slapping miserably at the sand fleas that had turned his skin to welts. The fleas worried all of them, but Joe Scali and some of the women suffered worst. Trin had not seen his friend smile in so long that he had almost forgotten that person. This Joe was full of worry and pessimism. Even if they found a place to live and thrive, Trin wondered if Joe would ever be able to see the lighter side of things again. Would any of them?

'They are buoyant enough,' Trin corrected him. 'But they are not built for the open sea.'

'Built for aristos to lounge around on in the evenings, sipping from their kiante bottles.'

Trin did not bother to turn and acknowledge the voice. Only one person among them spoke to him with such insolence. Djes and Joe Scali had lobbied for Cass Mulravey's presence here. It was better, they said, to keep her close. Yet her presence made him stiff with anger, worse even than the way he felt near Jilda. At least his madre understood her place.

'I would think twice before ridiculing them – or me, Cass Mulravey. We are your only protection.' Trin let threat enter his tone. It was time that the woman was put down.

She made a derisive sound but said no more. Irritatingly, though, she came and stood next to him.

'We will need shade and ropes, Principe. In such waters it will be easy to be swept away. The yachts have no sides.'

'We could knot weed together for rope and tie each person to the masthead,' suggested Djes. 'And make shades from the spine bushes.'

Trin visualised her idea. It could work. It would have to work. 'It will take us several days to prepare the ropes. Joe, I want you to desalinate as much water as you can and store it in the larger shells that we have collected. We will take extra with us in case we cannot stay close enough together. Mulravey, your women will collect the weed and knot it together.'

'And what will your men do, Pellegrini? Or will their "protection" be enough of a blessing?'

This time Trin did turn to her, making no attempt to disguise his annoyance. 'My men will take a yacht and return to the last island to collect spine bush. There is not enough here to both shade us and to tear down. And if you question me again, I will withdraw my protection and you will be left to your own resources.'

Mulravey rocked forward on her heels as if she might launch herself at him. Trin could smell her stale sweat and see the knots in her straggling hair. Her shape was mannish under her envirosuit, her breasts limp and flat.

'Please, Cass Mulravey, your women are so exhausted and weak – it is the better task for them,' said Djeserit. 'I can show them the strongest kelp. This trip will be our last.'

Mulravey exhaled slowly and settled back on her heels. 'You are right, Djeserit. Despite the fish you brought us, many of them are still so weak that they can barely walk. I'll gather those that can and bring them back here. You can show us where to find the best weed.' She turned and walked up the beach.

'You would have made a good diplomat, Djes,' said Joe Scali after Mulravey had gone. He had a respect in his voice that Trin had not heard before.

'Thank you for the food, Djeserit,' said Juno Genarro. 'I had not thought that raw fish could taste so good. You've saved us from starving, girl. And from giving up.'

The men's attention made her shy. Trin could tell that by the way she drew her legs to her chest. 'There is fresh water on the new island,' she said, deflecting

their comments. 'And caves. And the vegetation promises fruits and nuts.'

'Then I say we get on with it,' said Juno. 'Principe?'

'*Si*,' said Trinder thoughtfully. '*Si*.'

THALES

Thales nursed the gene gun on his lap, his eyes fixed on the Petri bubble. The Godhead had hired a taxi to take them back to the Arrivals Bell so they could speak privately. He was grateful to – and terrified by – Tekton in the same disturbing vortex of emotions.

The archiTects of his acquaintance had all been self-absorbed aesthetes. It was a manner that Thales felt comfortable around – for philosopers, though not always aesthetes, were indeed inclined to similar preoccupations.

But Tekton was something more than that. He had shot the balol without compunction and had seemed only interested in preserving the life of the filthy old man whom he had brought into the clinic for a specific reason. Human compassion did not appear to figure highly, if indeed at all, on Tekton's agenda – which made Thales nervous, for the Godhead appeared to be helping him. Thales could only deduce one thing from this: that Tekton had his own reasons for doing so.

Thales would not be fooled again by a veneer of philanthropy, as he had been with Gutnee Paraburd.

I can change. I can learn.

He suddenly longed to see Bethany. This longing came with a surprise realisation. He had come to rely on her opinion in such a short time. Despite her blunt ways, Bethany understood men of this calibre, had mingled with these calculating types all her life. Her own brother was one.

'And you say you travelled here on a biozoon piloted by a *female*. How does an educated young man from Scolar find himself on such a beast? I've heard they have the odour of a butchery.'

Thales lifted his gaze to meet his saviour's. Tekton was of a similar build to him, but his skin was unnaturally tight over his skeleton, and his face was without eyebrows or eyelashes, his head without hair. It created an effect of brittleness and witlessness that was clearly misleading. Tekton lacked neither energy nor perspicacity.

'I have never been in such an establishment, but it does remind me of the smell of vinegar-cured meats,' said Thales.

Tekton wrinkled his pert nose. 'How appalling.'

'You become accustomed to it, Godhead, as one does with anything, over time,' Thales added.

'I am not one to accustom myself to anything. But tell me how this came about – you and the biozoon? You mentioned blackmail – a word that one should never utter lightly.'

'There is nothing light about my situation, Godhead, except perhaps your intervention in it.' Then Thales told him how it had started: Gutnee and his deceptive courier mission, Sophos Mianos, and his escape with the Baronessa and her mercenaries.

'Can you tell me why a Latino noblewoman was meeting with OLOSS officials between Scolar and its shift station?'

'They were suspicious of her biozoon and did not wish it to come close to our planet. The Baronessa comes from a place called Araldis; a distant mining planet that has recently been overrun by an alien species. She was the only one to escape – saved by her ability to pilot the biozoon. She is fiercely determined to save those that are left – but OLOSS are not convinced.'

Tekton did not respond immediately and appeared to be listening to another voice. So Thales went back to contemplating the bubble of the gene gun. What were the contents intended to do, he wondered? If he still had access to Alambra he could ask her to research the function of the orbitofrontal cortex. He missed her voice in his head. Mouds were another thing to which one became accustomed.

'And this Latino woman is still with you?' asked Tekton abruptly.

'Yes. She is charged with returning me to Edo, as are the mercenaries. Then Lasper Farr will oblige her with a force to recapture her world.'

'Lasper Farr?' Tekton's thin-lipped mouth fell open in undisguised shock. '*Carnage* Farr?'

Thales nodded angrily. 'It is an apt name. At his best he is psychopathic. At his worst . . . who can say what such a man could do?'

'He is the one who has sent you here to retrieve the DNA? Or was it the man Gutnee?'

'Farr discovered that my blood contained a barrier substance used by couriers. He . . . questioned me at some length, and compelled me to come here and receive the DNA. I am to return it to him instead of to Gutnee.'

Tekton's lips curved in a sly smile. 'You could say that he saw an opportunity.'

Thales nodded again. 'To ensure my compliance he infected me with a bacterium that the barrier will not stop. I must return the DNA – and myself, obviously – to receive the antidote.' He stopped then. Sick of it all, and of himself. Perhaps he had told the Godhead too much about his situation. But leverage was what he needed, and that was something he sensed that Tekton could provide.

'Then our meeting is most providential, Thales Berniere. And I look forward to meeting the Latino Baronessa.'

'She is a most refined woman,' allowed Thales, 'who has been forced into poor company.'

'Aaah, yes,' said Tekton. 'That is something we must all zealously guard against.'

Thales nodded a third time. On that point, he and the Godhead were in complete agreement.

Bethany was waiting just inside the biozoon's egress scale. She flung herself upon Thales and clung to him.

Conscious of Tekton's presence, Thales tried to hold her away at a distance. But she would not be deterred.

He leaned back to peer down at her face. 'Bethany, this is Godhead Tekton, a tyro to the Entity on Belle-Monde.'

But Bethany either did not hear him or would not heed him. She raised her head and stared at him with tear-swollen eyes. 'Thales, the Extros have taken the Baronessa. Randall left us at the markets on the docks. We – we knew it wasn't safe so we started to head back here to *Insignia*. But they overran us – a bunch of siphonophores – I tried to grab her hand but it was like a wall between us. And when they'd gone, so was she. The biozoon let me on board, but it's distressed – can't you hear it?'

Thales listened. The creature's normally dull internal noises were sharper, the way it sounded when its system was altering pattern.

'I think she must have been taken off Rho Junction. The biozoon is getting ready to leave. What should we do? Should we get off? Josef hasn't returned yet.'

'You're the only one here?'

'Yes.' Bethany finally glanced at Tekton. 'Pardon me, Godhead, but our . . . friend has—'

'Yes, yes,' said the Godhead, speaking quickly. 'Tragic and worrying. May I offer a quick alternative?'

'Y-yes,' stammered Beth. She glanced at Thales for his agreement. 'I guess so.'

'Msr Berniere has apprised me briefly of your situation and I find myself in a position to offer some help. Not for the Baronessa, I'm afraid, but for you. I would offer you lodgings on a luxury ship and conveyance to Akouedo. And before you ask why, let me say that I am appalled at Msr Berniere's circumstances, so it seems the least I can do. The cost is incidental to me. However, time is crucial. It seems this biozoon has imminent plans to follow its Innate and, as you will understand, Thales, I have the need to avoid station sec. I do not wish to get caught up in untidy or prolonged investigations. There is a liner leaving within the half-hour and I have booked passage on it. It departs from the dock opposite this one.'

'I don't know that—' Bethany began to refuse but Thales grabbed her hand.

'Bethany, come with me,' he said.

'But what about Lasper?' she said.

Thales held up the gene gun. 'I have the DNA here. Surely Lasper will accept that and will provide me with the bacterium antidote.'

Some of the worry lines eased from Bethany's face. 'You didn't have the injection?'

'No.' He smiled. 'It will take time to tell the events as they happened but Godhead Tekton has made a generous offer, Beth. I want to take it.'

'But the Baronessa?'

'I am concerned for her too but the mercenaries will see to her safety,' he soothed. 'What could we do anyway?'

'And Josef?'

Thales frowned. 'Whose company would you prefer to be in – mine or his?'

Bethany chewed her lip in indecision. 'It's just that I owe Josef a debt of sorts. Without him I would not have escaped Dowl station, without him—'

Thales put his finger to her lips. 'Please, please come.'

Her stare searched his face. 'But what does it mean, Thales?'

'Freedom,' he whispered. 'For both of us.'

Bethany took a deep breath and kissed him. 'I have to leave Josef a message.'

Thales nodded. 'I will collect our things.'

Thales returned with a pitifully small bundle that contained both his and Bethany's belongings.

Tekton stood impatiently by the egress scale, shifting from one foot to the other. He was listening to his moud again and Thales felt a stab of envy.

'We must hurry. *The Last Aesthetic's* moud has contacted me to say that they will close boarding in a few minutes. The station has put a hold on incoming traffic and dis-embarkation is moving through more rapidly.'

'I've left Josef a message on his cabin intracast.' Bethany came up behind them. She glanced around. '*Insignia*'s starting to vibrate.' She pushed her hand into the pucker of the egress scale. When it peeled back Tekton led them out and along the docking tube.

At the entrance he turned to the right and caught the conveyor that took them on a loop around the venti-lation shaft that penetrated the centre of the docks.

Thales stared out at the markets that hugged the rim of the shaft: hundreds of stalls and booths selling food and trinkets and filter masks. A stretch of cato-plasma tubes like the ones in the Heijunka, advertised as cheap sleeping compartments.

Tekton got off the conveyor and directed them to a tube entrance bearing a humanesque-shaped hand as its symbol. The tube was almost opposite *Insignia* but nearly a full mesur away.

Thales pointed to the symbol. 'A good omen,' he said to Bethany. 'It's a Jain symbol called Ahisma.'

But she had stepped off the conveyor to the other side and was standing on her toes, peering back towards *Insignia*.

Both Tekton and Thales went across to her.

'You have a special friend whom you do not wish to leave?' Tekton enquired politely.

'Yes, in a way. At least, I would like to have seen him and . . . Oh! There! Thales, it's Josef.'

Thales followed the line of her out-thrust arm to where *Insignia* was docked. He could see Jo-Jo Rasterovich and the three mercenaries gathered around the mouth of the biozoon's tube.

'Josef!' Bethany shouted and waved her hands. 'Jo—'

Rasterovich saw her and waved back. He began to run towards the conveyor on his side but the white haired mercenary blocked his escape, grabbing him roughly.

Tekton clamped his hand over Bethany's wrist. 'This is not a time for problematical goodbyes, and anything that might require your deliberation means you will miss departure.'

'Beth!' pleaded Thales. 'Don't complicate this.' The Ahisma symbol had begun to flash. 'The liner is leaving.'

Beth swallowed as if relieving a dry throat and then nodded.

Tekton removed his hand.

She gave Jo-Jo one more wave and turned and followed after Thales.

JO-JO RASTEROVICH

'Beth! Wait! Don't go anywhere with that prick!' Jo-Jo tried to bellow but his throat was thick with allergy again. He started across the docks towards the conveyor but Rast Randall apprehended him in an untidy head-lock before he could set foot on it.

'What are you doing?' She wrestled him to a kneeling position before she loosened her hold. Her white hair was plastered to her head as if she'd been running – not just to catch him – and she stank of her sweat.

'She's – leaving – on that – liner with – Berniere and—'

Rast shook him. 'Listen! So what! We've got other problems. Fedor is still missing and the biozoon's prepping itself to depart.'

Jo-Jo glanced back, still panting from his exertion. His eyes were streaming and he dashed the moisture away. The Tau Crux symbol flashed the docked craft's intention to leave. 'But it's got no pilot.'

'It's a 'zoon. When their biologics start to buzz the station's just got to let them go.'

Jo-Jo looked back the other way. Bethany was disappearing into the tube with Thales and a slim Lostol wearing a bulky hat. Jo-Jo hadn't seen Tekton since Belle-Monde but he knew him in an instant. 'Fedor might be with them.'

'No. She's not.'

Jo-Jo frowned. 'How so sure?'

'I talked to every damn thing on this dock with a heartbeat – and to some without. The Extros took her. That's a fact. I'd say the 'zoon's following her. What are you going to do?'

Never – even in those terrible moments afloat in the vacuum of space – had Jo-Jo ever felt so utterly torn.

Tekton was the reason he was alive, the reason he hadn't ripped off his face-mask out in space and let his lungs flatten. Revenge had given him a reason to live and he'd grabbed it with utter and complete conviction. Every blink, every twitch of his muscles since then had been about achieving it.

Not only that, but something that he'd thought to be a small annoyance was turning into a large concern: his throat, the itch and the watering of his eyes. Lasper Farr had given him something in that inhaler back on Edo. As a priority he needed to get back into the Junction proper and find a booth where he could renew his HealthWatch and scan his immune system.

But Mira Fedor . . . he found it impossible to breathe even *thinking* that she was hurt or in pain. He wanted to slit Rast Randall open for her neglect; he wanted . . . *What do I want?*

'Rasterovich?' Rast was moving backwards towards the 'zoon, holding her hands up in question. Catchut and Latourn were already inside the tube.

But Jo-Jo couldn't answer. He was caught in a conflict. He waited for his minds to slide apart as they had done in times of stress ever since Sole had interfered' with him. The detestable sensation was preferable to paralysis.

But this time his mind remained glued together and completely opaque to thought.

Rast gave him a quick salute and dropped her hands. She turned and ran into the tube after her men.

Jo-Jo stood there. *Nothing* from his mind. He wiped his eyes again and coughed.

Nothing.

But slowly something else began to happen: a feeling in his chest, spreading with every breath, across his skin, into his heart, along his ribs; a searing feeling, but warm – warm and alive. A feeling that made him stronger . . . better, even.

Not a feeling to live for – a feeling to die for.

His heart had an answer for him. *Mira Fedor.*

Sole

mix'm mix'm round round
see'm soon
where'm came
luscious

EXTRAS

About the Author

Marianne de Pierres was born in Western Australia and now lives in Queensland with her husband, three sons and two cockatoos. She has a BA in Film and Television and a Postgraduate Certificate of Arts in Writing, Editing and Publishing. Her passions are books, basketball and avocados. She has been actively involved in promoting Speculative Fiction in Australia and is the co-founder of the Vision Writers Group, and ROR – wRiters On the Rise, a critiquing group for professional writers. She was also involved in the early planning stage of Clarion South. Marianne has published a variety of short fiction and is collaborating on a film project for Sydney-based Enchanter Productions. You can find out more about her at www.mariannedepierres.com

Find out more about Marianne de Pierres and other Orbit authors by registering for the free monthly newsletter at www.orbitbooks.net

if you enjoyed

CHAOS SPACE

look out for

SATURN RETURNS

by

Sean Williams

THIS WRECKAGE

The relics of art for ever decaying,
– the productions of nature for ever renewed.

Robert Charles Maturin

'I am not a decent man.'

The words were spoken in response to a question Imre Bergamasc couldn't hear. Although he knew they came from his own mouth, he knew also that the utterance was a memory, not something occurring in his present. He wasn't talking to anyone. He appeared, rather, to be lying on his back with his eyes closed, as though he had just woken from a deep sleep, but fully dressed in a soft jumpsuit made of material that whispered softly as he raised his hands to touch his chest and explore his face.

Something was wrong, or at least very different. He had breasts.

His eyes opened wide. A grey bulkhead greeted him, less than a meter from his face. He raised his head and looked down along his foreign, curved body. A coffin-like space enclosed him on all sides except his left, where it opened onto a larger chamber. The surface beneath him was padded: a bed of some kind, yes, but one of spartan proportions. There was room for just one person, and no space to sit up. Two narrow striplights provided the sole illumination, cold and characterless. The chamber beyond his bunk was dark and sounded empty.

His breathing became more rapid. He had no recollection at all of how he had arrived in such a place, or become female into the bargain. He was profoundly out of his depth. He was—

'Who are you?' asked a voice.

He jumped. The words came from a speaker built into the wall to his right that didn't seem to be functioning with perfect clarity, for the voice came with more than a hint of static.

'What's your name?' it asked him.

'Don't you know?' His own voice – real, not remembered – could have been a man's, contralto and throaty from disuse. He cleared his throat. The timbre didn't change. 'You brought me here, didn't you?'

Instead of answering him, the voice asked, 'Who do you think you are?'

'We could ask each other questions all day.' He lowered his head back onto the thin mattress, already drained by the short exchange. 'Tell me who you are, first. Then we can talk.'

'We are the Jinc, fifth ganglion of the Noh exploratory arm. Perhaps you have heard of us.' The voice addressing him sounded faintly hopeful but not expectant. 'We trawl the outer edge of the galaxy for clues to the nature of God.'

He suppressed a momentary discomfort on finding that he was addressing a group mind. He didn't know why that should bother him. 'God? Why?'

'We have reasons. In the course of our explorations, we found you.'

'What do you mean, you found me?'

'Your body, in a manner of speaking, drifting. We will provide full details shortly. You need know for now only that we spared no effort in restoring you to consciousness and, we hope, full physical fitness.'

He flexed his fingers. Despite the odd alteration in gender, he did feel fine enough. 'I'm well, I suppose. What happened to me? What was I doing so far from the Continuum?'

'Is that the last thing you remember, the Continuum?'

'Why would that be unusual?'

'We will explain. Your situation is unique, and we do expect there to be some injury to your memory. It would help us to know your name, if you do in fact know it.'

'Some injury...' He rubbed his forehead. An

alarming dizziness threatened to consume him as he tried to recall what had brought him to such a strait. His body, drifting on the galactic fringes; rescued by deep-space scavengers and turned into a woman; his memory impaired. 'My name is Imre Bergamasc,' he said. 'That I'm sure of. The rest . . .' He rubbed harder. His brain was as heavy and sluggish as lead. 'I don't know. I do have memories, but – I – they won't fall into place.' He kicked out suddenly, flailing his legs in an ill-advised attempt to swing out of his bunk and into the chamber beyond, there to stand and seek out his questioner, the voice known only through a speaker thus far, buzzing and removed.

Nausea overwhelmed him before he came close to succeeding. A flock of memories, beating at his mind like a storm of crows, drove him back into the bunk.

'I don't know,' he moaned into the speaker. 'I don't know who I am.'

'You said your name is Imre Bergamasc. Isn't that who you are?'

'I suppose it must be. It has to be.' He placed both hands over his eyes and felt cool wetness on his cheeks. 'Who is Imre Bergamasc? Do you know who he's supposed to be? I don't know, and I don't know how to find out.'

'Are you saying now that you're not Imre Bergamasc?' The speaker sounded puzzled and cautious – perhaps, even, oddly fearful.

'That's my name,' he said, 'so I must be. Right?'

The speaker fell silent. Imre wept softly to himself, seeing no way out of the terrible conundrum. He knew his name but didn't know who he was. Something in his mind wasn't working correctly. The uncertainty cut like acid deep into his thoughts. He couldn't think through that terrible block, now that he had confronted it. He was stuck, frozen, damaged.

A door in the chamber outside his bunk hissed open. Air shifted minutely as pressures equalised. He wiped his face and blinked his sight clear of tears. A hunched, monk-like figure had entered the room.

'We, the Jinc, will explain,' it said, coming to his side. Its voice was the same as the one before: thin and dusted with static. The speaker had been working perfectly. 'Please let us.'

He looked up into a face that seemed composed of nothing but gristle and grey skin, as animated as a corpse. Its eyes were shut, but its hands moved with all the purpose and certainty of the sighted. He reflexively recoiled when it reached for him with long, flexing fingers, but again he reined in that instinct. The Noh was a group mind distributed through the skulls of numerous willing hosts. The creature before him had no more individual will than his own foot, being the instrument through which the gestalt mind acted. It was a mouthpiece, not the mouth.

He nodded to his strange host and let himself be eased out of the bunk.

The Noh vessel was cramped and tortuous to navigate. Corridors little wider than the bunk in which he had woken snaked between sepulchral chambers that doubled or tripled functions in order to utilise the volumes they occupied with maximum efficiency. The room in which he had woken was, it transpired, normally reserved for medicinal purposes as well as bunking space for the mouthpieces roughly equating to doctors or nurses within the Jinc. The dispersed entity – who took its name as a parenthesis around a single parcel of the greater culture or creature known as the Noh – needed such functionaries just as an individual human needed an immune system. When components fell ill, repair was easier than replacement. Voyages through deep space demanded such careful use of resources, since the next stop might be hundreds of years Absolute away.

Imre could not have retraced the route he followed through the Jinc's vessel. He hoped he would not need to. Along the way he noted clues as to the physical nature of the ship: a spinning habitat providing centripetal gravity in a low-thrust environment; decentralised life support capable of isolating one segment of the vessel from another in case of a major catastrophe; numerous signs of age and wear indicating that the vessel had been in service for a considerable time, even by the standards of deep space. His guide negotiated the tight tunnels by application of well-practiced taps and kicks to anchor points and solid bulkheads. The sounds and smells of humanity were everywhere, even among the Jinc, where all notions of individuality had been subsumed. He smelled food and spices and sweat, and a faint stink of corruption, as though from a faulty water reclamation plant. The scents triggered memories he couldn't pin down: faces and feelings that were, for the moment, fragmentary and nothing less than frustrating. Somehow, he knew everything about centripetal gravity and water recla-mation plants but failed to piece together anything more substantial about himself than his name. That struck him as grossly unfair, and he hoped the Jinc would soon explain why that might be.

His guide brought him to an observation port at the very edge of the spinning habitat, where gravity approached half Earth Standard. Unfamiliar details made themselves felt as he stepped into the center of the port: the weight of his breasts; the width of his hips; the narrowness of his feet. He had no hair at all and no obvious markings on his skin. He had, as yet, not seen his own face, so couldn't tell how much it resembled the one glimpsed in his memory. That his new body possessed a suite of implants and cognitive modifications came as no surprise; such were standard in the Continuum. Only the most recalcitrant of people, Primes, rejected such technology and lived more or less as humans had hundreds of thousands of years ago.

A name drifted across his thoughts – Emlee Copas – and with it an image of a wiry, blond-haired woman with jade green eyes. Before he could pursue the recollection, the reflective black bulkheads of the port faded to transparency, and the full glory of the galaxy at close range confronted him.

He gasped. One hundred billion stars filled the view to his right, shining across all frequencies of the spectrum. To his left was mottled darkness, lit only by globular clusters and more distant aggregations of galaxies. The Noh vessel was still too close to discern the true shape of the Milky Way – the barred spiral that humanity had long ago spanned from end to end – but the central bulge was clearly visible, as was the thick, curving arc of one arm.

'Behold,' said the Jinc's mouthpiece, rather unnecessarily Bergamasc thought, until he realised that the wizened creature pointed not at the galaxy but at an object much closer to hand. 'This is your origin,' it said, indicating a long, grey cylinder with the rough proportions of an old-fashioned flashlight, hanging immobile with respect to the Jinc's vessel. Its size was impossible to determine without points of reference. 'Do you recognise it?'

Imre could only shake his head. 'What's it made of?' he asked, taking stock of starlight gleaming dully from undecorated metal. 'It looks like iron.'

The creature bowed its cowled head. 'The most stable element in the universe. This artifact was built to endure the ages.'

'How long has it been drifting out here?'

'Many centuries Absolute, at least. Its rest was disturbed, making a more precise date difficult to ascertain.'

'Disturbed how?'

'The Drum, as we call it, was discovered in pieces. Two crude but effective nuclear explosions had reduced it to little more than dust, which we gathered, mote by mote, from within the blast radius. Our painstaking reconstruction of the original artifact took longer than we anticipated, for much has been lost forever – including, we thought at first, its contents, for the Drum proved to be hollow.'

'What makes you sure there were contents at all? It could have been empty when destroyed.'

'That was our second thought. Someone built this artifact and set it adrift on the outer limits of human space in a stable orbit that would have seen it neither escape the Milky Way nor return to habitable regions. Then someone else, for unknown reasons, came along to steal its contents and eliminate the evidence.'

'A long way to come for a heist.'

'Indeed, and just as far for murder.'

Imre studied the expressionless face of the Jinc mouthpiece even though he knew it would reveal nothing. 'What do you mean, murder?'

'We have ascertained that the Drum was always empty of matter, but not information. Its interior wall was inscribed with a single groove, looping around and around like copper wire in a crude electric motor. The groove contained notches spaced at irregular intervals. When we examined those notches – played them, if you like, as one would once have played a record with a diamond needle – we quickly ascertained that they contained information. The Drum was a data storage device, strange and magnificent in its own way, and intended to last forever. That it might have done but for its deliberate destruction.'

'You managed to recover and decode the data,' he said, guessing ahead. The feeling of dizziness returned, and it had nothing to do with the vertiginous view. 'This must be where I come in.'

'Yes. The Drum preserved the life of a single person in hard-storage. We have reconstructed a large proportion of that person from what remained of the Drum. Who that person was, exactly, we couldn't tell. Now you are awake, we know.'

'How much do you know, really? The record preserved my name, but it got my gender wrong.'

'Gender is a matter of choice not biology, as it should be. It is one data point among trillions. We only had your genes to rely on for your physiognomy. They allow the possibility of a masculine form, but also several species of late-onset cancer as well. Would you have had us retain those tendencies too?'

'Of course not.'

'Then we can only apologise for assuming incorrectly regarding your gender. We had a one in two chance of getting it right. The mistake can be rectified, in time.'

'I'll think about it.' If reclaiming his past self and finding out who he had been was to become his priority – as seemed logical, given the lack of an alternative proposition – then adopting his prior physical form could be an important first step. In none of the memories clamoring for his attention was he female or any other gender but male. 'In the meantime, what should I do?'

'You may remain our guest, if you wish.'

Imre took a deep breath. So many thoughts ran through his brain at a time that it was hard to concentrate on just one. From the collision between them, he picked out several key notions. The Jinc was a long way from anywhere, so leaving might be difficult, perhaps even impossible, given that he had no vessel of his own or any belongings that he knew of. He had to assume that the Jinc was genuinely willing to keep him around, since it had gone to so much trouble to re-create him from the splinters of his outlandish personality backup. Only when that willingness ran out, perhaps in conjunction with its curiosity about his identity and past, would he have to make other plans. Until then, it seemed simplest to take the Jinc at its word and accept its hospitality.

Part of him, though, hated the thought. He had only the Jinc's word that any of this was true. There were other ways to edit memory, and only some of them were benign.

'You said that you were able to reconstruct "a large proportion" of the person I had once been,' he said. 'What about the rest? Where did that come from?'

'Extrapolation accounts for much of the missing genetic code,' said the Jinc, not flinching from the question at all. 'The rest came from a standard human template. Several neurological modules required direct intervention – functions of the brain, in other words, that simply did not work until we intervened – but we did everything we could to ensure that such alterations were kept to a minimum. Memory could not be repaired. Only you can put those pieces back together.'

'There's no single answer, then,' he said. 'I'm me plus some bits you made up. I'm not me mixed with someone else, though. You're definitely saying that.'

'Yes. It was not our intention to create a new persona. You are as close to the record of the Drum as we could make you.'

That was something, Imre supposed, even though intention was a guarantee of nothing.

'I'll stay until I can sort myself out,' he said. 'You've wasted enough resources on me already.'

'We do not think so.'

Imre studied the expressionless face of his guide, sensing a meaning hidden but unable to tease it free. He resolved then to spend as much time studying the Jinc as himself. If he could discover why it had gone to so much trouble to resurrect him from the dust of intergalactic space, that would go some way to revealing who it thought he might be.

And then, possessed with that knowledge, he could begin to wonder who had tried to kill him.

He had no plan of attack. Who had ever been in such a situation before? Not he, if the incomplete reminiscences at his disposal were anything to go by. There were uncountable such fractions, each needing to be lifted out of obscurity, examined, then rewritten in both the neurological and narrative senses back into his mind. He chose to let instinct be his sole guide, taking him where it willed throughout the Noh vessel, and beyond, to the Drum itself, where someone – his former self, presumably – had gone to painstaking effort to preserve him for posterity, only to see it blown to smithereens.

Moving around the Drum was easier than expected. The Jinc gave him a cowl and robe identical to the ones worn by its mouthpieces. A translucent microfilm provided him with air and maintained a comfortable temperature. It also adjusted the magnetic properties of the soles of his feet, enabling them to stick to the iron of the Drum's curving wall. It was easily thirty meters across and well over one hundred long. He walked for hours along the thin spiral decorating its wide interior. Less than a millimeter wide, it formed the single helix that had preserved the data comprising him and his body. The magnitude of the venture startled and shocked him. This was information engineering on a massive, hubristic scale. The Drum had been built to withstand everything the void threw at it. Only intelligence, deliberate and malicious, had ultimately done it in.

He could see places where the Jinc had failed to reassemble the Drum from its multitudinous bits. Tiny black dots marred its metallic grey surface where a resinous material filled in for the missing parts, offending a deep-seated need in him for neatness and order. He felt as though he were walking across a starscape in negative, one that arced up and around him in a powerful representation of the curvature of space. The real stars shone down either end of the Drum, where the Jinc had left open the construct's massive caps. Naked vacuum bathed the cylinder and its contents. The sound of his magnetic footsteps propagated through the metal in silent waves.

When he was done, he walked to where the short-range shuttle scoop waited to take him back to the Noh vessel. The Jinc's home looked like a giant neuron, all curves and distended spines with a semitransparent outer hull that gleamed liquidly in the light of the Milky Way. Imre could discern no front or rear. Similarly with the shuttle scoop, which was a large, seed-shaped vessel pockmarked with thirteen mouths that could, at will, distend vast magnetic vanes. The purpose of the vanes was simple: to suck up the dust and debris the Jinc encountered in its long, destinationless voyage. The remains of the Drum had been gathered in just such a fashion, the mouthpiece of the Jinc had told him. What the Jinc did with its normal harvest, Imre hadn't yet ascertained.

The mouthpiece awaited him in the scoop, as lifeless as ever. Perhaps it was the same one who had greeted him on his awakening, perhaps not. The distinction was meaningless. He told himself to stop thinking about it as an individual and treat it, in both his mind and every aspect of his behavior, as the Jinc itself.

'Did that trigger any memories?' the Jinc asked him as he reached the edge of the Drum and prepared to cross.

'I'm afraid not. I've never seen anything like i before.' He stepped carefully into the belly of the scoop disengaging his magnetic feet with relief. Fleetin g forces gripped him as the scoop accelerated away. ' suppose it was worth a try.'

'You sound disappointed.'

He was, but saw no point in dwelling on the fact Although the data had been encoded in the Drum with a fair degree of redundancy, nuclear blasts and wide dispersal were huge hurdles to overcome. The Jinc had done an amazing job to recover anything. 'The way I see it, I'm lucky to be here at all. Wherever we are, exactly.

The hunched figure beside him made no move to offer any information on that score, so he took it upon himself to ask.

'Show me where you've come from.'

A series of three-dimensional maps appeared around him. He waved them away.

'No. Pointing will be fine, while we're out here.'

The mouthpiece looked up at him. A long, wrinkled finger pointed through the transparent hull of the scoop at the splendid starscape ahead of them, tracing a line around the extremities of the galaxy. There was no clear purpose to the Jinc's past movements just as there was no obvious 'captain' aboard the ship. It was driven by collective will in directions unknown.

Imre's gaze slid from the outstretched finger outward to the galaxy, truly grasping its immensity for the first time. It filled one-half of his view, a tilted, glowing waterfall looming over the shuttle scoop and its passengers. Every speck was a star – one of a hundred thousand million, large and small, dead and alive, and none of them overlooked by humanity. The Continuum connected them all, whether by arcane quantum loops, stately webs of electro-magnetic radiation, or sluggish bullets of matter. The minds inhabiting the Milky Way ranged from as small as his, via gestalts as complex as the Jinc, to intelligences as large as the galaxy itself. Layer upon layer of sentience and civilisation stretched upward from the individual to heights he could barely imagine, and all of it had originated in one remarkable system, on one tiny world.

He staggered, not under the influence of acceleration or the immensity of the view, but from a flashback that burst in his skull like a Roman candle.

'What about the individual?' said Alphin Freer, an angular, high-cheeked man with iron grey eyes and neat black hair. 'Are we supposed to forget everything you told us – that we fought for?'

'The Forts are the big players in the galaxy now.' His own voice again, ringing in his ears. The disorientation was profound. He was undoubtedly in the scoop, but at the same time he was on the bridge of a burning ship. 'They may have had the Aces all along.'

'No shit,' said a big, scar-pitted soldier looming like a small mountain to one side, combat suit open to the waist. The green-eyed blonde beside him looked ready to cry.

'If you do this,' said Freer, 'you're as much a traitor to the human race as they are.'

'Listen to me.' Imre's reminiscence was full of anger, resentment, and frustration, but his voice conveyed nothing but entreaty. 'Whatever it takes to get us out of this – isn't that worth pursuing?'

'You really think we're getting out of this?'

The new voice came from behind him, silky and subtle like a stiletto blade. Imre turned – or remembered turning – and the recollection suddenly dissolved, leaving him with fleeting impressions of snakeskins and stab wounds.

He shook his head. The stars were making him feel light-headed.

'Are you unwell?' asked the Jinc. One cool, skeletal hand fell on his shoulder.

'I don't know,' Imre said. 'I think I'd like to lie down.'

'That can easily be arranged. You have been assigned a private berth. We will show you there now.'

'Thank you.' The Jinc's statement took a moment to sink in. 'A private berth, really?'

'We made it especially for you.'

It was, he supposed, somewhat less involved than plucking his pieces out of the void and putting them together again, but the thought still made him uncomfortable. 'I'd be happy enough in the sickbay.'

The Jinc didn't reply. As the scoop rolled into a new course, Imre held on and kept his eyes averted from the view.

* * *

Incoherent memories trickled down the crater wall of his mind, threatening an avalanche of incapacitating proportions.

The burning ship was called *Pelorus*, and it had been the flagship of an armada vast enough to cast a shadow across a solar system. Like many ships of the day, it had endured the ravages of interstellar space by sloughing away layers of hull in much the same fashion that humans shed dead skin cells. Across a voyage of several hundred light-years, every external surface might be completely replaced many times over while everything within remained pristine.

'In the same way,' a voice from his memory said, 'the Forts replace frags. But are they skin cells? I don't think so. A skin cell doesn't feel pain or loss. It doesn't feel anything at all. The comparison, and the practice, is odious.'

Humans had evolved vastly and without check across the galaxy. People came in all shapes and sizes and communicated by every imaginable means. No reliable method had been found to cross the light-speed barrier, but that was no deterrent. Where space would not break, time would happily bend. If a journey was to take a thousand years by the 'natural' tick of the clock, why not make the subjective ticks longer so the journey seemed to last only a decade, or a year, or a day, or even a minute? Indefinite life extension had been in common practice since before humanity left Earth. To grow old and die while visiting a neighbor – for anything less than a thousand light-years away was practically on one's doorstep – would be considered wasteful, even obscene. People shook hands across the constellations. They made conversations, and love, and war.

'This machine runs down.' That was the big, scarred man again. His accent was untraceable, wooden only in the sense that a forest was made of wood. 'So few of us are left.'

'That's a bleak outlook.' Imre's face hurt as though he had recently been laughing uproariously. Or screaming.

'Only gods walk on water.'

'Only idiots or fools would try. We're neither, right?'

'Amen. We're the new religion.'

An acrid wave of ozone swept that memory from the stage. A name took its place: the Corps. Just as humans in ancient times had formed friendships, allegiances, and armies, so too did affiliations spring up across the intergalactic gulfs. Some were necessarily loose; others were as tight as they had ever been. Some were between numerous discrete, different individuals; some consisted of multiple copies of one individual, propagated across the starscape like seeds, meeting up every millennium or so to exchange memories. Such singletons were themselves an ambiguous blend of individual and multiplicity. Novel pronouns and neologisms abounded as language struggled to keep up with numerous new ways to be. All were human, since they had sprung from the same ancient home as all known intelligent life, but not all were the same.

The Corps was just one of many affiliations caught in the middle. Imre Bergamasc – the man who had amassed the memories preserved in the Drum – had seen through many sets of eyes and lived in many bodies. He had none of the smeared awareness of the Jinc, however; each body had a keen sense of himself – and that, gradually, was how the revived Imre was coming to think of his former incarnation: Himself, the being that had preceded him in life's great adventure. There were bound to be more of him out there somewhere, unless whoever had destroyed the Drum had finished them off too. There were also, most likely, other members of the Corps.

Alphin Freer was definitely one of them: cool, remote, and knife-sharp. The big man whose name and origins wouldn't quite come, another; also the reticent blonde, Emlee Copas, with eyes of green stone. The fourth of his former companions was the woman whose voice had crawled down him like oil on a ship's hull. The five of them had been a team, he gradually surmised; soldiers of both kinds, war- and peacemakers, as circumstances demanded. Had they been friends? That he couldn't quite unpack. Certainly, they had been close; perhaps even co-dependent. At least one of them had been his lover, if the complex knot of emotional associations was anything to go by. Flesh and blood and pain and fucking, all wound up in one vicious tangle. If he pulled at it too hard, he feared he might strangle himself.

His own voice formed the backdrop to many of the memories – demanding, cajoling, commanding, ranting – but the words weren't always comprehensible. So many speeches: when had he ever found so much to say? Now, all he wanted was to close his ears and think. If he opened his mouth to answer the Jinc's questions, he feared the dusty, disconnected pieces of his mind might fall out.

Sloughing hulls and singletons in rows demanded that he keep it together as best he could. Whether he was divine or merely decent, or not even that, he owed it to himself to piece Himself together. Then he could stand back and decide who or what he had been. Soldier? Victim? Leader? Man?

He was in a bar. Three glasses of a pinkish liquid rested on the table before him. The big man glanced over his shoulder as though at a sudden sound. 'Something is wrong.'

Imre reached into the pocket of his uniform jacket for the Henschke Sloan sidearm he kept there, fully loaded. Before he could draw, a single shot discharged into the ceiling behind them, and a voice barked that they should stay seated.

He remembered nothing after that point.

But her name, the name of his lover, did eventually come to him: covert ops specialist Helwise MacPhedron, she of the liquid voice and thin, soft ribs that went down her waist like those of a snake.

Just thinking of her sent a shudder along his spine, but once again he didn't know why.